THE OXFORD SHERLOCK HOLMES

General Editor: OWEN DUDLEY EDWARDS

THE ADVENTURES OF SHERLOCK HOLMES

SIR ARTHUR CONAN DOYLE was born in Edinburgh in 1859 to Irish Catholic parents. A Jesuit pupil at Stonyhurst, he graduated in medicine from Edinburgh (1881), and won his doctorate (1885). He practised medicine at Southsea in the 1880s as well as in a Greenland whaler, a West African trader and (after 20 years' retirement) a Boer War hospital. His literary career began in *Chambers's Edinburgh Journal* before he was 20, and he invented Sherlock Holmes when 26. After moving to London he transferred Holmes and Watson to short stories in the newly launched *Strand* magazine (1891) where he remained the lead author. A master of the short story, Conan Doyle's other great series revolved around Brigadier Gerard and Napoleon, while of his longer stories the same mix of comedy with adventure characterized his historical and scientific fiction, with unforgettable heroes such as the minute bellicose Sir Nigel, the Puritan crook Decimus Saxon, and the Shavian egomaniac Professor Challenger. His influence on the detective story was omnipresent, but his own literary stature as a classic is only now receiving its scholarly due. He died in 1930.

RICHARD LANCELYN GREEN edited *The Uncollected Sherlock Holmes* and *The Further Adventures of Sherlock Holmes*. With John Michael Gibson, he compiled the Soho Series *Bibliography of A. Conan Doyle.*

OWEN DUDLEY EDWARDS, the general editor of The Oxford Sherlock Holmes, is Reader in History at the University of Edinburgh and author of *The Quest for Sherlock Holmes: A Biographical Study of Sir Arthur Conan Doyle.*

OXFORD WORLD'S CLASSICS

*For over 100 years Oxford World's Classics have brought
readers closer to the world's great literature. Now with over 700
titles—from the 4,000-year-old myths of Mesopotamia to the
twentieth century's greatest novels—the series makes available
lesser-known as well as celebrated writing.*

*The pocket-sized hardbacks of the early years contained
introductions by Virginia Woolf, T. S. Eliot, Graham Greene,
and other literary figures which enriched the experience of reading.
Today the series is recognized for its fine scholarship and
reliability in texts that span world literature, drama and poetry,
religion, philosophy and politics. Each edition includes perceptive
commentary and essential background information to meet the
changing needs of readers.*

OXFORD WORLD'S CLASSICS

=====

ARTHUR CONAN DOYLE

The Adventures of Sherlock Holmes

=====

Edited with an Introduction and Notes by
RICHARD LANCELYN GREEN

OXFORD
UNIVERSITY PRESS

OXFORD

UNIVERSITY PRESS

Great Clarendon Street, Oxford OX2 6DP

Oxford University Press is a department of the University of Oxford.
It furthers the University's objective of excellence in research, scholarship,
and education by publishing worldwide in

Oxford New York

Athens Auckland Bangkok Bogotá Buenos Aires Calcutta
Cape Town Chennai Dar es Salaam Delhi Florence Hong Kong Istanbul
Karachi Kuala Lumpur Madrid Melbourne Mexico City Mumbai
Nairobi Paris São Paulo Shanghai Singapore Taipei Tokyo Toronto Warsaw

with associated companies in Berlin Ibadan

Oxford is a registered trade mark of Oxford University Press
in the UK and in certain other countries

Published in the United States
by Oxford University Press Inc., New York

First published in the Oxford Sherlock Holmes 1993
First published as a World's Classics paperback 1994
Reissued as an Oxford World's Classics paperback 1999
Reissued 2008

British Library Cataloguing in Publication Data

Data available

Library of Congress Cataloging in Publication Data

Doyle, Arthur Conan, Sir, 1859–1930.
The adventures of Sherlock Holmes / Arthur Conan Doyle ; edited
with an introduction by Richard Lancelyn Green.
p. cm.—(Oxford world's classics) (The Oxford Sherlock Holmes)
Includes bibliographical references.
1. Holmes, Sherlock (Fictitious character)—Fiction. 2. Private
investigators—England—Fiction. 3. Detective and mystery stories,
English. I. Green, Richard Lancelyn. II. Title. III. Series.
IV. Series: Doyle, Arthur Conan, Sir, 1859–1930. Oxford Sherlock Holmes.
PR4622.A7 1994 823'.8—dc20 94–7786

ISBN 978–0–19–953695–5

2

Printed in Great Britain by
Clays Ltd, St Ives plc

CONTENTS

THE ADVENTURES OF
SHERLOCK HOLMES

ACKNOWLEDGEMENTS

GRATEFUL thanks are due to Brigadier J. N. Stisted for use of the family papers of Joseph Bell, to the Humanities Research Center, Austin, Texas (the Ellery Queen Collection) for permission to examine the MS of 'A Scandal in Bohemia', and to the several institutions holding Arthur Conan Doyle correspondence used in the preparation of this edition and of *The Return of Sherlock Holmes*.

GENERAL EDITOR'S PREFACE
TO THE SERIES

ARTHUR Conan Doyle told his *Strand* editor, Herbert Greenhough Smith (1855–1935), that 'A story always comes to me as an organic thing and I never can recast it without the Life going out of it.'[1]

On the whole, this certainly seems to describe Conan Doyle's method with the Sherlock Holmes stories, long and short. Such manuscript evidence as survives (approximately half the stories) generally bears this out: there is remarkably little revision. Sketches or scenarios are another matter. Conan Doyle was no more bound by these at the end of his literary life than at the beginning, whence scraps of paper survive to tell us of 221B Upper Baker Street where lived Ormond Sacker and J. Sherrinford Holmes. But very little such evidence is currently available for analysis.

Conan Doyle's relationship with his most famous creation was far from the silly label 'The Man Who Hated Sherlock Holmes': equally, there was no indulgence in it. Though the somewhat too liberal Puritan Micah Clarke was perhaps dearer to him than Holmes, Micah proved unable to sustain a sequel to the eponymous novel of 1889. By contrast, 'Sherlock' (as his creator irreverently alluded to him when not creating him) proved his capacity for renewal 59 times (which Conan Doyle called 'a striking example of the patience and loyalty of the British public'). He dropped Holmes in 1893, apparently into the Reichenbach Falls, as a matter of literary integrity: he did not intend to be written off as 'the Holmes man'. But public clamour turned Holmes into an economic asset that could not be ignored. Even so, Conan Doyle could not have continued to write about

---

[1] Undated letter, quoted by Cameron Hollyer, 'Author to Editor', *ACD: The Journal of the Arthur Conan Doyle Society*, 3 (1992), 19–20. Conan Doyle's remark was probably *à propos* 'The Red Circle' (*His Last Bow*).

Holmes without taking some pleasure in the activity, or indeed without becoming quietly proud of him.

Such Sherlock Holmes manuscripts as survive are frequently in private keeping, and very few have remained in Britain. In this series we have made the most of two recent facsimiles, of 'The Dying Detective' and 'The Lion's Mane'. In general, manuscript evidence shows Conan Doyle consistently underpunctuating, and to show the implications of this 'The Dying Detective' (*His Last Bow*) has been printed from the manuscript. 'The Lion's Mane', however, offers the one case known to us of drastic alterations in the surviving manuscript, from which it is clear from deletions that the story was entirely altered, and Holmes's role transformed, in the process of its creation.

Given Conan Doyle's general lack of close supervision of the Holmes texts, it is not always easy to determine his final wishes. In one case, it is clear that 'His Last Bow', as a deliberate contribution to war propaganda, underwent a ruthless revision at proof stage—although (as we note for the first time) this was carried out on the magazine text and lost when published in book form. But nothing comparable exists elsewhere.

In general, American texts of the stories are closer to the magazine texts than British book texts. Textual discrepancies, in many instances, may simply result from the conflicts of sub-editors. Undoubtedly, Conan Doyle did some re-reading, especially when returning to Holmes after an absence; but on the whole he showed little interest in the constitution of his texts. In his correspondence with editors he seldom alluded to proofs, discouraged ideas for revision, and raised few—if any—objections to editorial changes. For instance, we know that the *Strand*'s preference for 'Halloa' was not Conan Doyle's original usage, and in this case we have restored the original orthography. On the other hand, we also know that the *Strand* texts consistently eliminated anything (mostly expletives) of an apparently blasphemous character, but in the absence of manuscript confirmation we have normally been unable to restore what were probably stronger original versions. (In any case, it is perfectly possible that Conan Doyle, the consummate professional, may have come to exercise self-censorship in the certain knowledge that editorial changes would be imposed.)

Throughout the series we have corrected any obvious errors, though these are comparatively few: the instances are at all times noted. (For a medical man, Conan Doyle's handwriting was commendably legible, though his 'o' could look like an 'a'.) Regarding the order of individual stories, internal evidence makes it clear that 'A Case of Identity' (*Adventures*) was written before 'The Red-Headed League' and was intended to be so printed; but the 'League' was the stronger story and the *Strand*, in its own infancy, may have wanted the Holmes stories established as quickly as possible (at this point the future of both the Holmes series and the magazine was uncertain). Surviving letters show that the composition of 'The Solitary Cyclist' (*Return*) preceded that of 'The Dancing Men' (with the exception of the former's first paragraph, which was rewritten later); consequently, the order of these stories has been reversed. Similarly, the stories in *His Last Bow* and *The Case-Book of Sherlock Holmes* have been rearranged in their original order of publication, which—as far as is known—reflects the order of composition. The intention has been to allow readers to follow the fictional evolution of Sherlock Holmes over the forty years of his existence.

The one exception to this principle will be found in *His Last Bow*, where the final and eponymous story was actually written and published after *The Valley of Fear*, which takes its place in the Holmes canon directly after the magazine publication of the other stories in *His Last Bow*; but the removal of the title story to the beginning of the *Case-Book* would have been too radically pedantic and would have made *His Last Bow* ludicrously short. Readers will note that we have already reduced the extent of *His Last Bow* by returning 'The Cardboard Box' to its original location in the *Memoirs of Sherlock Holmes* (after 'Silver Blaze' and before 'The Yellow Face'). The removal of 'The Cardboard Box' from the original sequence led to the inclusion of its introductory passage in 'The Resident Patient': this, too, has been returned to its original position and the proper opening of 'The Resident Patient' restored. Generally, texts have been derived from first book publication collated with magazine texts and, where possible, manuscripts; in the case of 'The Cardboard Box' and 'The Resident Patient', however, we have employed the *Strand* texts, partly because of the restoration of the latter's opening, partly to give readers a flavour of the magazine in which the Holmes stories made their first, vital conquests.

In all textual decisions the overriding desire has been to meet the author's wishes, so far as these can be legitimately ascertained from documentary evidence or application of the rule of reason.

One final plea. If you come to these stories for the first time, proceed now to the texts themselves, putting the introductions and explanatory notes temporarily aside. Our introductions are not meant to introduce: Dr Watson will perform that duty, and no one could do it better. Then, when you have mastered the stories, and they have mastered you, come back to us.

OWEN DUDLEY EDWARDS

University of Edinburgh

INTRODUCTION

*T*HE *Adventures of Sherlock Holmes* was first published in
October 1892, but the popularity and fame of the
detective preceded the book and became apparent soon
after the first story appeared in the *Strand Magazine* for July
1891. The success was immediate and lasting and Arthur
Conan Doyle rose rapidly to prominence as a result. He had
already published one historical novel, *Micah Clarke* (1889),
and had completed another, *The White Company*, and on the
strength of these had decided to give up his medical practice
in Southsea to devote a greater part of his time to writing.
The idea had been discussed for over a year, but the decision became irrevocable after a visit to Berlin in November
1890 where he went in the hope of witnessing a demonstration
of Dr Robert Koch's consumption cure. He was unable to
gain access to it, but a chance encounter with Dr Malcolm
Morris, a Harley Street dermatologist, decided his future.
Doyle had worked on a part-time basis at the Portsmouth
Eye Hospital correcting refractions, so Morris suggested that
he should set himself up in London as an eye specialist
which would give him security and allow time for literary
work. It could easily be done, he said, if he were to 'put in
six months' work' in Vienna to bring himself up to date with
the latest developments.

Doyle acted upon the advice without delay. He returned
to London on 19 November 1890, reached Southsea three
days later, and by the end of the month had notified
his family of his intention to leave Southsea. A farewell
dinner was held in his honour on 12 December by the
Portsmouth Literary and Scientific Society, of which he had
been an honorary secretary, and on 18 December he closed
the doors of 1, Bush Villas for the last time. With his wife
Louisa he then went to Birmingham to stay with friends and
on Christmas Eve joined his mother at Masongill in north-
west Yorkshire.

On the last day of the year he set off for Vienna, which he reached on 5 January 1891. After a few days in a hotel, he and his wife found lodgings at the Pension Banfort in Universitaats Strasse, and in time he made his way to the Krankenhaus. However, his knowledge of technical German proved inadequate and most of the time was given over to the pleasures of Viennese society, skating, and writing—with the first three weeks entirely devoted to a short novel, *The Doings of Raffles Haw*, which he had agreed to do for *Answers*, the penny paper owned by Alfred Harmsworth (1865–1922), later Lord Northcliffe. He left Vienna for Semmering on 9 March, visited Venice and Milan, spent a few days in Paris, where he saw Professor Edmond Landolt, author of the standard work *The Refraction and Accommodation of the Eye and their Anomalies* (tr. C. M. Culver, Edinburgh, 1886), and was back in London on 24 March 1891.

The idea for the Sherlock Holmes short stories was then foremost in his mind and the writing of the first series coincided with his stay in London, which makes the period of particular significance. His search for accommodation took him to the area around the British Museum where he had stayed on previous occasions and he found suitable lodgings at 23 Montague Place, at the back of the Museum in the road which runs into Russell Square. It is possible (as the Census was taken on 5 April 1891) to name all those who shared the building with him. Mary Esther Gould, a spinster of 54, was the landlady and she lived with her sister Jane, a teacher at an elementary school. The boarders were Jane Sutherland, aged 64; Edwin J. Davies, an 18-year-old clerk; Frank and Percy Jefferson, licensed victuallers (who ran the Old King's Head in Bear Street), and Carl A. Falstedt, the Swedish Consul in Sydney (New South Wales), with his English wife, Cecilia. Two domestic servants, Mary Smith and Lillie Brereton completed the household—apart that is from A. Conan Doyle, aged 31, who described himself as an Ophthalmic Surgeon, and his wife, L. Conan Doyle, aged 33, and their baby daughter, Mary (born 1889). Doyle and his wife were isolated from the other lodgers as they had a self-contained suite of rooms, which included a sitting-room and a spare bedroom, but they presumably used a common dining-room when not taking their food in the neighbouring restaurants.

It took several days to find professional premises near Harley Street, but from 1 April (at an annual rent of £120) Doyle had the use of a front room and part use of a waiting-room at 2 Upper Wimpole Street (which was and is a separately numbered street between Wimpole Street and Devonshire Place). The waiting-room was shared with James Donelan, MB, while the consulting-room had formerly belonged to a dental surgeon called Alfred Hart. On the first day in the new premises and before he had arranged his furniture or signed on at the Royal Westminster Ophthalmic Hospital, he set to work on 'A Scandal in Bohemia' (or 'A Scandal of Bohemia' as it was first known). His pocket diary shows the speed at which the stories were written. The first was dispatched to Alexander Pollock Watt (1834–1914), his literary agent, on 3 April. On 10 April, 'A Case of Identity' was finished. On 20 April, 'The Red-Headed League' was sent off, and 'The Boscombe Valley Mystery' followed on 27 April.

The momentum would no doubt have continued, had he not succumbed to illness on 4 May. 'I was starting off for my usual trudge one morning from our lodgings when icy shivers passed over me, and I only got back in time to avoid a total collapse. It was a virulent attack of influenza, at a time when influenza was in its deadly prime.' For a week he was in grave danger and afterwards was 'as weak as a child and as emotional, but with a mind as clear as crystal'. By 18 May he was again at work and on that day dispatched the fifth adventure, 'The Five Orange Pips'. He also decided to 'cut the painter' and rely entirely on his pen for his livelihood. It was, he said, 'one of the great moments of exaltation of my life'. During June he looked at various suburban villas in South London—including one at 146 Selhurst Road, another at West Hill, Sydenham, and two in Tennison Road, South Norwood, and settled for 12 Tennison

Road for which he paid a yearly rent of £85. By the end of June he and his wife and baby daughter were settled in the new house. July was occupied writing a short novel called *Beyond the City*, and the last of the six Sherlock Holmes stories, 'The Man with the Twisted Lip', was dispatched at the beginning of August.

The short story was a staple of magazines, as were serialized novels; but Doyle felt that his use of two characters running through the stories was breaking new ground. In an interview in *Tit-Bits* (15 December 1900) he said that it had occurred to him that serial stories in magazines were a mistake because if the first number was missed the readers were debarred from the story, and he therefore thought of writing a serial without appearing to do so, with each instalment complete in itself and capable of being read on its own 'while each retained a connecting link with the one before and the one that was to come by means of its leading characters'. 'In this respect,' he said, 'I was a revolutionist, and I think I may fairly lay claim to the credit of being the inaugurator of a system which has since been worked by others with no little success.'

Sherlock Holmes was an obvious candidate for this treatment. He had made his first appearance in *A Study in Scarlet* in *Beeton's Christmas Annual* for 1887 and the character had been carefully constructed far beyond the requirements of a single story. The story had been well received by the few papers that troubled to review the annual; it was published as a shilling paperback the following year and reprinted the year after that. Andrew Lang (1844–1912) praised it in *Longman's Magazine*, and partly on the strength of his review *Lippincott's Magazine* commissioned a second story, which became *The Sign of the Four*, for its issue of February 1890.

The major sources of inspiration for the methods of Sherlock Holmes were the stories of Edgar Allan Poe (1809–49) and of Émile Gaboriau (1835–73), and at times Doyle copied them so faithfully that he appeared to be quoting from them.

Gaboriau, whose major novels appeared at the end of the 1860s, was widely acknowledged in the mid 1880s as the greatest exponent and true father of the detective novel. English translations of his works, such as *L'Affaire Lerouge* (1866) or *Monsieur Lecoq* (1869), were widely disseminated in paperback by Vizetelly & Co. from 1881, and many were read by Doyle before he started work on *A Study in Scarlet*. The detective story was then so closely associated with Gaboriau that imitators were spoken of as belonging to the 'Gaboriau school'. The great fault of his novels for those who wish to see them as detective stories is that the detective element is overlaid with digressions concerning the background to the crime. His detectives are shown to be fallible, because their analytical genius leads to inferences and logical conclusions dependent on facts which are then contradicted by later discoveries; but he provided the perfect model for Doyle. Holmes at times speaks with the voice of Lecoq or of Père Tabaret. He sometimes acts in the same manner. From time to time he uses the same devices and the same logic, and makes the same inferences. He could fairly be said to have been schooled in the methods of the 1860s.

Gaboriau provided the 'sensational' and the 'rational' elements, but the art came from Edgar Allan Poe, whose works were repeatedly mined by Doyle in his search for plots and ideas. The three stories concerning C. Auguste Dupin, 'The Murders in the Rue Morgue' (1841), 'The Mystery of Marie Rogêt' (1842–3), and 'The Purloined Letter' (1844) were written before the term 'detective' had been widely adopted but the format is recognizable as the direct fictional precursor of the short Sherlock Holmes stories. Dupin is more refined than the detectives who were derived from *Mémoires* (1828) of the ex-criminal first chief of the Brigade de Sureté (1812–25), Eugène François Vidocq (1775–1857). He is seen through the eyes of a narrator who is his companion (an essential element of the Sherlock Holmes stories); he uses logical analysis and inference, and is the greatest fictional exponent of 'ratiocination' and the first 'armchair detective'.

Sherlock Holmes as a detective owes much to his great predecessors; but if he is judged solely on that criterion, he might be found wanting. The first six adventures are not true crime stories, though crime plays its part. They are not true detective stories, though the detective is essential to them. They are fantasies and fairy stories, and their greatness lies not in applying and developing the methods of Gaboriau and Poe, but in their relation to the style, atmosphere, and ethos of the period. It is the anecdotal inconsequence of Oliver Wendell Holmes (1809–94); the free use of simile borrowed from George Meredith (1828–1909), the bright and brittle aestheticism of Oscar Wilde (1854–1900), and the humour and elegance of Robert Louis Stevenson (1850–94), which raise them above Doyle's other work. In these stories he was touched by greatness, partly by chance, partly by design. The strands of his character and of his reading were perfectly fused together, and the disparate elements formed themselves into an inimitable alloy.

Doyle read and re-read Oliver Wendell Holmes and from him came the warm conversational tone which makes Sherlock Holmes no less a friend of the reader than his namesake. 'The Genius of George Meredith' was the subject of a lecture by Doyle to the Portsmouth Literary and Scientific Society on 20 November 1888, in which he said that Meredith was a writer made to be imitated. 'The Methods of Mr Stevenson in Fiction' (*National Review*, January 1890) was an article which analysed Stevenson's style and revealed what Doyle had learned from it, notably the rich colouring, the sense of menace, and the humour. And he was also influenced by Oscar Wilde (whom he met in 1889), by the wit and the Bohemian *fin de siècle* gloss, the pithy aphorisms, and the eccentricities of genius which distinguish Holmes from his predecessors and transform him into what Paul Barolzy in *Walter Pater's Renaissance* (1987) calls the 'domesticated aesthete' who follows in the tradition of Poe, Charles Baudelaire (1821–67), Joris Karl Huysmans (1848–1907), and Wilde, yet falls short of true decadence and poses no threat within the cosy domesticity of Baker Street.

If Doyle learnt from his literary contemporaries it was the popular penny weeklies such as *Tit-Bits*, *Answers*, and *Cassell's Saturday Journal* that provided him with ideas and plots. Here, week after week, were short tit-bits of information, curious facts, and anecdotes, including tales of a reporter who had assumed the disguise of a beggar, of a man who had been threatened when a snake came through a ventilator, of an engineer who had been nearly crushed to death under a ship's crank, and of birds with diamonds in their crops. It was a rich and fertile hunting-ground, which few others would have thought to use, but it tallies with all that is known of him. He had contributed to *Cassell's Saturday Journal*; he had written for *Answers*, and had been reading *Tit-Bits* throughout the 1880s, and this partly explains why the stories succeed so well for they introduce touches of the bizarre. In the Sherlock Holmes stories his weaknesses became strengths. He made superficiality into a virtue. The veneer was appropriate. He could fabricate improbable plots, riddled with contradictions, and in doing so produce some of the most memorable stories in the English language. They might occasionally stretch the bounds of probability to breaking point but in the process they take on the character of fables.

Doyle could have legitimately dedicated *The Adventures of Sherlock Holmes* to the memory of Edgar Allan Poe, or he could have coupled Poe's name with that of Émile Gaboriau, or he could have dedicated it to Stevenson or Wilde, or to Wilkie Collins, another source of inspiration, or could have found a way of acknowledging his debt to *Tit-Bits*. Instead he dedicated it to Joseph Bell, who in the months before the book's publication was revealed as the model for Sherlock Holmes. It was from Bell, he said, that Sherlock Holmes had acquired his ability to surprise clients by revealing an intimate knowledge of their trade or employment, and it was this which he felt distinguished him from his predecessors: Holmes's powers were not limited to the search for clues about the mystery, but extended beyond it. This ability did not derive from Bell alone, nor was it his exclusive preserve, indeed several points by which a trade could be identified were listed in the columns of *Tit-Bits* ('Peculiarities of Workmen', 10 January 1891); yet Bell came to dominate discussion of Sherlock Holmes and to him went the credit of Holmes's distinctive powers. The fantasy was brought down to earth. Fifty more stories followed in which Sherlock Holmes continued to glow because of his glorious and glamorous past, while the mythic creation was often seen as no more than a well-loved character in the repertoire of a popular writer who had modelled it on his old teacher at Edinburgh.

Joseph Bell (1837–1911) was the son of an Edinburgh surgeon and was educated at the Edinburgh Academy and at Edinburgh University. He rose from dresser to Senior Surgeon and Consulting Surgeon at the Edinburgh Royal Infirmary, edited the *Edinburgh Medical Journal* for twenty-three years (1873–96), and wrote two books on surgery. He was a distinguished practitioner and fondly remembered by students, but it is thanks to Doyle, who attended his classes from 1877 to 1879, that he gained a form of immortality.

In an interview published in the *Bookman* in May 1892 Doyle told Raymond Blathwayt that Sherlock Holmes was the

literary embodiment, if I may so express it, of my memory of a professor of medicine at Edinburgh University, who would sit in the patients' waiting-room with a face like a Red Indian and diagnose the people as they came in, before even they had opened their mouths. He would tell them their symptoms, he would give them details of their lives, and he would hardly ever make a mistake. 'Gentlemen,' he would say to us students standing around, 'I am not quite sure whether this man is a cork-cutter or a slater. I observe a slight *callus*, or hardening, on one side of the forefinger, and a little thickening on the outside of his thumb, and that is a sure sign he is either one or the other.' His great faculty of deduction was at times highly dramatic. 'Ah!' he would say to another man, 'you are a soldier, a non-commissioned officer, and you have served in Bermuda. Now how did I know that, gentlemen? He came into the room without taking his hat off, as he would go into an orderly room. He was a soldier. A slight authoritative air, combined with his age, showed he was an N.C.O. A slight rash on the forehead tells me he was in Bermuda, and subject to a certain rash known only there.'

Further examples of Bell's intuitive powers were given by Doyle in an interview with Harry How in June 1892:

Case No. 1 would step up.

'I see,' said Mr Bell, 'you're suffering from drink. You even carry a flask in the inside pocket of your overcoat.'

Another case would come forward.

'Cobbler, I see.' Then he would turn to the students, and point out to them that the inside of the knee of the man's trousers was worn. That was where the man had rested the lapstone—a peculiarity only found in cobblers.

('A Day with Dr Conan Doyle', *Strand Magazine*, Aug. 1892)

And in the preface to the Author's Edition (1903, written in 1901), he said:

It was my own good fortune to have found the qualities of my hero in actual life, although it was towards the detection of disease rather than of crime that his remarkable talents were directed. Yet, as in my young student days, I saw and heard the ease with which my teacher reasoned from points which were hardly visible to me, and arrived at just conclusions from the most trivial details, there grew upon me the conviction that the resources of the human brain in this direction had never been appreciated, and that a scientific system might give results more remarkable than any of the arbitrary and inexplicable triumphs which so often fall to the lot of the detective in fiction. Monsieur Dupin had, of course, already demonstrated this, and I can only claim the very limited credit of doing it from a fresh model and from a new point of view.

After Doyle mentioned him in the interview of May 1892, Bell wrote in praise of the stories and denied that he had been more than a minor influence upon them. Doyle replied on 4 May 1892, saying:

It is most certainly to you that I owe Sherlock Holmes, and though in the stories I have the advantage of being able to place him in all sorts of dramatic positions I do not think that his analytical work is in the least an exaggeration of some effects which I have seen you produce in the outpatient ward. Round the centre of deduction and inference and observation which I have heard you inculcate I have tried to build up a man who pushed the thing as far as it would go—further occasionally—and I am so glad that the result has satisfied you, who are the critic with the most right to be severe.

Bell then offered an idea for a story about a 'bacteriological criminal'. Doyle told him that it might 'get beyond the average man, whose interest must be held from the first, and who won't be interested unless he thoroughly understands', but he asked for further details and said he would 'be very grateful for any "spotting of trade" tips, or anything else of a Sherlock Holmesy nature' which he might care to provide.[1] Doyle also asked Bell in the letter of 4 May 1892 if he might dedicate the volume to him: 'The book will come out about September and I should much like to inscribe your name upon the fly leaf, if the dedication will not be an intrusion. I am sure that no other name has as good a right to the place' (Brigadier J. N. Stisted Family Papers, Edinburgh).

Bell replied by return accepting the dedication; further letters were exchanged, and Doyle arranged for him to receive copies of his previous books. A long letter from Bell on his deductive methods in teaching, dated from Edinburgh on 16 June 1892 in response to an inquiry from Harry How, concluded the interview with Doyle, which appeared in the *Strand* in August. Thereafter Bell was to be forever associated with Sherlock Holmes. He became a part of the legend, tending to obscure the several divergent strands which make up the character. His importance can be

[1] The 'bacteriological criminal' may ultimately have been realized in the portrait of Culverton Smith, who uses such knowledge to murder his nephew and to attempt to murder Holmes, in 'The Dying Detective' (*His Last Bow*). Bell never saw the story, and it may, indeed, have been his death on 4 October 1911 and Conan Doyle's preparation of an obituary to appear in the *Daily Express* the following day, which resurrected the memory of his old teacher's idea. 'The Dying Detective' was the next Holmes story Doyle would write after composing his tribute to Bell, although it took some months to germinate and did not appear in the *Strand* until December 1913. It was probably the most substantial impact of a suggestion by Bell on the plots of the Holmes cycle [ODE].

exaggerated. The drawback with his skill (as far as the reader is concerned) is that his deductions (relating to a peculiar rash found only in Bermuda or a callus which is a peculiar to a cork-cutter) have to be taken on trust. Moreover, they are the stuff of parody and can all too quickly become ridiculous, at least to non-medical minds.

If Joseph Bell is part of the legend, so too is the *Strand Magazine* in which the Adventures of Sherlock Holmes first appeared. It was planned at the end of 1890 by George Newnes (1851–1910), who had made his fortune with *Tit-Bits*.

W. T Stead (1849–1912)—who had considered going into a partnership with Newnes for the new magazine, but had instead founded the *Review of Reviews*—described it in the *Index to Periodical Literature of the World* (covering the year 1891) thus:

The first number of this mid-monthly was brought out by Mr George Newnes, the well-known conductor of *Tit-Bits*, in January 1891. The ideal of the *Strand* is a six-penny *Harper* or *Scribner*, depending for its future chiefly upon translations from foreign authors, and for its circulation upon the number and quality of its illustrations. It has achieved a phenomenal success. It is well printed, smartly got up, and contains besides its foreign translations, occasional articles of current interest, and portraits of celebrities at various ages.[2]

Doyle may have taken a copy of the first issue with him to Vienna, but it is more probable that he did not see the magazine until his return—when he would certainly have had the March 1891 issue which contained one of his own stories, 'The Voice of Science'. This had been written the previous year and had been offered without success to the

[2] Stead's stern morality does not seem to have dictated his perusal of more than an issue or two of the *Strand*, instead of the year for which he purported to speak. He certainly throws ironic light on the idea of the *Strand* during his own involvement at the blueprint stage. And he enables us to grasp the magnitude of the revolution Sherlock Holmes wrought in its pages. If Stead failed to chart its impact (relying on his knowledge of pre-publication plans) he must have been almost alone [ODE].

English *Figaro*. It then went to A. P. Watt, the agent to whom Doyle had entrusted his literary affairs, and it was accepted by the editor of the *Strand* on 24 January 1891. It was not a notable story and was never collected in book form in its author's lifetime, nor did Doyle's name appear below the title at the head of the text, or even at its close, and it was only to be found in the list of contents at the front or later in the index to the first volume.

Some confusion surrounds the receipt of the next stories. The manuscript of 'A Scandal in Bohemia' is known to have been sent to A. P. Watt on 3 April 1891, as this is the date in Doyle's pocket-diary. Watt sent it to the *Strand Magazine* who received it on 6 April 1891—and this again is certain as the manuscript was date stamped. 'A Case of Identity' and 'The Red-Headed League' were sent to Watt separately, but were presumably offered together to the *Strand*. This seems probable as the order became confused and they were published out of sequence (so that 'The Red-Headed League' which mentions 'A Case of Identity' was published as the second story, rather than as the third). A fourth story followed soon after, and then came the hiatus caused by Doyle's illness. Doyle, however, spoke of three stories, rather than four, when he was interviewed by *Tit-Bits* in 1900. He explained that he had written them in his consulting-room to fill the time while waiting for patients. 'In this way I wrote three stories, which were afterwards published as part of the "Adventures of Sherlock Holmes". The editor liked them, seemed keen on them, and asked for more. The more he asked for the more I turned out, until I had done a dozen. That dozen constituted the volume which was afterwards published as *The Adventures of Sherlock Holmes*' (*Tit-Bits*, 15 December 1900).

There are three accounts by the editor of the *Strand*, Herbert Greenhough Smith (1855–1935), who helped to found the magazine in 1890 and remained as its editor until 1930 (the same year as Doyle's death)—and all are different. The first was given in a 'thumbnail sketch' published in *John O' London's Weekly* on 19 April 1919 (which refers to a description of the offices of *Tit-Bits* in Burleigh Street that were used by the *Strand* until new premises were opened in Southampton Row). He said:

Well I remember how, many years ago when the *Strand Magazine* was making its start in a tiny room at the top of a building in a street off the Strand—a sanctum approached through a room crammed with typewriters, with machines incessantly clicking—there came to me an envelope containing the first two stories of a series which were destined to become famous over all the world as the 'Adventures of Sherlock Holmes'. What a God-send to an editor jaded with wading through reams of impossible stuff! The ingenuity of plot, the limpid clearness of style, the perfect art of telling a story!

He used almost the same words in an obituary of Doyle in the *Strand* for September 1930, but mentions only one story: 'It was in 1891 that, as Editor of the *Strand Magazine*, I received the first of these stories which were destined to become famous over all the world as *The Adventures of Sherlock Holmes*.' He said he had cause to remember the occasion well, spoke of the *Strand* in its infancy, of the editor 'jaded with wading through reams of impossible stuff', and of his pleasure when he read the first story. 'I saw the great possibilities of a fine series, and said so to Sir Arthur, who has generously written in his memoirs how encouraged he was to go ahead.'

Finally in an interview with the *World's Press News* on 18 December 1930 to mark his retirement, he again varied his account. He said that Doyle had written two Sherlock Holmes novels and *The White Company* without creating 'any great sensation in the literary world':

Then he tried short stories, and A. P. Watt, his agent, sent me the first two of Sherlock's Adventures. I realized at once that here was the greatest short story writer since Edgar Allan Poe. I can still remember rushing in to Mr Newnes's room and thrusting the stories before his eyes. He read them with an appreciation equal to my own, and forthwith secured Conan Doyle to write the famous series of Adventures, which eventually ran to over fifty stories.

The probable chain of events must therefore be that the first story was accepted without comment, but that the special quality of Sherlock Holmes and the originality of the format was fully appreciated when the two subsequent stories arrived. Smith and Newnes must then have contacted Doyle and asked him to continue them. The price, which had initially been around £25, was raised to £35 for the later stories. Doyle had always envisaged a series, but he might perhaps have limited the number to four had he not been pressed to continue them. The fifth was written in May after he recovered from his illness, but he spent the whole of July writing *Beyond the City* and did not send off the sixth until August, so there was no sense of urgency.

By the end of April 1891 Smith had four stories which he could run as a series. This was done starting in July using the series title '*Adventures of Sherlock Holmes*', and below it he put 'Adventure I—A Scandal in Bohemia'. The following month he repeated the formula, 'Adventure II—The Red-Headed League', and so on until he reached the last of the six. The pressure from Greenhough Smith and Newnes only became insistent in October 1891 after the first stories had appeared in the *Strand*, and the request was at first refused. On 14 October 1891 Doyle told his mother that 'The *Strand* are simply imploring me to continue Holmes' and that he was writing by the same post to say that if they offered him £50 per story, irrespective of length, he might be induced to reconsider his decision. The *Strand* accepted his terms. By the end of October Doyle had written two of the new Sherlock Holmes stories ('The Blue Carbuncle' and 'The Speckled Band') and he wrote to his mother that he could see his way through a third, 'so that I should not have much trouble with the rest'. On 11 November he told her:

I have done five of the Sherlock Holmes stories of the new Series. They are 1. The Adventure of the Blue Carbuncle. 2. The Adventure of the Speckled Band. 3. The Adventure of the Noble Bachelor. 4. The Adventure of the Engineer's Thumb. 5. The Adventure of the Beryl Coronet. I think that they are up to the standard of the first series, & the twelve ought to make a rather

good book of the sort. I think of slaying Holmes in the sixth &
winding him up for good & all. He takes my mind from better
things. I think your golden haired idea has the making of a tale in
it, but I think it would be better not as a detective tale, but as a
separate one.[3]

He might have carried out his threat to kill Holmes had
not his mother restrained him. It was her influence, and
indeed her suggestion of a story about a girl who was
kidnapped and made to cut her hair so as to impersonate
another woman, which saved Holmes for a subsequent
series.

There was understandable relief in the new offices of the
Strand in October 1891 when Doyle agreed to write six
further stories, and mention of it was made when Doyle was
included among the 'Portraits of Celebrities at Different
Times of their Lives' in the December 1891 issue. The
accompanying note said: 'There are few better writers of
short stories than Mr Conan Doyle, and it gives us great
pleasure to announce that the extraordinary adventures of
Sherlock Holmes, which have proved so popular with our
readers during the past six months, will be continued in the
new year.'

There was no break between them, but the headings for
the new stories were different. It was the same series title,
followed by the number, thus: 'VII. The Adventure of the
Blue Carbuncle'. This clearly differentiates the two series
and would have posed problems on the contents page of the
first book edition, if it had had one. But Newnes, who
published the book using the *Strand Magazine* presses, with
the same size paper and the same heavy bevelled covers, did
not include a contents page, though he did make the titles
uniform within the text. The result was not entirely satisfactory as these appeared as 'The Adventures [*sic*] of a Scandal
in Bohemia', 'The Adventure of the Red-Headed League',

---

[3] ACD to Mary Doyle; MS facsimile in Dickson Carr, *Life* (facing p. 64);
other quotations taken from Dickson Carr, pp. 86–7. Carr was not a perfect
copyist.

'The Adventure of a Case of Identity', 'The Adventure of the Boscombe Valley Mystery', 'The Adventure of the Five Orange Pips', and 'The Adventure of the Man with the Twisted Lip'.

Today the chief importance of the magazine lies in the illustrations. These were by Sidney Edward Paget (1860–1908) and they are as closely associated with the text as 'Phiz' (Hablot Knight Browne) to Dickens or Sir John Tenniel to Lewis Carroll. They were greatly superior to the earlier illustrations, which now tend to be forgotten. There were several clumsy woodcuts for *A Study in Scarlet* in *Beeton's Christmas Annual*, and Doyle's father, Charles, had produced spindly drawings for the first separate edition of 1888. The first edition of *The Sign of Four* had an unattractive frontispiece by Charles Kerr (1858–1907), and Holmes had been shown wearing a deerstalker in the small woodcuts that accompanied a reprint of *The Sign of Four* in the *Bristol Observer*. But it was left to Sidney Paget to produce the definitive drawings, and they are still familiar because of the large number of copies of the magazine that were printed and the facsimiles made from it.

Paget probably received the commission in error, for the art editor is believed to have wanted his brother, Walter (1863–1935). Paget had no artistic pretensions, but his style was suitable, and it is hard now to imagine how any artist could have improved upon it. He established the popular conception of Sherlock Holmes, and in particular gave him the deerstalker and travelling cape which are now indelibly associated with him. These were first seen in the drawings for 'The Boscombe Valley Mystery' and used again in a scene in a railway carriage in 'Silver Blaze' (*Strand*, Dec. 1892). The furniture and backgrounds found in the drawings were based on Paget's own (as were many of the clothes), and his friends and relations were used as models. For Holmes he used his brother, Walter; for Dr Watson, there was Alfred Morris Butler who had been a contemporary at the Royal Academy School; and another face belonged to his brother-in-law, Stephen Martin.

Doyle's physical conception of his creation, however, was different. 'My own view of Sherlock Holmes,' he said in the interview with *Tit-Bits* (15 December 1900), '—I mean the man as I saw him in my imagination—was quite different from that which Mr Paget pictured in the *Strand Magazine*. I, however, am eminently pleased with his work, and quite understand the aspect which he gave to the character, and am even prepared to accept him now as Mr Paget drew him. In my own mind, however, he was a more beaky-nosed, hawk-faced man, approaching more to the Red Indian type, than the artist represented him, but, as I have said, Mr Paget's pictures please me very much.' This was evidently so from the beginning as Doyle had written to the editor of the *Strand* on 9 July 1891, immediately after the first story had appeared, saying: 'Should you see the Artist who did my "Sherlock Holmes", I wish you would tell him how very much I appreciate his rendering. I hope the blocks may be preserved so that my future publisher may have the refusal of them.' Paget went on to illustrate *The Memoirs of Sherlock Holmes*, *The Hound of the Baskervilles*, and *The Return of Sherlock Holmes*, but died before the other stories were published. Doyle paid him a further tribute in a speech at the Stoll Convention Dinner on 27 September 1921. 'In the early days it was Sidney Paget who illustrated those stories so well that he made a type which the whole English-reading race came to recognize, and I may say here that in his premature death English art lost a very great asset.'

The publication of the first short Sherlock Holmes stories in America was left to Samuel Sidney McClure (1857–1949) who had founded a newspaper syndicate in 1886. In his autobiography he says that he first heard of the name of Conan Doyle when he visited Andrew Lang at St Andrews during a visit to Britain in 1889. Lang, who was a reader for Longman's, told him that they were about to bring out *Micah Clarke*. If this were so, it would have been in February 1889 as the book was published on 25 February 1889. Lang also informed McClure that Doyle had written *A Study in*

Scarlet, which he highly recommended. 'On the train going down from Scotland,' McClure recalled, 'I bought the shilling-shocker at a news-stand, and as soon as I had read it decided to go after Doyle's stories for the syndicate.' He then elides this memory with the purchase of the short stories—which cannot have been before April or May 1891: 'I bought the first twelve Sherlock Holmes stories from Mr Watt, Conan Doyle's agent, and paid £12 ($60) apiece for them.' He explained that the syndicate inundated newspapers with fiction and articles in proof form, for which he would fix different rates according to their circulation and capacity to pay. The papers received copies of all the stories for use within a certain period, but they only paid for those for which they had space. Thus the length of the Sherlock Holmes stories was potentially problematic. 'The usual syndicate story ran about five thousand words, and these ran up to eight and nine thousand. We got a good many complaints from editors about their length, and it was not until nearly all of the first twelve of the Sherlock Holmes stories had been published that the editors of the papers I served began to comment favorably upon the series and that the public began to take a keen interest' (S.S. McClure, *My Autobiography*, 1914).

Syndication could produce large profits and this was not lost on Doyle, who was adept at promoting his own work. After *The Sign of the Four* had appeared in *Lippincott's Magazine*, he was asked by the editor of a regional British paper if it might have the second serial rights. Doyle checked with Lippincott and found that after a certain period the rights would revert to him and he could dispose of them as he wished. He therefore made a list of all the likely newspapers and wrote to the editors offering them the second use of the Sherlock Holmes story. Three accepted his offer (or four if one includes the initial request), but the exercise paid dividends later as it served as an introduction and the sudden fame of Sherlock Holmes made many editors realize the mistake they had made in refusing the story when it was offered.

Doyle's promotion of his stories is also evident in the text. The first of the short stories made a direct allusion to *A Study in Scarlet* and *The Sign of the Four* (which the editor of the *Strand* removed), and most of the *Adventures* referred to at least one of the short stories or novels which had preceded it. Even after Watt was employed as his agent, he remained in direct touch with his publishers and demanded the highest possible price for his stories. Nor did the self-promotion end there for he even paid to advertise *The Adventures of Sherlock Holmes*. The first English edition was published on 14 October 1892 in an edition of 10,000 copies and nearly 8,000 had been sold by December. Doyle then stepped in, and on 9 January 1893 he told A.P. Watt:

Newnes has nothing to do with the advertising. I enclose £25. Let the advertisement be twice a week in *Daily Telegraph*, *Daily News*, *Standard*, and *Pall Mall*, as long as money lasts.

Simply:

First edition of 10,000 nearly exhausted
The Adventures of Sherlock Holmes
by
A. Conan Doyle
[Gilt edges, 104 illustrations. 6s]
Newnes & Co., Southampton St.

Whether because of the advertisements or because of the popularity of the book (which had to compete with the bound volumes of the magazine that were printed in large numbers) the edition was soon exhausted; a further five thousand were printed in 1893 and another five thousand the following year. The American edition fared less well. Newspaper syndication was profitable for authors, but it was a diffuse system, wholly dependent on the whims of editors. Sherlock Holmes was not therefore a household name in America and the first American edition of the *Adventures*, which was published by Harpers on 15 October 1892, was kept to 4,500 copies. But the sales grew and the popularity of Sherlock Holmes increased when the stories which make up *The Memoirs of Sherlock Holmes* began appearing in

Harper's Weekly. The *Adventures* never afterwards went out of print.

The appearance of the first Holmes short stories coincided with a new copyright agreement between Britain and the United States—which ended the free-for-all piracy between the two countries. The first three 'Adventures', however, were not protected by copyright and were first published in pirated editions of *The Doings of Raffles Haw*, and later as separate editions or in any number of combinations. This may not have been of financial benefit to Doyle, but the existence of the pirate editions—which also included *A Study in Scarlet* and *The Sign of Four*—probably did more to make the name of Sherlock Holmes known in America than the initial syndication.

The Adventures of Sherlock Holmes was well received by the critics. Joseph Bell, to whom it was dedicated and by whom it was said to have been inspired, reviewed it in the *Bookman* for December 1892 (an essay afterwards used by the publishers Ward, Lock in a slightly shortened form as a preface to *A Study in Scarlet*, of which they owned the copyright, having bought it from the inexperienced author for £25). He began by dismissing much of the current journalism as intellectually barren, but found hope in the books which encouraged thought and stimulated observation. Among these he put the detective stories by Conan Doyle: 'He created a shrewd, quick-sighted, inquisitive man, half doctor, half virtuoso, with plenty of spare time, a retentive memory, and perhaps with the best gift of all—the power of unloading the mind of all the burden of trying to remember unnecessary details . . . to him the petty results of environment, the sign-manuals of labour, the stains of trade, the incidents of travel, have living interest, as they tend to satisfy an insatiable, almost inhuman, because impersonal curiosity.'

Bell was impressed by the character of Sherlock Holmes, but also praised Doyle as a 'born story teller': 'He has had the wit to devise excellent plots, interesting complications; he tells them in honest Saxon-English with directness and pith; and, above all his other merits, his stories are absolutely free from padding.' Doyle, he said, 'knows how delicious brevity is, how everything tends to be too long, and he has given us stories that we can read at a sitting between dinner and coffee, and we have not a chance to forget the beginning before we reach the end.' Of the stories themselves, he said: 'One man will enjoy "The Red-Headed League"; another "The Blue Carbuncle"; for the average reader "The Speckled Band" has special charms. The story of "The Five Orange Pips" will probably come home to the American, and "The Noble Bachelor" will interest Mayfair. In "The Engineer's Thumb" Mr Holmes has less to do, but what he does is done with his usual directness of action, guided by simplicity of method. Not one of the twelve is a failure, and the handsome volume in which they have been collected will be a prize for all those young and old who are not ashamed to read good stories.'

Praise also came from another person who had been an influence on the book (and who had known Joseph Bell in Edinburgh). Robert Louis Stevenson wrote to Doyle on 5 April 1893 thanking him for the many occasions on which he had made himself agreeable': 'It is now my turn; and I hope you will allow me to offer you my compliments on your very ingenious and very interesting adventures of Sherlock Holmes. That is the class of literature that I like when I have the toothache. As a matter of fact, it was a pleurisy I was enjoying when I took the volume up; and it will interest you as a medical man to know that the cure was for the moment effectual. Only one thing troubles me: can this be my old friend Joe Bell?' (*The Letters of Robert Louis Stevenson*, 1899).

Other critics were equally generous, and a review in the *Speaker* for 26 November 1892 may serve as an example. It spoke of the 'inimitable Sherlock Holmes' and said the stories were 'in the very first rank of their class' and proof that France was not the only country that could produce a Gaboriau: 'And then Mr Doyle, unlike Gaboriau, is never tedious. He does not prolong the agonies either of his reader or of the victims of the plots it is his business to unravel. The result is a volume which may be safely commended to all who like sensational stories of the best class, ingenious in plot, graceful in narration, and absorbing in interest.'

A less conventional review, though one which has had a prodigious progeny, was entitled 'The Real Sherlock Holmes' and appeared on 29 October 1892 in the *National Observer* (previously the *Scots Observer*, and in both identities edited by the crippled poet William Ernest Henley (1849–1903)). It was by 'Our Special Correspondent' who in view of the recent publication of some of his more celebrated cases had called upon the famous scientific detective 'for the purpose of elucidating if possible some of the more eventful and thrilling episodes in his adventures'. Sherlock Holmes was quoted as saying that he was less than happy with Mr Doyle's plagiarism, and he complained that the book was 'a garbled version of some very inferior incidents' in his professional career: 'I have been grossly misrepresented by him,' he said. 'Do you think I really made that blunder in "A Scandal in Bohemia"? Do you imagine I really had as little a finger in "The Engineer's Thumb" and "The Copper Beeches" as he makes out? And do you suppose I interfered as ineffectually in the "Five Pips" as he represents?' Obviously Doyle had heard of him through Dr Watson: 'With my name, and a fairly accurate account of those interesting cases of mine, "The Blue Carbuncle" and "The Speckled Band", he made a good start; and after that anything would sell[,] even stuff like "The Engineer's Thumb" or the "The Noble Husband" [*sic*].'

The reality of Sherlock Holmes was a quality which struck readers and critics alike. It was evident from the start and the stories seemed to lend themselves naturally to parody and pastiche. One of the first, 'My Evening with Sherlock Holmes', appeared in the *Speaker* on 28 November 1891; and the correspondence columns of *Tit-Bits* (which published letters addressed to the *Strand*) were inclined to treat him as a real person. On 23 January 1892 it replied to a letter from 'Buttons' who wished to know whether Sherlock Holmes 'is or is not an actual living person'. The editors were unable to say: 'As a matter of fact we have not made the personal acquaintance of Mr Sherlock Holmes, but we have read so much of his doings that we have made up our minds that if there is a mystery in connection with this office we shall endeavour to find out the whereabouts of Mr Sherlock Holmes and employ him to investigate it, and if when that time comes we should find that no such person is in existence we shall then be very much disappointed.'

In the *Saturday Review* for 6 May 1905, Max Beerbohm (1872–1956) resorted to Sherlockian pastiche when writing a review of a society thriller by E. Temple Thurston, *John Chilcote, MP*, in performance at the St James's Theatre starring the actor-manager George Alexander (1858–1918). Beerbohm feared that he might be getting old, and that his younger readers would not share his views of Sherlock Holmes: 'But I was at an impressionable age when he burst upon the world; and so he became a part of my life, and will never, I suppose, be utterly dislodged. I can not pass through Baker Street, even now, without thinking of him . . . My sentiment for Sherlock Holmes was never one of reverence unalloyed. Indeed, one of the secrets of his hold on me was that he so often amused me.'

T. S. Eliot (1888–1965) also succumbed to the spell and in a review of the collected edition of the short stories (*Criterion*, April 1929) wondered why this was so. The greatest of the Sherlock Holmes mysteries, he said, was 'that when we talk of him we invariably fall into the fancy of his existence'. Holmes was more real than Doyle and yet his reality was a reality of its own kind. He was open to criticism and yet remained the pre-eminent detective, the one which readers would prefer over all others:

It is of course, the dramatic ability, rather than the pure detective ability, that does it. But it is a dramatic ability applied with great cunning and concentration; it is not spilt about. The content of the story may be poor; but the form is nearly always perfect. We are so well worked up by the dramatic preparation that we accept the conclusion—even when, as in 'The Red-Headed League', it is perfectly obvious from the beginning.

'But every writer owes something to Holmes,' said Eliot.

And every critic of The Novel who has a theory about the reality of characters in fiction, would do well to consider Holmes. There is no rich humanity, no deep and cunning psychology and knowledge of the human heart about him; he is obviously a formula. He has not the reality of any great character of Dickens or Thackeray or George Eliot or Meredith or Hardy; or Jane Austen or the Brontës or Virginia Woolf or James Joyce: yet, as I suggested, he is just as real to us as Falstaff or the Wellers. He is not even a very good detective. But I am not sure that Sir Arthur Conan Doyle is not one of the great dramatic authors of his age.

Similarly Hesketh Pearson (1887–1964) (in *G.K.'s Weekly*, 5 October 1929), recognized that 'there is an illusion of truth even about the most improbable deductive achievements recorded by Watson'. Holmes 'bestrides the earth like a Colossus' but is always of the earth. 'His personality is so magnetic that even his improbabilities become him. One criticizes him, but one always returns to him. His faults no less than his virtues, endear him to us, because he is an old and intimate friend.'

For Edmund Wilson (1895–1972), imagination and style set the Sherlock Holmes stories in a different category from other mystery writers. 'My contention is,' he said in an article for the *New Yorker* (17 Feb. 1945), 'that Sherlock Holmes is literature on a humble but not ignoble level.' He described the stories as fairy tales (a term which Doyle himself had used) in which the central characters had become detached from their author and lived a life of their own. Holmes was a genie let out of a bottle. He was the result of a spell, made up of elements borrowed from Poe and Stevenson, but from which Doyle had developed his own vein of fantasy in which the reader could feel the presence of the 'sinister'. It was an epic over which hung 'an air of irrepressible comedy'.

The Adventures of Sherlock Holmes has the richest vein of fantasy of any work by Conan Doyle. It stands alongside *Treasure Island, The Wrong Box, The Picture of Dorian Gray*, and *Three Men in a Boat*, as an expression of its period. It is part dream, part comedy, and part illusion. It is Conan Doyle's greatest masterpiece, so strong at the start that the reader overlooks any weaknesses in the later stories. It is perhaps the peak of its creator's achievement.

RICHARD LANCELYN GREEN

NOTE ON THE TEXT

The text is based on the first edition (George Newnes, 1892), collated with the original appearances of the twelve stories in the *Strand Magazine* (July 1891–June 1892), except for 'A Scandal in Bohemia', which has also been collated with the MS.

SELECT BIBLIOGRAPHY

I. A. CONAN DOYLE: PRINCIPAL WORKS

(a) *Fiction*

A Study in Scarlet (Ward, Lock, & Co., 1888)
The Mystery of Cloomber (Ward & Downey, 1888)
Micah Clarke (Longmans, Green, & Co., 1889)
The Captain of the Pole-Star and Other Tales (Longmans, Green, & Co., 1890)
The Sign of the Four (Spencer Blackett, 1890)
The Firm of Girdlestone (Chatto & Windus, 1890)
The White Company (Smith, Elder, & Co., 1891)
The Adventures of Sherlock Holmes (George Newnes, 1892)
The Great Shadow (Arrowsmith, 1892)
The Refugees (Longmans, Green, & Co., 1893)
The Memoirs of Sherlock Holmes (George Newnes, 1893)
Round the Red Lamp (Methuen & Co., 1894)
The Stark Munro Letters (Longmans, Green, & Co., 1895)
The Exploits of Brigadier Gerard (George Newnes, 1896)
Rodney Stone (Smith, Elder, & Co., 1896)
Uncle Bernac (Smith, Elder, & Co., 1897)
The Tragedy of the Korosko (Smith, Elder, & Co., 1898)
A Duet With an Occasional Chorus (Grant Richards, 1899)
The Green Flag and Other Stories of War and Sport (Smith, Elder, & Co., 1900)
The Hound of the Baskervilles (George Newnes, 1902)
Adventures of Gerard (George Newnes, 1903)
The Return of Sherlock Holmes (George Newnes, 1905)
Sir Nigel (Smith, Elder, & Co., 1906)
Round the Fire Stories (Smith, Elder, & Co., 1908)
The Last Galley (Smith, Elder, & Co., 1911)
The Lost World (Hodder & Stoughton, 1912)
The Poison Belt (Hodder & Stoughton, 1913)
The Valley of Fear (Smith, Elder, & Co., 1915)
His Last Bow (John Murray, 1917)
Danger! and Other Stories (John Murray, 1918)
The Land of Mist (Hutchinson & Co., 1926)
The Case-Book of Sherlock Holmes (John Murray, 1927)
The Maracot Deep and Other Stories (John Murray, 1929)

The Complete Sherlock Holmes Short Stories (John Murray, 1928)
The Conan Doyle Stories (John Murray, 1929)
The Complete Sherlock Holmes Long Stories (John Murray, 1929)

(b) *Non-fiction*

The Great Boer War (Smith, Elder, & Co., 1900)
The Story of Mr George Edalji (T. Harrison Roberts, 1907)
Through the Magic Door (Smith, Elder, & Co., 1907)
The Crime of the Congo (Hutchinson & Co., 1909)
The Case of Oscar Slater (Hodder & Stoughton, 1912)
The German War (Hodder & Stoughton, 1914)
The British Campaign in France and Flanders (Hodder & Stoughton, 6 vols., 1916–20)
The Poems of Arthur Conan Doyle (John Murray, 1922)
Memories and Adventures (Hodder & Stoughton, 1924; revised edn., 1930)
The History of Spiritualism (Cassell & Co., 1926)

2. MISCELLANEOUS

A Bibliography of A. Conan Doyle (Soho Bibliographies 23: Oxford, 1983) by Richard Lancelyn Green and John Michael Gibson, with a foreword by Graham Greene, is the standard—and indispensable—source of bibliographical information, and of much else besides. Green and Gibson have also assembled and introduced *The Unknown Conan Doyle*, comprising *Uncollected Stories* (those never previously published in book form); *Essays on Photography* (documenting a little-known enthusiasm of Conan Doyle's during his time as a student and young doctor), both published in 1982; and *Letters to the Press* (1986). Alone, Richard Lancelyn Green has compiled (1) *The Uncollected Sherlock Holmes* (1983), an impressive assemblage of Holmesiana, containing almost all Conan Doyle's writing about his creation (other than the stories themselves) together with related material by Joseph Bell, J. M. Barrie, and Beverley Nichols; (2) *The Further Adventures of Sherlock Holmes* (1985), a selection of eleven apocryphal Holmes adventures by various authors, all diplomatically introduced; (3) *The Sherlock Holmes Letters* (1986), a collection of noteworthy public correspondence on Holmes and Holmesiana and far more valuable than its title suggests; and (4) *Letters to Sherlock Holmes* (1984), a powerful testimony to the power of the Holmes stories.

Though much of Conan Doyle's work is now readily available there are still gaps. Some of his very earliest fiction now only survives in rare piracies (apart, that is, from the magazines in which they were first published), including items of intrinsic genre interest such as 'The Gully of Bluemansdyke' (1881) and its sequel 'My Friend the Murderer' (1882), which both turn on the theme of the murderer-informer (handled very differently—and far better—in the Holmes story of 'The Resident Patient' (*Memoirs*)): both of these were used as book-titles for the same pirate collection first issued as *Mysteries and Adventures* (1889). Other stories achieved book publication only after severe pruning—for example, 'The Surgeon of Gaster Fell', reprinted in *Danger!* many years after magazine publication (1890). Some items given initial book publication were not included in the collected edition of *The Conan Doyle Stories*. Particularly deplorable losses were 'John Barrington Cowles' (1884: included subsequently in *Edinburgh Stories of Arthur Conan Doyle* (1981)), 'A Foreign Office Romance' (1894), 'The Club-Footed Grocer' (1898), 'A Shadow Before' (1898), and 'Danger!' (1914). Three of these may have been post-war casualties, as seeming to deal too lightheartedly with the outbreak of other wars; 'John Barrington Cowles' may have been dismissed as juvenile work; but why Conan Doyle discarded a story as good as 'The Club-Footed Grocer' would baffle even Holmes.

At the other end of his life, Conan Doyle's tidying impaired the survival of his most recent work, some of which well merited lasting recognition. *The Maracot Deep and Other Stories* appeared in 1929, a little over a month after *The Conan Doyle Stories*; 'Maracot' itself found a separate paperback life as a short novel; the two Professor Challenger stories, 'The Disintegration Machine' and 'When the World Screamed', were naturally included in John Murray's *The Professor Challenger Stories* (1952); but the fourth item, 'The Story of Spedegue's Dropper', passed beyond the ken of most of Conan Doyle's readers. These three stories show the author, in his seventieth year, still at the height of his powers.

In 1980 Gaslight Publications, of Bloomington, Ind., reprinted *The Mystery of Cloomber*, *The Firm of Girdlestone*, *The Doings of Raffles Haw* (1892), *Beyond the City* (1893), *The Parasite* (1894; also reprinted in *Edinburgh Stories of Arthur Conan Doyle*), *The Stark Munro Letters*, *The Tragedy of the Korosko*, and *A Duet*. *Memories and Adventures*, Conan Doyle's enthralling but impressionistic recollections, are best read in the revised (1930) edition. *Through the Magic Door* remains the best introduction to the literary mind of Conan Doyle, whilst some of his volumes on Spiritualism have autobiographical material of literary significance.

ACD: The Journal of the Arthur Conan Doyle Society (ed. Christopher Roden, David Stuart Davies [to 1991], and Barbara Roden [from 1992]), together with its newsletter, *The Parish Magazine*, is a useful source of critical and biographical material on Conan Doyle. The enormous body of 'Sherlockiana' is best pursued in *The Baker Street Journal*, published by Fordham University Press, or in the *Sherlock Holmes Journal* (Sherlock Holmes Society of London), itemized up to 1974 in the colossal *World Bibliography of Sherlock Holmes and Doctor Watson* (1974) by Ronald Burt De Waal (see also De Waal, *The International Sherlock Holmes* (1980)) and digested in *The Annotated Sherlock Holmes* (2 vols., 1968) by William S. Baring-Gould, whose industry has been invaluable for the Oxford Sherlock Holmes editors. Jack Tracy, *The Encyclopaedia Sherlockiana* (1979) is a very helpful compilation of relevant data. Those who can nerve themselves to consult it despite its title will benefit greatly from Christopher Redmond, *In Bed With Sherlock Holmes* (1984). The classic 'Sherlockian' work is Ronald A. Knox, 'Studies in the Literature of Sherlock Holmes', first published in *The Blue Book* (July 1912) and reprinted in his *Essays in Satire* (1928).

The serious student of Conan Doyle may perhaps deplore the vast extent of 'Sherlockian' literature, even though the size of this output is testimony in itself to the scale and nature of Conan Doyle's achievement. But there is undoubtedly some wheat amongst the chaff. At the head stands Dorothy L. Sayers, *Unpopular Opinions* (1946); also of some interest are T. S. Blakeney, *Sherlock Holmes: Fact or Fiction* (1932), H. W. Bell, *Sherlock Holmes and Dr Watson* (1932), Vincent Starrett, *The Private Life of Sherlock Holmes* (1934), Gavin Brend, *My Dear Holmes* (1951), S. C. Roberts, *Holmes and Watson* (1953) and Roberts's introduction to *Sherlock Holmes: Selected Stories* (Oxford: The World's Classics, 1951), James E. Holroyd, *Baker Street Byways* (1959), Ian McQueen, *Sherlock Holmes Detected* (1974), and Trevor H. Hall, *Sherlock Holmes and his Creator* (1978). One Sherlockian item certainly falls into the category of the genuinely essential: D. Martin Dakin, *A Sherlock Holmes Commentary* (1972), to which all the editors of the present series are indebted.

Michael Pointer, *The Public Life of Sherlock Holmes* (1975) contains invaluable information concerning dramatizations of the Sherlock Holmes stories for radio, stage, and the cinema; of complementary interest are Chris Steinbrunner and Norman Michaels, *The Films of Sherlock Holmes* (1978) and David Stuart Davies, *Holmes of the Movies* (1976), whilst Philip Weller with Christopher Roden, *The Life and Times of Sherlock Holmes* (1992) summarizes a great deal of useful information concerning Conan Doyle's life and Holmes's cases, and in addition is delightfully illustrated. The more concrete products of the Holmes industry are dealt with in Charles Hall, *The Sherlock Holmes Collection* (1987). For a useful retrospective view, Allen Eyles, *Sherlock Holmes: A Centenary Celebration* (1986) rises to the occasion. Both useful and engaging are Peter Haining, *The Sherlock Holmes Scrapbook* (1973) and Charles Viney, *Sherlock Holmes in London* (1989).

Of the many anthologies of Holmesiana, P. A. Shreffler (ed.), *The Baker Street Reader* (1984) is exceptionally useful. D. A. Redmond, *Sherlock Holmes: A Study in Sources* (1982) is similarly indispensable. Michael Hardwick, *The Complete Guide to Sherlock Holmes* (1986) is both reliable and entertaining; Michael Harrison, *In the Footsteps of Sherlock Holmes* (1958) is occasionally helpful.

For more general studies of the detective story, the standard history is Julian Symons, *Bloody Murder* (1972, 1985, 1992). Necessary but a great deal less satisfactory is Howard Haycraft, *Murder for Pleasure* (1942); of more value is Haycraft's critical anthology *The Art of the Mystery Story* (1946), which contains many choice period items. Both R. F. Stewart, *. . . And Always a Detective* (1980) and Colin Watson, *Snobbery with Violence* (1971) are occasionally useful. Dorothy Sayers's pioneering introduction to *Great Short Stories of Detection, Mystery and Horror* (First Series, 1928), despite some inspired howlers, is essential reading; Raymond Chandler's riposte, 'The Simple Art of Murder' (1944), is reprinted in Haycraft, *The Art of the Mystery Story* (see above). Less well known than Sayers's essay but with an equal claim to poineer status is E. M. Wrong's introduction to *Crime and Detection*, First Series (Oxford: The World's Classics, 1926). See also Michael Cox (ed.), *Victorian Tales of Mystery and Detection: An Oxford Anthology* (1992).

Amongst biographical studies of Conan Doyle one of the most distinguished is Jon L. Lellenberg's survey, *The Quest for Sir Arthur Conan Doyle* (1987), with a Foreword by Dame Jean Conan Doyle (much the best piece of writing on ACD by any member of his family). The four earliest biographers—the Revd John Lamond (1931), Hesketh Pearson (1943), John Dickson Carr (1949), and Pierre Nordon (1964)—all had access to the family archives, subsequently closed to researchers following a lawsuit; hence all four biographies contain valuable documentary material, though Nordon handles the evidence best (the French text is fuller than the English version, published in 1966). Of the others, Lamond seems only to have made little use of the material available to him;

Pearson is irreverent and wildly careless with dates; Dickson Carr has a strong fictionalizing element. Both he and Nordon paid a price for their access to the Conan Doyle papers by deferring to the far from impartial editorial demands of Adrian Conan Doyle; Nordon nevertheless remains the best available biography. The best short sketch is Julian Symons, *Conan Doyle* (1979) (and for the late Victorian milieu of the Holmes cycle some of Symons's own fiction, such as *The Blackheath Poisonings* and *The Detling Secret*, can be thoroughly recommended). Harold Orel (ed.), *Critical Essays on Sir Arthur Conan Doyle* (1992) is a good and varied collection, whilst Robin Winks, *The Historian as Detective* (1969) contains many insights and examples applicable to the Holmes corpus; Winks's *Detective Fiction: A Collection of Critical Essays* (1980) is an admirable working handbook, with a useful critical bibliography. Edmund Wilson's famous essay 'Mr Holmes, they were the footprints of a gigantic hound' (1944) may be found in his *Classics and Commercials: A Literary Chronicle of the Forties* (1950).

Specialized biographical areas are covered in Owen Dudley Edwards, *The Quest for Sherlock Holmes: A Biographical Study of Arthur Conan Doyle* (1983) and in Geoffrey Stavert, *A Study in Southsea: The Unrevealed Life of Dr Arthur Conan Doyle* (1987), which respectively assess the significance of the years up to 1882, and from 1882 to 1890. Alvin E. Rodin and Jack D. Key provide a thorough study of Conan Doyle's medical career and its literary implications in *Medical Casebook of Dr Arthur Conan Doyle* (1984). Peter Costello, in *The Real World of Sherlock Holmes: The True Crimes Investigated by Arthur Conan Doyle* (1991) claims too much, but it is useful to be reminded of events that came within Conan Doyle's orbit, even if they are sometimes tangential or even irrelevant. Christopher Redmond, *Welcome to America, Mr Sherlock Holmes* (1987) is a thorough account of Conan Doyle's tour of North America in 1894.

Other than Baring-Gould (see above), the only serious attempt to annotate the nine volumes of the Holmes cycle has been in the Longman Heritage of Literature series (1979–80), to which the present editors are also indebted. Of introductions to individual texts, H. R. F. Keating's to the *Adventures* and *The Hound of the Baskervilles* (published in one volume under the dubious title *The Best of Sherlock Holmes* (1992)) is worthy of particular mention.

A CHRONOLOGY OF ARTHUR CONAN DOYLE

1855   Charles Altamont Doyle, youngest son of the political cartoonist John Doyle ('HB'), and Mary Foley, his Irish landlady's daughter, marry in Edinburgh on 31 July.

1859   Arthur Ignatius Conan Doyle, third child and elder son of ten siblings, born at 11 Picardy Place, Edinburgh, on 22 May and baptized into the Roman Catholic religion of his parents.

1868–75 ACD commences two years' education under the Jesuits at Hodder, followed by five years at its senior sister college, Stonyhurst, both in the Ribble Valley, Lancashire; becomes a popular storyteller amongst his fellow-pupils, writes verses, edits a school paper, and makes one close friend, James Ryan of Glasgow and Ceylon. Doyle family resides at 3 Sciennes Hill Place, Edinburgh.

1875–6   ACD passes London Matriculation Examination at Stonyhurst and studies for a year in the Jesuit college at Feldkirch, Austria.

1876–7   ACD becomes a student of medicine at Edinburgh University on the advice of Bryan Charles Waller, now lodging with the Doyle family at 2 Argyle Park Terrace.

1877–80 Waller leases 23 George Square, Edinburgh as a 'consulting pathologist', with all the Doyles as residents. ACD continues medical studies, becoming surgeon's clerk to Joseph Bell at Edinburgh; also takes temporary medical assistantships at Sheffield, Ruyton (Salop), and Birmingham, the last leading to a close friendship with his employer's family, the Hoares. First story published, 'The Mystery of Sasassa Valley', in *Chambers's Journal* (6 Sept. 1879); first non-fiction published—'Gelseminum as a Poison', *British Medical Journal* (20 Sept. 1879). Sometime previously ACD sends 'The Haunted Grange of Goresthorpe' to *Blackwood's Edinburgh Magazine*, but it is filed and forgotten.

1880   (Feb.–Sept.) ACD serves as surgeon on the Greenland whaler *Hope* of Peterhead.

1881   ACD graduates MB, CM (Edin.); Waller and the Doyles
        living at 15 Lonsdale Terrace, Edinburgh.

1881–2 (Oct.–Jan.) ACD serves as surgeon on the steamer
        Mayumba to West Africa, spending three days with US
        Minister to Liberia, Henry Highland Garnet, black
        abolitionist leader, then dying. (July–Aug.) Visits Foley
        relatives in Lismore, Co. Waterford.

1882   Ill-fated partnership with George Turnavine Budd in
        Plymouth. ACD moves to Southsea, Portsmouth, in
        June. ACD published in *London Society*, *All the Year Round*,
        Lancet, and *British Journal of Photography*. Over the next
        eight years ACD becomes an increasingly successful
        general practitioner at Southsea.

1882–3 Breakup of the Doyle family in Edinburgh. Charles
        Altamont Doyle henceforth confined because of alcohol-
        ism and epilepsy. Mary Foley Doyle resident in Mason-
        gill Cottage on the Waller estate at Masongill, Yorkshire.
        Innes Doyle (b. 1873) resident with ACD as schoolboy
        and surgery page from Sept. 1882.

1883   'The Captain of the *Pole-Star*' published (*Temple Bar*,
        Jan.), as well as a steady stream of minor pieces. Works
        on *The Mystery of Cloomber*.

1884   ACD publishes 'J. Habakuk Jephson's Statement' (*Corn-
        hill Magazine*, Jan.), 'The Heiress of Glenmahowley'
        (*Temple Bar*, Jan.), 'The Cabman's Story' (*Cassell's Satur-
        day Journal*, May); working on *The Firm of Girdlestone*.

1885   Publishes 'The Man from Archangel' (*London Society*,
        Jan.). John Hawkins, briefly a resident patient with
        ACD, dies of cerebral meningitis. Louisa Hawkins, his
        sister, marries ACD. (Aug.) Travels in Ireland for honey-
        moon. Awarded Edinburgh MD.

1886   Writing *A Study in Scarlet*.

1887   *A Study in Scarlet* published in *Beeton's Christmas Annual*.

1888   (July) First book edition of *A Study in Scarlet* published by
        Ward, Lock; (Dec.) *The Mystery of Cloomber* published.

1889   (Feb.) *Micah Clarke* (ACD's novel of the Monmouth
        Rebellion of 1685) published. Mary Louise Conan
        Doyle, ACD's eldest child, born. Unauthorized publica-
        tion of *Mysteries and Adventures* (published later as *The*

Gully of Bluemansdyke and *My Friend the Murderer*). *The Sign of the Four* and Oscar Wilde's *The Picture of Dorian Gray* commissioned by Lippincott's.

1890   (Jan.) 'Mr [R. L.] Stevenson's Methods in Fiction' published in the *National Review*. (Feb.) *The Sign of the Four* published in *Lippincott's Monthly Magazine*; (Mar.) first authorized short-story collection, *The Captain of the Pole-star and other tales*, published; (Apr.) *The Firm of Girdlestone* published; (Oct.) first book edition of the *Sign* published by Spencer Blackett.

1891   ACD sets up as an eye specialist in 2 Upper Wimpole Street, off Harley Street, while living at Montague Place. Moves to South Norwood. (July–Dec.) The first six 'Adventures of Sherlock Holmes' published in George Newnes's *Strand Magazine*. (Oct.) *The White Company* published; *Beyond the City* first published in *Good Cheer*, the special Christmas number of *Good Words*.

1892   (Jan.–June) Six more Holmes stories published in the *Strand*, with another in Dec. (Mar.) *The Doings of Raffles Haw* published (first serialized in Alfred Harmsworth's penny paper *Answers*, Dec. 1891–Feb. 1892). (14 Oct.) *The Adventures of Sherlock Holmes* published by Newnes. (31 Oct.) Waterloo story *The Great Shadow* published. Alleyne Kingsley Conan Doyle born. Newnes republishes the *Sign*.

1893   'Adventures of Sherlock Holmes' (second series) continues in the *Strand*, to be published by Newnes as *The Memoirs of Sherlock Holmes* (Dec.), minus 'The Cardboard Box'. Holmes apparently killed in 'The Final Problem' (Dec.) to free ACD for 'more serious literary work'. (May) *The Refugees* published. *Jane Annie; or, the Good Conduct Prize* (musical comedy co-written with J. M. Barrie) fails at the Savoy Theatre. (10 Oct.) Charles Altamont Doyle dies.

1894   (Oct.) *Round the Red Lamp*, a collection of medical short stories, published, several for the first time. *The Stark Munro Letters*, a fictionalized autobiography, begun, to be concluded the following year. ACD on US lecture tour with Innes Doyle. (Dec.) *The Parasite* published; 'The Medal of Brigadier Gerard' published in the *Strand*.

1895   'The Exploits of Brigadier Gerard' published in the *Strand*.

1896   (Feb.) *The Exploits of Brigadier Gerard* published by Newnes. ACD settles at Hindhead, Surrey, to minimize effects of his wife's tuberculosis. (Nov.) *Rodney Stone*, a pre-Regency mystery, published. Self-pastiche, 'The Field Bazaar', appears in the Edinburgh University *Student* (20 Nov.).

1897   (May) Napoleonic novel *Uncle Bernac* published; three 'Captain Sharkey' pirate stories published in *Pearson's Magazine* (Jan., Mar., May). Home at Undershaw, Hindhead.

1898   (Feb.) *The Tragedy of the Korosko* published. (June) Publishes *Songs of Action*, a verse collection. (June–Dec.) Begins to publish 'Round the Fire Stories' in the *Strand*—'The Beetle Hunter', 'The Man with the Watches', 'The Lost Special', 'The Sealed Room', 'The Black Doctor', 'The Club-Footed Grocer', and 'The Brazilian Cat'. Ernest William Hornung (ACD's brother-in-law) creates A. J. Raffles and in 1899 dedicates the first stories to ACD.

1899   (Jan.–May) Concludes 'Round the Fire' series in the *Strand* with 'The Japanned Box', 'The Jew's Breast-Plate', 'B. 24', 'The Latin Tutor', and 'The Brown Hand'. (Mar.) Publishes *A Duet with an Occasional Chorus*, a version of his own romance. (Oct.–Dec.) 'The Croxley Master', a boxing story, published in the *Strand*. William Gillette begins 33 years starring in *Sherlock Holmes*, a play by Gillette and ACD.

1900   Accompanies volunteer-staffed Langman hospital as unofficial supervisor to support British forces in the Boer War. (Mar.) Publishes short-story collection, *The Green Flag and other stories of war and sport*. (Oct.) *The Great Boer War* published. Unsuccessful Liberal Unionist parliamentary candidate for Edinburgh Central.

1901   (Aug.) 'The Hound of the Baskervilles' begins serialization in the *Strand*, subtitled 'Another Adventure of Sherlock Holmes'.

1902   (Jan.) *The War in South Africa: Its Cause and Conduct* published. 'Sherlockian' higher criticism begun by Frank Sidgwick in the *Cambridge Review* (23 Jan.). (Mar.) *The Hound of the Baskervilles* published by Newnes. ACD accepts knighthood with reluctance.

1903   (Sept.) *Adventures of Gerard* published by Newnes (previously serialized in the *Strand*). (Oct.) 'The Return of

Sherlock Holmes' begins in the *Strand*. Author's Edition of ACD's major works published in twelve volumes by Smith, Elder and thirteen by D. Appleton & Co. of New York, with prefaces by ACD; many titles omitted.

1904   'Return of Sherlock Holmes' continues in the *Strand*; series designed to conclude with 'The Abbey Grange' (Sept.), but ACD develops earlier allusions and produces 'The Second Stain' (Dec.).

1905   (Mar.) *The Return of Sherlock Holmes* published by Newnes. (Dec.) Serialization of 'Sir Nigel' begun in the *Strand* (concluded Dec. 1906).

1906   (Nov.) Book publication of *Sir Nigel*. ACD defeated as Unionist candidate for Hawick District in general election. (4 July) Death of Louisa ('Touie'), Lady Conan Doyle. ACD deeply affected.

1907   ACD clears the name of George Edalji (convicted in 1903 of cattle-maiming). (18 Sept.) Marries Jean Leckie. (Nov.) Publishes *Through the Magic Door*, a celebration of his literary mentors (earlier version serialized in *Great Thoughts*, 1894).

1908   Moves to Windlesham, Crowborough, Sussex. (Jan.) Death of Sidney Paget. (Sept.) *Round the Fire Stories* published, including some not in earlier *Strand* series. (Sept.–Oct.) 'The Singular Experience of Mr John Scott Eccles' (later retitled as 'The Adventure of Wisteria Lodge') begins occasional series of Holmes stories in the *Strand*.

1909   ACD becomes President of the Divorce Law Reform Union (until 1919). Denis Percy Stewart Conan Doyle born. Takes up agitation against Belgian oppression in the Congo.

1910   (Sept.) 'The Marriage of the Brigadier', the last Gerard story, published in the *Strand*, and (Dec.) the Holmes story of 'The Devil's Foot'. ACD takes six-month lease on Adelphi Theatre; the play *The Speckled Band* opens there, eventually running to 346 performances. Adrian Malcolm Conan Doyle born.

1911   (Apr.) *The Last Galley* (short stories, mostly historical) published. Two more Holmes stories appear in the *Strand*: 'The Red Circle' (Mar., Apr.) and 'The Disappearance of Lady Frances Carfax' (Dec.). ACD declares for Irish Home Rule, under the influence of Sir Roger Casement.

1912   (Apr.–Nov.) The first Professor Challenger story, *The Lost World*, published in the *Strand*, book publication in Oct. Jean Lena Annette Conan Doyle (afterwards Air Commandant Dame Jean Conan Doyle, Lady Bromet) born.

1913   (Feb.) Writes 'Great Britain and the Next War' (*Fortnightly Review*). (Aug.) Second Challenger story, *The Poison Belt*, published. (Dec.) 'The Dying Detective' published in the *Strand*. ACD campaigns for a channel tunnel.

1914   (July) 'Danger!', warning of the dangers of a war-time blockade of Britain, published in the *Strand*. (4 Aug.) Britain declares war on Germany; ACD forms local volunteer force.

1914–15   (Sept.) *The Valley of Fear* begins serialization in the *Strand* (concluding May 1915).

1915   (27 Feb.) *The Valley of Fear* published by George H. Doran in New York. (June) *The Valley of Fear* published in London by Smith, Elder (transferred with rest of ACD stock to John Murray when the firm is sold on the death of Reginald Smith). Five Holmes films released in Germany (ten more during the war).

1916   (Apr., May) First instalments of *The British Campaign in France and Flanders 1914* appear in the *Strand*. (Aug.) *A Visit to Three Fronts* published. Sir Roger Casement convicted of high treason after Dublin Easter Week Rising and executed despite appeals for clemency by ACD and others.

1917   War censor interdicts ACD's history of the 1916 campaigns in the *Strand*. (Sept.) 'His Last Bow' published in the *Strand*. (Oct.) *His Last Bow* published by John Murray (includes 'The Cardboard Box').

1918   (Apr.) ACD publishes *The New Revelation*, proclaiming himself a Spiritualist. (Dec.) *Danger! and other stories* published. Permitted to resume accounts of 1916 and 1917 campaigns in the *Strand*, but that for 1918 never serialized. Death of eldest son, Captain Kingsley Conan Doyle, from influenza aggravated by war wounds.

1919   Death of Brigadier-General Innes Doyle, from post-war pneumonia.

1920–30   ACD engaged in world-wide crusade for Spiritualism.

1921–2   ACD's one-act play, *The Crown Diamond*, tours with Dennis Neilson-Terry as Holmes.

1921   (Oct.) 'The Mazarin Stone' (apparently based on *The Crown Diamond*) published in the *Strand*. Death of mother, Mary Foley Doyle.

1922   (Feb.–Mar.) 'The Problem of Thor Bridge' in the *Strand*. (July) John Murray publishes a collected edition of the non-Holmes short stories in six volumes: *Tales of the Ring and the Camp, Tales of Pirates and Blue Water, Tales of Terror and Mystery, Tales of Twilight and the Unseen, Tales of Adventure and Medical Life*, and (Nov.) *Tales of Long Ago* (Sept.) Collected edition of ACD's *Poems* published by Murray.

1923   (Mar.) 'The Creeping Man' published in the *Strand*.

1924   (Jan.) 'The Sussex Vampire' appears in the *Strand*. (June) 'How Watson Learned the Trick', ACD's own Holmes pastiche, appears in *The Book of the Queen's Dolls' House Library*. (Sept.) *Memories and Adventures* published (reprinted with additions and deletions 1930).

1925   (Jan.) 'The Three Garridebs' and (Feb.–Mar.) 'The Illustrious Client' published in the *Strand*. (July) *The Land of Mist*, a Spiritualist novel featuring Challenger, begins serialization in the *Strand*.

1926   (Mar.) *The Land of Mist* published. *Strand* publishes 'The Three Gables' (Oct.), 'The Blanched Soldier' (Nov.), and 'The Lion's Mane' (Dec.).

1927   *Strand* publishes 'The Retired Colourman' (Jan.), 'The Veiled Lodger' (Feb.), and 'Shoscombe Old Place' (Apr.). (June) Murray publishes *The Case-Book of Sherlock Holmes*.

1928   (Oct.) *The Complete Sherlock Holmes Short Stories* published by Murray.

1929   (June) *The Conan Doyle Stories* (containing the six separate volumes issued by Murray in 1922) published. (July) *The Maracot Deep and other stories*, ACD's last collection of his fictional work.

1930   (7 July, 8.30 a.m.) Death of Arthur Conan Doyle. 'Education never ends, Watson. It is a series of lessons with the greatest for the last' ('The Red Circle').

The Adventures of
Sherlock Holmes

To
MY OLD TEACHER
JOSEPH BELL, MD, &c.
OF
2 MELVILLE CRESCENT
EDINBURGH

A Scandal in Bohemia

TO Sherlock Holmes she is always *the* woman. I have seldom heard him mention her under any other name. In his eyes she eclipses and predominates the whole of her sex. It was not that he felt any emotion akin to love for Irene Adler.* All emotions, and that one particularly, were abhorrent to his cold, precise, but admirably balanced mind. He was, I take it, the most perfect reasoning and observing machine that the world has seen;* but, as a lover, he would have placed himself in a false position. He never spoke of the softer passions, save with a gibe and a sneer. They were admirable things for the observer—excellent for drawing the veil from men's motives and actions. But for the trained reasoner to admit such intrusions into his own delicate and finely adjusted temperament was to introduce a distracting factor* which might throw a doubt upon all his mental results. Grit in a sensitive instrument, or a crack in one of his own high-power lenses, would not be more disturbing than a strong emotion in a nature such as his. And yet there was but one woman to him, and that woman was the late Irene Adler,* of dubious and questionable memory.

I had seen little of Holmes since the singular chain of events which I have already narrated in a bold fashion under the heading of *The Sign of Four*. My marriage had, as he foretold, drifted us away from each other.* My own complete happiness, and the home-centred interests which rise up around the man who first finds himself master of his own establishment, were sufficient to absorb all my attention; while Holmes, who loathed every form of society with his whole Bohemian soul, remained in our lodgings in Baker Street, buried among his old books, and alternating from week to week between cocaine and ambition, the drowsiness of the drug, and the fierce energy of his own keen nature. He was still, as ever, deeply attracted by the study of crime, and occupied his immense faculties and extraordinary powers of observation in following out those clues, and clearing up those mysteries, which had been abandoned as hopeless by the official police.* From time to time I heard some vague account of his doings: of his summons to Odessa in the case of the Trepoff murder,* of his clearing up of the singular tragedy of the Atkinson brothers* at Trincomalee,* and finally of the mission which he had accomplished so delicately and successfully for the reigning family of Holland.* Beyond these signs of his activity, however, which I merely shared with all the readers of the daily press, I knew little of my former friend and companion.

One night—it was on the 20th of March, 1888—I was returning from a journey to a patient (for I had now returned to civil practice*), when my way led me through Baker Street. As I passed the well-remembered door, which must always be associated in my mind with my wooing, and with the dark incidents of the Study in Scarlet, I was seized with a keen desire to see Holmes again, and to know how he was employing his extraordinary powers. His rooms were brilliantly lit, and, even as I looked up, I saw his tall spare figure pass twice in a dark silhouette against the blind. He was pacing the room swiftly, eagerly, with his head sunk upon his chest, and his hands clasped behind him. To me, who knew his every mood and habit, his attitude and manner told their own story. He was at work again. He had risen out of his drug-created dreams, and was hot upon the scent of some new problem. I rang the bell, and was shown up to the chamber which had formerly been in part my own.

His manner was not effusive. It seldom was; but he was glad, I think, to see me. With hardly a word spoken, but with a kindly eye, he waved me to an armchair, threw across his case of cigars, and indicated a spirit case* and a gasogene* in the corner. Then he stood before the fire, and looked me over in his singular introspective fashion.

'Wedlock suits you,' he remarked. 'I think, Watson, that you have put on seven and a half pounds since I saw you.'

'Seven,' I answered.

'Indeed, I should have thought a little more. Just a trifle more, I fancy, Watson. And in practice again, I observe. You did not tell me that you intended to go into harness.'

'Then, how do you know?'

'I see it, I deduce it. How do I know that you have been getting yourself very wet lately, and that you have a most clumsy and careless servant girl?'

'My dear Holmes,' said I, 'this is too much. You would certainly have been burned* had you lived a few centuries ago. It is true that I had a country walk on Thursday and came home in a dreadful mess; but, as I have changed my clothes, I can't imagine how you deduce it. As to Mary Jane,* she is incorrigible, and my wife has given her notice; but there again I fail to see how you work it out.'

He chuckled to himself and rubbed his long nervous hands together.

'It is simplicity itself,' said he; 'my eyes tell me that on the inside of your left shoe, just where the firelight strikes it, the leather is scored by six almost parallel cuts. Obviously they have been caused by someone who has very carelessly scraped round the edges of the sole in order to remove crusted mud from it. Hence, you see, my double deduction that you had been out in vile weather, and that you had a particularly malignant boot-slitting specimen of the London slavey. As to your practice, if a gentleman walks into my rooms smelling of iodoform,* with a black mark of nitrate of silver* upon his right fore-finger, and a bulge on the side of his top hat to show where he has secreted his stethoscope,* I must be dull indeed if I do not pronounce him to be an active member of the medical profession.'

I could not help laughing at the ease with which he explained his process of deduction. 'When I hear you give your reasons,' I remarked, 'the thing always appears to me to be so ridiculously simple that I could easily do it myself, though at each successive instance of your reasoning I am baffled, until you explain your process. And yet I believe that my eyes are as good as yours.'

'Quite so,' he answered, lighting a cigarette, and throwing himself down into an armchair. 'You see, but you do not observe. The distinction is clear. For example, you have frequently seen the steps which lead up from the hall to this room.'

'Frequently.'

'How often?'

'Well, some hundreds of times.'

'Then how many are there?'

'How many! I don't know.'

'Quite so. You have not observed. And yet you have seen. That is just my point. Now, I know that there are seventeen steps, because I have both seen and observed. By the way, since you are interested in these little problems, and since you are good enough to chronicle one or two of my trifling experiences, you may be interested in this.' He threw over a sheet of thick, pink-tinted note-paper which had been lying open upon the table. 'It came by the last post,' said he. 'Read it aloud.'

The note was undated, and without either signature or address.

'There will call upon you tonight, at a quarter to eight o'clock,' it said, 'a gentleman who desires to consult you upon a matter of the very deepest moment. Your recent services to one of the Royal Houses of Europe have shown that you are one who may safely be trusted with matters which are of an importance which can hardly be exaggerated. This account of you we have from all quarters received. Be in your chamber then at that hour, and do not take it amiss if your visitor wear a mask.'

'This is indeed a mystery,' I remarked. 'What do you imagine that it means?'

'I have no data yet. It is a capital mistake to theorize before one has data. Insensibly one begins to twist facts to suit theories, instead of theories to suit facts. But the note itself. What do you deduce from it?'

I carefully examined the writing, and the paper upon which it was written.

'The man who wrote it was presumably well-to-do,' I remarked, endeavouring to imitate my companion's processes. 'Such paper could not be bought under half-a-crown* a packet. It is peculiarly strong and stiff.'

'Peculiar—that is the very word,' said Holmes. 'It is not an English paper at all. Hold it up to the light.'

I did so, and saw a large E with a small g, a P, and a large G with a small t woven into the texture of the paper.

'What do you make of that?' asked Holmes.

'The name of the maker, no doubt; or his monogram, rather.'

'Not at all. The G with the small t stands for "Gesell-schaft", which is the German for "Company". It is a customary contraction like our "Co.". P, of course, stands for "Papier". Now for the Eg. Let us glance at our Continental Gazetteer.'* He took down a heavy brown volume from his shelves. 'Eglow, Eglonitz*—here we are, Egria. It is in a German-speaking country—in Bohemia,* not far from Carlsbad.* "Remarkable as being the scene of the death of Wallenstein,* and for its numerous glass factories and paper mills."* Ha, ha, my boy, what do you make of that?' His eyes sparkled, and he sent up a great blue triumphant cloud from his cigarette.

'The paper was made in Bohemia,' I said.

'Precisely. And the man who wrote the note is a German. Do you note the peculiar construction of the sentence— "This account of you we have from all quarters received". A Frenchman or Russian could not have written that. It is the German who is so uncourteous to his verbs. It only remains, therefore, to discover what is wanted by this German who writes upon Bohemian paper, and prefers wearing a mask to showing his face. And here he comes, if I am not mistaken, to resolve all our doubts.'

As he spoke there was the sharp sound of horses' hoofs and grating wheels against the kerb, followed by a sharp pull at the bell. Holmes whistled.

'A pair, by the sound,' said he. 'Yes,' he continued, glancing out of the window. 'A nice little brougham* and a pair of beauties. A hundred and fifty guineas apiece. There's money in this case, Watson, if there is nothing else.'

'I think that I had better go, Holmes.'

'Not a bit, Doctor. Stay where you are. I am lost without my Boswell.* And this promises to be interesting. It would be a pity to miss it.'

'But your client—'

'Never mind him. I may want your help, and so may he. Here he comes. Sit down in that armchair, Doctor, and give us your best attention.'

A slow and heavy step, which had been heard upon the stairs and in the passage, paused immediately outside the door. Then there was a loud and authoritative tap.

'Come in!' said Holmes.

A man entered who could hardly have been less than six feet six inches in height, with the chest and limbs of a Hercules.* His dress was rich with a richness which would, in England, be looked upon as akin to bad taste. Heavy bands of astrakhan* were slashed across the sleeves and fronts of his double-breasted coat, while the deep blue cloak which was thrown over his shoulders was lined with flame-coloured silk, and secured at the neck with a brooch which consisted of a single flaming beryl. Boots which extended half-way up his calves, and which were trimmed at the tops with a rich brown fur, completed the impression of barbaric opulence which was suggested by his whole appearance. He carried a broad-brimmed hat in his hand, while he wore across the upper part of his face, extending down past the cheek-bones, a black vizard mask,* which he had apparently adjusted that very moment, for his hand was still raised to it as he entered. From the lower part of the face he appeared to be a man of strong character,* with a thick, hanging lip, and a long straight chin, suggestive of resolution pushed to the length of obstinacy.

'You had my note?' he asked, with a deep, harsh voice and a strongly marked German accent. 'I told you that I would call.' He looked from one to the other of us, as if uncertain which to address.

'Pray take a seat,' said Holmes. 'This is my friend and colleague, Dr Watson, who is occasionally good enough to help me in my cases. Whom have I the honour to address?'

'You may address me as the Count von Kramm,* a Bohemian nobleman. I understand that this gentleman, your friend, is a man of honour and discretion, whom I may trust with a matter of the most extreme importance. If not, I should much prefer to communicate with you alone.'

I rose to go, but Holmes caught me by the wrist and pushed me back into my chair. 'It is both, or none,' said he. 'You may say before this gentleman anything which you may say to me.'

The Count shrugged his broad shoulders. 'Then I must begin,' said he, 'by binding you both to absolute secrecy for two years, at the end of that time the matter will be of no importance. At present it is not too much to say that it is of such weight that it may have an influence upon European history.'

'I promise,' said Holmes.

'And I.'

'You will excuse this mask,' continued our strange visitor. 'The august person who employs me wishes his agent to be unknown to you, and I may confess at once that the title by which I have just called myself is not exactly my own.'

'I was aware of it,' said Holmes dryly.

'The circumstances are of great delicacy, and every pre-caution has to be taken to quench what might grow to be an immense scandal and seriously compromise one of the reigning families of Europe. To speak plainly, the matter implicates the great House of Ormstein, hereditary kings of Bohemia.*

'I was also aware of that,' murmured Holmes, settling himself down in his armchair, and closing his eyes.

Our visitor glanced with some apparent surprise at the languid, lounging figure of the man who had been no doubt depicted to him as the most incisive reasoner, and most energetic agent in Europe. Holmes slowly reopened his eyes, and looked impatiently at his gigantic client.

'If your Majesty would condescend to state your case,' he remarked, 'I should be better able to advise you.'

The man sprang from his chair, and paced up and down the room in uncontrollable agitation. Then, with a gesture of desperation, he tore the mask from his face and hurled it upon the ground. 'You are right,' he cried, 'I am the King. Why should I attempt to conceal it?'

'Why, indeed?' murmured Holmes. 'Your Majesty had not spoken before I was aware that I was addressing Wilhelm Gottsreich Sigismond von Ormstein, Grand Duke of Cassel-Felstein, and hereditary King of Bohemia.*

'But you can understand,' said our strange visitor, sitting down once more and passing his hand over his high, white forehead, 'you can understand that I am not accustomed to doing such business in my own person. Yet the matter was so delicate that I could not confide it to an agent without putting myself in his power. I have come *incognito** from Prague* for the purpose of consulting you.'

'Then, pray consult,' said Holmes, shutting his eyes once more.

'The facts are briefly these: Some five years ago, during a lengthy visit to Warsaw,* I made the acquaintance of the well-known adventuress Irene Adler. The name is no doubt familiar to you.'

'Kindly look her up in my index, Doctor,' murmured Holmes, without opening his eyes. For many years he had adopted a system of docketing all paragraphs concerning men and things, so that it was difficult to name a subject or a person on which he could not at once furnish information. In this case I found her biography sandwiched in between that of a Hebrew Rabbi* and that of a staff-commander who had written a monograph upon the deep-sea fishes.*

'Let me see,' said Holmes. 'Hum! Born in New Jersey in the year 1858. Contralto—hum! La Scala,* hum! Prima donna Imperial Opera of Warsaw*—Yes! Retired from operatic stage—ha! Living in London—quite so! Your Majesty, as I understand, became entangled with this young

person, wrote her some compromising letters, and is now
desirous of getting those letters back.'

'Precisely so. But how—'

'Was there a secret marriage?'

'None.'

'No legal papers or certificates?'

'None.'

'Then I fail to follow your Majesty. If this young person
should produce her letters for blackmailing or other purposes, how is she to prove their authenticity?'

'There is the writing.'

'Pooh, pooh! Forgery.'

'My private note-paper.'

'Stolen.'

'My own seal.'

'Imitated.'

'My photograph.'

'Bought.'

'We were both in the photograph.'

'Oh, dear! That is very bad! Your Majesty has indeed
committed an indiscretion.'

'I was mad—insane.'

'You have compromised yourself seriously.'

'I was only Crown Prince then. I was young. I am but
thirty now.'

'It must be recovered.'

'We have tried and failed.'

'Your Majesty must pay. It must be bought.'

'She will not sell.'

'Stolen, then.'

'Five attempts have been made. Twice burglars in my pay
ransacked her house. Once we diverted her luggage when
she travelled. Twice she has been waylaid. There has been
no result.'

'No sign of it?'

'Absolutely none.'

Holmes laughed. 'It is quite a pretty little problem,' said
he.

'But a very serious one to me,' returned the King, reproachfully.

'Very, indeed. And what does she propose to do with the photograph?'

'To ruin me.'

'But how?'

'I am about to be married.'

'So I have heard.'

'To Clotilde Lothman von Saxe-Meningen, second daughter of the King of Scandinavia.* You may know the strict principles of her family. She is herself the very soul of delicacy. A shadow of a doubt as to my conduct would bring the matter to an end.'

'And Irene Adler?'

'Threatens to send them the photograph. And she will do it. I know that she will do it. You do not know her, but she has a soul of steel. She has the face of the most beautiful of women, and the mind of the most resolute of men.* Rather than I should marry another woman, there are no lengths to which she would not go—none.'

'You are sure that she has not sent it yet?'

'I am sure.'

'And why?'

'Because she has said that she would send it on the day when the betrothal was publicly proclaimed. That will be next Monday.'

'Oh, then, we have three days yet,' said Holmes, with a yawn. 'That is very fortunate, as I have one or two matters of importance to look into just at present. Your Majesty will, of course, stay in London for the present?'

'Certainly. You will find me at the Langham,* under the name of the Count von Kramm.'

'Then I shall drop you a line to let you know how we progress.'

'Pray do so. I shall be all anxiety.'

'Then, as to money?'

'You have *carte blanche.*'*

'Absolutely?'

'I tell you that I would give one of the provinces* of my kingdom to have that photograph.'

'And for present expenses?'

The King took a heavy chamois leather bag from under his cloak, and laid it on the table.

'There are three hundred pounds in gold, and seven hundred in notes,' he said.

Holmes scribbled a receipt upon a sheet of his note-book, and handed it to him.

'And mademoiselle's address?' he asked.

'Is Briony Lodge, Serpentine Avenue, St John's Wood.'*

Holmes took a note of it. 'One other question,' said he. 'Was the photograph a cabinet?'*

'It was.'

'Then, good-night, your Majesty, and I trust that we shall soon have some good news for you. And good night, Watson,' he added, as the wheels of the Royal brougham rolled down the street. 'If you will be good enough to call tomorrow afternoon, at three o'clock, I should like to chat this little matter over with you.'

At three o'clock precisely I was at Baker Street, but Holmes had not yet returned. The landlady informed me that he had left the house shortly after eight o'clock in the morning. I sat down beside the fire, however, with the intention of awaiting him, however long he might be. I was already deeply interested in his inquiry, for, though it was surrounded by none of the grim and strange features which were associated with the two crimes which I have elsewhere recorded,* still, the nature of the case and the exalted station of his client gave it a character of its own. Indeed, apart from the nature of the investigation which my friend had on hand, there was something in his masterly grasp of a situation, and his keen, incisive reasoning, which made it a pleasure to me to study his system of work, and to follow the quick, subtle methods by which he disentangled the most inextricable mysteries. So accustomed was I to his invariable success that the very possibility of his failing had ceased to enter into my head.

It was close upon four before the door opened, and a drunken-looking groom, ill-kempt and side-whiskered with an inflamed face and disreputable clothes, walked into the room. Accustomed as I was to my friend's amazing powers in the use of disguises, I had to look three times before I was certain that it was indeed he. With a nod he vanished into the bedroom, whence he emerged in five minutes tweed-suited and respectable, as of old. Putting his hands into his pockets, he stretched out his legs in front of the fire, and laughed heartily for some minutes.

'Well, really!' he cried, and then he choked; and laughed again until he was obliged to lie back, limp and helpless, in the chair.

'What is it?'

'It's quite too funny. I am sure you could never guess how I employed my morning, or what I ended by doing.'

'I can't imagine. I suppose that you have been watching the habits, and perhaps the house, of Miss Irene Adler.'

'Quite so, but the sequel was rather unusual. I will tell you, however. I left the house a little after eight o'clock this morning, in the character of a groom out of work. There is a wonderful sympathy and freemasonry among horsey men. Be one of them, and you will know all that there is to know. I soon found Briony Lodge. It is a *bijou* villa,* with a garden at the back, but built out in front right up to the road, two stories. Chubb lock* to the door. Large sitting-room on the right side, well-furnished, with long windows almost to the floor, and those preposterous English window fasteners which a child could open. Behind there was nothing remarkable, save that the passage window could be reached from the top of the coach-house. I walked round it and examined it closely from every point of view, but without noting anything else of interest.

'I then lounged down the street, and found, as I expected, that there was a mews in a lane which runs down by one wall of the garden. I lent the ostlers a hand in rubbing down their horses, and I received in exchange twopence, a glass of half-and-half,* two fills of shag tobacco,* and as much information as I could desire about Miss Adler, to say nothing of half a dozen other people in the neighbourhood in whom I was not in the least interested, but whose biographies I was compelled to listen to.'

'And what of Irene Adler?' I asked.

'Oh, she has turned all the men's heads down in that part. She is the daintiest thing under a bonnet on this planet. So say the Serpentine Mews, to a man. She lives quietly, sings at concerts, drives out at five every day, and returns at seven sharp for dinner. Seldom goes out at other times, except when she sings. Has only one male visitor, but a good deal of him. He is dark, handsome, and dashing; never calls less than once a day, and often twice. He is a Mr Godfrey Norton,* of the Inner Temple.* See the advantages of a cabman as a confidant. They had driven him home a dozen times from Serpentine Mews, and knew all about him. When I had listened to all that they had to tell, I began to walk up and down near Briony Lodge once more, and to think over my plan of campaign.

'This Godfrey Norton was evidently an important factor in the matter. He was a lawyer. That sounded ominous. What was the relation between them, and what the object of his repeated visits? Was she his client, his friend, or his mistress? If the former, she had probably transferred the photograph to his keeping. If the latter, it was less likely. On the issue of this question depended whether I should continue my work at Briony Lodge, or turn my attention to the gentleman's chambers in the Temple. It was a delicate point, and it widened the field of my inquiry. I fear that I bore you with these details, but I have to let you see my little difficulties, if you are to understand the situation.'

'I am following you closely,' I answered.

'I was still balancing the matter in my mind when a hansom cab drove up to Briony Lodge, and a gentleman sprang out. He was a remarkably handsome man, dark, aquiline, and moustached—evidently the man of whom I had heard. He appeared to be in a great hurry, shouted to the cabman to wait, and brushed past the maid who opened the door with the air of a man who was thoroughly at home.

'He was in the house about half an hour, and I could catch glimpses of him, in the windows of the sitting-room, pacing up and down, talking excitedly and waving his arms. Of her I could see nothing. Presently he emerged, looking even more flurried than before. As he stepped up to the cab, he pulled a gold watch from his pocket and looked at it earnestly, "Drive like the devil" he shouted, "first to Gross and Hankey's in Regent Street,* and then to the church of St Monica in the Edgware Road.* Half a guinea* if you do it in twenty minutes!"

'Away they went, and I was just wondering whether I should not do well to follow them, when up the lane came a neat little landau,* the coachman with his coat only half buttoned, and his tie under his ear, while all the tags of his harness were sticking out of the buckles. It hadn't pulled up before she shot out of the hall door and into it. I only caught a glimpse of her at the moment, but she was a lovely woman, with a face that a man might die for.

' "The Church of St Monica, John," she cried, "and half a sovereign if you reach it in twenty minutes."

'This was quite too good to lose, Watson. I was just balancing whether I should run for it, or whether I should perch behind her landau, when a cab came through the street. The driver looked twice at such a shabby fare; but I jumped in before he could object. "The Church of St Monica," said I, "and half a sovereign* if you reach it in twenty minutes." It was twenty-five minutes to twelve,* and of course it was clear enough what was in the wind.

'My cabby drove fast. I don't think I ever drove faster, but the others were there before us. The cab and the landau with their steaming horses were in front of the door when I arrived. I paid the man, and hurried into the church. There was not a soul there save the two whom I had followed, and a surpliced clergyman, who seemed to be expostulating with them. They were all three standing in a knot in front of the altar. I lounged up the side aisle like any other idler who has dropped into a church. Suddenly, to my surprise, the three at the altar faced round to me, and Godfrey Norton came running as hard as he could towards me.

' "Thank God!" he cried. "You'll do. Come! Come!"

' "What then?" I asked.

' "Come, man, come, only three minutes, or it won't be legal."

'I was half dragged up to the altar, and before I knew where I was, I found myself mumbling responses* which were whispered in my ear, and vouching for things of which I knew nothing, and generally assisting in the secure tying up of Irene Adler, spinster, to Godfrey Norton, bachelor. It was all done in an instant, and there was the gentleman thanking me on the one side and the lady on the other, while the clergyman beamed on me in front. It was the most preposterous position in which I ever found myself in my life, and it was the thought of it that started me laughing just now. It seems that there had been some informality about their licence, that the clergyman absolutely refused to marry them without a witness of some sort, and that my lucky appearance saved the bridegroom from having to sally out into the streets in search of a best man. The bride gave me a sovereign, and I mean to wear it on my watch-chain in memory of the occasion.'*

'This is a very unexpected turn of affairs,' said I; 'and what then?'

'Well, I found my plans very seriously menaced. It looked as if the pair might take an immediate departure, and so necessitate very prompt and energetic measures on my part. At the church door, however, they separated, he driving back to the Temple, and she to her own house. "I shall drive out in the Park* at five as usual," she said as she left him. I heard no more. They drove away in different directions, and I went off to make my own arrangements.'

'Which are?'

'Some cold beef and a glass of beer,' he answered, ringing the bell. 'I have been too busy to think of food, and I am likely to be busier still this evening. By the way, Doctor, I shall want your co-operation.'

'I shall be delighted.'

'You don't mind breaking the law?'

'Not in the least.'

'Nor running a chance of arrest?'

'Not in a good cause.'

'Oh, the cause is excellent!'

'Then I am your man.'

'I was sure that I might rely on you.'

'But what is it you wish?'

'When Mrs Turner* has brought in the tray I will make it clear to you. Now,' he said, as he turned hungrily on the simple fare that our landlady had provided, 'I must discuss it while I eat, for I have not much time. It is nearly five now. In two hours we must be on the scene of action. Miss Irene, or Madame, rather, returns from her drive at seven. We must be at Briony Lodge to meet her.'

'And what then?'

'You must leave that to me. I have already arranged what is to occur. There is only one point on which I must insist. You must not interfere, come what may. You understand?'

'I am to be neutral?'

'To do nothing whatever. There will probably be some small unpleasantness. Do not join in it. It will end in my being conveyed into the house. Four or five minutes afterwards the sitting-room window will open. You are to station yourself close to that open window.'

'Yes.'

'You are to watch me, for I will be visible to you.'

'Yes.'

'And when I raise my hand—so—you will throw into the room what I give you to throw, and will, at the same time, raise the cry of fire. You quite follow me?'

'Entirely.'

'It is nothing very formidable,' he said, taking a long cigar-shaped roll from his pocket. 'It is an ordinary plumber's smoke rocket,* fitted with a cap at either end to make it self-lighting. Your task is confined to that. When you raise your cry of fire, it will be taken up by quite a number of people. You may then walk to the end of the street, and I will rejoin you in ten minutes. I hope that I have made myself clear?'

'I am to remain neutral, to get near the window, to watch you, and, at the signal, to throw in this object, then to raise the cry of fire, and to await you at the corner of the street.'

'Precisely.'

'Then you may entirely rely on me.'

'That is excellent. I think perhaps it is almost time that I prepared for the new *rôle* I have to play.'

He disappeared into his bedroom, and returned in a few minutes in the character of an amiable and simple-minded Non-conformist clergyman. His broad black hat, his baggy trousers, his white tie, his sympathetic smile, and general look of peering and benevolent curiosity, were such as Mr John Hare* alone could have equalled. It was not merely that Holmes changed his costume. His expression, his manner, his very soul seemed to vary with every fresh part that he assumed. The stage lost a fine actor, even as science lost an acute reasoner, when he became a specialist in crime.

It was a quarter past six when we left Baker Street, and it still wanted ten minutes to the hour when we found ourselves in Serpentine Avenue. It was already dusk, and the lamps were just being lighted as we paced up and down in front of Briony Lodge, waiting for the coming of its occupant. The house was just such as I had pictured it from Sherlock Holmes's succinct description, but the locality appeared to be less private than I expected. On the contrary, for a small street in a quiet neighbourhood, it was remarkably animated. There was a group of shabbily-dressed men smoking and laughing in a corner, a scissors-grinder with his wheel,* two guardsmen who were flirting with a nurse-girl,* and several well-dressed young men who were lounging up and down with cigars in their mouths.

'You see,' remarked Holmes, as we paced to and fro in front of the house, 'this marriage rather simplifies matters. The photograph becomes a double-edged weapon now. The chances are that she would be as averse to its being seen by

Mr Godfrey Norton, as our client is to its coming to the eyes of his Princess. Now the question is—Where are we to find the photograph?'

'Where, indeed?'

'It is most unlikely that she carries it about with her. It is cabinet size. Too large for easy concealment about a woman's dress. She knows that the King is capable of having her waylaid and searched. Two attempts of the sort have already been made. We may take it then that she does not carry it about with her.'

'Where, then?'

'Her banker or her lawyer. There is that double possibility. But I am inclined to think neither. Women are naturally secretive, and they like to do their own secreting. Why should she hand it over to anyone else? She could trust her own guardianship, but she could not tell what indirect or political influence might be brought to bear upon a business man. Besides, remember that she had resolved to use it within a few days. It must be where she can lay her hands upon it. It must be in her own house.'

'But it has twice been burgled.'

'Pshaw! They did not know how to look.'

'But how will you look?'

'I will not look.'

'What then?'

'I will get her to show me.'

'But she will refuse.'

'She will not be able to. But I hear the rumble of wheels. It is her carriage. Now carry out my orders to the letter.'

As he spoke, the gleam of the sidelights of a carriage came round the curve of the avenue. It was a smart little landau which rattled up to the door of Briony Lodge. As it pulled up, one of the loafing men at the corner dashed forward to open the door in the hope of earning a copper, but was elbowed away by another loafer who had rushed up with the same intention. A fierce quarrel broke out, which was increased by the two guardsmen, who took sides with one of the loungers, and by the scissors-grinder, who was equally hot upon the other side. A blow was struck, and in an instant the lady, who had stepped from her carriage, was the centre of a little knot of flushed and struggling men who struck savagely at each other with their fists and sticks. Holmes dashed into the crowd to protect the lady; but just as he reached her, he gave a cry and dropped to the ground, with the blood running freely down his face. At his fall the guardsmen took to their heels in one direction and the loungers in the other, while a number of better dressed people who had watched the scuffle without taking part in it, crowded in to help the lady and to attend to the injured man. Irene Adler, as I will still call her, had hurried up the steps; but she stood at the top with her superb figure outlined against the lights of the hall, looking back into the street.

'Is the poor gentleman much hurt?' she asked.

'He is dead,' cried several voices.

'No, no, there's life in him,' shouted another. 'But he'll be gone before you can get him to hospital.'

'He's a brave fellow,' said a woman. 'They would have had the lady's purse and watch if it hadn't been for him. They were a gang, and a rough one, too. Ah, he's breathing now.'

'He can't lie in the street. May we bring him in, marm?'

'Surely. Bring him into the sitting-room. There is a comfortable sofa. This way, please!'

Slowly and solemnly he was borne into Briony Lodge, and laid out in the principal room, while I still observed the proceedings from my post by the window. The lamps had been lit, but the blinds had not been drawn, so that I could see Holmes as he lay upon the couch. I do not know whether he was seized with compunction at that moment for the part he was playing, but I know that I never felt more heartily ashamed of myself in my life than when I saw the beautiful creature against whom I was conspiring, or the grace and kindliness with which she waited upon the injured man. And yet it would be the blackest treachery to Holmes to draw back now from the part which he had entrusted to me. I hardened my heart and took the smoke-rocket from under my ulster.* After all, I thought, we are not injuring her. We are but preventing her from injuring another.

Holmes had sat up upon the couch, and I saw him motion like a man who is in want of air. A maid rushed across and threw open the window. At the same instant I saw him raise his hand, and at the signal I tossed my rocket into the room with a cry of 'Fire'. The word was no sooner out of my mouth than the whole crowd of spectators, well dressed and ill—gentlemen, ostlers, and servant maids—joined in a general shriek of 'Fire'. Thick clouds of smoke curled into the room, and out at the open window. I caught a glimpse of rushing figures, and a moment later the voice of Holmes from within, assuring them that it was a false alarm. Slipping through the shouting crowd I made my way to the corner of the street, and in ten minutes was rejoiced to find my friend's arm in mine, and to get away from the scene of the uproar. He walked swiftly and in silence for some few minutes, until we had turned down one of the quiet streets which lead towards the Edgware Road.

'You did it very nicely, Doctor,' he remarked. 'Nothing could have been better. It is all right.'

'You have the photograph!'

'I know where it is.'

'And how did you find out?'

'She showed me, as I told you she would.'

'I am still in the dark.'

'I do not wish to make a mystery,' said he, laughing. 'The matter was perfectly simple. You, of course, saw that everyone in the street was an accomplice. They were all engaged for the evening.'

'I guessed as much.'

'Then, when the row broke out, I had a little moist red paint in the palm of my hand. I rushed forward, fell down, clapped my hand to my face, and became a piteous spectacle. It is an old trick.'

'That also I could fathom.'

24

'Then they carried me in. She was bound to have me in. What else could she do? And into her sitting-room which was the very room which I suspected. It lay between that and her bedroom, and I was determined to see which. They laid me on a couch, I motioned for air, they were compelled to open the window, and you had your chance.'

'How did that help you?'

'It was all-important. When a woman thinks that her house is on fire, her instinct is at once to rush to the thing which she values most. It is a perfectly overpowering impulse, and I have more than once taken advantage of it. In the case of the Darlington Substitution Scandal* it was of use to me, and also in the Arnsworth Castle business.* A married woman grabs at her baby—an unmarried one reaches for her jewel box. Now it was clear to me that our lady of to-day had nothing in the house more precious to her than what we are in quest of. She would rush to secure it. The alarm of fire was admirably done. The smoke and shouting was enough to shake nerves of steel. She responded beautifully. The photograph is in a recess behind a sliding panel just above the right bell-pull. She was there in an instant, and I caught a glimpse of it as she half drew it out. When I cried out that it was a false alarm, she replaced it, glanced at the rocket, rushed from the room, and I have not seen her since. I rose, and, making my excuses, escaped from the house. I hesitated whether to attempt to secure the photograph at once; but the coachman had come in, and as he was watching me narrowly, it seemed safer to wait. A little over-precipitance may ruin all.'

'And now?' I asked.

'Our quest is practically finished. I shall call with the King tomorrow, and with you, if you care to come with us. We will be shown into the sitting-room to wait for the lady, but it is probable that when she comes she may find neither us nor the photograph. It might be a satisfaction to His Majesty to regain it with his own hands.'

'And when will you call?'

'At eight in the morning. She will not be up, so that we shall have a clear field. Besides, we must be prompt, for this marriage may mean a complete change in her life and habits. I must wire to the King without delay.'

We had reached Baker Street, and had stopped at the door. He was searching his pockets for the key, when some one passing said:

'Good night, Mister Sherlock Holmes.'

There were several people on the pavement at the time, but the greeting appeared to come from a slim youth in an ulster who had hurried by.

'I've heard that voice before,' said Holmes, staring down the dimly lit street. 'Now, I wonder who the deuce that could have been.'

I slept at Baker Street that night, and we were engaged upon our toast and coffee when the King of Bohemia rushed into the room.

'You have really got it!' he cried, grasping Sherlock Holmes by either shoulder, and looking eagerly into his face.

'Not yet.'

'But you have hopes?'

'I have hopes.'

'Then, come. I am all impatience to be gone.'

'We must have a cab.'

'No, my brougham is waiting.'

'Then that will simplify matters.'

We descended, and started off once more for Briony Lodge.

'Irene Adler is married,' remarked Holmes.

'Married! When?'

'Yesterday.'

'But to whom?'

'To an English lawyer named Norton.'

'But she could not love him?'

'I am in hopes that she does.'

'And why in hopes?'

'Because it would spare your Majesty all fear of future annoyance. If the lady loves her husband, she does not love your Majesty. If she does not love your Majesty there is no reason why she should interfere with your Majesty's plan.'

'It is true. And yet—! Well! I wish she had been of my own station! What a queen she would have made!' He relapsed into a moody silence which was not broken until we drew up in Serpentine Avenue.

The door of Briony Lodge was open, and an elderly woman stood upon the steps. She watched us with a sardonic eye* as we stepped from the brougham.

'Mr Sherlock Holmes, I believe?' said she.

'I am Mr Holmes,' answered my companion, looking at her with a questioning and rather startled gaze.

'Indeed! My mistress told me that you were likely to call. She left this morning with her husband, by the 5.15 train from Charing Cross,* for the Continent.'

'What!' Sherlock Holmes staggered back, white with chagrin and surprise. 'Do you mean that she has left England?'

'Never to return.'

'And the papers?' asked the King, hoarsely. 'All is lost.'

'We shall see.' He pushed past the servant, and rushed into the drawing-room, followed by the King and myself. The furniture was scattered about in every direction, with dismantled shelves, and open drawers, as if the lady had hurriedly ransacked them before her flight. Holmes rushed at the bell-pull, tore back a small sliding shutter, and, plunging in his hand, pulled out a photograph and a letter. The photograph was of Irene Adler herself in evening dress, the letter was superscribed to 'Sherlock Holmes, Esq. To be left till called for.' My friend tore it open and we all three read it together. It was dated at midnight of the preceding night, and ran in this way:

My Dear Mr Sherlock Holmes,

You really did it very well. You took me in completely. Until after the alarm of fire, I had not a suspicion. But then, when I found how I had betrayed myself, I began to think. I had been warned against you months ago. I had been told that if the King employed an agent, it would certainly be you. And your address had been given me. Yet, with all this, you made me reveal what you wanted

27

to know. Even after I became suspicious, I found it hard to think evil of such a dear, kind old clergyman. But, you know, I have been trained as an actress myself. Male costume is nothing new to me. I often take advantage of the freedom which it gives. I sent John, the coachman, to watch you, ran upstairs, got into my walking clothes, as I call them, and came down just as you departed.

Well, I followed you to your door and so made sure that I was really an object of interest to the celebrated Mr Sherlock Holmes. Then I, rather imprudently, wished you good-night, and started for the Temple to see my husband.

We both thought the best resource was flight when pursued by so formidable an antagonist; so you will find the nest empty when you call to-morrow. As to the photograph, your client may rest in peace. I love and am loved by a better man than he. The King may do what he will without hindrance from one whom he has cruelly wronged. I keep it only to safeguard myself, and to preserve a weapon which will always secure me from any steps which he might take in the future. I leave a photograph which he might care to possess; and I remain, dear Mr Sherlock Holmes, very truly yours,
IRENE NORTON, *née* ADLER

'What a woman—oh, what a woman!' cried the King of Bohemia, when we had all three read this epistle. 'Did I not tell you how quick and resolute she was? Would she not have made an admirable queen? Is it not a pity she was not on my level?'*

'From what I have seen of the lady, she seems, indeed, to be on a very different level to your Majesty,' said Holmes, coldly. 'I am sorry that I have not been able to bring your Majesty's business to a more successful conclusion.'

'On the contrary, my dear sir,' cried the King. 'Nothing could be more successful. I know that her word is inviolate. The photograph is now as safe as if it were in the fire.'

'I am glad to hear your Majesty say so.'

'I am immensely indebted to you. Pray tell me in what way I can reward you. This ring—' He slipped an emerald snake ring from his finger and held it out upon the palm of his hand.

'Your Majesty has something which I should value even more highly,' said Holmes.

'You have but to name it.'

'This photograph!'

The King stared at him in amazement.

'Irene's photograph!' he cried. 'Certainly, if you wish it.'

'I thank your Majesty. Then there is no more to be done in the matter. I have the honour to wish you a very good morning.' He bowed, and, turning away without observing the hand which the King stretched out to him, he set off in my company for his chambers.

And that was how a great scandal threatened to affect the kingdom of Bohemia, and how the best plans of Mr Sherlock Holmes were beaten by a woman's wit. He used to make merry over the cleverness of women, but I have not heard him do it of late. And when he speaks of Irene Adler, or when he refers to her photograph, it is always under the honourable title of *the* woman.

A Case of Identity

'MY dear fellow,' said Sherlock Holmes, as we sat on either side of the fire in his lodgings at Baker Street, 'life is infinitely stranger than anything which the mind of man could invent.* We would not dare to conceive the things which are really mere commonplaces of existence. If we could fly out of that window hand in hand, hover over this great city, gently remove the roofs, and peep in at the queer things which are going on, the strange coincidences, the plannings, the cross-purposes, the wonderful chains of events, working through generations, and leading to the most *outré** results, it would make all fiction with its conventionalities and foreseen conclusions most stale and unprofitable.'*

'And yet I am not convinced of it,' I answered. 'The cases which come to light in the papers are, as a rule, bald enough, and vulgar enough. We have in our police reports realism pushed to its extreme limits, and yet the result is, it must be confessed, neither fascinating nor artistic.'

'A certain selection and discretion must be used in producing a realistic effect,' remarked Holmes. 'This is wanting in the police report, where more stress is laid perhaps upon the platitudes of the magistrate than upon the details, which to an observer contain the vital essence of the whole matter. Depend upon it there is nothing so unnatural as the commonplace.'

I smiled and shook my head. 'I can quite understand you thinking so,' I said. 'Of course, in your position of unofficial adviser and helper to everybody who is absolutely puzzled, throughout three continents, you are brought in contact with all that is strange and bizarre. But here'—I picked up the morning paper from the ground—'let us put it to a practical test. Here is the first heading upon which I come. "A husband's cruelty to his wife." There is half a column of print, but I know without reading it that it is all perfectly familiar to me. There is, of course, the other woman, the drink, the push, the blow, the bruise, the sympathetic sister or landlady. The crudest of writers could invent nothing more crude.'

'Indeed, your example is an unfortunate one for your argument,' said Holmes, taking the paper, and glancing his eye down it. 'This is the Dundas separation case,* and, as it happens, I was engaged in clearing up some small points in connection with it. The husband was a teetotaller, there was no other woman, and the conduct complained of was that he had drifted into the habit of winding up every meal by taking out his false teeth and hurling them at his wife, which you will allow is not an action likely to occur to the imagination of the average story-teller. Take a pinch of snuff, Doctor, and acknowledge that I have scored over you in your example.'

He held out his snuff-box of old gold, with a great amethyst in the centre of the lid.* Its splendour was in such contrast to his homely ways and simple life that I could not help commenting upon it.

'Ah,' said he, 'I forgot that I had not seen you for some weeks. It is a little souvenir from the King of Bohemia in return for my assistance in the case of the Irene Adler papers.'

'And the ring?' I asked, glancing at a remarkable brilliant which sparkled upon his finger.

'It was from the reigning family of Holland, though the matter in which I served them was of such delicacy that I cannot confide it even to you, who have been good enough to chronicle one or two of my little problems.'

'And have you any on hand just now?' I asked with interest.

'Some ten or twelve, but none which presents any feature of interest. They are important, you understand, without being interesting. Indeed, I have found that it is usually in unimportant matters that there is a field for observation, and for the quick analysis of cause and effect which gives the charm to an investigation. The larger crimes are apt to be the simpler, for the bigger the crime, the more obvious, as a rule, is the motive. In these cases, save for one rather intricate matter which has been referred to me from Marseilles, there is nothing which presents any features of interest. It is possible, however, that I may have something better before very many minutes are over, for this is one of my clients, or I am much mistaken.'

He had risen from his chair, and was standing between the parted blinds, gazing down into the dull, neutral-tinted London street. Looking over his shoulder I saw that on the pavement opposite there stood a large woman with a heavy fur boa round her neck, and a large curling red feather in a broad-brimmed hat which was tilted in a coquettish Du-chess-of-Devonshire fashion* over her ear. From under this great panoply* she peeped up in a nervous, hesitating fashion at our windows, while her body oscillated backwards and forwards, and her fingers fidgeted with her glove buttons. Suddenly, with a plunge, as of the swimmer who leaves the bank, she hurried across the road, and we heard the sharp clang of the bell.

'I have seen those symptoms before,' said Holmes, throwing his cigarette into the fire. 'Oscillation upon the pavement always means an *affaire du coeur*.* She would like advice, but is not sure that the matter is not too delicate for communication. And yet even here we may discriminate. When a woman has been seriously wronged by a man she no longer oscillates, and the usual symptom is a broken bell wire. Here we may take it that there is a love matter, but that the maiden is not so much angry as perplexed, or grieved. But here she comes in person to resolve our doubts.'

As he spoke there was a tap at the door, and the boy in buttons* entered to announce Miss Mary Sutherland,* while the lady herself loomed behind his small black figure like a full-sailed merchantman behind a tiny pilot boat. Sherlock Holmes welcomed her with the easy courtesy for which he was remarkable, and having closed the door, and bowed her into an armchair, he looked over her in the minute and yet abstracted fashion which was peculiar to him.

'Do you not find,' he said, 'that with your short sight it is a little trying to do so much typewriting?'

'I did at first,' she answered, 'but now I know where the letters are without looking.' Then, suddenly realizing the full purport of his words, she gave a violent start, and looked up with fear and astonishment upon her broad, good-humoured face. 'You've heard about me, Mr Holmes,' she cried, 'else how could you know all that?'

'Never mind,' said Holmes, laughing, 'it is my business to know things. Perhaps I have trained myself to see what others overlook. If not, why should you come to consult me?'

'I came to you, sir because I heard of you from Mrs Etherege,* whose husband you found so easy when the police and everyone had given him up for dead. Oh, Mr Holmes, I wish you would do as much for me. I'm not rich, but still I have a hundred a year in my own right, besides the little that I make by the machine, and I would give it all to know what has become of Mr Hosmer Angel.'*

'Why did you come away to consult me in such a hurry?' asked Sherlock Holmes, with his finger-tips together, and his eyes to the ceiling.

Again a startled look came over the somewhat vacuous face of Miss Mary Sutherland. 'Yes, I did bang out of the house,' she said, 'for it made me angry to see the easy way in which Mr Windibank*—that is, my father—took it all. He would not go to the police, and he would not go to you, and so at last, as he would do nothing, and kept on saying that there was no harm done, it made me mad, and I just on with my things and came right away to you.'

'Your father?' said Holmes. 'Your step-father, surely, since the name is different?'

'Yes, my step-father. I call him father, though it sounds funny, too, for he is only five years and two months older than myself.'

'And your mother is alive?'

'Oh, yes, mother is alive and well. I wasn't best pleased, Mr Holmes, when she married again so soon after father's death, and a man who was nearly fifteen years younger than herself. Father was a plumber in the Tottenham Court Road,* and he left a tidy business behind him, which mother carried on with Mr Hardy, the foreman, but when Mr Windibank came he made her sell the business, for he was very superior, being a traveller in wines. They got four thousand seven hundred for goodwill and interest, which wasn't near as much as father could have got if he had been alive.'

I had expected to see Sherlock Holmes impatient under this rambling and inconsequential narrative, but, on the contrary, he had listened with the greatest concentration of attention.

'Your own little income,' he asked, 'does it come out of the business?'

'Oh, no, sir, it is quite separate, and was left me by my uncle Ned* in Auckland. It is in New Zealand Stock,* paying 4½ per cent. Two thousand five hundred pounds was the amount, but I can only touch the interest.'

'You interest me extremely,' said Holmes. 'And since you draw so large a sum as a hundred a year, with what you earn into the bargain, you no doubt travel a little and indulge yourself in every way. I believe that a single lady can get on very nicely upon an income of about sixty pounds.'

'I could do with much less than that, Mr Holmes, but you understand that as long as I live at home I don't wish to be a burden to them, and so they have the use of the money just while I am staying with them. Of course that is only just for the time. Mr Windibank draws my interest every quarter, and pays it over to mother, and I find that I can do pretty well with what I earn at typewriting. It brings me twopence a sheet, and I can often do from fifteen to twenty sheets in a day.'

'You have made your position very clear to me,' said Holmes. 'This is my friend, Dr Watson, before whom you can speak as freely as before myself. Kindly tell us now all about your connection with Mr Hosmer Angel.'

A flush stole over Miss Sutherland's face, and she picked nervously at the fringe of her jacket. 'I met him first at the

34

gasfitters' ball,* she said. 'They used to send father tickets when he was alive, and then afterwards they remembered us, and sent them to mother. Mr Windibank did not wish us to go. He never did wish us to go anywhere. He would get quite mad if I wanted so much as to join a Sunday-school treat. But this time I was set on going, and I would go, for what right had he to prevent? He said the folk were not fit for us to know, when all father's friends were to be there. And he said that I had nothing fit to wear, when I had my purple plush* that I had never so much as taken out of the drawer. At last, when nothing else would do, he went off to France upon the business of the firm, but we went, mother and I, with Mr Hardy, who used to be our foreman, and it was there I met Mr Hosmer Angel.'

'I suppose,' said Holmes, 'that when Mr Windibank came back from France, he was very annoyed at your having gone to the ball.'

'Oh, well, he was very good about it. He laughed, I remember, and shrugged his shoulders, and said there was no use denying anything to a woman, for she would have her way.'

'I see. Then at the gasfitters' ball you met, as I understand, a gentleman called Mr Hosmer Angel.'

'Yes, sir. I met him that night, and he called next day to ask if we had got home all safe, and after that we met him—that is to say, Mr Holmes, I met him twice for walks, but after that father came back again, and Mr Hosmer Angel could not come to the house any more.'

'No?'

'Well, you know, father didn't like anything of the sort. He wouldn't have any visitors if he could help it, and he used to say that a woman should be happy in her own family circle. But then, as I used to say to mother, a woman wants her own circle to begin with, and I had not got mine yet.'

'But how about Mr Hosmer Angel? Did he make no attempt to see you?'

'Well, father was going off to France again in a week, and Hosmer wrote and said that it would be safer and better not to see each other until he had gone. We would write in the meantime, and he used to write every day. I took the letters in in the morning, so there was no need for father to know.'

'Were you engaged to the gentleman at this time?'

'Oh, yes, Mr Holmes. We were engaged after the first walk that we took. Hosmer—Mr Angel—was a cashier in an office in Leadenhall Street*—and—'

'What office?'

'That's the worst of it, Mr Holmes, I don't know.'

'Where did he live then?'

'He slept on the premises.'

'And you don't know his address?'

'No—except that it was Leadenhall Street.'

'Where did you address your letters, then?'

'To the Leadenhall Street Post Office, to be left till called for. He said that if they were sent to the office he would be chaffed by all the other clerks about having letters from a lady, so I offered to typewrite them, like he did his, but he wouldn't have that, for he said that when I wrote them they seemed to come from me but when they were typewritten he always felt that the machine had come between us. That will just show you how fond he was of me, Mr Holmes, and the little things that he would think of.'

'It was most suggestive,' said Holmes. 'It has long been an axiom of mine that the little things are infinitely the most important. Can you remember any other little things about Mr Hosmer Angel?'

'He was a very shy man, Mr Holmes. He would rather walk with me in the evening than in the daylight, for he said that he hated to be conspicuous. Very retiring and gentle-manly he was. Even his voice was gentle. He'd had the quinsy* and swollen glands when he was young, he told me, and it had left him with a weak throat, and a hesitating, whispering fashion of speech. He was always well-dressed, very neat and plain, but his eyes were weak, just as mine are, and he wore tinted glasses against the glare.'

'Well, and what happened when Mr Windibank, your step-father, returned to France?'

'Mr Hosmer Angel came to the house again, and pro-
posed that we should marry before father came back. He
was in dreadful earnest, and made me swear, with my hands
on the Testament,* that whatever happened I would always
be true to him. Mother said he was quite right to make me
swear, and that it was a sign of his passion. Mother was all
in his favour from the first, and was even fonder of him than
I was. Then, when they talked of marrying within the week,
I began to ask about father; but they both said never to
mind about father, but just to tell him afterwards, and
mother said she would make it all right with him. I didn't
quite like that, Mr Holmes. It seemed funny that I should
ask his leave, as he was only a few years older than me; but
I didn't want to do anything on the sly, so I wrote to father
at Bordeaux,* where the Company has its French offices,
but the letter came back to me on the very morning of the
wedding.'

'It missed him then?'

'Yes, sir, for he had started to England just before it
arrived.'

'Ha! that was unfortunate. Your wedding was arranged,
then, for the Friday. Was it to be in church?'

'Yes, sir, but very quietly. It was to be at St Saviour's, near
King's Cross,* and we were to have breakfast afterwards at
the St Pancras Hotel.* Hosmer came for us in a hansom,
but as there were two of us, he put us both into it, and
stepped himself into a four-wheeler which happened to
be the only other cab in the street. We got to the church
first, and when the four-wheeler drove up we waited for him
to step out, but he never did, and when the cabman got
down from the box and looked, there was no one there! The
cabman said he could not imagine what had become of
him, for he had seen him get in with his own eyes. That was
last Friday, Mr Holmes, and I have never seen or heard
anything since then to throw any light upon what became
of him.'

'It seems to me that you have been very shamefully
treated,' said Holmes.

'Oh no, sir! He was too good and kind to leave me so. Why, all the morning he was saying to me that, whatever happened, I was to be true; and that even if something quite unforeseen occurred to separate us, I was always to remember that I was pledged to him, and that he would claim his pledge sooner or later. It seemed strange talk for a wedding morning, but what has happened since gives a meaning to it.'

'Most certainly it does. Your own opinion is, then, that some unforeseen catastrophe has occurred to him?'

'Yes, sir. I believe that he foresaw some danger, or else he would not have talked so. And then I think that what he foresaw happened.'

'But you have no notion as to what it could have been?'

'None.'

'One more question. How did your mother take the matter?'

'She was angry, and said that I was never to speak of the matter again.'

'And your father? Did you tell him?'

'Yes, and he seemed to think, with me, that something had happened, and that I should hear of Hosmer again. As he said, what interest could anyone have in bringing me to the doors of the church, and then leaving me? Now, if he had borrowed my money, or if he had married me and got my money settled on him, there might be some reason; but Hosmer was very independent about money, and never would look at a shilling of mine. And yet what could have happened? And why could he not write? Oh, it drives me half mad to think of! and I can't sleep a wink at night.' She pulled a little handkerchief out of her muff, and began to sob heavily into it.

'I shall glance into the case for you,' said Holmes, rising, 'and I have no doubt that we shall reach some definite result. Let the weight of the matter rest upon me now, and do not let your mind dwell upon it further. Above all, try to let Mr Hosmer Angel vanish from your memory, as he has done from your life.'

'Then you don't think I'll see him again?'

'I fear not.'

'Then what has happened to him?'

'You will leave that question in my hands. I should like an accurate description of him, and any letters of his which you can spare.'

'I advertised for him in last Saturday's *Chronicle*,'* said she. 'Here is the slip, and here are four letters from him.'

'Thank you. And your address?'

'31 Lyon Place, Camberwell.'*

'Mr Angel's address you never had, I understand. Where is your father's place of business?'

'He travels for Westhouse & Marbank, the great claret importers* of Fenchurch Street.'*

'Thank you. You have made your statement very clearly. You will leave the papers here, and remember the advice which I have given you. Let the whole incident be a sealed book, and do not allow it to affect your life.'

'You are very kind, Mr Holmes, but I cannot do that. I shall be true to Hosmer. He shall find me ready when he comes back.'

For all the preposterous hat and the vacuous face, there was something noble in the simple faith of our visitor which compelled our respect. She laid her little bundle of papers upon the table, and went her way, with a promise to come again whenever she might be summoned.

Sherlock Holmes sat silent for a few minutes with his fingertips still pressed together, his legs stretched out in front of him, and his gaze directed upwards to the ceiling. Then he took down from the rack the old and oily clay pipe, which was to him as a counsellor, and, having lit it, he leaned back in his chair, with the thick blue cloud-wreaths spinning up from him, and a look of infinite languor in his face.

'Quite an interesting study, that maiden,' he observed. 'I found her more interesting than her little problem, which, by the way, is rather a trite one. You will find parallel cases, if you consult my index, in Andover in '77,* and there was something of the sort at The Hague* last year. Old as is the

idea, however, there were one or two details which were
new to me. But the maiden herself was most instructive.'

'You appear to read a good deal upon her which was quite
invisible to me,' I remarked.

'Not invisible, but unnoticed, Watson. You did not know
where to look, and so you missed all that was important. I
can never bring you to realize the importance of sleeves, the
suggestiveness of thumb-nails, or the great issues that may
hang from a bootlace.* Now what did you gather from that
woman's appearance? Describe it.'

'Well, she had a slate-coloured, broad-brimmed straw hat,
with a feather of a brickish red. Her jacket was black, with
black beads sewn upon it, and a fringe of little black jet*
ornaments. Her dress was brown, rather darker than coffee
colour, with a little purple plush at the neck and sleeves. Her
gloves were greyish, and were worn through at the right
forefinger. Her boots I didn't observe. She had small, round,
hanging gold ear-rings, and a general air of being fairly well
to do, in a vulgar, comfortable, easy-going way.'

Sherlock Holmes clapped his hands softly together and
chuckled.

''Pon my word, Watson, you are coming along wonderfully. You have really done very well indeed. It is true that
you have missed everything of importance, but you have hit
upon the method, and you have a quick eye for colour. Never
trust to general impressions, my boy, but concentrate yourself
upon details. My first glance is always at a woman's sleeve.
In a man it is perhaps better first to take the knee of the
trouser. As you observe, this woman had plush upon her
sleeves, which is a most useful material for showing traces.
The double line a little above the wrist, where the typewritist
presses against the table, was beautifully defined. The sewing-
machine, of the hand type, leaves a similar mark, but only on
the left arm, and on the side of it farthest from the thumb,
instead of being right across the broadest part, as this was. I
then glanced at her face, and observing the dint of a pince-nez
at either side of her nose, I ventured a remark upon short sight
and typewriting, which seemed to surprise her.'

'It surprised me.'

'But, surely, it was very obvious. I was then much surprised and interested on glancing down to observe that, though the boots which she was wearing were not unlike each other, they were really odd ones, the one having a slightly decorated toe-cap, and the other a plain one. One was buttoned only in the two lower buttons out of five, and the other at the first, third, and fifth. Now, when you see that a young lady, otherwise neatly dressed, has come away from home with odd boots, half-buttoned, it is no great deduction to say that she came away in a hurry.'

'And what else?' I asked, keenly interested, as I always was, by my friend's incisive reasoning.

'I noted, in passing, that she had written a note before leaving home, but after being fully dressed. You observed that her right glove was torn at the forefinger, but you did not apparently see that both glove and finger were stained with violet ink. She had written in a hurry, and dipped her pen too deep. It must have been this morning, or the mark would not remain clear upon the finger. All this is amusing, though rather elementary, but I must go back to business, Watson. Would you mind reading me the advertised description of Mr Hosmer Angel?'

I held the little printed slip to the light. 'Missing,' it said, 'on the morning of the 14th, a gentleman named Hosmer Angel. About 5 ft 7 in in height; strongly built, sallow complexion, black hair, a little bald in the centre, bushy, black side whiskers and moustache; tinted glasses, slight infirmity of speech. Was dressed, when last seen, in black frock-coat faced with silk, black waistcoat, gold Albert chain,* and grey Harris tweed trousers,* with brown gaiters over elastic-sided boots. Known to have been employed in an office in Leadenhall Street. Anybody bringing, etc., etc.'

'That will do,' said Holmes. 'As to the letters,' he continued, glancing over them, 'they are very commonplace. Absolutely no clue in them to Mr Angel, save that he quotes Balzac* once. There is one remarkable point, however, which will no doubt strike you.'

'They are typewritten,' I remarked.

'Not only that, but the signature is typewritten. Look at the neat little "Hosmer Angel" at the bottom. There is a date you see, but no superscription, except Leadenhall Street, which is rather vague. The point about the signature is very suggestive—in fact, we may call it conclusive.'

'Of what?'

'My dear fellow, is it possible you do not see how strongly it bears upon the case?'

'I cannot say that I do, unless it were that he wished to be able to deny his signature if an action for breach of promise were instituted.'

'No, that was not the point. However, I shall write two letters which should settle the matter. One is to a firm in the City, the other is to the young lady's step-father, Mr Windibank, asking him whether he could meet us here at six o'clock to-morrow evening. It is just as well that we should do business with the male relatives. And now, Doctor, we can do nothing until the answers to those letters come, so we may put our little problem upon the shelf for the interim.'

I had had so many reasons to believe in my friend's subtle powers of reasoning, and extraordinary energy in action, that I felt that he must have some solid grounds for the assured and easy demeanour with which he treated the singular mystery which he had been called upon to fathom. Only once had I known him to fail, in the case of the King of Bohemia and of the Irene Adler photograph, but when I looked back to the weird business of the Sign of Four, and the extraordinary circumstances connected with the Study in Scarlet, I felt that it would be a strange tangle indeed which he could not unravel.

I left him then, still puffing at his black clay pipe, with the conviction that when I came again on the next evening I would find that he held in his hands all the clues which would lead up to the identity of the disappearing bridegroom of Miss Mary Sutherland.

A professional case of great gravity was engaging my own attention at the time, and the whole of next day I was busy at the bedside of the sufferer. It was not until close upon six o'clock that I found myself free, and was able to spring into a hansom and drive to Baker Street, half afraid that I might be too late to assist at the *dénouement* of the little mystery.* I found Sherlock Holmes alone, however, half asleep, with his long, thin form curled up in the recesses of his armchair. A formidable array of bottles and test-tubes, with the pungent cleanly smell of hydrochloric acid, told me that he had spent his day in the chemical work which was so dear to him.

'Well, have you solved it?' I asked as I entered.

'Yes. It was the bisulphate of baryta.'*

'No, no, the mystery!' I cried.

'Oh, that! I thought of the salt that I have been working upon. There was never any mystery in the matter, though, as I said yesterday, some of the details are of interest. The only drawback is that there is no law, I fear, that can touch the scoundrel.'

'Who was he, then, and what was his object in deserting Miss Sutherland?'

The question was hardly out of my mouth, and Holmes had not yet opened his lips to reply, when we heard a heavy footfall in the passage, and a tap at the door.

'This is the girl's step-father, Mr James Windibank,' said Holmes. 'He has written to me to say that he would be here at six. Come in!'

The man who entered was a sturdy middle-sized fellow, some thirty years of age, clean shaven, and sallow skinned, with a bland, insinuating manner, and a pair of wonderfully sharp and penetrating grey eyes. He shot a questioning glance at each of us, placed his shiny top-hat upon the sideboard, and with a slight bow, sidled down into the nearest chair.

'Good evening, Mr James Windibank,' said Holmes. 'I think that this typewritten letter is from you, in which you made an appointment with me for six o'clock!'

'Yes, sir. I am afraid that I am a little late, but I am not quite my own master, you know. I am sorry that Miss Sutherland has troubled you about this little matter, for I think it is far better not to wash linen of this sort in public. It was quite against my wishes that she came, but she is a very excitable, impulsive girl, as you may have noticed, and she is not easily controlled when she has made up her mind on a point. Of course, I do not mind you so much, as you are not connected with the official police, but it is not pleasant to have a family misfortune like this noised abroad. Besides, it is a useless expense, for how could you possibly find this Hosmer Angel?'

'On the contrary,' said Holmes quietly; 'I have every reason to believe that I will succeed in discovering Mr Hosmer Angel.'

Mr Windibank gave a violent start, and dropped his gloves. 'I am delighted to hear it,' he said.

'It is a curious thing,' remarked Holmes, 'that a typewriter has really quite as much individuality as a man's handwriting.* Unless they are quite new, no two of them write exactly alike. Some letters get more worn than others, and some wear only on one side. Now, you remark in this note of yours, Mr Windibank, that in every case there is some little slurring over of the "e", and a slight defect in the tail of the "r". There are fourteen other characteristics, but those are the more obvious.'

'We do all our correspondence with this machine at the office, and no doubt it is a little worn,' our visitor answered, glancing keenly at Holmes with his bright little eyes.

'And now I will show you what is really a very interesting study, Mr Windibank,' Holmes continued. 'I think of writing another little monograph some of these days on the typewriter and its relation to crime. It is a subject to which I have devoted some little attention. I have here four letters which purport to come from the missing man. They are all typewritten. In each case, not only are the "e's" slurred and the "r's" tailless, but you will observe, if you care to use my magnifying lens, that the fourteen other characteristics to which I have alluded are there as well.'

Mr Windibank sprang out of his chair, and picked up his hat. 'I cannot waste time over this sort of fantastic talk, Mr

Holmes,' he said. 'If you can catch the man, catch him, and let me know when you have done it.'

'Certainly,' said Holmes, stepping over and turning the key in the door. 'I let you know, then, that I have caught him!'

'What! where?' shouted Mr Windibank, turning white to his lips, and glancing about him like a rat in a trap.

'Oh, it won't do—really it won't,' said Holmes, suavely. 'There is no possible getting out of it, Mr Windibank. It is quite too transparent, and it was a very bad compliment when you said it was impossible for me to solve so simple a question. That's right! Sit down, and let us talk it over.'

Our visitor collapsed into a chair with a ghastly face and a glitter of moisture on his brow. 'It—it's not actionable,' he stammered.

'I am very much afraid that it is not. But between ourselves, Windibank, it was as cruel, and selfish, and heartless a trick in a petty way as ever came before me. Now, let me just run over the course of events, and you will contradict me if I go wrong.'

The man sat huddled up in his chair, with his head sunk upon his breast, like one who is utterly crushed. Holmes stuck his feet up on the corner of the mantelpiece, and leaning back with his hands in his pockets, began talking, rather to himself, as it seemed, than to us.

'The man married a woman very much older than himself for her money,' said he, 'and he enjoyed the use of the money of the daughter as long as she lived with them. It was a considerable sum for people in their position, and the loss of it would have made a serious difference. It was worth an effort to preserve it. The daughter was of a good, amiable disposition, but affectionate and warm-hearted in her ways, so that it was evident that with her fair personal advantages, and her little income, she would not be allowed to remain single long. Now her marriage would mean, of course, the loss of a hundred a year, so what does her step-father do to prevent it? He takes the obvious course of keeping her at home, and forbidding her to seek the company of people of her own age. But soon he found that that would not answer for ever. She became restive, insisted upon her rights, and finally announced her positive intention of going to a certain ball. What does her clever step-father do then? He conceives an idea more creditable to his head than to his heart. With the connivance and assistance of his wife he disguised himself, covered those keen eyes with tinted glasses, masked the face with a moustache and a pair of bushy whiskers, sunk that clear voice into an insinuating whisper, and doubly secure on account of the girl's short sight, he appears as Mr Hosmer Angel, and keeps off other lovers by making love himself.'

'It was only a joke at first,' groaned our visitor. 'We never thought that she would have been so carried away.'

'Very likely not. However that may be, the young lady was very decidedly carried away, and having quite made up her mind that her step-father was in France, the suspicion of treachery never for an instant entered her mind. She was flattered by the gentleman's attentions, and the effect was increased by the loudly expressed admiration of her mother. Then Mr Angel began to call, for it was obvious that the matter should be pushed as far as it would go, if a real effect were to be produced. There were meetings, and an engagement, which would finally secure the girl's affections from turning towards anyone else. But the deception could not be kept up for ever. These pretended journeys to France were rather cumbrous. The thing to do was clearly to bring the business to an end in such a dramatic manner that it would leave a permanent impression upon the young lady's mind, and prevent her from looking upon any other suitor for some time to come. Hence those vows of fidelity exacted upon a Testament, and hence also the allusions to a possibility of something happening on the very morning of the wedding. James Windibank wished Miss Sutherland to be so bound to Hosmer Angel, and so uncertain as to his fate, that for ten years to come, at any rate, she would not listen to another man. As far as the church door he brought her, and then, as he could go no further, he conveniently vanished away by the old trick of stepping in at one door of a four-wheeler, and out at the other. I think that that was the chain of events, Mr Windibank!'

Our visitor had recovered something of his assurance while Holmes had been talking, and he rose from his chair now with a cold sneer upon his pale face.

'It may be so, or it may not, Mr Holmes,' said he, 'but if you are so very sharp you ought to be sharp enough to know that it is you who are breaking the law now, and not me. I have done nothing actionable from the first, but as long as you keep that door locked you lay yourself open to an action for assault and illegal constraint.'

'The law cannot, as you say, touch you,' said Holmes, unlocking and throwing open the door, 'yet there never was a man who deserved punishment more. If the young lady has a brother or a friend he ought to lay a whip across your shoulders. By Jove!' he continued, flushing up at the sight of the bitter sneer upon the man's face, 'it is not part of my duties to my client, but here's a hunting-crop* handy, and I think I shall just treat myself to—' He took two swift steps to the whip, but before he could grasp it there was a wild clatter of steps upon the stairs, the heavy hall door banged, and from the window we could see Mr James Windibank running at the top of his speed down the road.

'There's a cold-blooded scoundrel!' said Holmes, laughing, as he threw himself down into his chair once more. 'That fellow will rise from crime to crime until he does something very bad and ends on a gallows. The case has, in some respects, been not entirely devoid of interest.'

'I cannot now entirely see all the steps of your reasoning,' I remarked.

'Well, of course it was obvious from the first that this Mr Hosmer Angel must have some strong object for his curious conduct, and it was equally clear that the only man who really profited by the incident, as far as we could see, was the step-father. Then the fact that the two men were never together, but that the one always appeared when the other was away, was suggestive. So were the tinted spectacles and the curious voice, which both hinted at a disguise, as did the bushy whiskers. My suspicions were all confirmed by his peculiar action in typewriting his signature, which of course inferred that his handwriting was so familiar to her that she would recognize even the smallest sample of it. You see all these isolated facts, together with many minor ones, all pointed in the same direction.'

'And how did you verify them?'

'Having once spotted my man, it was easy to get corroboration. I knew the firm for which this man worked. Having taken the printed description, I eliminated everything from it which could be the result of a disguise—the whiskers, the glasses, the voice, and I sent it to the firm, with a request that they would inform me whether it answered the description of any of their travellers. I had already noticed the peculiarities of the typewriter, and I wrote to the man himself at his business address, asking him if he would come here. As I expected, his reply was typewritten, and revealed the same trivial but characteristic defects. The same post brought me a letter from Westhouse & Marbank, of Fenchurch Street, to say that the description tallied in every respect with that of their employee, James Windibank. *Voilà tout!*'*

'And Miss Sutherland?'

'If I tell her she will not believe me. You may remember the old Persian saying, "There is danger for him who taketh the tiger cub, and danger also for whoso snatches a delusion from a woman." There is as much sense in Hafiz as in Horace,* and as much knowledge of the world.'

The Red-Headed League

I HAD called upon my friend, Mr Sherlock Holmes, one day in the autumn of last year, and found him in deep conversation with a very stout, florid-faced, elderly gentleman, with fiery red hair. With an apology for my intrusion, I was about to withdraw, when Holmes pulled me abruptly into the room, and closed the door behind me.

'You could not possibly have come at a better time, my dear Watson,' he said, cordially.

'I was afraid that you were engaged.'

'So I am. Very much so.'

'Then I can wait in the next room.'

'Not at all. This gentleman, Mr Wilson, has been my partner and helper in many of my most successful cases, and I have no doubt that he will be of the utmost use to me in yours also.'

The stout gentleman half rose from his chair, and gave a bob of greeting, with a quick little questioning glance from his small, fat-encircled eyes.

'Try the settee,' said Holmes, relapsing into his armchair, and putting his fingertips together, as was his custom when in judicial moods. 'I know, my dear Watson, that you share my love of all that is bizarre and outside the conventions and humdrum routine of every-day life. You have shown your relish for it by the enthusiasm which has prompted you to chronicle, and, if you will excuse my saying so, somewhat to embellish so many of my own little adventures.'

'Your cases have indeed been of the greatest interest to me,' I observed.

'You will remember that I remarked the other day, just before we went into the very simple problem presented by Miss Mary Sutherland,* that for strange effects and extraordinary combinations we must go to life itself, which is always far more daring than any effort of the imagination.'

'A proposition which I took the liberty of doubting.'

'You did, Doctor, but none the less you must come round to my view, for otherwise I shall keep piling fact upon fact on you, until your reason breaks down under them and acknowledges me to be right. Now, Mr Jabez Wilson* here has been good enough to call upon me this morning, and to begin a narrative which promises to be one of the most singular which I have listened to for some time. You have heard me remark that the strangest and most unique things are very often connected not with the larger but with the smaller crimes, and occasionally, indeed, where there is room for doubt whether any positive crime has been committed. As far as I have heard, it is impossible for me to say whether the present case is an instance of crime or not, but the course of events is certainly among the most singular that I have ever listened to. Perhaps, Mr Wilson, you would have the great kindness to recommence your narrative. I ask you not merely because my friend Dr Watson has not heard the opening part, but also because the peculiar nature of the story makes me anxious to have every possible detail from your lips. As a rule, when I have heard some slight indication of the course of events I am able to guide myself by the thousands of other similar cases which occur to my memory. In the present instance I am forced to admit that the facts are, to the best of my belief, unique.'

The portly client puffed out his chest with an appearance of some little pride, and pulled a dirty and wrinkled newspaper from the inside pocket of his greatcoat. As he glanced down the advertisement column, with his head thrust forward, and the paper flattened out upon his knee, I took a good look at the man, and endeavoured after the fashion of my companion to read the indications which might be presented by his dress or appearance.

I did not gain very much, however, by my inspection. Our visitor bore every mark of being an average commonplace British tradesman, obese, pompous, and slow. He wore rather baggy grey shepherd's check trousers,* a not over-clean black frock-coat, unbuttoned in the front, and a drab waistcoat with a heavy brassy Albert chain, and a square pierced bit of metal dangling down as an ornament. A frayed top-hat, and a faded brown overcoat with a wrinkled velvet collar lay upon a chair beside him. Altogether, look as I would, there was nothing remarkable about the man save his blazing red head, and the expression of extreme chagrin and discontent upon his features.

Sherlock Holmes's quick eye took in my occupation, and he shook his head with a smile as he noticed my questioning glances. 'Beyond the obvious facts that he has at some time done manual labour, that he takes snuff, that he is a Freemason,* that he has been in China, and that he has done a considerable amount of writing lately, I can deduce nothing else.'

Mr Jabez Wilson started up in his chair, with his forefinger upon the paper, but his eyes upon my companion.

'How, in the name of good fortune, did you know that, Mr Holmes?' he asked. 'How did you know, for example, that I did manual labour? It's as true as gospel, and I began as a ship's carpenter.'

'Your hands, my dear sir. Your right hand is quite a size larger then your left.* You have worked with it, and the muscles are more developed.'

'Well, the snuff, then, and the Freemasonry?'

'I won't insult your intelligence by telling you how I read that, especially as, rather against the strict rules of your order,* you use an arc and compass breastpin.'*

'Ah, of course, I forgot that. But the writing?'

'What else can be indicated by that right cuff so very shiny for five inches, and the left one with the smooth patch near the elbow where you rest it upon the desk.'

'Well, but China?'

'The fish which you have tattooed immediately above your right wrist could only have been done in China.* I have made a small study of tattoo marks, and have even contributed to the literature of the subject. That trick of staining the fishes' scales of a delicate pink is quite peculiar to China. When, in addition, I see a Chinese coin hanging from your watch-chain,* the matter becomes even more simple.'

Mr Jabez Wilson laughed heavily. 'Well, I never!' said he. 'I thought at first you had done something clever, but I see that there was nothing in it after all.'

'I begin to think, Watson,' said Holmes, 'that I make a mistake in explaining. "Omne ignotum pro magnifico*," you know, and my poor little reputation, such as it is, will suffer shipwreck if I am so candid. Can you not find the advertisement, Mr Wilson?'

'Yes, I have got it now,' he answered, with his thick, red finger planted half-way down the column. 'Here it is. This is what began it all. You must read it for yourself, sir.'

I took the paper from him and read as follows:

TO THE RED-HEADED LEAGUE*—On account of the bequest of the late Ezekiah Hopkins,* of Lebanon, Penn., U.S.A.,* there is now another vacancy open which entitles a member of the League to a salary of four pounds a week for purely nominal services. All red-headed men who are sound in body and mind, and above the age of twenty-one years, are eligible. Apply in person on Monday, at eleven o'clock, to Duncan Ross, at the offices of the League, 7, Pope's Court, Fleet Street.*

'What on earth does this mean?' I ejaculated, after I had twice read over the extraordinary announcement.

Holmes chuckled, and wriggled in his chair, as was his habit when in high spirits. 'It is a little off the beaten track, isn't it?' said he. 'And now, Mr Wilson, off you go at scratch,* and tell us all about yourself, your household, and the effect which this advertisement had upon your fortunes. You will first make a note, Doctor, of the paper and the date.'

'It is the *Morning Chronicle*,* of April 27, 1890. Just two months ago.'*

'Very good. Now, Mr Wilson?'

'Well, it is just as I have been telling you, Mr Sherlock Holmes,' said Jabez Wilson, mopping his forehead, 'I have a small pawnbroker's business at Coburg Square, near the City.* It's not a very large affair, and of late years it has not done more than just give me a living. I used to be able to keep two assistants, but now I only keep one; and I would have a job to pay him, but that he is willing to come for half wages, so as to learn the business.'

'What is the name of this obliging youth?' asked Sherlock Holmes.

'His name is Vincent Spaulding,* and he's not such a youth either. It's hard to say his age. I should not wish a smarter assistant, Mr Holmes; and I know very well that he could better himself, and earn twice what I am able to give him. But after all, if he is satisfied, why should I put ideas in his head?'

'Why, indeed? You seem most fortunate in having an employee who comes under the full market price. It is not a common experience among employers in this age. I don't know that your assistant is not as remarkable as your advertisement.'

'Oh, he has his faults, too,' said Mr Wilson. 'Never was such a fellow for photography. Snapping away with a camera when he ought to be improving his mind, and then diving down into the cellar like a rabbit into its hole to develop his pictures. That is his main fault; but on the whole, he's a good worker. There's no vice in him.'

'He is still with you, I presume?'

'Yes, sir. He and a girl of fourteen, who does a bit of simple cooking, and keeps the place clean—that's all I have in the house, for I am a widower, and never had any family.* We live very quietly, sir, the three of us; and we keep a roof over our heads, and pay our debts, if we do nothing more.

'The first thing that put us out was that advertisement. Spaulding, he came down into the office just this day eight weeks with this very paper in his hand, and he says:

' "I wish to the Lord, Mr Wilson, that I was a red-headed man."

' "Why that?" I asks.

' "Why" says he, "here's another vacancy on the League of the Red-Headed Men. It's worth quite a little fortune to any man who gets it, and I understand that there are more vacancies than there are men, so that the trustees are at their wits' end what to do with the money. If my hair would only change colour, here's a nice little crib* all ready for me to step into."

' "Why, what is it, then?" I asked. You see, Mr Holmes, I am a very stay-at-home man, and, as my business came to me instead of my having to go to it, I was often weeks on end without putting my foot over the door-mat. In that way I didn't know much of what was going on outside, and I was always glad of a bit of news.

' "Have you never heard of the League of the Red-Headed Men?" he asked, with his eyes open.

' "Never."

' "Why, I wonder at that, for you are eligible yourself for one of the vacancies."

' "And what are they worth?" I asked.

' "Oh, merely a couple of hundred a year, but the work is slight, and it need not interfere much with one's other occupations."

'Well, you can easily think that that made me prick up my ears, for the business has not been over good for some years, and an extra couple of hundred would have been very handy.

' "Tell me all about it," said I.

' "Well," said he, showing me the advertisement, "you can see for yourself that the League has a vacancy, and there is the address where you should apply for particulars. As far as I can make out, the League was founded by an American millionaire, Ezekiah Hopkins, who was very peculiar in his ways. He was himself red-headed, and he had a great sympathy for all red-headed men; so, when he died, it was found that he had left his enormous fortune in the hands of trustees, with instructions to apply the interest to the providing of easy berths to men whose hair is of that colour. From all I hear it is splendid pay, and very little to do."

' "But," said I, "there would be millions of red-headed men who would apply."

' "Not so many as you might think," he answered. "You see, it is really confined to Londoners, and to grown men. This American had started from London when he was young, and he wanted to do the old town a good turn. Then, again, I have heard it is no use your applying if your hair is light red, or dark red, or anything but real, bright, blazing, fiery red. Now, if you cared to apply, Mr Wilson, you would just walk in; but perhaps it would hardly be worth your while to put yourself out of the way for the sake of a few hundred pounds."

'Now, it is a fact, gentlemen, as you may see for your-selves, that my hair is of a very full and rich tint, so that it seemed to me that, if there was to be any competition in the matter, I stood as good a chance as any man that I had ever met. Vincent Spaulding seemed to know so much about it that I thought he might prove useful, so I just ordered him to put up the shutters for the day, and to come right away with me. He was very willing to have a holiday, so we shut the business up, and started off for the address that was given us in the advertisement.

'I never hope to see such a sight as that again, Mr Holmes. From north, south, east, and west every man who had a shade of red in his hair had tramped into the City to answer the advertisement. Fleet Street was choked with red-headed folk, and Pope's Court looked like a coster's orange barrow.* I should not have thought there were so many in the whole country as were brought together by that single advertisement. Every shade of colour they were—straw, lemon, orange, brick, Irish-setter, liver, clay; but, as Spaulding said, there were not many who had the real vivid flame-coloured tint. When I saw how many were waiting I would have given it up in despair; but Spaulding would not hear of it. How he did it I could not imagine, but he pushed and pulled and butted until he got me through the crowd, and right up to the steps which led to the office. There was a double stream upon the stair, some going up in hope, and some coming back dejected; but we wedged in as well as we could, and soon found ourselves in the office.'

'Your experience has been a most entertaining one,' remarked Holmes, as his client paused and refreshed his memory with a huge pinch of snuff. 'Pray continue your very interesting statement.'

'There was nothing in the office but a couple of wooden chairs and a deal table, behind which sat a small man, with a head that was even redder than mine. He said a few words to each candidate as he came up, and then he always managed to find some fault in them which would disqualify them. Getting a vacancy did not seem to be such a very easy matter after all. However, when our turn came, the little man was more favourable to me than to any of the others, and he closed the door as we entered, so that he might have a private word with us.

' "This is Mr Jabez Wilson," said my assistant, "and he is willing to fill a vacancy in the League."

' "And he is admirably suited for it," the other answered. "He has every requirement. I cannot recall when I have seen anything so fine." He took a step backwards, cocked his head on one side, and gazed at my hair until I felt quite bashful. Then suddenly he plunged forward, wrung my hand, and congratulated me warmly on my success.

' "It would be injustice to hesitate," said he. "You will, however, I am sure, excuse me for taking an obvious precaution." With that he seized my hair in both his hands, and tugged until I yelled with the pain. "There is water in your eyes," said he, as he released me. "I perceive that all is as it should be. But we have to be careful, for we have twice been deceived by wigs and once by paint. I could tell you tales of cobbler's wax* which would disgust you with human nature." He stepped over to the window, and shouted through it at the top of his voice that the vacancy was filled. A groan of disappointment came up from below, and the folk all trooped away in different directions, until there was not a red head to be seen except my own and that of the manager.

' "My name," said he, "is Mr Duncan Ross,* and I am myself one of the pensioners upon the fund left by our noble benefactor. Are you a married man, Mr Wilson? Have you a family?"

'I answered that I had not.

'His face fell immediately.

' "Dear me!" he said gravely, "that is very serious indeed! I am sorry to hear you say that. The fund was, of course, for the propagation and spread of the red-heads as well as for their maintenance. It is exceedingly unfortunate that you should be a bachelor."

'My face lengthened at this, Mr Holmes, for I thought that I was not to have the vacancy after all; but after thinking it over for a few minutes, he said that it would be all right.

' "In the case of another," said he, "the objection might be fatal, but we must stretch a point in favour of a man with such a head of hair as yours. When shall you be able to enter upon your new duties?"

' "Well, it is a little awkward, for I have a business already," said I.

' "Oh, never mind about that, Mr Wilson!" said Vincent Spaulding. "I shall be able to look after that for you."

' "What would be the hours?" I asked.

' "Ten to two."

'Now a pawnbroker's business is mostly done of an evening, Mr Holmes, especially Thursday and Friday evening, which is just before pay-day; so it would suit me very well to earn a little in the mornings. Besides, I knew that my assistant was a good man, and that he would see to anything that turned up.

' "That would suit me very well," said I. "And the pay?"

' "Is four pounds a week."

' "And the work?"

' "Is purely nominal."

' "What do you call purely nominal?"

' "Well, you have to be in the office, or at least in the building, the whole time. If you leave, you forfeit your whole position for ever. The will is very clear upon that point. You don't comply with the conditions if you budge from the office during that time."

' "It's only four hours a day, and I should not think of leaving," said I.

' "No excuse will avail," said Mr Duncan Ross, "neither sickness, nor business, nor anything else. There you must stay, or you lose your billet."

' "And the work?"

' "Is to copy out the *Encyclopedia Britannica*.* There is the first volume of it in that press.* You must find your own ink, pens, and blotting-paper, but we provide this table and chair. Will you be ready to-morrow?"*

' "Certainly," I answered.

' "Then good-bye, Mr Jabez Wilson, and let me congratulate you once more on the important position which you have been fortunate enough to gain." He bowed me out of the room, and I went home with my assistant, hardly knowing what to say or do, I was so pleased at my own good fortune.

'Well, I thought over the matter all day, and by evening I was in low spirits again; for I had quite persuaded myself that the whole affair must be some great hoax or fraud, though what its object might be I could not imagine. It seemed altogether past belief that anyone could make such a will, or that they would pay a sum for doing anything so simple as copying out the *Encyclopedia Britannica*. Vincent Spaulding did what he could to cheer me up, but by bedtime I had reasoned myself out of the whole thing. However, in the morning I determined to have a look at it anyhow, so I bought a penny bottle of ink, and with a quill pen, and seven sheets of foolscap paper, I started off for Pope's Court.

'Well, to my surprise and delight everything was as right as possible. The table was set out ready for me, and Mr Duncan Ross was there to see that I got fairly to work. He started me off upon the letter A,* and then he left me; but he would drop in from time to time to see that all was right with me. At two o'clock he bade me good-day, complimented me upon the amount that I had written, and locked the door of the office after me.

'This went on day after day, Mr Holmes, and on Saturday the manager came in and planked down* four golden sovereigns for my week's work. It was the same next week, and the same the week after. Every morning I was there at ten, and every afternoon I left at two. By degrees Mr Duncan Ross took to coming in only once of a morning, and then, after a time, he did not come in at all. Still, of course, I never dared to leave the room for an instant, for I was not sure when he might come, and the billet was such a good one, and suited me so well, that I would not risk the loss of it.

'Eight weeks passed away like this, and I had written about Abbots, and Archery, and Armour, and Architecture, and Attica,* and hoped with diligence that I might get on to the B's before very long. It cost me something in foolscap, and I had pretty nearly filled a shelf with my writings. And then suddenly the whole business came to an end.'

'To an end?'

'Yes, sir. And no later than this morning. I went to my work as usual at ten o'clock, but the door was shut and locked, with a little square of cardboard hammered on to the middle of the panel with a tack. Here it is, and you can read for yourself.'

He held up a piece of white cardboard, about the size of a sheet of note-paper. It read in this fashion:

THE RED-HEADED LEAGUE IS DISSOLVED.
OCT. 9, 1890.

Sherlock Holmes and I surveyed this curt announcement and the rueful face behind it, until the comical side of the affair so completely overtopped every other consideration that we both burst out into a roar of laughter.

'I cannot see that there is anything very funny,' cried our client, flushing up to the roots of his flaming head. 'If you can do nothing better than laugh at me, I can go elsewhere.'

'No, no,' cried Holmes, shoving him back into the chair from which he had half risen. 'I really wouldn't miss your case for the world. It is most refreshingly unusual. But there is, if you will excuse me saying so, something just a little funny about it. Pray what steps did you take when you found the card upon the door?'

'I was staggered, sir. I did not know what to do. Then I called at the offices round, but none of them seemed to know anything about it. Finally, I went to the landlord, who is an accountant living on the ground floor, and I asked him if he could tell me what had become of the Red-Headed League. He said that he had never heard of any such body. Then I asked him who Mr Duncan Ross was. He answered that the name was new to him.

' "Well," said I, "the gentleman at No. 4."*

' "What, the red-headed man?"

' "Yes."

' "Oh," said he, "his name was William Morris.* He was a solicitor, and was using my room as a temporary convenience until his new premises were ready. He moved out yesterday."

' "Where could I find him?"

' "Oh, at his new offices. He did tell me the address. Yes, 17 King Edward Street, near St Paul's."*

'I started off, Mr Holmes, but when I got to that address it was a manufactory of artificial knee-caps,* and no one in it had ever heard of either Mr William Morris, or Mr Duncan Ross.'

'And what did you do then?' asked Holmes.

'I went home to Saxe-Coburg Square, and I took the advice of my assistant. But he could not help me in any way. He could only say that if I waited I should hear by post. But that was not quite good enough, Mr Holmes. I did not wish to lose such a place without a struggle, so, as I had heard that you were good enough to give advice to poor folk who were in need of it, I came right away to you.'

'And you did very wisely,' said Holmes. 'Your case is an exceedingly remarkable one, and I shall be happy to look into it. From what you have told me I think that it is possible that graver issues hang from it than might at first sight appear.'

'Grave enough!' said Mr Jabez Wilson. 'Why, I have lost four pounds a week.'

'As far as you are personally concerned,' remarked Holmes, 'I do not see that you have any grievance against this extraordinary league. On the contrary, you are, as I understand, richer by some thirty pounds, to say nothing of the minute knowledge which you have gained on every subject which comes under the letter A. You have lost nothing by them.'

'No, sir. But I want to find out about them, and who they are, and what their object was in playing this prank—if it was a prank—upon me. It was a pretty expensive joke for them, for it cost them two-and-thirty pounds.*

'We shall endeavour to clear up these points for you. And, first, one or two questions, Mr Wilson. This assistant of yours who first called your attention to the advertisement—how long had he been with you?'

'About a month then.'

'How did he come?'

'In answer to an advertisement.'

'Was he the only applicant?'

'No, I had a dozen.'

'Why did you pick him?'

'Because he was handy, and would come cheap.'

'At half wages, in fact.'

'Yes.'

'What is he like, this Vincent Spaulding?'

'Small, stout-built, very quick in his ways, no hair on his face, though he's not short of thirty. Has a white splash of acid upon his forehead.'

Holmes sat up in his chair in considerable excitement. 'I thought as much,' said he. 'Have you ever observed that his ears are pierced for ear-rings?'

'Yes, sir. He told me that a gipsy had done it for him when he was a lad.'

'Hum!' said Holmes, sinking back in deep thought. 'He is still with you?'

'Oh, yes, sir; I have only just left him.'

'And has your business been attended to in your absence?'

'Nothing to complain of, sir. There's never very much to do of a morning.'

'That will do, Mr Wilson. I shall be happy to give you an opinion upon the subject in the course of a day or two. To-day is Saturday,* and I hope that by Monday we may come to a conclusion.'

'Well, Watson,' said Holmes, when our visitor had left us, 'what do you make of it all?'

'I make nothing of it,' I answered, frankly. 'It is a most mysterious business.'

'As a rule,' said Holmes, 'the more bizarre a thing is the less mysterious it proves to be. It is your commonplace, featureless crimes which are really puzzling, just as a commonplace face is the most difficult to identify. But I must be prompt over this matter.'

'What are you going to do, then?' I asked.

'To smoke,' he answered. 'It is quite a three-pipe problem, and I beg that you won't speak to me for fifty minutes.' He curled himself up in his chair, with his thin knees drawn up to his hawk-like nose,* and there he sat with his eyes closed and his black clay pipe thrusting out like the bill of some strange bird. I had come to the conclusion that he had dropped asleep, and indeed was nodding myself, when he suddenly sprang out of his chair with the gesture of a man who had made up his mind, and put his pipe down upon the mantelpiece.

'Sarasate* plays at the St James's Hall* this afternoon,' he remarked. 'What do you think, Watson? Could your patients spare you for a few hours?'

'I have nothing to do to-day. My practice is never very absorbing.'

'Then put on your hat, and come. I am going through the City first, and we can have some lunch on the way. I observe that there is a good deal of German music on the programme which is rather more to my taste than Italian or French. It is introspective, and I want to introspect.* Come along!'

We travelled by the Underground as far as Aldersgate;*
and a short walk took us to Saxe-Coburg Square, the scene
of the singular story which we had listened to in the
morning. It was a pokey, little, shabby-genteel place, where
four lines of dingy two-storied brick houses looked out into
a small railed-in enclosure, where a lawn of weedy grass and
a few clumps of faded laurel bushes made a hard fight
against a smoke-laden and uncongenial atmosphere. Three
gilt balls* and a brown board with 'JABEZ WILSON' in white
letters upon a corner house, announced the place where our
red-headed client carried on his business. Sherlock Holmes
stopped in front of it with his head on one side and looked
it all over, with his eyes shining brightly between puckered
lids. Then he walked slowly up the street and then down
again to the corner, still looking keenly at the houses. Finally
he returned to the pawnbroker's, and, having thumped vigorously upon the pavement with his stick two or three times,
he went up to the door and knocked. It was instantly opened
by a bright-looking, clean-shaven young fellow, who asked
him to step in.

'Thank you,' said Holmes, 'I only wished to ask you how
you would go from here to the Strand.'

'Third right, fourth left,' answered the assistant promptly,
closing the door.

'Smart fellow, that,' observed Holmes as we walked away.
'He is, in my judgement, the fourth smartest man in London, and for daring I am not sure that he has not a claim
to be third. I have known something of him before.'

'Evidently,' said I, 'Mr Wilson's assistant counts for a good
deal in this mystery of the Red-Headed League. I am sure
that you inquired your way merely in order that you might
see him.'

'Not him.'

'What then?'

'The knees of his trousers.'*

'And what did you see?'

'What I expected to see.'

'Why did you beat the pavement?'

'My dear Doctor, this is a time for observation, not for talk. We are spies in an enemy's country. We know something of Saxe-Coburg Square. Let us now explore the paths which lie behind it.'

The road in which we found ourselves as we turned round the corner from the retired Saxe-Coburg Square presented as great a contrast to it as the front of a picture does to the back. It was one of the main arteries which convey the traffic of the City to the north and west.* The roadway was blocked with the immense stream of commerce flowing in a double tide inwards and outwards, while the footpaths were black with the hurrying swarm of pedestrians. It was difficult to realize as we looked at the line of fine shops and stately business premises that they really abutted on the other side upon the faded and stagnant square which we had just quitted.

'Let me see,' said Holmes, standing at the corner, and glancing along the line, 'I should like just to remember the order of the houses here. It is a hobby of mine to have an exact knowledge of London. There is Mortimer's, the tobacconist,* the little newspaper shop, the Coburg branch of the City and Suburban Bank,* the Vegetarian Restaurant, and McFarlane's carriage-building *depôt*. That carries us right on to the other block. And now, Doctor, we've done our work, so it's time we had some play. A sandwich and a cup of coffee, and then off to violin-land, where all is sweetness, and delicacy, and harmony, and there are no red-headed clients to vex us with their conundrums.'

My friend was an enthusiastic musician being himself not only a very capable performer, but a composer of no ordinary merit.* All the afternoon he sat in the stalls wrapped in the most perfect happiness, gently waving his long thin fingers in time to the music, while his gently smiling face and his languid, dreamy eyes were as unlike those of Holmes the sleuth-hound, Holmes the relentless, keen-witted, ready-handed criminal agent, as it was possible to conceive. In his singular character the dual nature alternately asserted itself* and his extreme exactness and astuteness represented, as I

have often thought, the reaction against the poetic and con-
templative mood which occasionally predominated in him.
The swing of his nature took him from extreme languor to
devouring energy; and, as I knew well, he was never so truly
formidable as when, for days on end, he had been lounging
in his arm-chair amid his improvisations and his black-
letter* editions. Then it was that the lust of the chase would
suddenly come upon him, and that his brilliant reasoning
power would rise to the level of intuition, until those who
were unacquainted with his methods would look askance at
him as on a man whose knowledge was not that of other
mortals. When I saw him that afternoon so enwrapped in
the music at St James's Hall I felt that an evil time might be
coming upon those whom he had set himself to hunt down.

'You want to go home, no doubt, Doctor,' he remarked,
as we emerged.

'Yes, it would be as well.'

'And I have some business to do which will take some
hours. This business at Coburg Square is serious.'

'Why serious?'

'A considerable crime is in contemplation. I have every
reason to believe that we shall be in time to stop it. But
to-day being Saturday rather complicates matters. I shall
want your help to-night.'

'At what time?'

'Ten will be early enough.'

'I shall be at Baker Street at ten.'

'Very well. And I say, Doctor! there may be some little
danger, so kindly put your army revolver in your pocket.'
He waved his hand, turned on his heel, and disappeared in
an instant among the crowd.

I trust that I am not more dense than my neighbours, but
I was always oppressed with a sense of my own stupidity in
my dealings with Sherlock Holmes. Here I had heard what
he had heard, I had seen what he had seen, and yet from
his words it was evident that he saw clearly not only what
had happened, but what was about to happen, while to me
the whole business was still confused and grotesque. As I

drove home to my house in Kensington I thought over it all, from the extraordinary story of the red-headed copier of the *Encyclopedia* down to the visit to Saxe-Coburg Square, and the ominous words with which he had parted from me. What was this nocturnal expedition, and why should I go armed? Where were we going, and what were we to do? I had the hint from Holmes that this smooth-faced pawn-broker's assistant was a formidable man—a man who might play a deep game. I tried to puzzle it out, but gave it up in despair, and set the matter aside until night should bring an explanation.

It was a quarter past nine when I started from home and made my way across the Park, and so through Oxford Street to Baker Street.* Two hansoms* were standing at the door, and, as I entered the passage, I heard the sound of voices from above. On entering his room, I found Holmes in anim-ated conversation with two men, one of whom I recognized as Peter Jones, the official police agent;* while the other was a long, thin, sad-faced man, with a very shiny hat and oppressively respectable frock-coat.

'Ha! our party is complete,' said Holmes, buttoning up his pea-jacket,* and taking his heavy hunting-crop from the rack. 'Watson, I think you know Mr Jones, of Scotland Yard? Let me introduce you to Mr Merryweather,* who is to be our companion in tonight's adventure.'

'We're hunting in couples again, Doctor, you see,' said Jones in his consequential way. 'Our friend here is a wonderful man for starting a chase. All he wants is an old dog to help him to do the running down.'

'I hope a wild goose may not prove to be the end of our chase,' observed Mr Merryweather gloomily.

'You may place considerable confidence in Mr Holmes, sir,' said the police agent loftily. 'He has his own little methods, which are, if he won't mind my saying so, just a little too theoretical and fantastic, but he has the makings of a detective in him. It is not too much to say that once or twice, as in that business of the Sholto murder and the Agra treasure,* he has been more nearly correct than the official force.'

'Oh, if you say so, Mr Jones, it is all right!' said the stranger, with deference. 'Still, I confess that I miss my rubber.* It is the first Saturday night for seven-and-thirty years that I have not had my rubber.'

'I think you will find,' said Sherlock Holmes, 'that you will play for a higher stake tonight than you have ever done yet, and that the play will be more exciting. For you, Mr Merryweather, the stake will be some thirty thousand pounds; and for you, Jones, it will be the man upon whom you wish to lay your hands.'

'John Clay, the murderer, thief, smasher, and forger.* He's a young man, Mr Merryweather, but he is at the head of his profession, and I would rather have my bracelets on him than on any criminal in London. He's a remarkable man, is young John Clay. His grandfather was a Royal Duke,* and he himself has been to Eton and Oxford. His brain is as cunning as his fingers, and though we meet signs of him at every turn, we never know where to find the man himself. He'll crack a crib in Scotland one week, and be raising money to build an orphanage in Cornwall the next.* I've been on his track for years, and have never set eyes on him yet.'

'I hope that I may have the pleasure of introducing you tonight. I've had one or two little turns also with Mr John Clay, and I agree with you that he is at the head of his profession. It is past ten, however, and quite time that we started. If you two will take the first hansom, Watson and I will follow in the second.'

Sherlock Holmes was not very communicative during the long drive, and lay back in the cab humming the tunes which he had heard in the afternoon. We rattled through an endless labyrinth of gas-lit streets until we emerged into Farringdon Street.*

'We are close there now,' my friend remarked. 'This fellow Merryweather is a bank director and personally interested in the matter. I thought it as well to have Jones with us also. He is not a bad fellow, though an absolute imbecile in his profession. He has one positive virtue. He is as brave as a bulldog, and as tenacious as a lobster if he gets his claws upon anyone. Here we are, and they are waiting for us.'

We had reached the same crowded thoroughfare in which we had found ourselves in the morning. Our cabs were dismissed, and, following the guidance of Mr Merryweather, we passed down a narrow passage, and through a side door, which he opened for us. Within there was a small corridor, which ended in a very massive iron gate. This also was opened, and led down a flight of winding stone steps, which terminated at another formidable gate. Mr Merryweather stopped to light a lantern, and then conducted us down a dark, earth-smelling passage, and so, after opening a third door, into a huge vault or cellar, which was piled all round with crates and massive boxes.

'You are not very vulnerable from above,' Holmes remarked, as he held up the lantern and gazed about him.

'Nor from below,' said Mr Merryweather, striking his stick upon the flags which lined the floor. 'Why, dear me, it sounds quite hollow!' he remarked, looking up in surprise.

'I must really ask you to be a little more quiet,' said Holmes severely. 'You have already imperilled the whole success of our expedition. Might I beg that you would have the goodness to sit down upon one of those boxes, and not to interfere?'

The solemn Mr Merryweather perched himself upon a crate, with a very injured expression upon his face, while Holmes fell upon his knees upon the floor, and, with the lantern and a magnifying lens, began to examine minutely the cracks between the stones. A few seconds sufficed to satisfy him for he sprang to his feet again, and put his glass in his pocket.

'We have at least an hour before us,' he remarked, 'for they can hardly take any steps until the good pawnbroker is safely in bed. Then they will not lose a minute, for the sooner they do their work the longer time they will have for their escape. We are at present, Doctor—as no doubt you have divined—in the cellar of the City branch of one of the principal London banks. Mr Merryweather is the chairman of directors, and he will explain to you that there are reasons why the more daring criminals of London should take a considerable interest in this cellar at present.'

'It is our French gold,' whispered the director. 'We have had several warnings that an attempt might be made upon it.'

'Your French gold?'

'Yes. We had occasion some months ago to strengthen our resources, and borrowed, for that purpose, thirty thousand napoleons* from the Bank of France. It has become known that we have never had occasion to unpack the money, and that it is still lying in our cellar. The crate upon which I sit contains two thousand napoleons packed between layers of lead foil. Our reserve of bullion is much larger at present than is usually kept in a single branch office, and the directors have had misgivings upon the subject.'

'Which were very well justified,' observed Holmes. 'And now it is time that we arranged our little plans. I expect that within an hour matters will come to a head. In the meantime, Mr Merryweather, we must put the screen over that dark lantern.'*

'And sit in the dark?'

'I am afraid so. I had brought a pack of cards in my pocket, and I thought that, as we were a *partie carrée,** you might have your rubber after all. But I see that the enemy's preparations have gone so far that we cannot risk the presence of a light. And, first of all, we must choose our positions. These are daring men, and, though we shall take them at a disadvantage they may do us some harm, unless we are careful. I shall stand behind this crate, and do you conceal yourself behind those. Then, when I flash a light upon them, close in swiftly. If they fire, Watson, have no compunction about shooting them down.'

I placed my revolver, cocked, upon the top of the wooden case behind which I crouched. Holmes shot the slide across the front of his lantern, and left us in pitch darkness—such an absolute darkness as I have never before experienced. The smell of hot metal remained to assure us that the light was still there, ready to flash out at a moment's notice. To me, with my nerves worked up to a pitch of expectancy, there was something depressing and subduing in the sudden gloom, and in the cold, dank air of the vault.

'They have but one retreat,' whispered Holmes. 'That is back through the house into Saxe-Coburg Square. I hope that you have done what I asked you, Jones?'

'I have an inspector and two officers waiting at the front door.'

'Then we have stopped all the holes. And now we must be silent and wait.'

What a time it seemed! From comparing notes afterwards it was but an hour and a quarter, yet it appeared to me that the night must have almost gone, and the dawn be breaking above us. My limbs were weary and stiff, for I feared to change my position, yet my nerves were worked up to the highest pitch of tension, and my hearing was so acute that I could not only hear the gentle breathing of my companions, but I could distinguish the deeper, heavier in-breath of the bulky Jones from the thin sighing note of the bank director. From my position I could look over the case in the direction of the floor. Suddenly my eyes caught the glint of a light.

At first it was but a lurid spark upon the stone pavement. Then it lengthened out until it became a yellow line, and then, without any warning or sound, a gash seemed to open and a hand appeared, a white, almost womanly hand, which felt about in the centre of the little area of light. For a minute or more the hand, with its writhing fingers, protruded out of the floor. Then it was withdrawn as suddenly as it appeared, and all was dark again save the single lurid spark, which marked a chink between the stones.

Its disappearance, however, was but momentary. With a rending, tearing sound, one of the broad, white stones turned over upon its side and left a square gaping hole through which streamed the light of a lantern. Over the edge there peeped a clean-cut, boyish face, which looked keenly about it, and then, with a hand on either side of the aperture, drew itself shoulder high and waist high until one

70

knee rested upon the edge. In another instant he stood at the side of the hole, and was hauling after him a companion, lithe and small like himself, with a pale face and a shock of very red hair.

'It's all clear,' he whispered. 'Have you the chisel and the bags. Great Scott! Jump, Archie, jump, and I'll swing for it!'*

Sherlock Holmes had sprung out and seized the intruder by the collar. The other dived down the hole, and I heard the sound of rending cloth as Jones clutched at his skirts.* The light flashed upon the barrel of a revolver, but Holmes's hunting-crop came down on the man's wrist, and the pistol clinked upon the stone floor.

'It's no use, John Clay,' said Holmes blandly; 'you have no chance at all.'

'So I see,' the other answered, with the utmost coolness. 'I fancy that my pal is all right, though I see you have got his coat-tails.'

'There are three men waiting for him at the door,' said Holmes.

'Oh, indeed. You seem to have done the thing very completely. I must compliment you.'

'And I you,' Holmes answered. 'Your red-headed idea was very new and effective.'

'You'll see your pal again presently,' said Jones. 'He's quicker at climbing down holes than I am. Just hold out while I fix the derbies.'*

'I beg that you will not touch me with your filthy hands,' remarked our prisoner, as the handcuffs clattered upon his wrists. 'You may not be aware that I have royal blood in my veins. Have the goodness also when you address me always to say "sir" and "please".'

'All right,' said Jones, with a stare and a snigger. 'Well, would you please, sir, march upstairs, where we can get a cab to carry your highness to the police-station.'

'That is better,' said John Clay, serenely. He made a sweeping bow to the three of us, and walked quietly off in the custody of the detective.

'Really, Mr Holmes,' said Mr Merryweather, as we followed them from the cellar, 'I do not know how the bank can thank you or repay you. There is no doubt that you have detected and defeated in the most complete manner one of the most determined attempts at bank robbery that have ever come within my experience.'

'I have had one or two little scores of my own to settle with Mr John Clay,' said Holmes. 'I have been at some small expense over this matter, which I shall expect the bank to refund, but beyond that I am amply repaid by having had an experience which is in many ways unique, and by hearing the very remarkable narrative of the Red-Headed League.'

'You see, Watson,' he explained in the early hours of the morning, as we sat over a glass of whisky-and-soda in Baker Street, 'it was perfectly obvious from the first that the only possible object of this rather fantastic business of the advertisement of the League, and the copying of the *Encyclopedia*, must be to get this not over-bright pawnbroker out of the way for a number of hours every day. It was a curious way of managing it, but really it would be difficult to suggest a better. The method was no doubt suggested to Clay's ingenious mind by the colour of his accomplice's hair. The four pounds a week was a lure which must draw him, and what was it to them, who were playing for thousands? They put in the advertisement; one rogue has the temporary office, the other rogue incites the man to apply for it, and together they manage to secure his absence every morning in the week. From the time that I heard of the assistant having come for half-wages, it was obvious to me that he had some strong motive for securing the situation.'

'But how could you guess what the motive was?'

'Had there been women in the house, I should have suspected a mere vulgar intrigue. That, however, was out of the question. The man's business was a small one, and there was nothing in his house which could account for such elaborate preparations and such an expenditure as they

were at. It must then be something out of the house. What
could it be? I thought of the assistant's fondness for photography, and his trick of vanishing into the cellar. The cellar!
There was the end of this tangled clue. Then I made
inquiries as to this mysterious assistant, and found that I had
to deal with one of the coolest and most daring criminals in
London. He was doing something in the cellar—something
which took many hours a day for months on end. What
could it be, once more? I could think of nothing save that
he was running a tunnel to some other building.

'So far I had got when we went to visit the scene of action.
I surprised you by beating upon the pavement with my
stick. I was ascertaining whether the cellar stretched out in
front or behind. It was not in front. Then I rang the bell,
and, as I hoped, the assistant answered it. We have had some
skirmishes, but we had never set eyes on each other before.
I hardly looked at his face. His knees were what I wished to
see. You must yourself have remarked how worn, wrinkled
and stained they were. They spoke of those hours of burrowing. The only remaining point was what they were burrowing
for. I walked round the corner, saw the City and Suburban
Bank abutted on our friend's premises, and felt that I had
solved my problem. When you drove home after the concert
I called upon Scotland Yard, and upon the chairman of the
bank directors, with the result that you have seen.'

'And how could you tell that they would make their
attempt to-night?' I asked.

'Well, when they closed their League offices that was a
sign that they cared no longer about Mr Jabez Wilson's
presence; in other words, that they had completed their
tunnel. But it was essential that they should use it soon, as
it might be discovered, or the bullion might be removed.
Saturday would suit them better than any other day, as it
would give them two days for their escape.* For all these
reasons I expected them to come to-night.'

'You reasoned it out beautifully,' I exclaimed in unfeigned
admiration. 'It is so long a chain, and yet every link rings
true.'

'It saved me from ennui,* he answered, yawning. 'Alas, I already feel it closing in upon me! My life is spent in one long effort to escape from the commonplaces of existence. These little problems help me to do so.'

'And you are a benefactor of the race,' said I.

He shrugged his shoulders. 'Well, perhaps, after all, it is of some little use,' he remarked. ' "L'homme c'est rien— l'œuvre c'est tout," as Gustave Flaubert wrote to George Sand.'*

The Boscombe Valley Mystery

WE were seated at breakfast one morning, my wife and I, when the maid brought in a telegram. It was from Sherlock Holmes, and ran in this way:

'Have you a couple of days to spare? Have just been wired* for from the West of England in connection with Boscombe Valley* tragedy. Shall be glad if you will come with me. Air and scenery perfect. Leave Paddington* by the 11.15.'

'What do you say, dear?' said my wife, looking across at me. 'Will you go?'

'I really don't know what to say. I have a fairly long list at present.'

'Oh, Anstruther would do your work for you.* You have been looking a little pale lately. I think that the change would do you good, and you are always so interested in Mr Sherlock Holmes's cases.'

'I should be ungrateful if I were not, seeing what I gained* through one of them,' I answered. 'But if I am to go I must pack at once, for I have only half an hour.'

My experience of camp life in Afghanistan had at least had the effect of making me a prompt and ready traveller. My wants were few and simple, so that in less than the time stated I was in a cab with my valise, rattling away to Paddington Station. Sherlock Holmes was pacing up and down the platform, his tall, gaunt figure made even gaunter and taller by his long grey travelling-cloak and close-fitting cloth cap.*

'It is really very good of you to come, Watson,' said he. 'It makes a considerable difference to me, having someone with me on whom I can thoroughly rely. Local aid is always either worthless or else biassed. If you will keep the two corner seats I shall get the tickets.'

We had the carriage to ourselves save for an immense litter of papers which Holmes had brought with him.

Among these he rummaged and read, with intervals of note-taking and of meditation, until we were past Reading. Then he suddenly rolled them all into a gigantic ball, and tossed them up on to the rack.

'Have you heard anything of the case?' he asked.

'Not a word. I have not seen a paper for some days.'

'The London press has not had very full accounts. I have just been looking through all the recent papers in order to master the particulars. It seems, from what I gather, to be one of those simple cases which are so extremely difficult.'

'That sounds a little paradoxical.'

'But it is profoundly true. Singularity is almost invariably a clue. The more featureless and commonplace a crime is, the more difficult it is to bring it home. In this case, however, they have established a very serious case against the son of the murdered man.'

'It is a murder, then?'

'Well, it is conjectured to be so. I shall take nothing for granted until I have the opportunity of looking personally into it. I will explain the state of things to you, as far as I have been able to understand it, in a very few words.

'Boscombe Valley is a country district not very far from Ross, in Herefordshire.* The largest landed proprietor in that part is a Mr John Turner,* who made his money in Australia, and returned some years ago to the old country. One of the farms which he held, that of Hatherley,* was let to Mr Charles McCarthy,* who was also an ex-Australian. The men had known each other in the Colonies,* so that it was not unnatural that when they came to settle down they should do so as near each other as possible. Turner was apparently the richer man, so McCarthy became his tenant, but still remained, it seems, upon terms of perfect equality, as they were frequently together. McCarthy had one son, a lad of eighteen, and Turner had an only daughter of the same age, but neither of them had wives living. They appear to have avoided the society of the neighbouring English families, and to have led retired lives, though both the McCarthys were fond of sport, and were frequently seen at the race meetings of the neighbourhood. McCarthy kept two servants—a man and a girl. Turner had a considerable household, some half dozen at the least. That is as much as I have been able to gather about the families. Now for the facts.

'On June 3—that is, on Monday last*—McCarthy left his house at Hatherley about three in the afternoon, and walked down to the Boscombe Pool, which is a small lake formed by the spreading out of the stream which runs down the Boscombe Valley. He had been out with his serving-man in the morning at Ross, and he had told the man that he must hurry, as he had an appointment of importance to keep at three. From that appointment he never came back alive.

'From Hatherley Farm-house to the Boscombe Pool is a quarter of a mile, and two people saw him as he passed over this ground. One was an old woman, whose name is not mentioned, and the other was William Crowder,* a game-keeper in the employ of Mr Turner. Both these witnesses depose that Mr McCarthy was walking alone. The game-keeper adds that within a few minutes of his seeing Mr McCarthy pass he had seen his son, Mr James McCarthy, going the same way with a gun under his arm. To the best of his belief, the father was actually in sight at the time, and the son was following him. He thought no more of the matter until he heard in the evening of the tragedy that had occurred.

'The two McCarthys were seen after the time when William Crowder, the gamekeeper, lost sight of them. The Boscombe Pool is thickly wooded round, with just a fringe of grass and of reeds round the edge. A girl of fourteen, Patience Moran,* who is the daughter of the lodge-keeper of the Boscombe Valley Estate, was in one of the woods picking flowers. She states that while she was there she saw, at the border of the wood and close by the lake, Mr McCarthy and his son, and that they appeared to be having a violent quarrel. She heard Mr McCarthy the elder using very strong language to his son, and she saw the latter raise up his hand as if to strike his father. She was so frightened

by their violence that she ran away, and told her mother
when she reached home that she had left the two McCarthys
quarrelling near Boscombe Pool, and that she was afraid that
they were going to fight. She had hardly said the words when
young Mr McCarthy came running up to the lodge to say
that he had found his father dead in the wood, and to ask for
the help of the lodge-keeper. He was much excited, without
either his gun or his hat, and his right hand and sleeve were
observed to be stained with fresh blood. On following him
they found the dead body of his father stretched out upon
the grass beside the Pool. The head had been beaten in by
repeated blows of some heavy and blunt weapon. The
injuries were such as might very well have been inflicted by
the butt-end of his son's gun, which was found lying on the
grass within a few paces of the body. Under these circumstances the young man was instantly arrested, and a verdict
of "Wilful Murder" having been returned at the inquest on
Tuesday, he was on Wednesday brought before the magis-
trates at Ross, who have referred the case to the next
Assizes.* Those are the main facts of the case as they came
out before the coroner and at the police-court.'

'I could hardly imagine a more damning case,' I remarked. 'If ever circumstantial evidence pointed to a criminal it does so here.'

'Circumstantial evidence is a very tricky thing,' answered
Holmes, thoughtfully; 'it may seem to point very straight to
one thing, but if you shift your own point of view a little,
you may find it pointing in an equally uncompromising
manner to something entirely different. It must be confessed,
however, that the case looks exceedingly grave against the
young man, and it is very possible that he is indeed the
culprit. There are several people in the neighbourhood,
however, and among them Miss Turner, the daughter of the
neighbouring landowner, who believe in his innocence, and
who have retained Lestrade,* whom you may remember in
connection with the Study in Scarlet, to work out the case
in his interest. Lestrade, being rather puzzled, has referred
the case to me, and hence it is that two middle-aged

gentlemen are flying westward at fifty miles an hour, instead of quietly digesting their breakfasts at home.'

'I am afraid,' said I, 'that the facts are so obvious that you will find little credit to be gained out of this case.'

'There is nothing more deceptive than an obvious fact,' he answered, laughing. 'Besides, we may chance to hit upon some other obvious facts which may have been by no means obvious to Mr Lestrade. You know me too well to think that I am boasting when I say that I shall either confirm or destroy his theory by means which he is quite incapable of employing, or even of understanding. To take the first example to hand, I very clearly perceive that in your bedroom the window is upon the right-hand side, and yet I question whether Mr Lestrade would have noted even so self-evident a thing as that.'

'How on earth—!'

'My dear fellow, I know you well. I know the military neatness which characterizes you. You shave every morning, and in this season you shave by the sunlight, but since your shaving is less and less complete as we get further back on the left side, until it becomes positively slovenly as we get round the angle of the jaw, it is surely very clear that that side is less well illuminated than the other. I could not imagine a man of your habits looking at himself in an equal light, and being satisfied with such a result. I only quote this as a trivial example of observation and inference. Therein lies my *métier*,* and it is just possible that it may be of some service in the investigation which lies before us. There are one or two minor points which were brought out in the inquest, and which are worth considering.'

'What are they?'

'It appears that his arrest did not take place at once, but after the return to Hatherley Farm. On the inspector of constabulary informing him that he was a prisoner, he remarked that he was not surprised to hear it, and that it was no more than his deserts. This observation of his had the natural effect of removing any traces of doubt which might have remained in the minds of the coroner's jury.'

'It was a confession,' I ejaculated.

'No, for it was followed by a protestation of innocence.'

'Coming on the top of such a damning series of events, it was at least a most suspicious remark.'

'On the contrary,' said Holmes, 'it is the brightest rift which I can at present see in the clouds. However innocent he might be, he could not be such an absolute imbecile as not to see that the circumstances were very black against him. Had he appeared surprised at his own arrest, or feigned indignation at it, I should have looked upon it as highly suspicious, because such surprise or anger would not be natural under the circumstances, and yet might appear to be the best policy to a scheming man. His frank acceptance of the situation marks him as either an innocent man, or else as a man of considerable self-restraint and firmness. As to his remark about his deserts, it was also not unnatural if you consider that he stood by the dead body of his father, and that there is no doubt that he had that very day so far forgotten his filial duty as to bandy words with him, and even, according to the little girl whose evidence is so important, to raise his hand as if to strike him. The self-reproach and contrition which are displayed in his remark appear to me to be the signs of a healthy mind, rather than of a guilty one.'

I shook my head. 'Many men have been hanged on far slighter evidence,' I remarked.

'So they have. And many men have been wrongfully hanged.'

'What is the young man's own account of the matter?'

'It is, I am afraid, not very encouraging to his supporters, though there are one or two points in it which are suggestive. You will find it here, and may read it for yourself.'

He picked out from his bundle a copy of the local Herefordshire paper,* and having turned down the sheet, he pointed out the paragraph in which the unfortunate young man had given his own statement of what had occurred. I settled myself down in the corner of the carriage, and read it very carefully. It ran in this way:

'Mr James McCarthy, the only son of the deceased, was then called, and gave evidence as follows: "I had been away from home for three days at Bristol, and had only just returned upon the morning of last Monday, the 3rd. My father was absent from home at the time of my arrival, and I was informed by the maid that he had driven over to Ross with John Cobb,* the groom. Shortly after my return I heard the wheels of his trap in the yard, and looking out of my window, I saw him get out and walk rapidly out of the yard, though I was not aware in which direction he was going. I then took my gun, and strolled out in the direction of the Boscombe Pool, with the intention of visiting the rabbit warren which is upon the other side. On my way I saw William Crowder, the gamekeeper, as he has stated in his evidence; but he is mistaken in thinking that I was following my father. I had no idea that he was in front of me. When about a hundred yards from the Pool I heard a cry of 'Cooee!'* which was a usual signal between my father and myself. I then hurried forward, and found him standing by the Pool. He appeared to be much surprised at seeing me, and asked me rather roughly what I was doing there. A conversation ensued, which led to high words, and almost to blows, for my father was a man of a very violent temper. Seeing that his passion was becoming ungovernable, I left him, and returned towards Hatherley Farm. I had not gone more than one hundred and fifty yards, however, when I heard a hideous outcry behind me, which caused me to run back again. I found my father expiring on the ground, with his head terribly injured. I dropped my gun, and held him in my arms, but he almost instantly expired. I knelt beside him for some minutes, and then made my way to Mr Turner's lodge-keeper, his house being the nearest, to ask for assistance. I saw no one near my father when I returned, and I have no idea how he came by his injuries. He was not a popular man, being somewhat cold and forbidding in his manners; but he had, as far as I know, no active enemies. I know nothing further of the matter."

81

'The Coroner: Did your father make any statement to you before he died?

'Witness: He mumbled a few words, but I could only catch some allusion to a rat.

'The Coroner: What did you understand by that?

'Witness: It conveyed no meaning to me. I thought that he was delirious.

'The Coroner: What was the point upon which you and your father had this final quarrel?

'Witness: I should prefer not to answer.

'The Coroner: I am afraid that I must press it.

'Witness: It is really impossible for me to tell you. I can assure you that it has nothing to do with the sad tragedy which followed.

'The Coroner: That is for the Court to decide. I need not point out to you that your refusal to answer will prejudice your case considerably in any future proceedings which may arise.

'Witness: I must still refuse.

'The Coroner: I understand that the cry of "Cooee" was a common signal between you and your father?

'Witness: It was.

'The Coroner: How was it, then, that he uttered it before he saw you, and before he even knew that you had returned from Bristol?

'Witness (with considerable confusion): I do not know.

'A Juryman: Did you see nothing which aroused your suspicions when you returned on hearing the cry, and found your father fatally injured?

'Witness: Nothing definite.

'The Coroner: What do you mean?

'Witness: I was so disturbed and excited as I rushed out into the open, that I could think of nothing except my father. Yet I have a vague impression that as I ran forward something lay upon the ground to the left of me. It seemed to me to be something grey in colour, a coat of some sort, or a plaid* perhaps. When I rose from my father I looked round for it, but it was gone.

'Do you mean that it disappeared before you went for help?

'Yes, it was gone.

'You cannot say what it was?

'No, I had a feeling something was there.

'How far from the body?

'A dozen yards or so.

'And how far from the edge of the wood?

'About the same.

'Then if it was removed it was while you were within a dozen yards of it?

'Yes, but with my back towards it.

'This concluded the examination of the witness.'

'I see,' said I, as I glanced down the column, 'that the coroner in his concluding remarks was rather severe upon young McCarthy. He calls attention, and with reason, to the discrepancy about his father having signalled to him before seeing him, also to his refusal to give details of his conversation with his father, and his singular account of his father's dying words. They are all, as he remarks, very much against the son.'

Holmes laughed softly to himself, and stretched himself out upon the cushioned seat. 'Both you and the coroner have been at some pains,' said he, 'to single out the very strongest points in the young man's favour. Don't you see that you alternately give him credit for having too much imagination and too little? Too little, if he could not invent a cause of quarrel which would give him the sympathy of the jury; too much, if he evolved from his own inner consciousness anything so *outré* as a dying reference to a rat, and the incident of the vanishing cloth. No, sir, I shall approach this case from the point of view that what this young man says is true, and we shall see whither that hypothesis will lead us. And now here is my pocket Petrarch,* and not another word shall I say of this case until we are on the scene of action. We lunch at Swindon,* and I see that we shall be there in twenty minutes.'

It was nearly four o'clock when we at last, after passing through the beautiful Stroud Valley* and over the broad gleaming Severn,* found ourselves at the pretty little country town of Ross. A lean, ferret-like man, furtive and sly-looking, was waiting for us upon the platform. In spite of the light brown dustcoat* and leather leggings which he wore in deference to his rustic surroundings, I had no difficulty in recognizing Lestrade, of Scotland Yard. With him we drove to the 'Hereford Arms',* where a room had already been engaged for us.

'I have ordered a carriage,' said Lestrade, as we sat over a cup of tea. 'I knew your energetic nature, and that you would not be happy until you had been on the scene of the crime.'

'It was very nice and complimentary of you,' Holmes answered. 'It is entirely a question of barometric pressure.'*

Lestrade looked startled. 'I do not quite follow,' he said.

'How is the glass? Twenty-nine,* I see. No wind, and not a cloud in the sky. I have a caseful of cigarettes here which need smoking, and the sofa is very much superior to the usual country hotel abomination. I do not think that it is probable that I shall use the carriage to-night.'

Lestrade laughed indulgently. 'You have, no doubt, already formed your conclusions from the newspapers,' he said. 'The case is as plain as a pikestaff,* and the more one goes into it the plainer it becomes. Still, of course, one can't refuse a lady, and such a very positive one, too. She had heard of you, and would have your opinion, though I repeatedly told her that there was nothing which you could do which I had not already done. Why, bless my soul! here is her carriage at the door.'

He had hardly spoken before there rushed into the room one of the most lovely young women that I have ever seen in my life. Her violet eyes* shining, her lips parted, a pink flush upon her cheeks, all thought of her natural reserve lost in her overpowering excitement and concern.

'Oh, Mr Sherlock Holmes!' she cried, glancing from one to the other of us, and finally, with a woman's quick intuition, fastening upon my companion, 'I am so glad that you have come. I have driven down to tell you so. I know that James didn't do it. I know it, and I want you to start upon your work knowing it, too. Never let yourself doubt upon that point. We have known each other since we were little children, and I know his faults as no one else does; but he is too tender-hearted to hurt a fly. Such a charge is absurd to anyone who really knows him.'

'I hope we may clear him, Miss Turner,' said Sherlock Holmes. 'You may rely upon my doing all that I can.'

'But you have read the evidence. You have formed some conclusion? Do you not see some loophole, some flaw? Do you not yourself think that he is innocent?'

'I think that it is very probable.'

'There now!' she cried, throwing back her head and looking defiantly at Lestrade. 'You hear! He gives me hope.'

Lestrade shrugged his shoulders. 'I am afraid that my colleague has been a little quick in forming his conclusions,' he said.

'But he is right. Oh! I know that he is right. James never did it. And about his quarrel with his father. I am sure that the reason why he would not speak about it to the coroner was because I was concerned in it.'

'In what way?' asked Holmes.

'It is no time for me to hide anything. James and his father had many disagreements about me. Mr McCarthy was very anxious that there should be a marriage between us. James and I have always loved each other as brother and sister, but of course he is young and has seen very little of life yet, and—and—well, he naturally did not wish to do anything like that yet. So there were quarrels, and this, I am sure, was one of them.

'And your father?' asked Holmes. 'Was he in favour of such a union?'

'No, he was averse to it also. No one but Mr McCarthy was in favour of it.' A quick blush passed over her fresh young face as Holmes shot one of his keen, questioning glances at her.

'Thank you for this information,' said he. 'May I see your father if I call to-morrow?'

'I am afraid the doctor won't allow it.'

'The doctor?'

'Yes, have you not heard? Poor father has never been strong for years back, but this has broken him down completely. He has taken to his bed, and Dr Willows says that he is a wreck, and that his nervous system is shattered. Mr McCarthy was the only man alive who had known dad in the old days in Victoria.'*

'Ha! In Victoria! That is important.'

'Yes, at the mines.'

'Quite so; at the gold mines, where, as I understand, Mr Turner made his money.'

'Yes, certainly.'

'Thank you, Miss Turner. You have been of material assistance to me.'

'You will tell me if you have any news tomorrow. No doubt you will go to the prison to see James. Oh, if you do, Mr Holmes, do tell him that I know him to be innocent.'

'I will, Miss Turner.'

'I must go home now, for dad is very ill, and he misses me so if I leave him. Good-bye, and God help you in your undertaking.' She hurried from the room as impulsively as she had entered, and we heard the wheels of her carriage rattle off down the street.

'I am ashamed of you, Holmes,' said Lestrade with dignity, after a few minutes' silence. 'Why should you raise up hopes which you are bound to disappoint? I am not over-tender of heart, but I call it cruel.'

'I think that I see my way to clearing James McCarthy,' said Holmes. 'Have you an order to see him in prison?'

'Yes, but only for you and me.'

'Then I shall reconsider my resolution about going out. We have still time to take a train to Hereford* and see him to-night?'

'Ample.'

'Then let us do so. Watson, I fear that you will find it very slow, but I shall only be away a couple of hours.'

I walked down to the station with them, and then wandered through the streets of the little town, finally returning to the hotel, where I lay upon the sofa and tried to interest myself in a yellow-backed novel.* The puny plot of the story was so thin, however, when compared to the deep mystery through which we were groping, and I found my attention wander so constantly from the fiction to the fact, that I at last flung it across the room, and gave myself up entirely to a consideration of the events of the day. Supposing that this unhappy young man's story was absolutely true, then what hellish thing, what absolutely unforeseen and extraordinary calamity, could have occurred between the time when he parted from his father and the moment when, drawn back by his screams, he rushed into the glade? It was something terrible and deadly. What could it be? Might not the nature of the injuries reveal something to my medical instincts? I rang the bell, and called for the weekly country paper, which contained a verbatim account of the inquest. In the surgeon's deposition it was stated that the posterior third of the left parietal bone and the left half of the occipital bone had been shattered* by a heavy blow from a blunt weapon. I marked the spot upon my own head. Clearly such a blow must have been struck from behind. That was to some extent in favour of the accused, as when seen quarrelling he was face to face with his father. Still, it did not go for very much, for the older man might have turned his back before the blow fell. Still, it might be worth while to call Holmes's attention to it. Then there was the peculiar dying reference to a rat. What could that mean? It could not be delirium. A man dying from a sudden blow does not commonly become delirious. No, it was more likely to be an attempt to explain how he met his fate. But what could it indicate? I cudgelled my brains to find some possible explanation. And then the incident of the grey cloth, seen by young McCarthy. If that were true, the murderer must have dropped some part of his dress, presumably his overcoat, in his flight, and must have had the hardihood to return and carry it away at the instant when the son was kneeling with his back turned not a dozen paces off. What a tissue of mysteries and improbabilities the whole thing was! I did not wonder at Lestrade's opinion, and yet I had so much faith in Sherlock Holmes's insight that I could not lose hope as long as every fresh fact seemed to strengthen his conviction of young McCarthy's innocence.

It was late before Sherlock Holmes returned. He came back alone, for Lestrade was staying in lodgings in the town.

'The glass still keeps very high,' he remarked, as he sat down. 'It is of importance that it should not rain before we are able to go over the ground. On the other hand, a man should be at his very best and keenest for such nice work as that, and I did not wish to do it when fagged by a long journey. I have seen young McCarthy.'

'And what did you learn from him?'

'Nothing.'

'Could he throw no light?'

'None at all. I was inclined to think at one time that he knew who had done it, and was screening him or her, but I am convinced now that he is as puzzled as everyone else. He is not a very quick-witted youth, though comely to look at, and, I should think, sound at heart.'

'I cannot admire his taste,' I remarked, 'if it is indeed a fact that he was averse to a marriage with so charming a young lady as this Miss Turner.'

'Ah, thereby hangs a rather painful tale.* This fellow is madly, insanely in love with her, but some two years ago, when he was only a lad, and before he really knew her, for she had been away five years at a boarding-school, what does the idiot do but get into the clutches of a barmaid in Bristol, and marry her at a registry office! No one knows a word of the matter, but you can imagine how maddening it must be to him to be upbraided for not doing what he would give his very eyes to do, but what he knows to be absolutely impossible. It was sheer frenzy of this sort which made him throw his hands up into the air when his father, at their last interview, was goading him on to propose to Miss Turner.

On the other hand, he had no means of supporting himself, and his father, who was by all accounts a very hard man, would have thrown him over utterly had he known the truth. It was with his barmaid wife that he had spent the last three days in Bristol, and his father did not know where he was. Mark that point. It is of importance. Good has come out of evil, however, for the barmaid, finding from the papers that he is in serious trouble, and likely to be hanged, has thrown him over utterly, and has written to him to say that she has a husband already in the Bermuda Dockyard,* so that there is really no tie between them. I think that that bit of news has consoled young McCarthy for all that he has suffered.'

'But if he is innocent, who has done it?'

'Ah! who? I would call your attention very particularly to two points. One is that the murdered man had an appointment with some one at the Pool, and that the some one could not have been his son, for his son was away, and he did not know when he would return. The second is that the murdered man was heard to cry "Cooee!" before he knew that his son had returned. Those are the crucial points upon which the case depends. And now let us talk about George Meredith,* if you please, and we shall leave minor points until tomorrow.'

There was no rain, as Holmes had foretold, and the morning broke bright and cloudless. At nine o'clock Lestrade called for us with the carriage, and we set off for Hatherley Farm and the Boscombe Pool.

'There is serious news this morning,' Lestrade observed. 'It is said that Mr Turner, of the Hall, is so ill that his life is despaired of.'

'An elderly man, I presume?' said Holmes.

'About sixty; but his constitution has been shattered by his life abroad, and he has been in failing health for some time. This business has had a very bad effect upon him. He was an old friend of McCarthy's, and, I may add, a great benefactor to him, for I have learned that he gave him Hatherley Farm rent free.'

'Indeed! That is interesting,' said Holmes.

'Oh, yes! In a hundred other ways he has helped him. Everybody about here speaks of his kindness to him.'

'Really! Does it not strike you as a little singular that this McCarthy, who appears to have had little of his own, and to have been under such obligations to Turner, should still talk of marrying his son to Turner's daughter, who is, presumably, heiress to the estate, and that in such a very cocksure manner, as if it was merely a case of a proposal and all else would follow? It is the more strange since we know that Turner himself was averse to the idea. The daughter told us as much. Do you not deduce something from that?'

'We have got to the deductions and the inferences,' said Lestrade, winking at me. 'I find it hard enough to tackle facts, Holmes, without flying away after theories and fancies.'

'You are right,' said Holmes demurely; 'you do find it very hard to tackle the facts.'

'Anyhow, I have grasped one fact which you seem to find it difficult to get hold of,' replied Lestrade with some warmth.

'And that is?'

'That McCarthy, senior, met his death from McCarthy, junior, and that all theories to the contrary are the merest moonshine.'*

'Well, moonshine is a brighter thing than fog,' said Holmes, laughing. 'But I am very much mistaken if this is not Hatherley Farm upon the left.'

'Yes, that is it.' It was a widespread, comfortable-looking building, two-storied, slate-roofed, with great yellow blotches of lichen upon the grey walls. The drawn blinds and the smokeless chimneys, however, gave it a stricken look, as though the weight of this horror still lay heavy upon it. We called at the door, when the maid, at Holmes's request, showed us the boots which her master wore at the time of his death, and also a pair of the son's, though not the pair which he had then had. Having measured these very carefully from seven or eight different points, Holmes desired to be led to the courtyard, from which we all followed the winding track which led to Boscombe Pool.

Sherlock Holmes was transformed* when he was hot upon such a scent as this. Men who had only known the quiet thinker and logician of Baker Street would have failed to recognize him. His face flushed and darkened. His brows were drawn into two hard, black lines, while his eyes shone out from beneath them with a steely glitter. His face was bent downwards, his shoulders bowed, his lips compressed, and the veins stood out like whip-cord* in his long, sinewy neck. His nostrils seemed to dilate with a purely animal lust for the chase, and his mind was so absolutely concentrated upon the matter before him, that a question or remark fell unheeded upon his ears, or at the most, only provoked a quick, impatient snarl in reply. Swiftly and silently he made his way along the track which ran through the meadows, and so by way of the woods to the Boscombe Pool. It was damp, marshy ground, as is all that district, and there were marks of many feet, both upon the path and amid the short grass which bounded it on either side. Sometimes Holmes would hurry on, sometimes stop dead, and once he made quite a little *détour* into the meadow. Lestrade and I walked behind him, the detective indifferent and contemptuous, while I watched my friend with the interest which sprang from the conviction that every one of his actions was directed towards a definite end.

The Boscombe Pool, which is a reed-girt sheet of water some fifty yards across, is situated at the boundary between the Hatherley Farm and the private park of the wealthy Mr Turner. Above the woods which lined it upon the further side we could see the red jutting pinnacles which marked the site of the rich landowner's dwelling. On the Hatherley side of the Pool, the woods grew very thick, and there was a narrow belt of sodden grass twenty paces across between the edge of the trees and the reeds which lined the lake. Lestrade showed us the exact spot at which the body had been found, and indeed, so moist was the ground, that I could plainly see the traces which had been left by the fall of the stricken man. To Holmes, as I could see by his eager face and peering eyes, very many other things were to be read upon the trampled grass. He ran round, like a dog who is picking up a scent, and then turned upon my companion.

'What did you go into the Pool for?' he asked.

'I fished about with a rake. I thought there might be some weapon or other trace. But how on earth—?'

'Oh, tut, tut! I have no time. That left foot of yours with its inward twist is all over the place. A mole could trace it, and there it vanishes among the reeds. Oh, how simple it would all have been had I been here before they came like a herd of buffalo, and wallowed all over it. Here is where the party with the lodge-keeper came, and they have covered all tracks for six or eight feet round the body. But here are three separate tracks of the same feet.' He drew out a lens,* and lay down upon his waterproof to have a better view, talking all the time rather to himself than to us. 'These are young McCarthy's feet. Twice he was walking, and once he ran swiftly so that the soles are deeply marked, and the heels hardly visible. That bears out his story. He ran when he saw his father on the ground. Then here are the father's feet as he paced up and down. What is this, then? It is the butt-end of the gun as the son stood listening. And this? Ha, ha! What have we here? Tip-toes, tip-toes! Square, too, quite unusual boots! They come, they go, they come again—of course that was for the cloak. Now where did they come from?' He ran up and down, sometimes losing, sometimes finding the track, until we were well within the edge of the wood and under the shadow of a great beech, the largest tree in the neighbourhood. Holmes traced his way to the farther side of this, and lay down once more upon his face with a little cry of satisfaction. For a long time he remained there, turning over the leaves and dried sticks, gathering up what seemed to me to be dust into an envelope, and examining with his lens not only the ground, but even the bark of the tree as far as he could reach. A jagged stone was lying among the moss, and this also he carefully examined and retained. Then he followed a pathway through the wood until he came to the high-road, where all traces were lost.

'It has been a case of considerable interest,' he remarked, returning to his natural manner. 'I fancy that this grey house on the right must be the lodge. I think that I will go in and have a word with Moran, and perhaps write a little note. Having done that, we may drive back to our luncheon. You may walk to the cab, and I shall be with you presently.'

It was about ten minutes before we regained our cab, and drove back into Ross, Holmes still carrying with him the stone which he had picked up in the wood.

'This may interest you, Lestrade,' he remarked, holding it out. 'The murder was done with it.'

'I see no marks.'

'There are none.'

'How do you know, then?'

'The grass was growing under it. It had only lain there a few days. There was no sign of a place whence it had been taken. It corresponds with the injuries. There is no sign of any other weapon.'

'And the murderer?'

'Is a tall man, left-handed, limps with the right leg,* wears thick-soled shooting-boots and a grey cloak, smokes Indian cigars, uses a cigar-holder, and carries a blunt penknife in his pocket. There are several other indications, but these may be enough to aid us in our search.'

Lestrade laughed. 'I am afraid that I am still a sceptic,' he said. 'Theories are all very well, but we have to deal with a hard-headed British jury.'

'*Nous verrons*,' answered Holmes calmly. 'You work your own method, and I shall work mine. I shall be busy this afternoon, and shall probably return to London by the evening train.'

'And leave your case unfinished?'

'No, finished.'

'But the mystery?'

'It is solved.'

'Who was the criminal, then?'

'The gentleman I describe.'

'But who is he?'

'Surely it would not be difficult to find out. This is not such a populous neighbourhood.'

Lestrade shrugged his shoulders. 'I am a practical man,' he said, 'and I really cannot undertake to go about the country looking for a left-handed gentleman with a game leg. I should become the laughing-stock of Scotland Yard.'

'All right,' said Holmes quietly. 'I have given you the chance. Here are your lodgings. Good-bye. I shall drop you a line before I leave.'

Having left Lestrade at his rooms we drove to our hotel, where we found lunch upon the table. Holmes was silent and buried in thought, with a pained expression upon his face, as one who finds himself in a perplexing position.

'Look here, Watson,' he said, when the cloth was cleared; 'just sit down in this chair and let me preach to you for a little. I don't quite know what to do, and I should value your advice. Light a cigar, and let me expound.'

'Pray do so.'

'Well, now, in considering this case there are two points about young McCarthy's narrative which struck us both instantly, although they impressed me in his favour and you against him. One was the fact that his father should, according to his account, cry "Cooee!" before seeing him. The other was his singular dying reference to a rat. He mumbled several words, you understand, but that was all that caught the son's ear. Now from this double point our research must commence, and we will begin it by presuming that what the lad says is absolutely true.'

'What of this "Cooee!" then?'

'Well, obviously it could not have been meant for the son. The son, as far as he knew, was in Bristol. It was mere chance that he was within earshot. The "Cooee!" was meant to attract the attention of whoever it was that he had the appointment with. But "Cooee" is a distinctly Australian cry, and one which is used between Australians. There is a strong presumption that the person whom McCarthy expected to meet at Boscombe Pool was someone who had been in Australia.'

'What of the rat, then?'

Sherlock Holmes took a folded paper from his pocket and flattened it out on the table. 'This is a map of the Colony of Victoria,' he said. 'I wired to Bristol for it last night.' He put his hand over part of the map. 'What do you read?' he asked.

'ARAT,' I read.

'And now?' he raised his hand.

'BALLARAT.'*

'Quite so. That was the word the man uttered, and of which his son only caught the last two syllables. He was trying to utter the name of his murderer. So-and-so of Ballarat.'

'It is wonderful!' I exclaimed.

'It is obvious. And now, you see, I had narrowed the field down considerably. The possession of a grey garment was a third point which, granting the son's statement to be correct, was a certainty. We have come now out of mere vagueness to the definite conception of an Australian from Ballarat with a grey cloak.'

'Certainly.'

'And one who was at home in the district, for the Pool can only be approached by the farm or by the estate, where strangers could hardly wander.'

'Quite so.'

'Then comes our expedition of to-day. By an examination of the ground I gained the trifling details which I gave to that imbecile Lestrade, as to the personality of the criminal.'

'But how did you gain them?'

'You know my method. It is founded upon the observance of trifles.'

'His height I know that you might roughly judge from the length of his stride. His boots, too, might be told from their traces.'

'Yes, they were peculiar boots.'

'But his lameness?'

'The impression of his right foot was always less distinct than his left. He put less weight upon it. Why? Because he limped—he was lame.'

'But his left-handedness?'

'You were yourself struck by the nature of the injury as recorded by the surgeon at the inquest. The blow was struck from immediately behind, and yet was upon the left side. Now, how can that be unless it were by a left-handed man? He had stood behind that tree during the interview between the father and son. He had even smoked there. I found the ash of a cigar, which my special knowledge of tobacco ashes enabled me to pronounce as an Indian cigar. I have, as you know, devoted some attention to this, and written a little monograph on the ashes of 140 different varieties of pipe, cigar, and cigarette tobacco.* Having found the ash, I then looked round and discovered the stump among the moss where he had tossed it. It was an Indian cigar, of the variety which are rolled in Rotterdam.'

'And the cigar-holder?'

'I could see that the end had not been in his mouth. Therefore he used a holder. The tip had been cut off, not bitten off, but the cut was not a clean one, so I deduced a blunt penknife.'

'Holmes,' I said, 'you have drawn a net round this man from which he cannot escape, and you have saved an innocent human life as truly as if you had cut the cord which was hanging him. I see the direction in which all this points. The culprit is—'

'Mr John Turner,' cried the hotel waiter, opening the door of our sitting-room, and ushering in a visitor.

The man who entered was a strange and impressive figure. His slow, limping step and bowed shoulders gave the appearance of decrepitude, and yet his hard, deep-lined, craggy features, and his enormous limbs showed that he was possessed of unusual strength of body and of character. His tangled beard, grizzled hair, and outstanding, drooping eyebrows combined to give an air of dignity and power to his appearance, but his face was of an ashen white, while his lips and the corners of his nostrils were tinged with a shade of blue. It was clear to me at a glance that he was in the grip of some deadly and chronic disease.

'Pray sit down on the sofa,' said Holmes gently. 'You had my note?'

'Yes, the lodge-keeper brought it up. You said that you wished to see me here to avoid scandal.'

'I thought people would talk if I went to the Hall.'

'And why did you wish to see me?' He looked across at my companion with despair in his weary eyes, as though his question were already answered.

'Yes,' said Holmes, answering the look rather than the words. 'It is so. I know all about McCarthy.'

The old man sank his face in his hands. 'God help me!' he cried. 'But I would not have let the young man come to harm. I give you my word that I would have spoken out if it went against him at the Assizes.'

'I am glad to hear you say so,' said Holmes, gravely.

'I would have spoken now had it not been for my dear girl. It would break her heart—it will break her heart when she hears that I am arrested.'

'It may not come to that,' said Holmes.

'What!'

'I am no official agent. I understand that it was your daughter who required my presence here, and I am acting in her interests. Young McCarthy must be got off, however.'

'I am a dying man,' said old Turner. 'I have had diabetes for years. My doctor says it is a question whether I shall live a month. Yet I would rather die under my own roof than in a gaol.'

Holmes rose and sat down at the table with his pen in his hand and a bundle of paper before him. 'Just tell us the truth,' he said. 'I shall jot down the facts. You will sign it, and Watson here can witness it. Then I could produce your confession at the last extremity to save young McCarthy. I promise you that I shall not use it unless it is absolutely needed.'

'It's as well,' said the old man; 'it's a question whether I shall live to the Assizes, so it matters little to me, but I should wish to spare Alice the shock. And now I will make the thing clear to you; it has been a long time in the acting, but will not take me long to tell.

'You didn't know this dead man, McCarthy. He was a devil incarnate. I tell you that. God keep you out of the clutches of such a man as he. His grip has been upon me these twenty years, and he has blasted my life. I'll tell you first how I came to be in his power.

'It was in the early 'sixties at the diggings.* I was a young chap then, hot-blooded and reckless, ready to turn my hand to anything; I got among bad companions, took to drink, had no luck with my claim, took to the bush, and, in a word became what you would call over here a highway robber. There were six of us, and we had a wild, free life of it, sticking up a station from time to time, or stopping the wagons on the road to the diggings. Black Jack of Ballarat was the name I went under, and our party is still remembered in the colony as the Ballarat Gang.

'One day a gold convoy came down from Ballarat to Melbourne, and we lay in wait for it and attacked it. There were six troopers* and six of us, so it was a close thing, but we emptied four of their saddles at the first volley. Three of our boys were killed, however, before we got the swag. I put my pistol to the head of the wagon-driver,* who was this very man McCarthy. I wish to the Lord that I had shot him then, but I spared him, though I saw his wicked little eyes fixed on my face, as though to remember every feature. We got away with the gold, became wealthy men, and made our way over to England without being suspected. There I parted from my old pals, and determined to settle down to a quiet and respectable life. I bought this estate, which chanced to be in the market, and I set myself to do a little good with my money, to make up for the way in which I had earned it. I married, too, and though my wife died young, she left me my dear little Alice. Even when she was just a baby her wee hand seemed to lead me down the right path as nothing else had ever done. In a word, I turned over a new leaf, and did my best to make up for the past. All was going well when McCarthy laid his grip upon me.

'I had gone up to town about an investment, and I met him in Regent Street with hardly a coat to his back or a boot to his foot.

' "Here we are, Jack," says he, touching me on the arm; "we'll be as good as a family to you. There's two of us, me and my son, and you can have the keeping of us. If you don't—it's a fine, law-abiding country is England, and there's always a policeman within hail."

'Well, down they came to the West Country, there was no shaking them off, and there they have lived rent free on my best land ever since. There was no rest for me, no peace, no forgetfulness; turn where I would, there was his cunning, grinning face at my elbow. It grew worse as Alice grew up, for he soon saw I was more afraid of her knowing my past than of the police. Whatever he wanted he must have, and whatever it was I gave him without question, land, money, houses, until at last he asked for a thing which I could not give. He asked for Alice.

'His son, you see, had grown up, and so had my girl, and as I was known to be in weak health, it seemed a fine stroke to him that his lad should step into the whole property. But there I was firm. I would not have his cursed stock mixed with mine; not that I had any dislike to the lad, but his blood was in him, and that was enough. I stood firm. McCarthy threatened. I braved him to do his worst. We were to meet at the Pool midway between our houses to talk it over.

'When I went down there I found him talking with his son, so I smoked a cigar, and waited behind a tree until he should be alone. But as I listened to his talk all that was black and bitter in me seemed to come uppermost. He was urging his son to marry my daughter with as little regard for what she might think as if she were a slut from off the streets. It drove me mad to think that I and all that I held most dear should be in the power of such a man as this.

Could I not snap the bond? I was already a dying and a desperate man. Though clear of mind and fairly strong of limb, I knew that my own fate was sealed. But my memory and my girl! Both could be saved, if I could but silence that foul tongue. I did it, Mr Holmes. I would do it again. Deeply as I have sinned, I have led a life of martyrdom to atone for it. But that my girl should be entangled in the same meshes which held me was more than I could suffer. I struck him down with no more compunction than if he had been some foul and venomous beast. His cry brought back his son; but I had gained the cover of the wood, though I was forced to go back to fetch the cloak which I had dropped in my flight. That is the true story, gentlemen, of all that occurred.'

'Well, it is not for me to judge you,' said Holmes, as the old man signed the statement which had been drawn out. 'I pray that we may never be exposed to such a temptation.'

'I pray not, sir. And what do you intend to do?'

'In view of your health, nothing. You are yourself aware that you will soon have to answer for your deed at a higher court than the Assizes. I will keep your confession, and, if McCarthy is condemned, I shall be forced to use it. If not, it shall never be seen by mortal eye; and your secret, whether you be alive or dead, shall be safe with us.'

'Farewell! then,' said the old man solemnly. 'Your own death-beds, when they come, will be the easier for the thought of the peace which you have given to mine.' Tottering and shaking in all his giant frame, he stumbled slowly from the room.

'God help us!' said Holmes, after a long silence. 'Why does Fate play such tricks with poor helpless worms? I never hear of such a case as this that I do not think of Baxter's words, and say: "There, but for the grace of God, goes Sherlock Holmes." '*

James McCarthy was acquitted at the Assizes, on the strength of a number of objections which had been drawn out by Holmes, and submitted to the defending counsel. Old

Turner lived for seven months after our interview, but he is now dead; and there is every prospect that the son and daughter may come to live happily together, in ignorance of the black cloud which rests upon their past.

The Five Orange Pips

WHEN I glance over my notes and records of the Sherlock Holmes cases between the years '82 and '90, I am faced by so many which present strange and interesting features, that it is no easy matter to know which to choose and which to leave. Some, however, have already gained publicity through the papers, and others have not offered a field for those peculiar qualities which my friend possessed in so high a degree, and which it is the object of these papers to illustrate. Some, too, have baffled his analytical skill, and would be, as narratives, beginnings without an ending, while others have been but partially cleared up, and have their explanations founded rather upon conjecture and surmise than on that absolute logical proof which was so dear to him. There is, however, one of these last which was so remarkable in its details and so startling in its results, that I am tempted to give some account of it, in spite of the fact that there are points in connection with it which never have been, and probably never will be, entirely cleared up.

The year '87 furnished us with a long series of cases of greater or less interest, of which I retain the records. Among my headings under this one twelve months, I find an account of the adventure of the Paradol Chamber,* of the Amateur Mendicant Society, who held a luxurious club in the lower vault of a furniture warehouse,* of the facts connected with the loss of the British barque *Sophy Anderson*,* of the singular adventures of the Grice Patersons in the island of Uffa,* and finally of the Camberwell poisoning case.* In the latter, as may be remembered, Sherlock Holmes was able, by winding up the dead man's watch, to prove that it had been wound up two hours ago, and that therefore the deceased had gone to bed within that time—a deduction which was of the greatest importance in clearing up the case. All these I may sketch out at some future date, but none of them present such singular features as the strange train of circumstances which I have now taken up my pen to describe.

It was in the latter days of September, and the equinoctial gales* had set in with exceptional violence. All day the wind had screamed and the rain had beaten against the windows, so that even here in the heart of great, hand-made London we were forced to raise our minds for the instant from the routine of life, and to recognize the presence of those great elemental forces which shriek at mankind through the bars of his civilization, like untamed beasts in a cage. As evening drew in the storm grew louder and louder, and the wind cried and sobbed like a child in the chimney.* Sherlock Holmes sat moodily at one side of the fireplace cross-indexing his records of crime, whilst I at the other was deep in one of Clark Russell's fine sea stories,* until the howl of the gale from without seemed to blend with the text, and the splash of the rain to lengthen out into the long swash of the sea waves. My wife was on a visit to her aunt's,* and for a few days I was a dweller once more in my old quarters at Baker Street.

'Why,' said I, glancing up at my companion, 'that was surely the bell? Who could come tonight? Some friend of yours, perhaps?'

'Except yourself I have none,' he answered. 'I do not encourage visitors.'

'A client, then?'

'If so, it is a serious case. Nothing less would bring a man out on such a day, and at such an hour. But I take it that it is more likely to be some crony of the landlady's.'

Sherlock Holmes was wrong in his conjecture, however, for there came a step in the passage, and a tapping at the door. He stretched out his long arm to turn the lamp away from himself and towards the vacant chair upon which a newcomer must sit. 'Come in!' said he.

The man who entered was young, some two-and-twenty at the outside, well groomed and trimly clad, with something of refinement and delicacy in his bearing. The streaming umbrella which he held in his hand, and his long shining waterproof told of the fierce weather through which he had come. He looked about him anxiously in the glare of the lamp, and I could see that his face was pale and his eyes heavy, like those of a man who is weighed down with some great anxiety.

'I owe you an apology,' he said, raising his golden *pince-nez* to his eyes. 'I trust that I am not intruding. I fear that I have brought some traces of the storm and the rain into your snug chamber.'

'Give me your coat and umbrella,' said Holmes. 'They may rest here on the hook, and will be dry presently. You have come up from the south-west, I see.'

'Yes, from Horsham.'*

'That clay and chalk mixture which I see upon your toe-caps is quite distinctive.'*

'I have come for advice.'

'That is easily got.'

'And help.'

'That is not always so easy.'

'I have heard of you, Mr Holmes. I heard from Major Prendergast how you saved him in the Tankerville Club Scandal.'*

'Ah, of course. He was wrongfully accused of cheating at cards.'

'He said that you could solve anything.'

'He said too much.'

'That you are never beaten.'

'I have been beaten four times—three times by men and once by a woman.'

'But what is that compared with the number of your successes?'

'It is true that I have been generally successful.'

'Then you may be so with me.'

'I beg that you will draw your chair up to the fire, and favour me with some details as to your case.'

'It is no ordinary one.'

'None of those which come to me are. I am the last court of appeal.'

'And yet I question, sir, whether, in all your experience, you have ever listened to a more mysterious and inexplicable chain of events than those which have happened in my own family.'

'You fill me with interest,' said Holmes. 'Pray give us the essential facts from the commencement, and I can afterwards question you as to those details which seem to me to be most important.'

The young man pulled his chair up, and pushed his wet feet out towards the blaze.

'My name,' said he, 'is John Openshaw,* but my own affairs have, so far as I can understand it, little to do with this awful business. It is a hereditary matter, so in order to give you an idea of the facts, I must go back to the commencement of the affair.

'You must know that my grandfather had two sons—my uncle Elias and my father Joseph. My father had a small factory at Coventry, which he enlarged at the time of the invention of bicycling.* He was the patentee of the Openshaw unbreakable tyre,* and his business met with such success that he was able to sell it, and to retire upon a handsome competence.

'My uncle Elias* emigrated to America when he was a young man, and became a planter in Florida, where he was reported to have done very well. At the time of the war* he fought in Jackson's army,* and afterwards under Hood,* where he rose to be a colonel. When Lee laid down his arms* my uncle returned to his plantation, where he remained for three or four years. About 1869 or 1870 he came back to Europe, and took a small estate in Sussex, near Horsham. He had made a very considerable fortune in the States, and his reason for leaving them was his aversion to the negroes,* and his dislike of the Republican policy in extending the franchise to them.* He was a singular man, fierce and quick-tempered, very foul-mouthed when he was angry, and of a most retiring disposition. During all the years that he lived at Horsham I doubt if ever he set foot in the town. He had a garden and two or three fields round his house, and there he would take his exercise, though very often for weeks on end he would never leave his room. He drank a great deal of brandy, and smoked very heavily, but he would see no society, and did not want any friends, not even his own brother.

'He didn't mind me, in fact he took a fancy to me, for at the time when he saw me first I was a youngster of twelve or so. That would be in the year 1878, after he had been eight or nine years in England. He begged my father to let me live with him, and he was very kind to me in his way. When he was sober he used to be fond of playing backgammon and draughts with me, and he would make me his representative both with the servants and with the tradespeople, so that by the time that I was sixteen I was quite master of the house. I kept all the keys, and could go where I liked and do what I liked, so long as I did not disturb him in his privacy. There was one singular exception, however, for he had a single room, a lumber-room up among the attics, which was invariably locked, and which he would never permit either me or anyone else to enter. With a boy's curiosity I have peeped through the keyhole, but I was never able to see more than such a collection of old trunks and bundles as would be expected in such a room.

'One day—it was in March, 1883—a letter with a foreign stamp lay upon the table in front of the Colonel's plate. It was not a common thing for him to receive letters, for his bills were all paid in ready money, and he had no friends of any sort. "From India!" said he, as he took it up, "Pondicherry* post-mark! What can this be?" Opening it hurriedly, out there jumped five little dried orange pips, which pattered down upon his plate. I began to laugh at this, but the laugh was struck from my lips at the sight of his face. His lip had fallen, his eyes were protruding, his skin the colour of putty, and he glared at the envelope which he still held in his trembling hand. "K. K. K.," he shrieked, and then: "My God, my God, my sins have overtaken me."

' "What is it, uncle!" I cried.

' "Death," said he, and rising from the table he retired to his room, leaving me palpitating with horror. I took up the envelope, and saw scrawled in red ink upon the inner flap, just above the gum, the letter K three times repeated. There was nothing else save the five dried pips. What could be the reason of his overpowering terror? I left the breakfast-table, and as I ascended the stairs I met him coming down with an old rusty key, which must have belonged to the attic, in one hand, and a small brass box, like a cash box, in the other.

' "They may do what they like, but I'll checkmate them still," said he, with an oath. "Tell Mary that I shall want a fire in my room today, and send down to Fordham,* the Horsham lawyer."

'I did as he ordered, and when the lawyer arrived I was asked to step up to the room. The fire was burning brightly, and in the grate there was a mass of black, fluffy ashes, as of burned paper, while the brass box stood open and empty beside it. As I glanced at the box I noticed, with a start, that upon the lid were printed the treble K which I had read in the morning upon the envelope.

' "I wish you, John," said my uncle, "to witness my will. I leave my estate, with all its advantages and all its disadvantages to my brother, your father, whence it will, no doubt, descend to you. If you can enjoy it in peace, well and good! If you find you cannot, take my advice, my boy, and leave it to your deadliest enemy. I am sorry to give you such a two-edged thing, but I can't say what turn things are going to take. Kindly sign the paper where Mr Fordham shows you."

'I signed the paper as directed, and the lawyer took it away with him. The singular incident made, as you may think, the deepest impression upon me, and I pondered over it, and turned it every way in my mind without being able to make anything of it. Yet I could not shake off the vague feeling of dread which it left behind it, though the sensation grew less keen as the weeks passed, and nothing happened to disturb the usual routine of our lives. I could see a change in my uncle, however. He drank more than ever, and he was less inclined for any sort of society. Most of his time he would spend in his room, with the door locked upon the inside, but sometimes he would emerge in a sort of drunken frenzy and would burst out of the house and tear about the garden with a revolver in his hand, screaming out that he was afraid of no man, and that he was not to be cooped up, like a sheep in a pen, by man or devil. When these hot fits were over, however, he would rush tumultuously in at the door, and lock and bar it behind him, like a man who can brazen it out no longer against the terror which lies at the roots of his soul. At such times I have seen his face even on a cold day, glisten with moisture as though it were new raised from a basin.

'Well, to come to an end of the matter, Mr Holmes, and not to abuse your patience, there came a night when he made one of those drunken sallies from which he never came back. We found him, when we went to search for him, face downwards in a little green-scummed pool, which lay at the foot of the garden. There was no sign of any violence, and the water was but two feet deep, so that the jury, having regard to his known eccentricity, brought in a verdict of suicide. But I, who knew how he winced from the very thought of death, had much ado to persuade myself that he had gone out of his way to meet it. The matter passed, however, and my father entered into possession of the estate, and of some fourteen thousand pounds, which lay to his credit at the bank.'

'One moment,' Holmes interposed. 'Your statement is, I foresee, one of the most remarkable to which I have ever listened. Let me have the date of the reception by your uncle of the letter, and the date of his supposed suicide.'

'The letter arrived on March the 10th, 1883. His death was seven weeks later, upon the night of the 2nd of May.'

'Thank you. Pray proceed.'

'When my father took over the Horsham property, he, at my request, made a careful examination of the attic, which had been always locked up. We found the brass box there, although its contents had been destroyed. On the inside of the cover was a paper label, with the initials K. K. K. repeated upon it, and "Letters, memoranda, receipts and a register" written beneath. These, we presume, indicated the nature of the papers which had been destroyed by Colonel Openshaw. For the rest, there was nothing of much importance in the attic, save a great many scattered papers and notebooks bearing upon my uncle's life in America. Some of them were of the war time, and showed that he had done his duty well, and had borne the repute of being a brave soldier. Others were of a date during the reconstruction of the Southern States,* and were mostly concerned with politics, for he had evidently taken a strong part in opposing the carpet-bag politicians* who had been sent down from the North.

'Well, it was the beginning of '84, when my father came to live at Horsham, and all went as well as possible with us until the January of '85. On the fourth day after the New Year I heard my father give a sharp cry of surprise as we sat together at the breakfast-table. There he was, sitting with a newly opened envelope in one hand and five dried orange pips in the out-stretched palm of the other one. He had always laughed at what he called my cock-and-bull story* about the Colonel, but he looked very puzzled and scared now that the same thing had come upon himself.

' "Why, what on earth does this mean, John?" he stammered.

'My heart had turned to lead. "It is K. K. K.," said I.

'He looked inside the envelope. "So it is," he cried. "Here are the very letters. But what is this written above them?"

' "Put the papers on the sun-dial," I read, peeping over his shoulder.

' "What papers? What sun-dial?" he asked.

' "The sun-dial in the garden. There is no other," said I; "but the papers must be those that are destroyed."

' "Pooh!" said he, gripping hard at his courage. "We are in a civilized land here, and we can't have tomfoolery of this kind. Where does the thing come from?"

' "From Dundee,"* I answered, glancing at the postmark.

' "Some preposterous practical joke," said he. "What have I to do with sun-dials and papers? I shall take no notice of such nonsense."

' "I should certainly speak to the police," I said.

' "And be laughed at for my pains. Nothing of the sort."

' "Then let me do so."

' "No, I forbid you. I won't have a fuss made over such nonsense."

'It was in vain to argue with him, for he was a very obstinate man. I went about, however, with a heart which was full of forebodings.

'On the third day after the coming of the letter my father went from home to visit an old friend of his, Major Free-body,* who is in command of one of the forts upon Ports-down Hill.* I was glad that he should go, for it seemed to me that he was further from danger when he was away from home. In that, however, I was in error. Upon the second day of his absence I received a telegram from the Major, implor-ing me to come at once. My father had fallen over one of the deep chalk-pits which abound in the neighbourhood, and was lying senseless, with a shattered skull. I hurried to him, but he passed away without having ever recovered his consciousness. He had, as it appears, been returning from Fareham* in the twilight, and as the country was unknown to him, and the chalk-pit unfenced, the jury had no hesitation in bringing in a verdict of "Death from accidental causes". Carefully as I examined every fact connected with his death, I was unable to find anything which could suggest the idea of murder. There were no signs of violence, no footmarks, no robbery, no record of strangers having been seen upon the roads. And yet I need not tell you that my mind was far from at ease, and that I was well-nigh certain that some foul plot had been woven round him.

'In this sinister way I came into my inheritance. You will ask me why I did not dispose of it? I answer because I was well convinced that our troubles were in some way depend-ent upon an incident in my uncle's life, and that the danger would be as pressing in one house as in another.

'It was in January, '85, that my poor father met his end, and two years and eight months have elapsed since then. During that time I have lived happily at Horsham, and I had begun to hope that this curse had passed away from the family, and that it had ended with the last generation. I had begun to take comfort too soon, however; yesterday morning the blow fell in the very shape in which it had come upon my father.'

The young man took from his waistcoat a crumpled envelope, and, turning to the table, he shook out upon it five little dried orange pips.

'This is the envelope,' he continued. 'The postmark is London—eastern division.* Within are the very words which were upon my father's last message. "K. K. K."; and then "Put the papers on the sundial".'

'What have you done?' asked Holmes.

'Nothing.'

'Nothing?'

'To tell the truth'—he sank his face into his thin, white hands—'I have felt helpless. I have felt like one of those poor rabbits when the snake is writhing towards it. I seem to be in the grasp of some resistless, inexorable evil, which no foresight and no precautions can guard against.'

'Tut! Tut!' cried Sherlock Holmes. 'You must act, man, or you are lost. Nothing but energy can save you. This is no time for despair.'*

'I have seen the police.'

'Ah?'

'But they listened to my story with a smile. I am convinced that the inspector has formed the opinion that the letters are all practical jokes, and that the deaths of my relations were really accidents, as the jury stated, and were not to be connected with the warnings.'

Holmes shook his clenched hands in the air. 'Incredible imbecility!' he cried.

'They have, however, allowed me a policeman, who may remain in the house with me.'

'Has he come with you to-night?'

'No. His orders were to stay in the house.'

Again Holmes raved in the air.

'Why did you come to me?' he said; 'and, above all, why did you not come at once?'

'I did not know. It was only to-day that I spoke to Major Prendergast about my trouble, and was advised by him to come to you.'

'It is really two days since you had the letter. We should have acted before this. You have no further evidence, I suppose, than that which you have placed before us—no suggestive detail which might help us?'

'There is one thing,' said John Openshaw. He rummaged in his coat pocket, and drawing out a piece of discoloured, blue-tinted paper, he laid it out upon the table. 'I have some remembrance,' said he, 'that on the day when my uncle burned the papers I observed that the small, unburned margins which lay amid the ashes were of this particular colour. I found this single sheet upon the floor of his room, and I am inclined to think that it may be one of the papers which had, perhaps, fluttered out from among the others, and in that way escaped destruction. Beyond the mention of pips, I do not see that it helps us much. I think myself that it is a page from some private diary. The writing is undoubtedly my uncle's.'

Holmes moved the lamp, and we both bent over the sheet of paper, which showed by its ragged edge that it had indeed been torn from a book. It was headed 'March, 1869', and beneath were the following enigmatical notices:*

4th. Hudson came. Same old platform.

7th. Set the pips on McCauley, Paramore, and John Swain of St Augustine.

9th. McCauley cleared.

10th. John Swain cleared.

12th. Visited Paramore. All well.

'Thank you!' said Holmes, folding up the paper and returning it to our visitor. 'And now you must on no account lose another instant. We cannot spare time even to discuss what you have told me. You must get home instantly, and act.'

'What shall I do?'

'There is but one thing to do. It must be done at once. You must put this piece of paper which you have shown us into the brass box which you have described. You must also put in a note to say that all the other papers were burned by your uncle, and that this is the only one which remains. You must assert that in such words as will carry conviction with them. Having done this, you must at once put the box out upon the sun-dial, as directed. Do you understand?'

'Entirely.'

'Do not think of revenge, or anything of the sort, at present. I think that we may gain that by means of the law; but we have our web to weave, while theirs is already woven. The first consideration is to remove the pressing danger which threatens you. The second is to clear up the mystery, and to punish the guilty parties.'

'I thank you,' said the young man, rising, and pulling on his overcoat. 'You have given me fresh life and hope. I shall certainly do as you advise.'

'Do not lose an instant. And, above all, take care of yourself in the meanwhile, for I do not think that there can be a doubt that you are threatened by a very real and imminent danger. How do you go back?'

'By train from Waterloo.'*

'It is not yet nine. The streets will be crowded, so I trust that you may be in safety. And yet you cannot guard yourself too closely.'

'I am armed.'

'That is well. To-morrow I shall set to work upon your case.'

'I shall see you at Horsham, then?'

'No, your secret lies in London. It is there that I shall seek it.'

'Then I shall call upon you in a day, or in two days, with news as to the box and the papers. I shall take your advice in every particular.' He shook hands with us, and took his leave. Outside the wind still screamed, and the rain splashed and pattered against the windows. This strange, wild story

seemed to have come to us from amid the mad elements—
blown in upon us like a sheet of sea-weed in a gale—and
now to have been re-absorbed by them once more.

Sherlock Holmes sat for some time in silence with his
head sunk forward, and his eyes bent upon the red glow of
the fire. Then he lit his pipe, and leaning back in his chair
he watched the blue smoke rings as they chased each other
up to the ceiling.

'I think, Watson,' he remarked at last, 'that of all our cases
we have had none more fantastic than this.'

'Save, perhaps, the Sign of Four.'

'Well, yes. Save, perhaps, that. And yet this John Openshaw seems to me to be walking amid even greater perils
than did the Sholtos.'*

'But have you,' I asked, 'formed any definite conception
as to what these perils are?'

'There can be no question as to their nature,' he
answered.

'Then what are they? Who is this K.K.K., and why does
he pursue this unhappy family?'

Sherlock Holmes closed his eyes, and placed his elbows
upon the arms of his chair, with his finger-tips together. 'The
ideal reasoner,' he remarked, 'would, when he has once
been shown a single fact in all its bearings, deduce from it
not only all the chain of events which led up to it, but also
all the results which would follow from it. As Cuvier could
correctly describe a whole animal by the contemplation of a
single bone,* so the observer who has thoroughly understood one link in a series of incidents, should be able
accurately to state all the other ones, both before and after.
We have not yet grasped the results which the reason alone
can attain to. Problems may be solved in the study which
have baffled all those who have sought a solution by the aid
of their senses. To carry the art, however, to its highest
pitch, it is necessary that the reasoner should be able to
utilize all the facts which have come to his knowledge, and
this in itself implies, as you will readily see, a possession of
all knowledge, which, even in these days of free education

and encyclopedias, is a somewhat rare accomplishment. It is not so impossible, however, that a man should possess all knowledge which is likely to be useful to him in his work, and this I have endeavoured in my case to do. If I remember rightly, you on one occasion, in the early days of our friendship, defined my limits in a very precise fashion.'

'Yes,' I answered, laughing. 'It was a singular document.* Philosophy, astronomy, and politics were marked at zero, I remember. Botany variable, geology profound as regards the mud-stains from any region within fifty miles of town, chemistry eccentric, anatomy unsystematic, sensational literature and crime records unique, violin player, boxer, swordsman, lawyer, and self-poisoner by cocaine and tobacco. Those, I think, were the main points of my analysis.'

Holmes grinned at the last item. 'Well,' he said, 'I say now, as I said then, that a man should keep his little brain attic stocked with all the furniture that he is likely to use, and the rest he can put away in the lumber-room of his library, where he can get it if he wants it. Now, for such a case as the one which has been submitted to us tonight, we need certainly to muster all our resources. Kindly hand me down the letter K of the American Encyclopedia* which stands upon the shelf beside you. Thank you. Now let us consider the situation, and see what may be deduced from it. In the first place, we may start with a strong presumption that Colonel Openshaw had some very strong reason for leaving America. Men at his time of life do not change all their habits, and exchange willingly the charming climate of Florida for the lonely life of an English provincial town. His extreme love of solitude in England suggests the idea that he was in fear of someone or something, which drove him from America. As to what it was he feared, we can only deduce that by considering the formidable letters which were received by himself and his successors. Did you remark the postmarks of those letters?'

'The first was from Pondicherry, the second from Dundee, and the third from London.'

'From East London. What do you deduce from that?'

'They are all sea-ports. That the writer was on board a ship.'

'Excellent. We have already a clue. There can be no doubt that the probability—the strong probability—is that the writer was on board of a ship. And now let us consider another point. In the case of Pondicherry seven weeks elapsed between the threat and its fulfilment, in Dundee it was only some three or four days. Does that suggest anything?'

'A greater distance to travel.'

'But the letter had also a greater distance to come.'

'Then I do not see the point.'

'There is at least a presumption that the vessel in which the man or men are is a sailing ship. It looks as if they always sent their singular warning or token before them when starting upon their mission. You see how quickly the deed followed the sign when it came from Dundee. If they had come from Pondicherry in a steamer they would have arrived almost as soon as their letter. But as a matter of fact seven weeks elapsed. I think that those seven weeks represented the difference between the mail boat which brought the letter, and the sailing vessel which brought the writer.'

'It is possible.'

'More than that. It is probable. And now you see the deadly urgency of this new case, and why I urged young Openshaw to caution. The blow has always fallen at the end of the time which it would take the senders to travel the distance. But this one comes from London, and therefore we cannot count upon delay.'

'Good God!' I cried. 'What can it mean, this relentless persecution?'

'The papers which Openshaw carried are obviously of vital importance to the person or persons in the sailing ship. I think that it is quite clear that there must be more than one of them. A single man could not have carried out two deaths in such a way as to deceive a coroner's jury. There must have been several in it, and they must have been men of resource and determination. Their papers they mean to

have, be the holder of them who it may. In this way you see
K.K.K. ceases to be the initials of an individual, and
becomes the badge of a society.'

'But of what society?'

'Have you never——' said Sherlock Holmes, bending forward and sinking his voice——'have you never heard of the
Ku Klux Klan?'

'I never have.'

Holmes turned over the leaves of the book upon his knee.
'Here it is,' said he presently, ' "Ku Klux Klan. A name
derived from a fanciful resemblance to the sound produced
by cocking a rifle.* This terrible secret society was formed
by some ex-Confederate soldiers in the Southern States after
the Civil War, and it rapidly formed local branches in
different parts of the country, notably in Tennessee, Louisiana,
the Carolinas, Georgia, and Florida. Its power was used for
political purposes, principally for the terrorizing of the negro
voters, and the murdering or driving from the country of
those who were opposed to its views. Its outrages were
usually preceded by a warning sent to the marked man in
some fantastic but generally recognized shape—a sprig of
oak leaves in some parts, melon seeds or orange pips in
others.* On receiving this the victim might either openly
abjure his former ways, or might fly from the country. If he
braved the matter out, death would unfailingly come upon
him, and usually in some strange and unforeseen manner.
So perfect was the organization of the society, and so system-
atic its methods, that there is hardly a case upon record
where any man succeeded in braving it with impunity, or in
which any of its outrages were traced home to the perpetrators.
For some years the organization flourished, in spite of the
efforts of the United States Government, and of the better
classes of the community in the South. Eventually, in the year
1869, the movement rather suddenly collapsed,* although
there have been sporadic outbreaks of the same sort since
that date."

'You will observe,' said Holmes, laying down the volume,
'that the sudden breaking up of the society was coincident

with the disappearance of Openshaw from America with
their papers. It may well have been cause and effect. It is no
wonder that he and his family have some of the more
implacable spirits upon their track. You can understand that
this register and diary may implicate some of the first men
in the South, and that there may be many who will not sleep
easy at night until it is recovered.'

'Then the page which we have seen—'

'Is such as we might expect. It ran, if I remember right,
"sent the pips to A, B, and C"—that is, sent the society's
warning to them. Then there are successive entries that A
and B cleared, or left the country, and finally that C was
visited, with, I fear, a sinister result for C. Well, I think,
Doctor, that we may let some light into this dark place,
and I believe that the only chance young Openshaw has in
the meantime is to do what I have told him. There is
nothing more to be said or to be done tonight, so hand me
over my violin and let us try to forget for half an hour the
miserable weather, and the still more miserable ways of our
fellow-men.'

It had cleared in the morning, and the sun was shining with
a subdued brightness through the dim veil which hangs over
the great city. Sherlock Holmes was already at breakfast
when I came down.

'You will excuse me for not waiting for you,' said he; 'I
have, I foresee, a very busy day before me in looking into
this case of young Openshaw's.'

'What steps will you take?' I asked.

'It will very much depend upon the results of my first
inquiries. I may have to go down to Horsham after all.'

'You will not go there first?'

'No, I shall commence with the City. Just ring the bell,
and the maid will bring up your coffee.

As I waited, I lifted the unopened newspaper from the
table and glanced my eye over it. It rested upon a heading
which sent a chill to my heart.

'Holmes,' I cried, 'you are too late.'

'Ah!' said he, laying down his cup, 'I feared as much. How was it done?' He spoke calmly, but I could see that he was deeply moved.

'My eye caught the name of Openshaw, and the heading "Tragedy near Waterloo Bridge".* Here is the account: "Between nine and ten last night Police Constable Cook, of the H Division,* on duty near Waterloo Bridge, heard a cry for help and a splash in the water. The night, however, was extremely dark and stormy, so that, in spite of the help of several passers-by, it was quite impossible to effect a rescue. The alarm, however, was given, and by the aid of the water police, the body was eventually recovered. It proved to be that of a young gentleman whose name, as it appears from an envelope which was found in his pocket, was John Openshaw, and whose residence is near Horsham. It is conjectured that he may have been hurrying down to catch the last train from Waterloo station, and that in his haste and the extreme darkness, he missed his path and walked over the edge of one of the small landing-places for river steamboats. The body exhibited no traces of violence, and there can be no doubt that the deceased had been the victim of an unfortunate accident, which should have the effect of calling the attention of the authorities to the condition of the riverside landing-stages." '

We sat in silence for some minutes, Holmes more depressed and shaken than I had ever seen him.

'That hurts my pride, Watson,' he said at last. 'It is a petty feeling, no doubt, but it hurts my pride. It becomes a personal matter with me now, and, if God sends me health, I shall set my hand upon this gang. That he should come to me for help, and that I should send him away to his death—!' He sprang from his chair, and paced about the room in uncontrollable agitation, with a flush upon his sallow cheeks, and a nervous clasping and unclasping of his long, thin hands.

'They must be cunning devils,' he exclaimed at last. 'How could they have decoyed him down there? The Embankment* is not on the direct line to the station. The bridge, no doubt, was too crowded, even on such a night, for their purpose. Well, Watson, we shall see who will win in the long run. I am going out now!'

'To the police?'

'No; I shall be my own police. When I have spun the web they may take the flies, but not before.'

All day I was engaged in my professional work, and it was late in the evening before I returned to Baker Street. Sherlock Holmes had not come back yet. It was nearly ten o'clock before he entered, looking pale and worn. He walked up to the sideboard, and, tearing a piece from the loaf, he devoured it voraciously, washing it down with a long draught of water.

'You are hungry,' I remarked.

'Starving. It had escaped my memory. I have had nothing since breakfast.'

'Nothing?'

'Not a bite. I had no time to think of it.'

'And how have you succeeded?'

'Well.'

'You have a clue?'

'I have them in the hollow of my hand. Young Openshaw shall not remain long unavenged. Why, Watson, let us put their own devilish trade-mark upon them. It is well thought of!'

'What do you mean?'

He took an orange from the cupboard, and tearing it to pieces, he squeezed out the pips upon the table. Of these he took five, and thrust them into an envelope. On the inside of the flap he wrote, 'S.H. for J. O.' Then he sealed it and addressed it to 'Captain James Calhoun,* Barque *Lone Star*, Savannah, Georgia.'*

'That will await him when he enters port,' said he, chuckling. 'It may give him a sleepless night. He will find it as sure a precursor of his fate as Openshaw did before him.'

'And who is this Captain Calhoun?'

'The leader of the gang. I shall have the others, but he first.'

'How did you trace it, then?'

He took a large sheet of paper from his pocket, all covered with dates and names.

'I have spent the whole day,' said he, 'over Lloyd's registers and the files of old papers,* following the future career of every vessel which touched at Pondicherry in January and in February in '83. There were thirty-six ships of fair tonnage which were reported there during those months. Of these, one, the *Lone Star* instantly attracted my attention, since, although it was reported as having cleared from London, the name is that which is given to one of the States of the Union.'

'Texas, I think.'

'I was not and am not sure which; but I knew that the ship must have an American origin.'

'What then?'

'I searched the Dundee records, and when I found that the barque *Lone Star* was there in January, '85, my suspicion became a certainty. I then inquired as to vessels which lay at present in the port of London.'

'Yes?'

'The *Lone Star* had arrived here last week. I went down to the Albert Dock,* and found that she had been taken down the river by the early tide this morning, homeward bound to Savannah. I wired to Gravesend,* and learned that she had passed some time ago, and as the wind is easterly, I have no doubt that she is now past the Goodwins,* and not very far from the Isle of Wight.'

'What will you do, then?'

'Oh, I have my hand upon him. He and the two mates are, as I learn, the only native-born Americans in the ship. The others are Finns and Germans. I know also that they were all three away from the ship last night. I had it from the stevedore, who has been loading their cargo. By the time their sailing ship reaches Savannah the mail-boat will have carried this letter, and the cable will have informed the police of Savannah that these three gentlemen are badly wanted here upon a charge of murder.'

There is ever a flaw, however, in the best laid of human plans,* and the murderers of John Openshaw were never to receive the orange pips which would show them that another, as cunning and resolute as themselves, was upon their track. Very long and severe were the equinoctial gales of that year. We waited long for news of the *Lone Star* of Savannah, but none ever reached us. We did at last hear that somewhere far out in the Atlantic a shattered sternpost of a boat was seen swinging in the trough of a wave, with the letters 'L. S.' carved upon it,* and that is all which we shall ever know of the fate of the *Lone Star*.

The Man with the Twisted Lip

ISA* WHITNEY, brother of the late Elias Whitney,* D.D.,
Principal of the Theological College of St George's,* was
much addicted to opium. The habit grew upon him, as I
understand, from some foolish freak when he was at college,
for having read De Quincey's description of his dreams and
sensations,* he had drenched his tobacco with laudanum* in
an attempt to produce the same effects. He found, as so
many more have done, that the practice is easier to attain
than to get rid of, and for many years he continued to be a
slave to the drug, an object of mingled horror and pity to
his friends and relatives. I can see him now, with yellow,
pasty face, drooping lids and pin-point pupils, all huddled in
a chair, the wreck and ruin of a noble man.

One night—it was in June, '89—there came a ring to my
bell, about the hour when a man gives his first yawn, and
glances at the clock. I sat up in my chair, and my wife laid
her needlework down in her lap and made a little face of
disappointment.

'A patient!' said she. 'You'll have to go out.'

I groaned, for I was newly come back from a weary
day.

We heard the door open, a few hurried words, and then
quick steps upon the linoleum. Our own door flew open,
and a lady, clad in some dark-coloured stuff with a black
veil, entered the room.

'You will excuse my calling so late,' she began, and then,
suddenly losing her self-control, she ran forward, threw her
arms about my wife's neck, and sobbed upon her shoulder.
'Oh! I'm in such trouble!' she cried; 'I do so want a little
help.'

'Why,' said my wife, pulling up her veil, 'It is Kate
Whitney. How you startled me, Kate! I had not an idea who
you were when you came in.'

'I didn't know what to do, so I came straight to you.' That was always the way. Folk who were in grief came to my wife like birds to a lighthouse.

'It was very sweet of you to come. Now, you must have some wine and water, and sit here comfortably and tell us all about it. Or should you rather that I sent James* off to bed?'

'Oh, no, no. I want the Doctor's advice and help too. It's about Isa. He has not been home for two days. I am so frightened about him!'

It was not the first time that she had spoken to us of her husband's trouble, to me as a doctor, to my wife as an old friend and school companion. We soothed and comforted her by such words as we could find. Did she know where her husband was? Was it possible that we could bring him back to her?

It seemed that it was. She had the surest information that of late he had, when the fit was on him, made use of an opium den in the furthest east of the City. Hitherto his orgies had always been confined to one day, and he had come back, twitching and shattered, in the evening. But now the spell had been upon him eight-and-forty hours, and he lay there, doubtless, among the dregs of the docks, breathing in the poison or sleeping off the effects. There he was to be found, she was sure of it, at the 'Bar of Gold',* in Upper Swandam Lane.* But what was she to do? How could she, a young and timid woman, make her way into such a place, and pluck her husband out from among the ruffians who surrounded him?

There was the case, and of course there was but one way out of it. Might I not escort her to this place? And then, as a second thought, why should she come at all? I was Isa Whitney's medical adviser, and as such I had influence over him. I could manage it better if I were alone. I promised her on my word that I would send him home in a cab within two hours if he were indeed at the address which she had given me. And so in ten minutes I had left my armchair and cheery sitting-room behind me, and was speeding eastward in a hansom on a strange errand, as it seemed to me at the time, though the future only could show how strange it was to be.

But there was no great difficulty in the first stage of my adventure. Upper Swandam Lane is a vile alley lurking behind the high wharves which line the north side of the river to the east of London Bridge. Between a slop shop,* and a gin shop,* approached by a steep flight of steps leading down to a black gap like the mouth of a cave, I found the den of which I was in search. Ordering my cab to wait, I passed down the steps, worn hollow in the centre by the ceaseless tread of drunken feet, and by the light of a flickering oil lamp above the door I found the latch and made my way into a long, low room, thick and heavy with the brown opium smoke, and terraced with wooden berths, like the forecastle of an emigrant ship.

Through the gloom one could dimly catch a glimpse of bodies lying in strange fantastic poses, bowed shoulders, bent knees, heads thrown back and chins pointing upwards, with here and there a dark, lack-lustre eye* turned upon the newcomer. Out of the black shadows there glimmered little red circles of light, now bright, now faint, as the burning poison waxed or waned in the bowls of the metal pipes. The most lay silent, but some muttered to themselves, and others talked together in a strange, low, monotonous voice, their conversation coming in gushes, and then suddenly tailing off into silence, each mumbling out his own thoughts, and paying little heed to the words of his neighbour. At the further end was a small brazier of burning charcoal,* beside which on a three-legged wooden stool there sat a tall, thin old man, with his jaw resting upon his two fists, and his elbows upon his knees, staring into the fire.

As I entered, a sallow Malay attendant had hurried up with a pipe for me and a supply of the drug, beckoning me to an empty berth.

'Thank you, I have not come to stay,' said I. 'There is a friend of mine here, Mr Isa Whitney, and I wish to speak with him.'

There was a movement and an exclamation from my right, and, peering through the gloom, I saw Whitney, pale, haggard, and unkempt, staring out at me.

'My God! It's Watson,' said he. He was in a pitiable state of reaction, with every nerve in a twitter. 'I say, Watson, what o'clock is it?'

'Nearly eleven.'

'Of what day?'

'Of Friday, June 19th.'*

'Good heavens! I thought it was Wednesday. It *is* Wednesday. What d'you want to frighten a chap for?' He sank his face on to his arms, and began to sob in a high treble key.

'I tell you that it is Friday, man. Your wife has been waiting this two days for you. You should be ashamed of yourself!'

'So I am. But you've got mixed, Watson, for I have only been here a few hours, three pipes, four pipes—I forget how many. But I'll go home with you. I wouldn't frighten Kate—poor little Kate. Give me your hand! Have you a cab?'

'Yes, I have one waiting.'

'Then I shall go in it. But I must owe something. Find what I owe, Watson. I am all off colour. I can do nothing for myself.'

I walked down the narrow passage between the double row of sleepers, holding my breath to keep out the vile, stupefying fumes of the drug, and looking about for the manager. As I passed the tall man who sat by the brazier I felt a sudden pluck at my skirt,* and a low voice whispered, 'Walk past me, and then look back at me.' The words fell quite distinctly upon my ear. I glanced down. They could only have come from the old man at my side, and yet he sat now as absorbed as ever, very thin, very wrinkled, bent with age, an opium pipe dangling down from between his knees, as though it had dropped in sheer lassitude from his fingers. I took two steps forward and looked back. It took all my self-control to prevent me from breaking out into a cry of astonishment. He had turned his back so that none could see him but I. His form had filled out, his wrinkles were gone, the dull eyes had regained their fire, and there, sitting by the fire, and grinning at my surprise, was none other than Sherlock Holmes. He made a slight motion to me to approach him, and instantly, as he turned his face half round to the company once more, subsided into a doddering, loose-lipped senility.

'Holmes!' I whispered, 'what on earth are you doing in this den?'

'As low as you can,' he answered, 'I have excellent ears. If you would have the great kindness to get rid of that sottish friend of yours, I should be exceedingly glad to have a little talk with you.'

'I have a cab outside.'

'Then pray send him home in it. You may safely trust him, for he appears to be too limp to get into any mischief. I should recommend you also to send a note by the cabman to your wife to say that you have thrown in your lot with me. If you will wait outside, I shall be with you in five minutes.'

It was difficult to refuse any of Sherlock Holmes's requests, for they were always so exceedingly definite, and put forward with such an air of mastery. I felt, however, that when Whitney was once confined in the cab, my mission was practically accomplished; and for the rest, I could not wish anything better than to be associated with my friend in one of those singular adventures which were the normal condition of his existence. In a few minutes I had written my note, paid Whitney's bill, led him out to the cab, and seen him driven through the darkness. In a very short time a decrepit figure had emerged from the opium den, and I was walking down the street with Sherlock Holmes. For two streets he shuffled along with a bent back and an uncertain foot. Then, glancing quickly round, he straightened himself out and burst into a hearty fit of laughter.

'I suppose, Watson,' said he, 'that you imagine that I have added opium-smoking to cocaine injections and all the other little weaknesses on which you have favoured me with your medical views.'

'I was certainly surprised to find you there.'

'But not more so than I to find you.'

'I came to find a friend.'

'And I to find an enemy!'

'An enemy?'

'Yes, one of my natural enemies, or, shall I say, my natural prey. Briefly, Watson, I am in the midst of a very remarkable inquiry, and I have hoped to find a clue in the incoherent ramblings of these sots, as I have done before now. Had I been recognized in that den my life would not have been worth an hour's purchase, for I have used it before now for my own purposes, and the rascally Lascar* who runs it has sworn vengeance upon me. There is a trap-door at the back of that building, near the corner of Paul's Wharf,* which could tell some strange tales of what has passed through it upon the moonless nights.'

'What! You do not mean bodies?'

'Aye, bodies, Watson. We should be rich men if we had a thousand pounds for every poor devil who has been done to death in that den. It is the vilest murder-trap on the whole riverside, and I fear Neville St Clair has entered it never to leave it more. But our trap should be here!' He put his two fore-fingers between his teeth and whistled shrilly, a signal which was answered by a similar whistle from the distance, followed shortly by the rattle of wheels and the clink of horse's hoofs.

'Now, Watson,' said Holmes, as a tall dog-cart dashed up through the gloom, throwing out two golden tunnels of yellow light from its side-lanterns, 'you'll come with me, won't you?'

'If I can be of use.'

'Oh, a trusty comrade is always of use. And a chronicler still more so. My room at The Cedars* is a double-bedded one.'

'The Cedars?'

'Yes; that is Mr St Clair's house. I am staying there while I conduct the inquiry.'

'Where is it, then?'

'Near Lee, in Kent. We have a seven-mile drive before us.'

'But I am all in the dark.'

'Of course you are. You'll know all about it presently. Jump up here! All right, John, we shall not need you. Here's half-a-crown. Look out for me to-morrow about eleven. Give her her head! So long, then!'

He flicked the horse with his whip, and we dashed away through the endless succession of sombre and deserted streets, which widened gradually, until we were flying across a broad balustraded bridge,* with the murky river flowing sluggishly beneath us. Beyond lay another broad wilderness of bricks and mortar, its silence broken only by the heavy, regular footfall of the policeman, or the songs and shouts of some belated party of revellers. A dull wrack* was drifting slowly across the sky, and a star or two twinkled dimly here and there through the rifts of the clouds. Holmes drove in silence, with his head sunk upon his breast, and the air of a man who is lost in thought, whilst I sat beside him curious to learn what this new quest might be which seemed to tax his powers so sorely, and yet afraid to break in upon the current of his thoughts. We had driven several miles, and were beginning to get to the fringe of the belt of suburban villas, when he shook himself, shrugged his shoulders, and lit up his pipe with the air of a man who has satisfied himself that he is acting for the best.

'You have a grand gift of silence, Watson,'* said he. 'It makes you quite invaluable as a companion. 'Pon my word, it is a great thing for me to have someone to talk to, for my own thoughts are not over-pleasant. I was wondering what I should say to this dear little woman to-night when she meets me at the door.'

'You forget that I know nothing about it.'

'I shall just have time to tell you the facts of the case before we get to Lee. It seems absurdly simple, and yet, somehow, I can get nothing to go upon. There's plenty of thread, no doubt, but I can't get the end of it in my hand. Now, I'll state the case clearly and concisely to you, Watson, and maybe you may see a spark where all is dark to me.'

'Proceed, then.'

'Some years ago—to be definite, in May, 1884—there came to Lee a gentleman, Neville St Clair by name, who appeared to have plenty of money. He took a large villa, laid out the grounds very nicely, and lived generally in good style. By degrees he made friends in the neighbourhood, and in 1887 he married the daughter of a local brewer, by whom he has now had two children. He had no occupation, but was interested in several companies, and went into town as a rule in the morning, returning by the 5.14 from Cannon Street* every night. Mr St Clair is now 37 years of age, is a man of temperate habits, a good husband, a very affectionate father, and a man who is popular with all who know him. I may add that his whole debts at the present moment, as far as we have been able to ascertain, amount to £88 10s., while he has £220 standing to his credit in the Capital and Counties Bank.* There is no reason, therefore, to think that money troubles have been weighing upon his mind.

'Last Monday Mr Neville St Clair went into town rather earlier than usual, remarking before he started that he had two important commissions to perform, and that he would bring his little boy home a box of bricks. Now, by the merest chance his wife received a telegram upon this same Monday, very shortly after his departure, to the effect that a small parcel of considerable value which she had been expecting was waiting for her at the offices of the Aberdeen Shipping Company.* Now, if you are well up in your London, you will know that the office of the company is in Fresno Street,* which branches out of Upper Swandam Lane, where you found me to-night. Mrs St Clair had her lunch, started for the City, did some shopping, proceeded to the Company's office, got her packet, and found herself exactly at 4.35 walking through Swandam Lane on her way back to the station. Have you followed me so far?'

'It is very clear.'

'If you remember, Monday was an exceedingly hot day, and Mrs St Clair walked slowly, glancing about in the hope of seeing a cab, as she did not like the neighbourhood in which she found herself. While she walked in this way down

Swandam Lane she suddenly heard an ejaculation or cry, and was struck cold to see her husband looking down at her,* and, as it seemed to her, beckoning to her from a second-floor window. The window was open, and she distinctly saw his face, which she describes as being terribly agitated. He waved his hands frantically to her, and then vanished from the window so suddenly that it seemed to her that he had been plucked back by some irresistible force from behind. One singular point which struck her quick feminine eye was that, although he wore some dark coat, such as he had started to town in, he had on neither collar nor necktie.

'Convinced that something was amiss with him, she rushed down the steps—for the house was none other than the opium den in which you found me to-night—and, running through the front room, she attempted to ascend the stairs which led to the first floor. At the foot of the stairs, however, she met this Lascar scoundrel, of whom I have spoken, who thrust her back, and, aided by a Dane, who acts as assistant there, pushed her out into the street. Filled with the most maddening doubts and fears, she rushed down the lane, and, by rare good fortune, met, in Fresno Street, a number of constables with an inspector, all on their way to their beat. The inspector and two men accompanied her back, and, in spite of the continued resistance of the proprietor, they made their way to the room in which Mr St Clair had last been seen. There was no sign of him there. In fact, in the whole of that floor there was no one to be found, save a crippled wretch of hideous aspect, who, it seems, made his home there. Both he and the Lascar stoutly swore that no one else had been in the front room during that afternoon. So determined was their denial that the inspector was staggered, and had almost come to believe that Mrs St Clair had been deluded when, with a cry, she sprang at a small deal box which lay upon the table, and tore the lid from it. Out there fell a cascade of children's bricks. It was the toy which he had promised to bring home.

'This discovery, and the evident confusion which the cripple showed, made the inspector realize that the matter was serious. The rooms were carefully examined, and results all pointed to an abominable crime. The front room was plainly furnished as a sitting-room, and led into a small bedroom, which looked out upon the back of one of the wharves. Between the wharf and the bedroom window is a narrow strip, which is dry at low tide, but is covered at high tide with at least four and a half feet of water. The bedroom window was a broad one, and opened from below. On examination traces of blood were to be seen upon the window-sill, and several scattered drops were visible upon the wooden floor of the bedroom. Thrust away behind a curtain in the front room were all the clothes of Mr Neville St Clair, with the exception of his coat. His boots, his socks, his hat, and his watch—all were there. There were no signs of violence upon any of these garments, and there were no other traces of Mr Neville St Clair. Out of the window he must apparently have gone, for no other exit could be discovered, and the ominous bloodstains upon the sill gave little promise that he could save himself by swimming, for the tide was at its very highest at the moment of the tragedy.

'And now as to the villains who seemed to be immediately implicated in the matter. The Lascar was known to be a man of the vilest antecedents, but as by Mrs St Clair's story he was known to have been at the foot of the stair within a few seconds of her husband's appearance at the window, he could hardly have been more than an accessory to the crime. His defence was one of absolute ignorance, and he protested that he had no knowledge as to the doings of Hugh Boone,* his lodger, and that he could not account in any way for the presence of the missing gentleman's clothes.

'So much for the Lascar manager. Now for the sinister cripple who lives upon the second floor of the opium den, and who was certainly the last human being whose eyes rested upon Neville St Clair. His name is Hugh Boone, and his hideous face is one which is familiar to every man who goes much to the City. He is a professional beggar,* though in order to avoid the police regulations he pretends to a small trade in wax vestas.* Some little distance down Threadneedle Street* upon the left hand side there is, as you may have remarked, a small angle in the wall. Here it is that the creature takes his daily seat, cross-legged, with his tiny stock of matches on his lap, and as he is a piteous spectacle a small rain of charity descends into the greasy leather cap which lies upon the pavement before him. I have watched this fellow more than once, before ever I thought of making his professional acquaintance, and I have been surprised at the harvest which he has reaped in so short a time. His appearance, you see, is so remarkable that no one can pass him without observing him. A shock of orange hair, a pale face disfigured by a horrible scar, which, by its contraction, has turned up the outer edge of his upper lip, a bull-dog chin, and a pair of very penetrating dark eyes, which present a singular contrast to the colour of his hair, all mark him out from amid the common crowd of mendicants, and so, too, does his wit, for he is ever ready with a reply to any piece of chaff which may be thrown at him by the passers-by. This is the man whom we now learn to have been the lodger at the opium den, and to have been the last man to see the gentleman of whom we are in quest.'

'But a cripple!' said I. 'What could he have done single-handed against a man in the prime of life?'

'He is a cripple in the sense that he walks with a limp; but, in other respects, he appears to be a powerful and well-nurtured man. Surely your medical experience would tell you, Watson, that weakness in one limb is often compensated for by exceptional strength in the others.'

'Pray continue your narrative.'

'Mrs St Clair had fainted at the sight of the blood* upon the window, and she was escorted home in a cab by the police, as her presence could be of no help to them in their investigations. Inspector Barton,* who had charge of the case, made a very careful examination of the premises, but without finding anything which threw any light upon the matter. One mistake had been made in not arresting Boone instantly, as he was allowed some few minutes during which he might have communicated with his friend the Lascar, but this fault was soon remedied, and he was seized and searched, without anything being found which could incriminate him. There were, it is true, some bloodstains upon his right shirt-sleeve, but he pointed to his ring finger, which had been cut near the nail, and explained that the bleeding came from there, adding that he had been to the window not long before, and that the stains which had been observed there came doubtless from the same source. He denied strenuously having ever seen Mr Neville St Clair, and swore that the presence of the clothes in his room was as much a mystery to him as to the police. As to Mrs St Clair's assertion, that she had actually seen her husband at the window, he declared that she must have been either mad or dreaming. He was removed, loudly protesting, to the police station, while the inspector remained upon the premises in the hope that the ebbing tide might afford some fresh clue.

'And it did, though they hardly found upon the mudbank what they had feared to find. It was Neville St Clair's coat, and not Neville St Clair, which lay uncovered as the tide receded. And what do you think they found in the pockets?'

'I cannot imagine.'

'No, I don't think you will guess. Every pocket stuffed with pennies and halfpennies—four hundred and twenty-one pennies, and two hundred and seventy halfpennies. It was no wonder that it had not been swept away by the tide. But a human body is a different matter. There is a fierce eddy between the wharf and the house. It seemed likely enough that the weighted coat had remained when the stripped body had been sucked away into the river.'

'But I understand that all the other clothes were found in the room. Would the body be dressed in a coat alone?'

'No, sir, but the facts might be met speciously enough. Suppose that this man Boone had thrust Neville St Clair through the window, there is no human eye which could have seen the deed. What would he do then? It would of course instantly strike him that he must get rid of the tell-tale garments. He would seize the coat then, and be in the act of throwing it out when it would occur to him that it would swim and not sink. He has little time, for he had heard the scuffle downstairs when the wife tried to force her way up, and perhaps he has already heard from his Lascar confederate that the police are hurrying up the street. There is not an instant to be lost. He rushes to some secret hoard, where he has accumulated the fruits of his beggary, and he stuffs all the coins upon which he can lay his hands into the pockets to make sure of the coat's sinking. He throws it out, and would have done the same with the other garments had not he heard the rush of steps below, and only just had time to close the window when the police appeared.'

'It certainly sounds feasible.'

'Well, we will take it as a working hypothesis for want of a better. Boone, as I have told you, was arrested and taken to the station, but it could not be shown that there had ever before been anything against him. He had for years been known as a professional beggar, but his life appeared to have been a very quiet and innocent one. There the matter stands at present, and the questions which have to be solved, what Neville St Clair was doing in the opium den, what happened to him when there, where he is now, and what Hugh Boone had to do with his disappearance, are all as far from solution as ever. I confess that I cannot recall any case within my experience which looked at the first glance so simple, and yet which presented such difficulties.'

Whilst Sherlock Holmes had been detailing this singular series of events we had been whirling through the outskirts of the great town until the last straggling houses had been left behind, and we rattled along with a country hedge upon either side of us. Just as he finished, however, we drove through two scattered villages, where a few lights still glimmered in the windows.

'We are on the outskirts of Lee,' said my companion. 'We have touched on three English counties* in our short drive, starting in Middlesex, passing over an angle of Surrey, and ending in Kent. See that light among the trees? That is The Cedars, and beside that lamp sits a woman whose anxious ears have already, I have little doubt, caught the clink of our horse's feet.'

'But why are you not conducting the case from Baker Street?' I asked.

'Because there are many inquiries which must be made out here. Mrs St Clair has mostly kindly put two rooms at my disposal, and you may rest assured that she will have nothing but a welcome for my friend and colleague. I hate to meet her, Watson, when I have no news of her husband. Here we are. Whoa, there, whoa!'

We had pulled up in front of a large villa which stood within its own grounds. A stable-boy had run out to the horse's head, and, springing down, I followed Holmes up the small, winding gravel drive which led to the house. As we approached, the door flew open, and a little blonde woman stood in the opening, clad in some sort of light *mousseline-de-soie,** with a touch of fluffy pink chiffon at her neck and wrists. She stood with her figure outlined against the flood of light, one hand upon the door, one half raised in eagerness, her body slightly bent, her head and face protruded, with eager eyes and parted lips, a standing question.

'Well?' she cried, 'well?' And then, seeing that there were two of us, she gave a cry of hope which sank into a groan as she saw that my companion shook his head and shrugged his shoulders.

'No good news?'

'None.'*

'No bad?'

'No.'

'Thank God for that. But come in. You must be weary, for you have had a long day.'

'This is my friend, Dr Watson. He has been of most vital use to me in several of my cases, and a lucky chance has made it possible for me to bring him out and associate him with this investigation.'

'I am delighted to see you,' said she, pressing my hand warmly. 'You will, I am sure, forgive anything which may be wanting in our arrangements, when you consider the blow which has come so suddenly upon us.'

'My dear madam,' said I, 'I am an old campaigner,* and if I were not, I can very well see that no apology is needed. If I can be of any assistance, either to you or to my friend here, I shall be indeed happy.'

'Now, Mr Sherlock Holmes,' said the lady as we entered a well-lit dining-room, upon the table of which a cold supper had been laid out. 'I should very much like to ask you one or two plain questions, to which I beg that you will give a plain answer.'

'Certainly, madam.'

'Do not trouble about my feelings. I am not hysterical, nor given to fainting. I simply wish to hear your real, real opinion.'

'Upon what point?'

'In your heart of hearts, do you think that Neville is alive?'

Sherlock Holmes seemed to be embarrassed by the question. 'Frankly now!' she repeated, standing upon the rug, and looking keenly down at him, as he leaned back in a basket chair.

'Frankly, then, madam, I do not.'

'You think that he is dead?'

'I do.'

'Murdered?'

'I don't say that. Perhaps.'

'And on what day did he meet his death?'

'On Monday.'

'Then perhaps, Mr Holmes, you will be good enough to explain how it is that I have received this letter from him today?'

Sherlock Holmes sprang out of his chair as if he had been galvanized.*

'What!' he roared.

'Yes, today.' She stood smiling, holding up a little slip of paper in the air.

'May I see it?'

'Certainly.'

He snatched it from her in his eagerness, and smoothing it out upon the table, he drew over the lamp, and examined it intently. I had left my chair, and was gazing at it over his shoulder. The envelope was a very coarse one, and was stamped with the Gravesend* post-mark, and with the date of that very day, or rather of the day before, for it was considerably after midnight.

'Coarse writing!' murmured Holmes. 'Surely this is not your husband's writing, madam.'

'No, but the enclosure is.'

'I perceive also that whoever addressed the envelope had to go and inquire as to the address.'

'How can you tell that?'

'The name, you see, is in perfectly black ink, which has dried itself. The rest is of the greyish colour which shows that blotting-paper has been used. If it had been written straight off, and then blotted, none would be of a deep black shade. This man has written the name, and there has then been a pause before he wrote the address, which can only mean that he was not familiar with it. It is, of course, a trifle, but there is nothing so important as trifles. Let us now see the letter! Ha! there has been an enclosure here!'

'Yes, there was a ring. His signet ring.'

'And you are sure that this is your husband's hand?'

'One of his hands.'*

'One?'

'His hand when he wrote hurriedly. It is very unlike his usual writing, and yet I know it well.'

' "Dearest, do not be frightened. All will come well. There is a huge error which it may take some little time to rectify. Wait in patience.—Neville." Written in pencil upon a fly-leaf of a book,* octavo size, no watermark. Hum!—Posted to-day in Gravesend by a man with a dirty thumb. Ha! And the flap has been gummed, if I am not very much in error, by a person who has been chewing tobacco. And you have no doubt that it is your husband's hand, madam?'

'None. Neville wrote those words.'

'And they were posted to-day at Gravesend. Well, Mrs St Clair, the clouds lighten, though I should not venture to say that the danger is over.'

'But he must be alive, Mr Holmes.'

'Unless this is a clever forgery to put us on the wrong scent. The ring, after all, proves nothing. It may have been taken from him.'

'No, no; it is, it is, it is his very own writing!'

'Very well. It may, however, have been written on Monday, and only posted to-day.'

'That is possible.'

'If so, much may have happened between.'

'Oh, you must not discourage me, Mr Holmes. I know that all is well with him. There is so keen a sympathy between us that I should know if evil came upon him.* On the very day that I saw him last he cut himself in the bedroom, and yet I in the dining-room rushed upstairs instantly with the utmost certainty that something had happened. Do you think that I would respond to such a trifle, and yet be ignorant of his death?'

'I have seen too much not to know that the impression of a woman may be more valuable than the conclusion of an analytical reasoner. And in this letter you certainly have a very strong piece of evidence to corroborate your view. But if your husband is alive and able to write letters, why should he remain away from you?'

'I cannot imagine. It is unthinkable.'

'And on Monday he made no remarks before leaving you?'

'No.'

'And you were surprised to see him in Swandam Lane?'

'Very much so.'

'Was the window open?'

'Yes.'

'Then he might have called to you?'

'He might.'

'He only, as I understand, gave an inarticulate cry?'

'Yes.'

'A call for help, you thought?'

'Yes. He waved his hands.'

'But it might have been a cry of surprise. Astonishment at the unexpected sight of you might cause him to throw up his hands.'

'It is possible.'

'And you thought he was pulled back?'

'He disappeared so suddenly.'

'He might have leaped back. You did not see anyone else in the room?'

'No, but this horrible man confessed to having been there, and the Lascar was at the foot of the stairs.'

'Quite so. Your husband, as far as you could see, had his ordinary clothes on?'

'But without his collar or tie. I distinctly saw his bare throat.'

'Had he ever spoken of Swandam Lane?'

'Never.'

'Had he ever shown any signs of having taken opium?'

'Never.'

'Thank you, Mrs St Clair. Those are the principal points about which I wished to be absolutely clear. We shall now have a little supper and then retire, for we may have a very busy day to-morrow.'

A large and comfortable double-bedded room had been placed at our disposal, and I was quickly between the sheets, for I was weary after my night of adventure. Sherlock Holmes was a man, however, who when he had an unsolved problem upon his mind would go for days, and even for a week, without rest, turning it over, rearranging his facts, looking at it from every point of view, until he had either fathomed it, or convinced himself that his data were insufficient. It was soon evident to me that he was now preparing for an all-night sitting. He took off his coat and waistcoat, put on a large blue dressing-gown,* and then wandered about the room collecting pillows from his bed, and cusions from the sofa and armchairs. With these he constructed a sort of Eastern divan,* upon which he perched himself cross-legged, with an ounce of shag tobacco and a box of matches laid out in front of him. In the dim light of the lamp I saw him sitting there, an old brier pipe between his lips, his eyes fixed vacantly upon the corner of the ceiling, the blue smoke curling up from him, silent, motionless, with the light shining upon his strong-set aquiline features. So he sat as I dropped off to sleep, and so he sat when a sudden ejaculation caused me to wake up, and I found the summer sun shining into the apartment. The pipe was still between his lips, the smoke still curled upwards, and the room was full of a dense tobacco haze, but nothing remained of the heap of shag which I had seen upon the previous night.

'Awake, Watson?' he asked.

'Yes.'

'Game for a morning drive?'

'Certainly.'

'Then dress. No one is stirring yet, but I know where the stable-boy sleeps, and we shall soon have the trap out.' He chuckled to himself as he spoke, his eyes twinkled, and he seemed a different man to the sombre thinker of the previous night.

As I dressed I glanced at my watch. It was no wonder that no one was stirring. It was twenty-five minutes past four. I had hardly finished when Holmes returned with the news that the boy was putting in the horse.

'I want to test a little theory of mine,' said he, pulling on his boots. 'I think, Watson, that you are now standing in the presence of one of the most absolute fools in Europe. I deserve to be kicked from here to Charing Cross.* But I think I have the key of the affair now.'

'And where is it?' I asked, smiling.

'In the bath-room,' he answered. 'Oh, yes, I am not joking,' he continued, seeing my look of incredulity. 'I have just been there, and I have taken it out, and I have got it in this Gladstone bag.* Come on, my boy, and we shall see whether it will not fit the lock.'

We made our way downstairs as quietly as possible; and out into the bright morning sunshine. In the road stood our horse and trap, with the half-clad stable-boy waiting at the head. We both sprang in, and away we dashed down the London road. A few country carts were stirring, bearing in vegetables to the metropolis, but the lines of villas on either side were as silent and lifeless as some city in a dream.

'It has been in some points a singular case,' said Holmes, flicking the horse on into a gallop. 'I confess that I have been as blind as a mole, but it is better to learn wisdom late, than never to learn it at all.'

In town, the earliest risers were just beginning to look sleepily from their windows as we drove through the streets of the Surrey side. Passing down the Waterloo Bridge Road we crossed over the river, and dashing up Wellington Street wheeled sharply to the right, and found ourselves in Bow Street.* Sherlock Holmes was well known to the Force, and the two constables at the door saluted him. One of them held the horse's head while the other led us in.

'Who is on duty?' asked Holmes.

'Inspector Bradstreet,* sir.'

'Ah, Bradstreet, how are you?' A tall, stout official had come down the stone-flagged passage, in a peaked cap and frogged jacket.* 'I wish to have a word with you, Bradstreet.'

'Certainly, Mr Holmes. Step into my room here.'

It was a small office-like room, with a huge ledger upon the table, and a telephone projecting from the wall. The inspector sat down at his desk.

'What can I do for you, Mr Holmes?'

'I called about that beggarman, Boone*—the one who was charged with being concerned in the disappearance of Mr Neville St Clair, of Lee.'

'Yes. He was brought up and remanded for further inquiries.'

'So I heard. You have him here?'

'In the cells.'

'Is he quiet?'

'Oh, he gives no trouble. But he is a dirty scoundrel.'

'Dirty?'

'Yes, it is all we can do to make him wash his hands, and his face is as black as a tinker's. Well, when once his case has been settled he will have a regular prison bath; and I think, if you saw him you would agree with me that he needed it.'

'I should like to see him very much.'

'Would you? That is easily done. Come this way. You can leave your bag.'

'No, I think that I'll take it.'

'Very good. Come this way, if you please.' He led us down a passage, opened a barred door, passed down a winding stair, and brought us to a white-washed corridor with a line of doors on each side.

'The third on the right is his,' said the inspector. 'Here it is!' He quietly shot back a panel in the upper part of the door, and glanced through.

'He is asleep,' said he. 'You can see him very well.'

We both put our eyes to the grating. The prisoner lay with his face towards us, in a very deep sleep, breathing slowly and heavily. He was a middle-sized man, coarsely clad as became his calling, with a coloured shirt protruding through the rent in his tattered coat. He was, as the inspector had said, extremely dirty, but the grime which covered his face could not conceal its repulsive ugliness. A broad weal from an old scar ran across it from eye to chin, and by its contraction had turned up one side of the upper lip, so that three teeth were exposed in a perpetual snarl. A shock of very bright red hair grew low over his eyes and forehead.

'He's a beauty, isn't he?' said the inspector.

'He certainly needs a wash,' remarked Holmes. 'I had an idea that he might, and I took the liberty of bringing the tools with me.' He opened his Gladstone bag as he spoke, and took out, to my astonishment, a very large bath sponge.

'He! he! You are a funny one,' chuckled the inspector.

'Now, if you will have the great goodness to open that door very quietly, we will soon make him cut a much more respectable figure.'

'Well, I don't know why not,' said the inspector. 'He doesn't look a credit to the Bow Street cells, does he?' He slipped his key into the lock, and we all very quietly entered the cell. The sleeper half turned, and then settled down once more into a deep slumber. Holmes stooped to the water jug, moistened his sponge, and then rubbed it twice vigorously across and down the prisoner's face.

'Let me introduce you,' he shouted, 'to Mr Neville St Clair, of Lee, in the county of Kent.'

Never in my life have I seen such a sight. The man's face peeled off under the sponge like the bark from a tree. Gone was the coarse brown tint! Gone, too, the horrid scar which had seamed it across, and the twisted lip which had given the repulsive sneer to the face! A twitch brought away the tangled red hair, and there, sitting up in his bed, was a pale, sad-faced, refined-looking man, black-haired and smooth-skinned, rubbing his eyes, and staring about him with sleepy bewilderment. Then suddenly realizing the exposure, he broke into a scream, and threw himself down with his face to the pillow.

'Great heaven!' cried the inspector, 'it is, indeed, the missing man. I know him from the photograph.'

The prisoner turned with the reckless air of a man who abandons himself to his destiny. 'Be it so,' said he. 'And pray what am I charged with?'

'With making away with Mr Neville St—Oh, come, you can't be charged with that, unless they make a case of attempted suicide of it,' said the inspector, with a grin. 'Well, I have been twenty-seven years in the Force, but this really takes the cake.'

'If I am Mr Neville St Clair, then it is obvious that no crime has been committed, and that, therefore, I am illegally detained.'

'No crime, but a very great error has been committed,' said Holmes. 'You would have done better to have trusted your wife.'

'It was not the wife, it was the children,' groaned the prisoner. 'God help me, I would not have them ashamed of their father. My God! What an exposure! What can I do?'

Sherlock Holmes sat down beside him on the couch, and patted him kindly on the shoulder.

'If you leave it to a court of law to clear the matter up,' said he, 'of course you can hardly avoid publicity. On the other hand, if you convince the police authorities that there is no possible case against you, I do not know that there is any reason that the details should find their way into the papers. Inspector Bradstreet would, I am sure, make notes upon anything which you might tell us, and submit it to the proper authorities. The case would then never go into court at all.'

'God bless you!' cried the prisoner passionately. 'I would have endured imprisonment, aye, even execution, rather than have left my miserable secret as a family blot to my children.

'You are the first who have ever heard my story. My father was a schoolmaster in Chesterfield,* where I received an excellent education. I travelled in my youth, took to the stage, and finally became a reporter on an evening paper in London. One day my editor wished to have a series of articles upon begging in the metropolis, and I volunteered to supply them. There was the point from which all my adventures started. It was only by trying begging as an amateur that I could get the facts upon which to base my articles. When an actor I had, of course, learned all the secrets of making up, and had been famous in the green-room* for my skill. I took advantage now of my attainments. I painted my face, and to make myself as pitiable as possible I made a good scar and fixed one side of my lip in a twist by the aid of a small slip of flesh-coloured plaster. Then with a red head of hair, and an appropriate dress, I took my station in the busiest part of the City, ostensibly as a match-seller, but really as a beggar. For seven hours I plied my trade, and when I returned home in the evening I found, to my surprise, that I had received no less than twenty-six shillings and fourpence.

'I wrote my articles, and thought little more of the matter until, some time later, I backed a bill* for a friend, and had a writ served upon me for £25. I was at my wits' end where to get the money, but a sudden idea came to me. I begged a fortnight's grace from the creditor, asked for a holiday from my employers, and spent the time in begging in the City under my disguise. In ten days I had the money, and had paid the debt.

'Well, you can imagine how hard it was to settle down to arduous work at two pounds a week, when I knew that I could earn as much in a day by smearing my face with a little paint, laying my cap on the ground, and sitting still. It was a long fight between my pride and the money, but the dollars* won at last, and I threw up reporting, and sat day after day in the corner which I had first chosen, inspiring pity by my ghastly face, and filling my pockets with coppers. Only one man knew my secret. He was the keeper of a low den in which I used to lodge in Swandam Lane, where I could every morning emerge as a squalid beggar and in the evening transform myself into a well-dressed man about town. This fellow, a Lascar, was well paid by me for his rooms, so that I knew that my secret was safe in his possession.

'Well, very soon I found that I was saving considerable sums of money. I do not mean that any beggar in the streets of London could earn seven hundred pounds a year—which is less than my average takings—but I had exceptional advantages in my power of making up, and also in a facility in repartee, which improved by practice, and made me quite a recognized character in the City. All day a stream of pennies, varied by silver, poured in upon me, and it was a very bad day upon which I failed to take two pounds.

'As I grew richer I grew more ambitious, took a house in the country, and eventually married, without anyone having a suspicion as to my real occupation. My dear wife knew that I had business in the City. She little knew what.

'Last Monday I had finished for the day, and was dressing in my room above the opium den, when I looked out of the window, and saw, to my horror and astonishment, that my wife was standing in the street, with her eyes fixed full upon me. I gave a cry of surprise, threw up my arms to cover my face, and rushing to my confidant, the Lascar, entreated him to prevent anyone from coming up to me. I heard her voice downstairs, but I knew that she could not ascend. Swiftly I threw off my clothes, pulled on those of a beggar, and put on my pigments and wig. Even a wife's eyes could not pierce so complete a disguise. But then it occurred to me that there might be a search in the room and that the clothes might betray me. I threw open the window, re-opening by my violence a small cut which I had inflicted upon myself in the bedroom that morning. Then I seized my coat, which was weighted by the coppers which I had just transferred to it from the leather bag in which I carried my takings. I hurled it out of the window, and it disappeared into the Thames. The other clothes would have followed, but at that moment there was a rush of constables up the stair, and a few minutes after I found, rather, I confess, to my relief, that instead of being identified as Mr Neville St Clair, I was arrested as his murderer.

'I do not know that there is anything else for me to explain. I was determined to preserve my disguise as long as possible, and hence my preference for a dirty face. Knowing that my wife would be terribly anxious, I slipped off my ring, and confided it to the Lascar at a moment when no constable was watching me, together with a hurried scrawl, telling her that she had no cause to fear.'

'That note only reached her yesterday,' said Holmes.

'Good God! What a week she must have spent.'

'The police have watched this Lascar,' said Inspector Bradstreet, 'and I can quite understand that he might find it difficult to post a letter unobserved. Probably he handed it to some sailor customer of his, who forgot all about it for some days.'

'That was it,' said Holmes, nodding approvingly, 'I have no doubt of it. But have you never been prosecuted for begging?'

'Many times; but what was a fine to me?'

'It must stop here, however,' said Bradstreet. 'If the police are to hush this thing up, there must be no more of Hugh Boone.'

'I have sworn it by the most solemn oaths which a man can take.'

'In that case I think that it is probable that no further steps may be taken. But if you are found again, then all must come out. I am sure, Mr Holmes, that we are very much indebted to you for having cleared the matter up. I wish I knew how you reach your results.'

'I reached this one,' said my friend, 'by sitting upon five pillows and consuming an ounce of shag. I think, Watson, that if we drive to Baker Street we shall just be in time for breakfast.'

The Blue Carbuncle

I HAD called upon my friend Sherlock Holmes upon the second morning after Christmas, with the intention of wishing him the compliments of the season. He was lounging upon the sofa in a purple dressing gown, a pipe-rack within his reach upon the right, and a pile of crumpled morning papers, evidently newly studied, near at hand. Beside the couch was a wooden chair, and on the angle of the back hung a very seedy and disreputable hard felt hat, much the worse for wear, and cracked in several places. A lens and a forceps lying upon the seat of the chair suggested that the hat had been suspended in this manner for the purpose of examination.

'You are engaged,' said I; 'perhaps I interrupt you.'

'Not at all. I am glad to have a friend with whom I can discuss my results. The matter is a perfectly trivial one' (he jerked his thumb in the direction of the old hat), 'but there are points in connection with it which are not entirely devoid of interest, and even of instruction.'

I seated myself in his armchair, and warmed my hands before his crackling fire, for a sharp frost had set in, and the windows were thick with the ice crystals. 'I suppose,' I remarked, 'that, homely as it looks, this thing has some deadly story linked on to it—that it is the clue which will guide you in the solution of some mystery, and the punishment of some crime.'

'No, no. No crime,' said Sherlock Holmes, laughing. 'Only one of those whimsical little incidents which will happen when you have four million human beings all jostling each other within the space of a few square miles.* Amid the action and reaction of so dense a swarm of humanity, every possible combination of events may be expected to take place, and many a little problem will be presented which may be striking and bizarre without being criminal. We have already had experience of such.'

'So much so,' I remarked, 'that, of the last six cases which I have added to my notes, three have been entirely free of any legal crime.'

'Precisely. You allude to my attempt to recover the Irene Adler papers, to the singular case of Miss Mary Sutherland, and to the adventure of the man with the twisted lip. Well, I have no doubt that this small matter will fall into the same innocent category. You know Peterson, the commissionaire?'*

'Yes.'

'It is to him that this trophy belongs.'

'It is his hat.'

'No, no; he found it. Its owner is unknown. I beg that you will look upon it, not as a battered billycock,* but as an intellectual problem. And, first, as to how it came here. It arrived upon Christmas morning, in company with a good fat goose, which is, I have no doubt, roasting at this moment in front of Peterson's fire. The facts are these. About four o'clock on Christmas morning, Peterson, who, as you know, is a very honest fellow, was returning from some small jollification, and was making his way homewards down Tottenham Court Road. In front of him he saw, in the gaslight, a tallish man, walking with a slight stagger, and carrying a white goose slung over his shoulder. As he reached the corner of Goodge Street a row broke out between this stranger and a little knot of roughs. One of the latter knocked off the man's hat, on which he raised his stick to defend himself, and, swinging it over his head, smashed the shop window behind him. Peterson had rushed forward to protect the stranger from his assailants, but the man, shocked at having broken the window, and seeing an official-looking person in uniform rushing towards him, dropped his goose, took to his heels and vanished amid the labyrinth of small streets which lie at the back of Tottenham Court Road. The roughs had also fled at the appearance of Peterson, so that he was left in possession of the field of battle, and also of the spoils of victory in the shape of this battered hat and a most unimpeachable Christmas goose.'

'Which surely he restored to their owner?'

'My dear fellow, there lies the problem. It is true that "For Mrs Henry Baker" was printed upon a small card which was tied to the bird's left leg, and it is also true that the initials "H. B."* are legible upon the lining of this hat; but, as there are some thousands of Bakers, and some hundreds of Henry Bakers in this city of ours,* it is not easy to restore lost property to any one of them.'

'What, then, did Peterson do?'

'He brought round both hat and goose to me on Christmas morning, knowing that even the smallest problems are of interest to me. The goose we retained until this morning, when there were signs that, in spite of the slight frost, it would be well that it should be eaten without unnecessary delay. Its finder has carried it off, therefore, to fulfil the ultimate destiny of a goose, while I continue to retain the hat of the unknown gentleman who lost his Christmas dinner.'

'Did he not advertise?'

'No.'

'Then, what clue could you have as to his identity?'

'Only as much as we can deduce.'

'From his hat?'

'Precisely.'

'But you are joking. What can you gather from this old battered felt?'

'Here is my lens. You know my methods. What can you gather yourself as to the individuality of the man who has worn this article?'

I took the tattered object in my hands, and turned it over rather ruefully. It was a very ordinary black hat of the usual round shape, hard and much the worse for wear. The lining had been of red silk, but was a good deal discoloured. There was no maker's name; but, as Holmes had remarked, the initials 'H. B.' were scrawled upon one side. It was pierced in the brim for a hat-securer, but the elastic was missing. For the rest, it was cracked, exceedingly dusty, and spotted in several places, although there seemed to have been some attempt to hide the discoloured patches by smearing them with ink.

'I can see nothing,' said I, handing it back to my friend.

'On the contrary, Watson, you can see everything. You fail, however, to reason from what you see. You are too timid in drawing your inferences.'

'Then, pray tell me what it is that you can infer from this hat?'

He picked it up, and gazed at it in the peculiar introspective fashion which was characteristic of him. 'It is perhaps less suggestive than it might have been,' he remarked, 'and yet there are a few inferences which are very distinct, and a few others which represent at least a strong balance of probability. That the man was highly intellectual is of course obvious upon the face of it, and also that he was fairly well-to-do within the last three years, although he has now fallen upon evil days. He had foresight, but has less now than formerly, pointing to a moral retrogression, which, when taken with the decline of his fortunes, seems to indicate some evil influence, probably drink, at work upon him. This may account also for the obvious fact that his wife has ceased to love him.'

'My dear Holmes!'

'He has, however, retained some degree of self-respect,' he continued, disregarding my remonstrance. 'He is a man who leads a sedentary life, goes out little, is out of training entirely, is middle-aged, has grizzled hair which he has had cut within the last few days, and which he anoints with lime-cream. These are the more patent facts which are to be deduced from his hat. Also, by the way, that it is extremely improbable that he has gas laid on his house.'

'You are certainly joking, Holmes.'

'Not in the least. Is it possible that even now when I give you these results you are unable to see how they are attained?'

'I have no doubt that I am very stupid; but I must confess that I am unable to follow you. For example, how did you deduce that this man was intellectual?'

For answer Holmes clapped the hat upon his head. It came right over the forehead and settled upon the bridge of his nose. 'It is a question of cubic capacity,' said he: 'a man with so large a brain must have something in it.'

'The decline of his fortunes, then?'

'This hat is three years old. These flat brims curled at the edge came in then. It is a hat of the very best quality. Look at the band of ribbed silk, and the excellent lining. If this man could afford to buy so expensive a hat three years ago, and has had no hat since, then he has assuredly gone down in the world.'

'Well, that is clear enough, certainly. But how about the foresight, and the moral retrogression?'

Sherlock Holmes laughed. 'Here is the foresight,' said he, putting his finger upon the little disc and loop of the hat-securer. 'They are never sold upon hats. If this man ordered one, it is a sign of a certain amount of foresight, since he went out of his way to take this precaution against the wind. But since we see that he has broken the elastic, and has not troubled to replace it, it is obvious that he has less foresight now than formerly, which is a distinct proof of a weakening nature. On the other hand, he has endeavoured to conceal some of these stains upon the felt by daubing them with ink, which is a sign that he has not entirely lost his self-respect.'

'Your reasoning is certainly plausible.'

'The further points, that he is middle-aged, that his hair is grizzled, that it has been recently cut, and that he uses lime-cream, are all to be gathered from a close examination of the lower part of the lining. The lens discloses a large number of hair ends, clean cut by the scissors of the barber. They all appear to be adhesive, and there is a distinct odour of lime-cream. This dust, you will observe, is not the gritty, grey dust of the street, but the fluffy brown dust of the house, showing that it has been hung up indoors most of the time; while the marks of moisture upon the inside are proof positive that the wearer perspired very freely, and could, therefore, hardly be in the best of training.'

'But his wife—you said that she had ceased to love him.'

'This hat has not been brushed for weeks. When I see you, my dear Watson, with a week's accumulation of dust upon your hat, and when your wife allows you to go out in such a state, I shall fear that you also have been unfortunate enough to lose your wife's affection.'

'But he might be a bachelor.'

'Nay, he was bringing home the goose as a peace-offering to his wife. Remember the card upon the bird's leg.'

'You have an answer to everything. But how on earth do you deduce that the gas is not laid on in the house?'

'One tallow stain, or even two, might come by chance; but, when I see no less than five, I think that there can be little doubt that the individual must be brought into frequent contact with burning tallow—walks upstairs at night probably with his hat in one hand and a guttering candle in the other. Anyhow, he never got tallow stains from a gas jet. Are you satisfied?'

'Well, it is very ingenious,' said I, laughing; 'but since, as you said just now, there has been no crime committed, and no harm done save the loss of a goose, all this seems to be rather a waste of energy.'

Sherlock Holmes had opened his mouth to reply, when the door flew open, and Peterson the commissionaire rushed into the apartment with flushed cheeks and the face of a man who is dazed with astonishment.

'The goose, Mr Holmes! The goose, sir!' he gasped.

'Eh! What of it, then? Has it returned to life, and flapped off through the kitchen window?' Holmes twisted himself round upon the sofa to get a fairer view of the man's excited face.

'See here, sir! See what my wife found in its crop!'* He held out his hand, and displayed upon the centre of the palm a brilliantly scintillating blue stone, rather smaller than a bean in size, but of such purity and radiance that it twinkled like an electric point in the dark hollow of his hand.

Sherlock Holmes sat up with a whistle. 'By Jove, Peterson, said he, 'this is treasure-trove indeed! I suppose you know what you have got?'

'A diamond, sir! A precious stone! It cuts into glass as though it were putty.'

'It's more than a precious stone. It's *the* precious stone.'

'Not the Countess of Morcar's blue carbuncle?'* I ejaculated.

'Precisely so. I ought to know its size and shape, seeing that I have read the advertisement about it in *The Times* every day lately. It is absolutely unique,* and its value can only be conjectured, but the reward offered of a thousand pounds is certainly not within a twentieth part of the market price.'*

'A thousand pounds! Great Lord of mercy!' The commissionaire plumped down into a chair, and stared from one to the other of us.

'That is the reward, and I have reason to know that there are sentimental considerations in the background which would induce the Countess to part with half of her fortune if she could but recover the gem.'

'It was lost, if I remember aright, at the Hotel Cosmopolitan,'* I remarked.

'Precisely so, on the 22nd of December, just five days ago. John Horner,* a plumber, was accused of having abstracted it from the lady's jewel-case. The evidence against him was so strong that the case has been referred to the Assizes.* I have some account of the matter here, I believe.' He rummaged amid his newspapers, glancing over the dates, until at last he smoothed one out, doubled it over, and read the following paragraph:

' "Hotel Cosmopolitan Jewel Robbery. John Horner, 26, plumber, was brought up upon the charge of having upon the 22nd inst., abstracted from the jewel-case of the Countess of Morcar the valuable gem known as the blue carbuncle. James Ryder,* upper-attendant* at the hotel, gave his evidence to the effect that he had shown Horner up to the dressing-room of the Countess of Morcar upon the day of the robbery, in order that he might solder the second bar of the grate,* which was loose. He had remained with Horner some little time but had finally been called away. On returning, he found that Horner had disappeared, that the bureau had been forced open, and that the small morocco casket* in which, as it afterwards transpired, the Countess was accustomed to keep her jewel, was lying empty upon the dressing-table. Ryder instantly gave the alarm, and Horner was arrested the same evening; but the stone could not be found either upon his person or in his rooms. Catherine Cusack, maid to the Countess, deposed to having heard Ryder's cry of dismay on discovering the robbery, and to having rushed into the room, where she found matters were as described by the last witness. Inspector Bradstreet, B Division,* gave evidence as to the arrest of Horner, who struggled frantically, and protested his innocence in the strongest terms. Evidence of a previous conviction for robbery having been given against the prisoner, the magistrate refused to deal summarily with the offence, but referred it to the Assizes. Horner, who had shown signs of intense emotion during the proceedings, fainted away at the conclusion, and was carried out of court."

'Hum! So much for the police-court,' said Holmes thoughtfully, tossing aside his paper. 'The question for us now to solve is the sequence of events from a rifled jewel-case at one end to the crop of a goose in Tottenham Court Road at the other. You see, Watson, our little deductions have suddenly assumed a much more important and less innocent aspect. Here is the stone; the stone came from the goose, and the goose came from Mr Henry Baker, the gentleman with the bad hat and all the other characteristics with which I have bored you. So now we must set ourselves very seriously to finding this gentleman, and ascertaining what part he has played in this little mystery. To do this, we must try the simplest means first, and these lie undoubtedly in an advertisement in all the evening papers. If this fail, I shall have recourse to other methods.'

'What will you say?'

'Give me a pencil, and that slip of paper. Now, then: "Found at the corner of Goodge Street, a goose and a black felt hat. Mr Henry Baker can have the same by applying at 6.30 this evening at 221 B Baker Street." That is clear and concise.'

'Very. But will he see it?'

'Well, he is sure to keep an eye on the papers, since, to a poor man, the loss was a heavy one. He was clearly so scared by his mischance in breaking the window, and by the approach of Peterson, that he thought of nothing but flight; but since then he must have bitterly regretted the impulse which caused him to drop his bird. Then, again, the introduction of his name will cause him to see it, for every one who knows him will direct his attention to it. Here you are, Peterson, run down to the advertising agency,* and have this put in the evening papers.'

'In which, sir?'

'Oh, in the *Globe, Star, Pall Mall, St James's Gazette, Evening News, Standard, Echo,** and any others that occur to you.'*

'Very well, sir. And this stone?'

'Ah, yes. I shall keep the stone. Thank you. And, I say, Peterson, just buy a goose on your way back, and leave it here with me, for we must have one to give to this gentleman in place of the one which your family is now devouring.'

When the commissionaire had gone, Holmes took up the stone and held it against the light. 'It's a bonny thing,' said he. 'Just see how it glints and sparkles. Of course it is a nucleus and focus of crime. Every good stone is. They are the devil's pet baits. In the larger and older jewels every facet may stand for a bloody deed. This stone is not yet twenty years old. It was found in the banks of the Amoy River in Southern China,* and is remarkable in having every characteristic of the carbuncle, save that it is blue in shade, instead of ruby red. In spite of its youth, it has already a sinister history. There have been two murders, a vitriol-throwing,* a suicide, and several robberies brought about for the sake of this forty-grain weight* of crystallized charcoal.* Who would think that so pretty a toy would be a purveyor to the gallows and the prison?* I'll lock it up in my strong-box, now, and drop a line to the Countess to say that we have it.'

'Do you think this man Horner is innocent?'

'I cannot tell.'

'Well, then, do you imagine that this other one, Henry Baker, had anything to do with the matter?'

'It is, I think, much more likely that Henry Baker is an absolutely innocent man, who had no idea that the bird which he was carrying was of considerably more value than if it were made of solid gold. That, however, I shall determine by a very simple test, if we have an answer to our advertisement.'

'And you can do nothing until then?'

'Nothing.'

'In that case I shall continue my professional round. But I shall come back in the evening at the hour you have mentioned, for I should like to see the solution of so tangled a business.'

'Very glad to see you. I dine at seven. There is a woodcock,* I believe. By the way, in view of recent occurrences, perhaps I ought to ask Mrs Hudson to examine its crop.'

I had been delayed at a case, and it was a little after half-past six when I found myself in Baker Street once more. As I approached the house I saw a tall man in a Scotch bonnet,* with a coat which was buttoned up to his chin, waiting outside in the bright semicircle which was thrown from the fanlight. Just as I arrived, the door was opened, and we were shown up together to Holmes's room.

'Mr Henry Baker, I believe,' said he, rising from his armchair, and greeting his visitor with the easy air of geniality which he could so readily assume. 'Pray take this chair by the fire, Mr Baker. It is a cold night, and I observe that your circulation* is more adapted for summer than for winter. Ah, Watson, you have just come at the right time. Is that your hat, Mr Baker?'

'Yes, sir, that is undoubtedly my hat.'

He was a large man, with rounded shoulders, a massive head, and a broad, intelligent face, sloping down to a pointed beard of grizzled brown. A touch of red in nose and cheeks, with a slight tremor of his extended hand, recalled Holmes's surmise as to his habits. His rusty black frock-coat was buttoned right up in front, with the collar turned up, and his lank wrists protruded from his sleeves without a sign of cuff or shirt. He spoke in a low staccato fashion, choosing his words with care, and gave the impression generally of a man of learning and letters who had had ill-usage at the hands of fortune.

'We have retained these things for some days,' said Holmes, 'because we expected to see an advertisement from you giving your address. I am at a loss to know now why you did not advertise.'

Our visitor gave a rather shame-faced laugh. 'Shillings have not been so plentiful with me as they once were,' he remarked. 'I had no doubt that the gang of roughs who assaulted me had carried off both my hat and the bird. I did not care to spend more money in a hopeless attempt at recovering them.'

'Very naturally. By the way, about the bird—we were compelled to eat it.'

'To eat it!' Our visitor half rose from his chair in his excitement.

'Yes; it would have been no use to anyone had we not done so. But I presume that this other goose upon the side-board, which is about the same weight and perfectly fresh, will answer your purpose equally well?'

'Oh, certainly, certainly!' answered Mr Baker, with a sigh of relief.

'Of course, we still have the feathers, legs, crop, and so on of your own bird, if you so wish—'

The man burst into a hearty laugh. 'They might be useful to me as relics of my adventure,' said he, 'but beyond that I can hardly see what use the *disjecta membra** of my late acquaintance are going to be to me. No, sir, I think that, with your permission, I will confine my attentions to the excellent bird which I perceive upon the sideboard.'

Sherlock Holmes glanced sharply across at me with a slight shrug of his shoulders.

'There is your hat, then, and there your bird,' said he. 'By the way, would it bore you to tell me where you got the other one from? I am somewhat of a fowl fancier, and I have seldom seen a better-grown goose.'

'Certainly, sir,' said Baker, who had risen and tucked his newly-gained property under his arm. 'There are a few of us who frequent the "Alpha" Inn near the Museum*—we are to be found in the Museum itself during the day, you understand. This year our good host, Windigate* by name, instituted a goose-club, by which, on consideration of some few pence every week, we were each to receive a bird at Christmas. My pence were duly paid, and the rest is familiar to you. I am much indebted to you, sir, for a Scotch bonnet is fitted neither to my years nor my gravity.' With a comical pomposity of manner he bowed solemnly to both of us, and strode off upon his way.

'So much for Mr Henry Baker,' said Holmes, when he had closed the door behind him. 'It is quite certain that he knows nothing whatever about the matter. Are you hungry, Watson?'

'Not particularly.'

'Then I suggest that we turn our dinner into a supper, and follow up this clue while it is still hot.'

'By all means.'

It was a bitter night, so we drew on our ulsters and wrapped cravats about our throats. Outside, the stars were shining coldly in a cloudless sky, and the breath of the passers-by blew out into smoke like so many pistol shots. Our footfalls rang out crisply and loudly as we swung through the doctors' quarter, Wimpole Street, Harley Street, and so through Wigmore Street* into Oxford Street. In a quarter of an hour we were in Bloomsbury at the "Alpha" Inn, which is a small public-house at the corner of one of the streets which run down into Holborn. Holmes pushed open the door of the private bar, and ordered two glasses of beer from the ruddy-faced, white-aproned landlord.

'Your beer should be excellent if it is as good as your geese,' he said.

'My geese!' The man seemed surprised.

'Yes. I was speaking only half an hour ago to Mr Henry Baker, who was a member of your goose-club.'

'Ah! yes, I see. But you see, sir, them's not *our* geese.'

'Indeed! Whose, then?'

'Well, I got the two dozen from a salesman in Covent Garden.'

'Indeed! I know some of them. Which was it?'

'Breckinridge* is his name.'

'Ah! I don't know him. Well, here's your good health, landlord, and prosperity to your house. Good-night!

'Now for Mr Breckinridge,' he continued, buttoning up his coat, as we came out into the frosty air. 'Remember, Watson, that though we have so homely a thing as a goose at one end of this chain, we have at the other a man who will certainly get seven years' penal servitude, unless we can establish his innocence. It is possible that our inquiry may but confirm his guilt; but, in any case, we have a line of investigation which has been missed by the police, and which a singular chance has placed in our hands. Let us follow it out to the bitter end. Faces to the south, then, and quick march!'

We passed across Holborn, down Endell Street,* and so through a zigzag of slums of Covent Garden Market.* One of the largest stalls bore the name of Breckinridge upon it, and the proprietor, a horsey-looking man with a sharp face and trim side-whiskers, was helping a boy to put up the shutters.

'Good evening, it's a cold night,' said Holmes.

The salesman nodded, and shot a questioning glance at my companion.

'Sold out of geese, I see,' continued Holmes, pointing at the bare slabs of marble.

'Let you have five hundred to-morrow morning.'

'That's no good.'

'Well, there are some on the stall with the gas flare.'

'Oh, but I was recommended to you.'

'Who by?'

'The landlord of the "Alpha".'

'Ah, yes; I sent him a couple of dozen.'

'Fine birds they were, too. Now where did you get them from?'

To my surprise the question provoked a burst of anger from the salesman.

'Now then, mister,' said he, with his head cocked and his arms akimbo, 'what are you driving at? Let's have it straight, now.'

'It is straight enough. I should like to know who sold you the geese which you supplied to the "Alpha".'

'Well, then, I shan't tell you. So now!'

'Oh, it is a matter of no importance; but I don't know why you should be so warm over such a trifle.'

'Warm! You'd be as warm, maybe, if you were pestered as I am. When I pay good money for a good article there should be an end of the business; but it's "Where are the geese?" and "Who did you sell the geese to?" and "What will you take for the geese?" One would think they were the only geese in the world, to hear the fuss that is made over them.'

'Well, I have no connection with any other people who have been making inquiries,' said Holmes carelessly. 'If you won't tell us the bet is off, that is all. But I'm always ready to back my opinion on a matter of fowls, and I have a fiver on it that the bird I ate is country bred.'

'Well, then, you've lost your fiver, for it's town bred,' snapped the salesman.

'It's nothing of the kind.'

'I say it is.'

'I don't believe you.'

'D'you think you know more about fowls than I, who have handled them ever since I was a nipper? I tell you, all those birds that went to the "Alpha" were town bred.'

'You'll never persuade me to believe that.'

'Will you bet, then?'

'It's merely taking your money, for I know that I am right. But I'll have a sovereign on with you, just to teach you not to be obstinate.'

The salesman chuckled grimly. 'Bring me the books, Bill,' said he.

The small boy brought round a small thin volume and a great greasy-backed one, laying them out together beneath the hanging lamp.

'Now then, Mr Cocksure,' said the salesman, 'I thought that I was out of geese, but before I finish you'll find that there is still one left in my shop. You see this little book?'

'Well?'

'That's the list of the folk from whom I buy. D'you see? Well, then, here on this page are the country folk, and the numbers after their names are where their accounts are in the big ledger. Now, then! You see this other page in red ink? Well, that is a list of my town suppliers. Now, look at that third name, Just read it out to me.'

'Mrs Oakshott,* 117, Brixton Road*—249,' read Holmes.

'Quite so. Now turn that up in the ledger.'

Holmes turned to the page indicated. 'Here you are, "Mrs Oakshott, 117, Brixton Road, egg and poultry supplier." '

'Now, then, what's the last entry?'

' "December 22. Twenty-four geese at 7s 6d." '

'Quite so. There you are. And underneath?'

' "Sold to Mr Windigate of the 'Alpha' at 12s." '

'What have you say now?'

Sherlock Holmes looked deeply chagrined. He drew a sovereign from his pocket and threw it down upon the slab, turning away with the air of a man whose disgust is too deep for words. A few yards off he stopped under a lamp-post, and laughed in the hearty, noiseless fashion which was peculiar to him.

'When you see a man with whiskers of that cut and the "*Pink 'Un*"* protruding out of his pocket, you can always draw him by a bet,' said he. 'I dare say that if I had put a hundred pounds down in front of him that man would not have given me such complete information as was drawn from him by the idea that he was doing me on a wager. Well, Watson, we are, I fancy, nearing the end of our quest, and the only point which remains to be determined is whether we should go on to this Mrs Oakshott tonight, or whether we should reserve it for to-morrow. It is clear from what that surly fellow said that there are others besides ourselves who are anxious about the matter, and I should—'

His remarks were suddenly cut short by a loud hubbub which broke out from the stall which we had just left. Turning round we saw a little rat-faced fellow, standing in the centre of the circle of yellow light which was thrown by the swinging lamp, while Breckinridge the salesman, framed in the door of his stall, was shaking his fists fiercely at the cringing figure.

'I've had enough of you and your geese,' he shouted. 'I wish you were all at the devil together. If you come pestering me any more with your silly talk I'll set the dog at you. You bring Mrs Oakshott here and I'll answer her, but what have you to do with it? Did I buy the geese off you?'

'No: but one of them was mine all the same,' whined the little man.

'Well, then, ask Mrs Oakshott for it.'

'She told me to ask you.'

'Well, you can ask the King of Proosia,* for all I care. I've had enough of it. Get out of this!' He rushed fiercely forward, and the inquirer flitted away into the darkness.

'Ha, this may save us a visit to Brixton Road,' whispered Holmes. 'Come with me, and we will see what is to be made of this fellow.' Striding through the scattered knots of people who lounged round the flaring stalls, my companion speedily overtook the little man and touched him upon the shoulder. He sprang round, and I could see in the gaslight that every vestige of colour had been driven from his face.

'Who are you, then? What do you want?' he asked in a quavering voice.

'You will excuse me,' said Holmes, blandly, 'but I could not help overhearing the questions which you put to the salesman just now. I think that I could be of assistance to you.' .

'You? Who are you? How could you know anything of the matter?'

'My name is Sherlock Holmes. It is my business to know what other people don't know.'*

'But you can know nothing of this?'

'Excuse me, I know everything of it. You are endeavouring to trace some geese which were sold by Mrs Oakshott,
of Brixton Road, to a salesman named Breckinridge, by him
in turn to Mr Windigate, of the "Alpha", and by him to his
club, of which Mr Henry Baker is a member.'

'Oh, sir, you are the very man whom I have longed to
meet,' cried the little fellow, with outstreched hands and
quivering fingers. 'I can hardly explain to you how interested I am in this matter.'

Sherlock Holmes hailed a four-wheeler* which was passing. 'In that case we had better discuss it in a cosy room
rather than in this windswept market-place,' said he. 'But
pray tell me, before we go further, who it is that I have the
pleasure of assisting.'

The man hesitated for an instant. 'My name is John
Robinson,'* he answered, with a sidelong glance.

'No, no; the real name,' said Holmes sweetly. 'It is always
awkward doing business with an *alias*.'

A flush sprang to the white cheeks of the stranger. 'Well,
then,' said he, 'my real name is James Ryder.'

'Precisely so. Head attendant at the Hotel Cosmopolitan.
Pray step into the cab, and I shall soon be able to tell you
everything which you would wish to know.'

The little man stood glancing from one to the other of us
with half-frightened, half-hopeful eyes, as one who is not
sure whether he is on the verge of a windfall or of a
catastrophe. Then he stepped into the cab, and in half an
hour we were back in the sitting-room at Baker Street.
Nothing had been said during our drive, but the high, thin
breathing of our new companion, and the claspings and
unclaspings of his hands, spoke of the nervous tension within
him.

'Here we are!' said Holmes cheerily, as we filed into the
room. 'The fire looks very seasonable in this weather. You
look cold, Mr Ryder. Pray take the basket chair.* I will just
put on my slippers before we settle this little matter of yours.
Now, then! You want to know what became of those geese?'

'Yes, sir.'

'Or rather, I fancy, of that goose. It was one bird, I imagine, in which you were interested—white, with a black bar across the tail.'

Ryder quivered with emotion. 'Oh, sir,' he cried, 'can you tell me where it went to?'

'It came here.'

'Here?'

'Yes, and a most remarkable bird it proved. I don't wonder that you should take an interest in it. It laid an egg after it was dead—the bonniest, brightest little blue egg that was ever seen. I have it here in my museum.'

Our visitor staggered to his feet, and clutched the mantelpiece with his right hand. Holmes unlocked his strong-box, and held up the blue carbuncle, which shone out like a star, with a cold, brilliant, many-pointed radiance. Ryder stood glaring with a drawn face, uncertain whether to claim or to disown it.

'The game's up, Ryder,' said Holmes quietly. 'Hold up, man, or you'll be into the fire. Give him an arm back into his chair, Watson. He's not got blood enough to go in for felony with impunity. Give him a dash of brandy. So! Now he looks a little more human. What a shrimp it is, to be sure!'

For a moment he had staggered and nearly fallen, but the brandy brought a tinge of colour into his cheeks, and he sat staring with frightened eyes at his accuser.

'I have almost every link in my hands, and all the proofs which I could possibly need, so there is little which you need tell me. Still, that little may as well be cleared up to make the case complete. You had heard, Ryder, of this blue stone of the Countess of Morcar's?'

'It was Catherine Cusack who told me of it,' said he, in a crackling voice.

'I see. Her ladyship's waiting-maid. Well the temptation of sudden wealth so easily acquired was too much for you, as it has been for better men before you; but you were not very scrupulous in the means you used. It seems to me, Ryder, that there is the making of a very pretty villain in you. You knew that this man Horner, the plumber, had been concerned in some such matter before, and that suspicion would rest the more readily upon him. What did you do, then? You made some small job in my lady's room—you and your confederate Cusack—and you managed that he should be the man sent for. Then, when he had left, you rifled the jewel-case, raised the alarm, and had this unfortunate man arrested. You then—'

Ryder threw himself down suddenly upon the rug, and clutched at my companion's knees. 'For God's sake, have mercy!' he shrieked. 'Think of my father! Of my mother! It would break their hearts. I never went wrong before! I never will again. I swear it. I'll swear it on a Bible. Oh, don't bring it into court! For Christ's sake, don't!'

'Get back into your chair! said Holmes sternly. 'It is very well to cringe and crawl now, but you thought little enough of this poor Horner in the dock for a crime of which he knew nothing.'

'I will fly, Mr Holmes. I will leave the country, sir. Then the charge against him will break down.'

'Hum! We will talk about that. And now let us hear a true account of the next act. How came the stone into the goose, and how came the goose into the open market? Tell us the truth, for there lies your only hope of safety.'

Ryder passed his tongue over his parched lips. 'I will tell you it just as it happened, sir,' said he. 'When Horner had been arrested, it seemed to me that it would be best for me to get away with the stone at once, for I did not know at what moment the police might not take it into their heads to search me and my room. There was no place about the hotel where it would be safe. I went out, as if on some commission, and I made for my sister's house. She had married a man named Oakshott, and lived in Brixton Road, where she fattened fowls for the market. All the way there every man I met seemed to me to be a policeman or a detective, and for all that it was a cold night, the sweat was pouring down my face before I came to the Brixton Road. My sister asked me what was the matter, and why I was so pale; but I told her that I had been upset by the jewel robbery at the hotel. Then I went into the back-yard, and smoked a pipe, and wondered what it would be best to do.

'I had a friend once called Maudsley,* who went to the bad, and has just been serving his time in Pentonville.* One day he had met me, and fell into talk about the ways of thieves and how they could get rid of what they stole. I knew that he would be true to me, for I knew one or two things about him, so I made up my mind to go right on to Kilburn,* where he lived and take him into my confidence. He would show me how to turn the stone into money. But how to get to him in safety? I thought of the agonies I had gone through in coming from the hotel. I might at any moment be seized and searched, and there would be the stone in my waistcoat pocket. I was leaning against the wall at the time, and looking at the geese which were waddling about round my feet, and suddenly an idea came into my head which showed me how I could beat the best detective that ever lived.

'My sister had told me some weeks before that I might have the pick of her geese for a Christmas present, and I knew that she was always as good as her word. I would take my goose now, and in it I would carry my stone to Kilburn. There was a little shed in the yard, and behind this I drove one of the birds, a fine big one, white, with a barred tail.* I caught it, and, prising its bill open, I thrust the stone down its throat as far as my finger could reach. The bird gave a gulp, and I felt the stone pass along its gullet and down into its crop. But the creature flapped and struggled, and out came my sister to know what was the matter. As I turned to speak to her the brute broke loose, and fluttered off among the others.

' "Whatever were you doing with that bird, Jem?" says she.

' "Well," said I, "you said you'd give me one for Christmas, and I was feeling which was the fattest."

' "Oh," says she, "we've set yours aside for you. Jem's bird, we call it. It's the big, white one over yonder. There's twenty-six of them, which makes one for you, and one for us, and two dozen for the market."

' "Thank you, Maggie," says I; "but if it is all the same to you I'd rather have that one I was handling just now."

' "The other is a good three pound heavier," she said, "and we fattened it expressly for you."

' "Never mind. I'll have the other, and I'll take it now," said I.

' "Oh, just as you like," said she, a little huffed. "Which is it you want, then?"

' "That white one, with the barred tail, right in the middle of the flock."

' "Oh, very well. Kill it and take it with you."

'Well, I did what she said, Mr Holmes, and I carried the bird all the way to Kilburn. I told my pal what I had done, for he was a man that it was easy to tell a thing like that to. He laughed until he choked, and we got a knife and opened the goose. My heart turned to water, for there was no sign of the stone, and I knew that some terrible mistake had occurred. I left the bird, rushed back to my sister's, and hurried into the back yard. There was not a bird to be seen there.

' "Where are they all, Maggie?" I cried.

' "Gone to the dealer's."

' "Which dealer's?"

' "Breckinridge, of Covent Garden."

' "But was there another with a barred tail?" I asked, "the same as the one I chose?"

' "Yes, Jem, there were two barred-tailed ones, and I could never tell them apart.'

'Well, then, of course, I saw it all, and I ran off as hard as my feet would carry me to this man Breckinridge; but he had sold the lot at once, and not one word would he tell me as to where they had gone. You heard him yourselves to-night. Well, he has always answered me like that. My sister thinks that I am going mad. Sometimes I think that I am myself. And now—now I am myself a branded thief, without ever having touched the wealth for which I sold my character.

God help me! God help me!' He burst into convulsive sobbing, with his face buried in his hands.

There was a long silence, broken only by his heavy breathing, and by the measured tapping of Sherlock Holmes's finger-tips upon the edge of the table. Then my friend rose, and threw open the door.

'Get out!' said he.

'What, sir! Oh, heaven bless you!'

'No more words. Get out!'

And no more words were needed. There was a rush, a clatter upon the stairs, the bang of a door, and the crisp rattle of running footfalls from the street.

'After all, Watson,' said Holmes, reaching up his hand for his clay pipe, 'I am not retained by the police to supply their deficiencies. If Horner were in danger it would be another thing, but this fellow will not appear against him, and the case must collapse. I suppose that I am commuting a felony,* but it is just possible that I am saving a soul.* This fellow will not go wrong again. He is too terribly frightened. Send him to gaol now, and you make him a gaol-bird for life. Besides, it is the season of forgiveness. Chance has put in our way a most singular and whimsical problem, and its solution is its own reward. If you will have the goodness to touch the bell, Doctor, we will begin another investigation, in which also a bird will be the chief feature.'

The Speckled Band

IN glancing over my notes of the seventy odd cases in which I have during the last eight years studied the methods of my friend Sherlock Holmes, I find many tragic, some comic, a large number merely strange, but none commonplace; for, working as he did rather for the love of his art than for the acquirement of wealth, he refused to associate himself with any investigation which did not tend towards the unusual, and even the fantastic. Of all these varied cases, however, I cannot recall any which presented more singular features than that which was associated with the well-known Surrey family of the Roylotts of Stoke Moran.* The events in question occurred in the early days of my association with Holmes, when we were sharing rooms as bachelors, in Baker Street. It is possible that I might have placed them upon record before, but a promise of secrecy was made at the time, from which I have only been freed during the last month by the untimely death of the lady to whom the pledge was given. It is perhaps as well that the facts should now come to light, for I have reasons to know there are widespread rumours as to the death of Dr Grimesby Roylott* which tend to make the matter even more terrible than the truth.

It was early in April, in the year '83, that I woke one morning to find Sherlock Holmes standing, fully dressed, by the side of my bed. He was a late riser as a rule, and, as the clock on the mantelpiece showed me that it was only a quarter past seven, I blinked up at him in some surprise, and perhaps just a little resentment, for I was myself regular in my habits.

'Very sorry to knock you up, Watson,' said he, 'but it's the common lot this morning. Mrs Hudson has been knocked up, she retorted upon me, and I on you.'

'What is it, then? A fire?'

'No, a client. It seems that a young lady has arrived in a considerable state of excitement, who insists upon seeing me. She is waiting now in the sitting-room. Now, when young ladies wander about the metropolis at this hour of the morning, and knock sleepy people up out of their beds, I presume that it is something very pressing which they have to communicate. Should it prove to be an interesting case, you would, I am sure, wish to follow it from the outset. I thought at any rate that I should call you, and give you the chance.'

'My dear fellow, I would not miss it for anything.'

I had no keener pleasure than in following Holmes in his professional investigations, and in admiring the rapid deductions, as swift as intuitions, and yet always founded on a logical basis, with which he unravelled the problems which were submitted to him. I rapidly threw on my clothes, and was ready in a few minutes to accompany my friend down to the sitting-room. A lady dressed in black and heavily veiled, who had been sitting in the window, rose as we entered.

'Good morning, madam,' said Holmes, cheerily. 'My name is Sherlock Holmes. This is my intimate friend and associate, Dr Watson, before whom you can speak as freely as before myself. Ha, I am glad to see that Mrs Hudson has had the good sense to light the fire. Pray draw up to it, and I shall order you a cup of hot coffee, for I observe that you are shivering.'

'It is not cold which makes me shiver,' said the woman in a low voice, changing her seat as requested.

'What then?'

'It is fear, Mr Holmes. It is terror.' She raised her veil as she spoke, and we could see that she was indeed in a pitiable state of agitation, her face all drawn and grey, with restless, frightened eyes, like those of some hunted animal. Her features and figure were those of a woman of thirty, but her hair was shot with premature grey, and her expression was weary and haggard. Sherlock Holmes ran her over with one of his quick, all-comprehensive glances.

'You must not fear,' said he, soothingly, bending forward and patting her forearm. 'We shall soon set matters right, I have no doubt. You have come in by train this morning, I see.'

'You know me, then?'

'No, but I observe the second half of a return ticket in the palm of your left glove. You must have started early and yet you had a good drive in a dog-cart,* along heavy roads, before you reached the station.'

The lady gave a violent start, and stared in bewilderment at my companion.

'There is no mystery, my dear madam,' said he, smiling. 'The left arm of your jacket is spattered with mud in no less than seven places. The marks are perfectly fresh. There is no vehicle save a dog-cart which throws up mud in that way, and then only when you sit on the left-hand side of the driver.'

'Whatever your reasons may be, you are perfectly correct,' said she. 'I started from home before six, reached Leatherhead* at twenty past, and came in by the first train to Waterloo. Sir, I can stand this strain no longer, I shall go mad if it continues. I have no one to turn to—none, save only one, who cares for me, and he, poor fellow, can be of little aid. I have heard of you, Mr Holmes; I have heard of you from Mrs Farintosh,* whom you helped in the hour of her sore need. It was from her that I had your address. Oh, sir, do you not think you could help me too, and at least throw a little light through the dense darkness which surrounds me? At present it is out of my power to reward you for your services, but in a month or two I shall be married, with the control of my own income, and then at least you shall not find me ungrateful.'

Holmes turned to his desk, and unlocking it, drew out a small case-book which he consulted.

'Farintosh,' said he. 'Ah, yes, I recall the case; it was concerned with an opal tiara. I think it was before your time, Watson. I can only say, madam, that I shall be happy to devote the same care to your case as I did to that of your friend. As to reward, my profession is its reward; but you are at liberty to defray whatever expenses I may be put to, at the time which suits you best. And now I beg that you will lay before us everything that may help us in forming an opinion upon the matter.'

'Alas!' replied our visitor. 'The very horror of my situation lies in the fact that my fears are so vague, and my suspicions depend so entirely upon small points, which might seem trivial to another, that even he to whom of all others I have a right to look for help and advice looks upon all that I tell him about it as the fancies of a nervous woman. He does not say so, but I can read it from his soothing answers and averted eyes. But I have heard, Mr Holmes, that you can see deeply into the manifold wickedness of the human heart. You may advise me how to walk amid the dangers which encompass me.'

'I am all attention, madam.'

'My name is Helen Stoner, and I am living with my step-father, who is the last survivor of one of the oldest Saxon families in England;* the Roylotts of Stoke Moran, on the western border of Surrey.'

Holmes nodded his head. 'The name is familiar to me,' said he.

'The family was at one time among the richest in England, and the estate extended over the borders into Berkshire in the north, and Hampshire in the west. In the last century, however, four successive heirs were of a dissolute and wasteful disposition, and the family ruin was eventually completed by a gambler, in the days of the Regency. Nothing was left save a few acres of ground, and the two-hundred-year-old house, which is itself crushed under a heavy mortgage. The last squire dragged out his existence there, living the horrible life of an aristocratic pauper; but his only son, my stepfather, seeing that he must adapt himself to the new conditions, obtained an advance from a relative, which enabled him to take a medical degree, and went out to Calcutta, where, by his professional skill and his force of character, he established a large practice. In a fit of anger, however, caused by some robberies which had been perpetrated in the house, he beat his native butler to death, and narrowly escaped a capital sentence. As it was, he suffered a long term of imprisonment, and afterwards returned to England a morose and disappointed man.

'When Dr Roylott was in India he married my mother, Mrs Stoner, the young widow of Major-General Stoner, of the Bengal Artillery.* My sister Julia and I were twins, and we were only two years old at the time of my mother's re-marriage. She had a considerable sum of money, not less than a thousand a year, and this she bequeathed to Dr Roylott entirely whilst we resided with him, with a provision that a certain annual sum should be allowed to each of us in the event of our marriage. Shortly after our return to England my mother died—she was killed eight years ago in a railway accident near Crewe.* Dr Roylott then abandoned his attempts to establish himself in practice in London, and took us to live with him in the ancestral house at Stoke Moran. The money which my mother had left was enough for all our wants, and there seemed no obstacle to our happiness.

'But a terrible change came over our stepfather about this time. Instead of making friends and exchanging visits with our neighbours, who had at first been overjoyed to see a Roylott of Stoke Moran back in the old family seat, he shut himself up in his house, and seldom came out save to indulge in ferocious quarrels with whoever might cross his path. Violence of temper approaching to mania has been hereditary in the men of the family, and in my stepfather's case it had, I believe, been intensified by his long residence in the tropics. A series of disgraceful brawls took place, two of which ended in the police-court, until at last he became the terror of the village, and the folks would fly at his approach, for he is a man of immense strength, and absolutely uncontrollable in his anger.

'Last week he hurled the local blacksmith over a parapet into a stream and it was only by paying over all the money that I could gather together that I was able to avert another public exposure. He had no friends at all save the wandering gipsies, and he would give these vagabonds leave to encamp upon the few acres of bramble-covered land which represent the family estate, and would accept in return the hospitality of their tents, wandering away with them sometimes for weeks on end.* He has a passion also for Indian animals,* which are sent over to him by a correspondent,* and he has at this moment a cheetah and a baboon, which wander freely over his grounds, and are feared by the villagers almost as much as their master.

'You can imagine from what I say that my poor sister Julia and I had no great pleasure in our lives. No servant would stay with us, and for a long time we did all the work of the house. She was but thirty at the time of her death, and yet her hair had already begun to whiten, even as mine has.'

'Your sister is dead, then?'

'She died just two years ago, and it is of her death that I wish to speak to you. You can understand that, living the life which I have described, we were little likely to see anyone of our own age and position. We had, however, an aunt, my mother's maiden sister, Miss Honoria Westphail,* who lives near Harrow,* and we were occasionally allowed to pay short visits at this lady's house. Julia went there at Christmas two years ago, and met there a half-pay Major of Marines,* to whom she became engaged. My stepfather learned of the engagement when my sister returned, and offered no objection to the marriage; but within a fortnight of the day which had been fixed for the wedding, the terrible event occurred which has deprived me of my only companion.'

Sherlock Holmes had been leaning back in his chair with his eyes closed, and his head sunk in a cushion, but he half opened his lids now, and glanced across at his visitor.

'Pray be precise as to details,' said he.

'It is easy for me to be so, for every event of that dreadful time is seared into my memory. The manor house is, as I have already said, very old, and only one wing is now inhabited. The bedrooms in this wing are on the ground floor, the sitting-rooms being in the central block of the buildings. Of these bedrooms the first is Dr Roylott's, the second my sister's, and the third my own. There is no communication between them, but they all open out into the same corridor. Do I make myself plain?'

'Perfectly so.'

'The windows of the three rooms open out upon the lawn. That fatal night Dr Roylott had gone to his room early, though we knew that he had not retired to rest, for my sister was troubled by the smell of the strong Indian cigars which it was his custom to smoke. She left her room, therefore, and came into mine, where she sat for some time, chatting about her approaching wedding. At eleven o'clock she rose to leave me, but she paused at the door and looked back.

' "Tell me, Helen," said she, "have you ever heard anyone whistle in the dead of the night?"

' "Never," said I.

' "I suppose that you could not possibly whistle yourself in your sleep?"

' "Certainly not. But why?"

' "Because during the last few nights I have always, about three in the morning, heard a low clear whistle. I am a light sleeper, and it has awakened me. I cannot tell where it came from—perhaps from the next room, perhaps from the lawn. I thought that I would just ask you whether you had heard it."

' "No, I have not. It must be those wretched gipsies in the plantation."

' "Very likely. And yet if it were on the lawn I wonder that you did not hear it also."

' "Ah, but I sleep more heavily than you."

' "Well, it is of no great consequence, at any rate," she smiled back at me, closed my door, and a few moments later I heard her key turn in the lock.'

'Indeed,' said Holmes. 'Was it your custom always to lock yourselves in at night?'

'Always.'

'And why?'

'I think that I mentioned to you that the Doctor kept a cheetah and a baboon. We had no feeling of security unless our doors were locked.'

'Quite so. Pray proceed with your statement.'

'I could not sleep that night. A vague feeling of impending misfortune impressed me. My sister and I, you will recollect, were twins, and you know how subtle are the links which bind two souls which are so closely allied. It was a wild night. The wind was howling outside, and the rain was beating and splashing against the windows. Suddenly, amidst all the hubbub of the gale, there burst forth the wild scream of a terrified woman. I knew that it was my sister's voice. I sprang from my bed, wrapped a shawl round me, and rushed into the corridor. As I opened my door I seemed to hear a low whistle, such as my sister described, and a few moments later a clanging sound, as if a mass of metal had fallen. As I ran down the passage my sister's door was unlocked, and revolved slowly upon its hinges.* I stared at it horror-stricken, not knowing what was about to issue from it. By the light of the corridor lamp I saw my sister appear at the opening, her face blanched with terror, her hands groping for help, her whole figure swaying to and fro like that of a drunkard. I ran to her and threw my arms round her, but at that moment her knees seemed to give way and she fell to the ground. She writhed as one who is in terrible pain, and her limbs were dreadfully convulsed. At first I thought that she had not recognized me, but as I bent over her she suddenly shrieked out in a voice which I shall never forget, "Oh, my God! Helen! It was the band! The speckled band!" There was something else which she would fain have said, and she stabbed with her finger into the air in the direction of the Doctor's room, but a fresh convulsion seized her and choked her words. I rushed out, calling loudly for my stepfather, and I met him hastening from his room in his dressing-gown. When he reached my sister's side she was unconscious, and though he poured brandy down her throat, and sent for medical aid from the village, all efforts were in vain, for she slowly sank and died without having recovered her consciousness. Such was the dreadful end of my beloved sister.'

'One moment,' said Holmes: 'are you sure about this whistle and metallic sound? Could you swear to it?'

'That was what the county coroner asked me at the inquiry.* It is my strong impression that I heard it, and yet among the crash of the gale, and the creaking of an old house, I may possibly have been deceived.'

'Was your sister dressed?'

'No, she was in her nightdress. In her right hand was found the charred stump of a match, and in her left a matchbox.'

'Showing that she had struck a light and looked about her when the alarm took place. That is important. And what conclusions did the coroner come to?'

'He investigated the case with great care, for Dr Roylott's conduct had long been notorious in the county, but he was unable to find any satisfactory cause of death. My evidence showed that the door had been fastened upon the inner side, and the windows were blocked by old-fashioned shutters with broad iron bars, which were secured every night. The walls were carefully sounded, and were shown to be quite solid all round, and the flooring was also thoroughly examined, with the same result. The chimney is wide, but is barred up by four large staples. It is certain, therefore, that my sister was quite alone when she met her end. Besides, there were no marks of any violence upon her.'

'How about poison?'

'The doctors examined her for it, but without success.'

'What do you think that this unfortunate lady died of, then?'

'It is my belief that she died of pure fear and nervous shock, though what it was which frightened her I cannot imagine.'

'Were there gipsies in the plantation at the time?'

'Yes, there are nearly always some there.'

'Ah, and what did you gather from this allusion to a band—a speckled band?'

'Sometimes I have thought that it was merely the wild talk of delirium, sometimes that it may have referred to some band of people, perhaps to these very gipsies in the plantation. I do not know whether the spotted handkerchiefs which so many of them wear over their heads might have suggested the strange adjective which she used.'

Holmes shook his head like a man who is far from being satisfied.

'These are very deep waters,' said he; 'pray go on with your narrative.'

'Two years have passed since then, and my life has been until lately lonelier than ever. A month ago, however, a dear friend, whom I have known for many years, has done me the honour to ask my hand in marriage. His name is Armitage*—Percy Armitage—the second son of Mr Armitage, of Crane Water, near Reading.* My stepfather has offered no opposition to the match, and we are to be married in the course of the spring. Two days ago some repairs were started in the west wing of the building, and my bedroom wall has been pierced, so that I have had to move into the chamber in which my sister died, and to sleep in the very bed in which she slept. Imagine, then, my thrill of terror when last night, as I lay awake, thinking over her terrible fate, I suddenly heard in the silence of the night the low whistle which had been the herald of her own death. I sprang up and lit the lamp, but nothing was to be seen in the room. I was too shaken to go to bed again, however, so I dressed, and as soon as it was daylight I slipped down, got a dog-cart at the Crown Inn,* which is opposite, and drove to Leatherhead, from whence I have come on this morning, with the one object of seeing you and asking your advice.'

'You have done wisely,' said my friend. 'But have you told me all?'

'Yes, all.'

'Miss Stoner, you have not. You are screening your stepfather.'

'Why, what do you mean?'

For answer Holmes pushed back the frill of black lace which fringed the hand that lay upon our visitor's knee. Five little livid spots, the marks of four fingers and a thumb, were printed upon the white wrist.

'You have been cruelly used,' said Holmes.

The lady coloured deeply, and covered over her injured wrist. 'He is a hard man,' she said, 'and perhaps he hardly knows his own strength.'

There was a long silence, during which Holmes leaned his chin upon his hands and stared into the crackling fire.

'This is very deep business,' he said at last. 'There are a thousand details which I should desire to know before I decide upon our course of action. Yet we have not a moment to lose. If we were to come to Stoke Moran to-day, would it be possible for us to see over these rooms without the knowledge of your stepfather?'

'As it happens, he spoke of coming into town to-day upon some most important business. It is probable that he will be away all day, and that there would be nothing to disturb you. We have a housekeeper now, but she is old and foolish, and I could easily get her out of the way.'

'Excellent. You are not averse to this trip, Watson?'

'By no means.'

'Then we shall both come. What are you going to do yourself?'

'I have one or two things which I would wish to do now that I am in town. But I shall return by the twelve o'clock train, so as to be there in time for your coming.'

'And you may expect us early in the afternoon. I have myself some small business matters to attend to. Will you not wait and breakfast?'

'No, I must go. My heart is lightened already since I have confided my trouble to you. I shall look forward to seeing you again this afternoon.' She dropped her thick black veil over her face, and glided from the room.

'And what do you think of it all, Watson?' asked Sherlock Holmes, leaning back in his chair.

'It seems to me to be a most dark and sinister business.'

'Dark enough, and sinister enough.'

'Yet if the lady is correct in saying that the flooring and walls are sound, and that the door, window, and chimney are impassable, then her sister must have been undoubtedly alone when she met her mysterious end.'

'What becomes, then, of these nocturnal whistles, and what of the very peculiar words of the dying woman?'

'I cannot think.'

'When you combine the ideas of whistles at night, the presence of a band of gipsies who are on intimate terms with this old doctor, the fact that we have every reason to believe that the doctor has an interest in preventing his stepdaughter's marriage, the dying allusion to a band, and finally, the fact that Miss Helen Stoner heard a metallic clang, which might have been caused by one of those metal bars which secured the shutters falling back into their place, I think there is good ground to think that the mystery may be cleared along those lines.'

'But what, then, did the gipsies do?'

'I cannot imagine.'

'I see many objections to any such a theory.'

'And so do I. It is precisely for that reason that we are going to Stoke Moran this day. I want to see whether the objections are fatal, or if they may be explained away. But what, in the name of the devil!'

The ejaculation had been drawn from my companion by the fact that our door had been suddenly dashed open, and that a huge man framed himself in the aperture. His costume was a peculiar mixture of the professional and of the agricultural, having a black top-hat, a long frock-coat, and a pair of high gaiters,* with a hunting-crop swinging in his hand. So tall was he that his hat actually brushed the cross bar of the doorway, and his breadth seemed to span it across from side to side. A large face, seared with a thousand wrinkles, burned yellow with the sun, and marked with every evil passion, was turned from one to the other of us, while his deep-set, bile-shot eyes,* and the high thin fleshless nose, gave him somewhat the resemblance to a fierce old bird of prey.

'Which of you is Holmes?' asked this apparition.

'My name, sir, but you have the advantage of me,' said my companion, quietly.

'I am Dr Grimesby Roylott, of Stoke Moran.'

'Indeed, Doctor,' said Holmes, blandly. 'Pray take a seat.'

'I will do nothing of the kind. My stepdaughter has been here. I have traced her. What has she been saying to you?'

'It is a little cold for the time of the year,' said Holmes.

'What has she been saying to you?' screamed the old man furiously.

'But I have heard that the crocuses promise well,' continued my companion imperturbably.

'Ha! You put me off, do you?' said our new visitor, taking a step forward, and shaking his hunting-crop. 'I know you, you scoundrel! I have heard of you before. You are Holmes the meddler.'

My friend smiled.

'Holmes the busybody!'

His smile broadened.

'Holmes the Scotland Yard jack-in-office.'*

Holmes chuckled heartily. 'Your conversation is most entertaining,' said he. 'When you go out close the door, for there is a decided draught.'

'I will go when I have had my say. Don't you dare to meddle with my affairs. I know that Miss Stoner has been here—I traced her! I am a dangerous man to fall foul of! See here.' He stepped swiftly forward, seized the poker, and bent it into a curve with his huge brown hands.

'See that you keep yourself out of my grip,' he snarled, and hurling the twisted poker into the fireplace, he strode out of the room.

'He seems a very amiable person,' said Holmes, laughing. 'I am not quite so bulky, but if he had remained I might have shown him that my grip was not much more feeble than his own.' As he spoke he picked up the steel poker, and with a sudden effort straightened it out again.*

'Fancy his having the insolence to confound me with the official detective force! This incident gives zest to our investigation, however, and I only trust that our little friend will not suffer from her imprudence in allowing this brute to trace her. And now, Watson, we shall order breakfast, and afterwards I shall walk down to Doctors' Commons,* where I hope to get some data which may help us in this matter.'

It was nearly one o'clock when Sherlock Holmes returned from his excursion. He held in his hand a sheet of blue paper, scrawled over with notes and figures.

'I have seen the will of the deceased wife,' said he. 'To determine its exact meaning I have been obliged to work out the present prices of the investments with which it is concerned. The total income, which at the time of the wife's death was little short of £1,100, is now through the fall in agricultural prices* not more than £750. Each daughter can claim an income of £250, in case of marriage. It is evident, therefore, that if both girls had married, this beauty would have had a mere pittance, while even one of them would cripple him to a serious extent. My morning's work has not been wasted, since it has proved that he has the very strongest motives for standing in the way of anything of the sort. And now, Watson, this is too serious for dawdling, especially as the old man is aware that we are interesting ourselves in his affairs, so if you are ready we shall call a cab and drive to Waterloo. I should be very much obliged if you would slip your revolver into your pocket. An Eley's No. 2* is an excellent argument with gentlemen who can twist steel pokers into knots. That and a tooth-brush are, I think, all that we need.'

At Waterloo we were fortunate in catching a train for Leatherhead, where we hired a trap* at the station inn, and drove for four or five miles through the lovely Surrey lanes. It was a perfect day, with a bright sun and a few fleecy clouds in the heavens. The trees and wayside hedges were just throwing out their first green shoots, and the air was full of the pleasant smell of the moist earth. To me at least there was a strange contrast between the sweet promise of the spring and this sinister quest upon which we were engaged. My companion sat in front of the trap, his arms folded, his hat pulled down over his eyes, and his chin sunk upon his breast, buried in the deepest thought. Suddenly, however, he started, tapped me on the shoulder, and pointed over the meadows.

'Look there!' said he.

A heavily-timbered park stretched up in a gentle slope, thickening into a grove at the highest point. From amidst the branches there jutted out the grey gables and high roof-tree of a very old mansion.

'Stoke Moran?' said he.

'Yes, sir, that be the house of Dr Grimesby Roylott,' remarked the driver.

'There is some building going on there,' said Holmes: 'that is where we are going.'

'There's the village,' said the driver, pointing to a cluster of roofs some distance to the left; 'but if you want to get to the house, you'll find it shorter to go over this stile, and so by the footpath over the fields. There it is, where the lady is walking.'

'And the lady, I fancy, is Miss Stoner,' observed Holmes, shading his eyes. 'Yes, I think we had better do as you suggest.'

We got off, paid our fare, and the trap rattled back on its way to Leatherhead.

'I thought it as well,' said Holmes, as we climbed the stile, 'that this fellow should think we had come here as architects, or on some definite business. It may stop his gossip. Good afternoon, Miss Stoner. You see that we have been as good as our word.'

Our client of the morning had hurried forward to meet us with a face which spoke her joy. 'I have been waiting so eagerly for you,' she cried, shaking hands with us warmly. 'All has turned out splendidly. Dr Roylett has gone to town, and it is unlikely that he will be back before evening.'

'We have had the pleasure of making the Doctor's acquaintance,' said Holmes, and in a few words he sketched out what had occurred. Miss Stoner turned white to the lips as she listened.

'Good heavens!' she cried, 'he has followed me, then.'

'So it appears.'

'He is so cunning that I never know when I am safe from him. What will he say when he returns?'

'He must guard himself, for he may find that there is someone more cunning than himself upon his track. You must lock yourself from him to-night. If he is violent, we shall take you away to your aunt's at Harrow. Now, we must make the best use of our time, so kindly take us at once to the rooms which we are to examine.'

The building was of grey, lichen-blotched stone, with a high central portion, and two curving wings, like the claws of a crab, thrown out on each side. In one of these wings the windows were broken, and blocked with wooden boards, while the roof was partly caved in, a picture of ruin. The central portion was in little better repair, but the right-hand block was comparatively modern, and the blinds in the windows, with the blue smoke curling up from the chimneys, showed that this was where the family resided. Some scaffolding had been erected against the end wall, and the stonework had been broken into, but there were no signs of any workmen at the moment of our visit. Holmes walked slowly up and down the ill-trimmed lawn, and examined with deep attention the outsides of the windows.

'This, I take it, belongs to the room in which you used to sleep, the centre one to your sister's, and the one next to the main building to Dr Roylott's chamber?'

'Exactly so. But I am now sleeping in the middle one.'

'Pending the alterations, as I understand. By the way, there does not seem to be any very pressing need for repairs at that end wall.'

'There were none. I believe that it was an excuse to move me from my room.'

'Ah! that is suggestive. Now, on the other side of this narrow wing runs the corridor from which these three rooms open. There are windows in it, of course?'

'Yes, but very small ones. Too narrow for anyone to pass through.'

'As you both locked your doors at night, your rooms were unapproachable from that side. Now, would you have the kindness to go into your room, and to bar your shutters.'

Miss Stoner did so, and Holmes, after a careful examination through the open window, endeavoured in every way to force the shutter open, but without success. There was no slit through which a knife could be passed to raise the bar. Then with his lens he tested the hinges, but they were of solid iron, built firmly into the massive masonry. 'Hum!' said he, scratching his chin in some perplexity, 'my theory certainly presents some difficulties. No one could pass these shutters if they were bolted. Well, we shall see if the inside throws any light upon the matter.'

A small side-door led into the whitewashed corridor from which the three bedrooms opened. Holmes refused to examine the third chamber, so we passed at once to the second, that in which Miss Stoner was now sleeping, and in which her sister had met her fate. It was a homely little room, with a low ceiling and a gaping fireplace, after the fashion of old country houses. A brown chest of drawers stood in one corner, a narrow white-counterpaned bed in another, and a dressing-table on the left-hand side of the window. These articles, with two small wickerwork chairs, made up all the furniture in the room, save for a square of Wilton carpet* in the centre. The boards round and the panelling of the walls were brown, worm-eaten oak, so old and discoloured that it may have dated from the original building of the house. Holmes drew one of the chairs into a corner and sat silent, while his eyes travelled round and round and up and down, taking in every detail of the apartment.

'Where does that bell communicate with?' he asked at last, pointing to a thick bell-rope which hung down beside the bed, the tassel actually lying upon the pillow.

'It goes to the housekeeper's room.'

'It looks newer than the other things?'

'Yes, it was only put there a couple of years ago.'

'Your sister asked for it, I suppose?'

'No, I never heard of her using it. We used always to get what we wanted for ourselves.'

'Indeed, it seemed unnecessary to put so nice a bell-pull there. You will excuse me for a few minutes while I satisfy myself as to this floor.' He threw himself down upon his face with his lens in his hand, and crawled swiftly backwards and forwards, examining minutely the cracks between the boards. Then he did the same with the woodwork with which the chamber was panelled. Finally he walked over to the bed and spent some time in staring at it, and in running his eye up and down the wall. Finally he took the bell-rope in his hand and gave it a brisk tug.

'Why, it's a dummy,' said he.

'Won't it ring?'

'No, it is not even attached to a wire. This is very interesting. You can see now that it is fastened to a hook just above where the little opening of the ventilator is.'

'How very absurd! I never noticed that before.'

'Very strange!' muttered Holmes, pulling at the rope. 'There are one or two very singular points about this room. For example, what a fool a builder must be to open a ventilator into another room, when, with the same trouble, he might have communicated with the outside air!'

'That is also quite modern,' said the lady.

'Done about the same time as the bell-rope?' remarked Holmes.

'Yes, there were several little changes carried out about that time.'

'They seem to have been of a most interesting character— dummy bell-ropes, and ventilators which do not ventilate. With your permission, Miss Stoner, we shall now carry our researches into the inner apartment.'

Dr Grimesby Roylott's chamber was larger than that of his stepdaughter, but was as plainly furnished. A camp bed,* a small wooden shelf full of books, mostly of a technical character, an armchair beside the bed, a plain wooden chair against the wall, a round table, and a large iron safe were the principal things which met the eye. Holmes walked slowly round and examined each and all of them with the keenest interest.

'What's in here?' he asked, tapping the safe.

'My stepfather's business papers.'

'Oh! you have seen inside then?'

'Only once, some years ago. I remember that it was full of papers.'

'There isn't a cat in it, for example?'

'No. What a strange idea!'

'Well, look at this!' He took up a small saucer of milk which stood on the top of it.

'No; we don't keep a cat. But there is a cheetah and a baboon.'

'Ah, yes, of course! Well, a cheetah is just a big cat, and yet a saucer of milk does not go very far in satisfying its wants, I daresay. There is one point which I should wish to determine.' He squatted down in front of the wooden chair, and examined the seat of it with the greatest attention.

'Thank you. That is quite settled,' said he, rising and putting his lens in his pocket. 'Hello! here is something interesting!'

The object which had caught his eye was a small dog lash hung on one corner of the bed. The lash, however, was curled upon itself, and tied so as to make a loop of whipcord.

'What do you make of that, Watson?'

'It's a common enough lash. But I don't know why it should be tied.'

'That is not quite so common, is it? Ah, me! it's a wicked world, and when a clever man turns his brain to crime it is the worst of all. I think that I have seen enough now, Miss Stoner, and, with your permission, we shall walk out upon the lawn.'

I had never seen my friend's face so grim, or his brow so dark, as it was when we turned from the scene of his investigation. We had walked several times up and down the lawn, neither Miss Stoner nor myself liking to break in upon his thoughts before he roused himself from his reverie.

'It is very essential, Miss Stoner,' said he, 'that you should absolutely follow my advice in every respect.'

'I shall most certainly do so.'

'The matter is too serious for any hesitation. Your life may depend upon your compliance.'

'I assure you that I am in your hands.'

'In the first place, both my friend and I must spend the night in your room.'

Both Miss Stoner and I gazed at him in astonishment.

'Yes, it must be so. Let me explain. I believe that that is the village inn over there?'

'Yes, that is the "Crown".'

'Very good. Your windows would be visible from there?'

'Certainly.'

'You must confine yourself to your room, on pretence of a headache, when your stepfather comes back. Then when you hear him retire for the night, you must open the shutters of your window, undo the hasp,* put your lamp there as a signal to us, and then withdraw with everything which you are likely to want into the room which you used to occupy. I have no doubt that, in spite of the repairs, you could manage there for one night.'

'Oh, yes, easily.'

'The rest you will leave in our hands.'

'But what will you do?'

'We shall spend the night in your room, and we shall investigate the cause of this noise which has disturbed you.'

'I believe, Mr Holmes, that you have already made up your mind,' said Miss Stoner, laying her hand upon my companion's sleeve.

'Perhaps I have.'

'Then for pity's sake tell me what was the cause of my sister's death.'

'I should prefer to have clearer proofs before I speak.'

'You can at least tell me whether my own thought is correct, and if she died from some sudden fright.'

'No, I do not think so. I think that there was probably some more tangible cause. And now, Miss Stoner, we must leave you, for if Dr Roylott returned and saw us, our journey would be in vain. Good-bye, and be brave, for if you will do what I have told you, you may rest assured that we shall soon drive away the dangers that threaten you.'

Sherlock Holmes and I had no difficulty in engaging a bedroom and sitting-room at the Crown Inn. They were on the upper floor, and from our window we could command a view of the avenue gate, and of the inhabited wing of Stoke Moran Manor House. At dusk we saw Dr Grimesby Roylott drive past, his huge form looming up beside the little figure of the lad who drove him. The boy had some slight difficulty in undoing the heavy iron gates, and we heard the hoarse roar of the Doctor's voice, and saw the fury with which he shook his clenched fists at him. The trap drove on, and a few minutes later we saw a sudden light spring up among the trees as the lamp was lit in one of the sitting-rooms.

'Do you know, Watson,' said Holmes, as we sat together in the gathering darkness, 'I have really some scruples as to taking you tonight. There is a distinct element of danger.'

'Can I be of assistance?'

'Your presence might be invaluable.'

'Then I shall certainly come.'

'It is very kind of you.'

'You speak of danger. You have evidently seen more in these rooms than was visible to me.'

'No, but I fancy that I may have deduced a little more. I imagine that you saw all that I did.'

'I saw nothing remarkable save the bell-rope, and what purpose that could answer I confess is more than I can imagine.'

'You saw the ventilator, too?'

'Yes, but I do not think that it is such a very unusual thing to have a small opening between two rooms. It was so small that a rat could hardly pass through.'

'I knew that we should find a ventilator before ever we came to Stoke Moran.'

'My dear Holmes!'

'Oh, yes, I did. You remember in her statement she said that her sister could smell Dr Roylott's cigar. Now, of course that suggests at once that there must be a communication between the two rooms. It could only be a small one, or it would have been remarked upon at the Coroner's inquiry. I deduced a ventilator.'

'But what harm can there be in that?'

'Well, there is at least a curious coincidence of dates. A ventilator is made, a cord is hung, and a lady who sleeps in the bed dies. Does not that strike you?'

'I cannot as yet see any connection.'

'Did you observe anything very peculiar about that bed?'

'No.'

'It was clamped to the floor. Did you ever see a bed fastened like that before?'

'I cannot say that I have.'

'The lady could not move her bed. It must always be in the same relative position to the ventilator and to the rope—for so we may call it, since it was clearly never meant for a bell-pull.'

'Holmes,' I cried, 'I seem to see dimly what you are hitting at. We are only just in time to prevent some subtle and horrible crime.'

'Subtle enough, and horrible enough. When a doctor does go wrong, he is the first of criminals. He has nerve and he has knowledge. Palmer and Pritchard* were among the heads of their profession. This man strikes even deeper, but, I think, Watson, that we shall be able to strike deeper still. But we shall have horrors enough before the night is over: for goodness' sake let us have a quiet pipe, and turn our minds for a few hours to something more cheerful.'

About nine o'clock the light among the trees was extinguished, and all was dark in the direction of the Manor House. Two hours passed slowly away, and then, suddenly, just at the stroke of eleven, a single bright light shone out right in front of us.

'That is our signal,' said Holmes, springing to his feet; 'it comes from the middle window.'

As we passed out he exchanged a few words with the landlord, explaining that we were going on a late visit to an acquaintance, and that it was possible that we might spend the night there. A moment later we were out on the dark road, a chill wind blowing in our faces, and one yellow light twinkling in front of us through the gloom to guide us on our sombre errand.

There was little difficulty in entering the grounds, for unrepaired breaches gaped in the old park wall.* Making our way among the trees, we reached the lawn, crossed it, and were about to enter through the window, when out from a clump of laurel bushes there darted what seemed to be a hideous and distorted child, who threw itself on the grass with writhing limbs, and then ran swiftly across the lawn into the darkness.

'My God!' I whispered, 'did you see it?'

Holmes was for the moment as startled as I. His hand closed like a vice upon my wrist in his agitation. Then he broke into a low laugh, and put his lips to my ear.

'It is a nice household,' he murmured. 'That is the baboon.'

I had forgotten the strange pets which the doctor affected. There was a cheetah, too; perhaps we might find it upon our shoulders at any moment. I confess that I felt easier in my mind when, after following Holmes's example and slipping off my shoes, I found myself inside the bedroom. My companion noiselessly closed the shutters, moved the lamp on to the table, and cast his eyes round the room. All was as we had seen it in the day-time. Then creeping up to me and making a trumpet of his hand, he whispered into my ear again so gently that it was all that I could do to distinguish the words:

'The least sound would be fatal to our plans.'

I nodded to show that I had heard.

'We must sit without a light. He would see it through the ventilator.'

I nodded again.

'Do not go to sleep; your very life may depend upon it. Have your pistol ready in case we should need it. I will sit on the side of the bed, and you in that chair.'

I took out my revolver and laid it on the corner of the table.

Holmes had brought up a long thin cane, and this he placed upon the bed beside him. By it he laid the box of matches and the stump of a candle. Then he turned down the lamp and we were left in darkness.

How shall I ever forget that dreadful vigil? I could not hear a sound, not even the drawing of a breath, and yet I knew that my companion sat open-eyed, within a few feet of me, in the same state of nervous tension in which I was myself. The shutters cut off the least ray of light, and we waited in absolute darkness. From outside came the occasional cry of a night-bird, and once at our very window a long drawn, cat-like whine, which told us that the cheetah was indeed at liberty. Far away we could hear the deep tones of the parish clock, which boomed out every quarter of an hour. How long they seemed, those quarters! Twelve struck, and one, and two, and three, and still we sat waiting silently for whatever might befall.

Suddenly there was the momentary gleam of a light up in the direction of the ventilator, which vanished immediately, but was succeeded by a strong smell of burning oil and heated metal. Someone in the next room had lit a dark lantern.* I heard a gentle sound of movement, and then all was silent once more, though the smell grew stronger. For half an hour I sat with straining ears. Then suddenly another sound became audible—a very gentle, soothing sound, like that of a small jet of steam escaping continually from a kettle. The instant that we heard it, Holmes sprang from the bed, struck a match, and lashed furiously with his cane at the bell-pull.

'You see it. Watson?' he yelled. 'You see it?'

But I saw nothing. At the moment when Holmes struck the light I heard a low, clear whistle, but the sudden glare flashing into my weary eyes made it impossible for me to tell what it was at which my friend lashed so savagely. I could, however, see that his face was deadly pale, and filled with horror and loathing.

He had ceased to strike, and was gazing up at the ventilator, when suddenly there broke from the silence of the night the most horrible cry to which I have ever listened. It swelled up louder and louder, a hoarse yell of pain and fear and anger all mingled in the one dreadful shriek. They say that away down in the village, and even in the distant parsonage, that cry raised the sleepers from their beds. It struck cold to our hearts, and I stood gazing at Holmes, and he at me, until the last echoes of it had died away into the silence from which it rose.

'What can it mean?' I gasped.

'It means that it is all over,' Holmes answered. 'And perhaps, after all, it is for the best. Take your pistol, and we shall enter Dr Roylott's room.'

With a grave face he lit the lamp, and led the way down the corridor. Twice he struck at the chamber door without any reply from within. Then he turned the handle and entered, I at his heels, with the cocked pistol in my hand.

It was a singular sight which met our eyes. On the table stood a dark lantern with the shutter half open, throwing a brilliant beam of light upon the iron safe, the door of which was ajar. Beside this table, on the wooden chair, sat Dr Grimesby Roylott, clad in a long grey dressing-gown, his bare ankles protruding beneath, and his feet thrust into red heelless Turkish slippers. Across his lap lay the short stock with the long lash which we had noticed during the day. His chin was cocked upwards, and his eyes were fixed in a dreadful rigid stare at the corner of the ceiling. Round his brow he had a peculiar yellow band, with brownish speckles, which seemed to be bound tight round his head. As we entered he made neither sound nor motion.

'The band! the speckled band!' whispered Holmes.

I took a step forward: in an instant his strange headgear began to move, and there reared itself from among his hair the squat diamond-shaped head and puffed neck of a loathsome serpent.

'It is a swamp adder!'* cried Holmes—'the deadliest snake in India. He has died within ten seconds of being bitten.

Violence does, in truth, recoil upon the violent, and the schemer falls into the pit which he digs for another.* Let us thrust this creature back into its den, and we can then remove Miss Stoner to some place of shelter, and let the county police know what has happened.'

As he spoke he drew the dog whip swiftly from the dead man's lap, and throwing the noose round the reptile's neck, he drew it from its horrid perch, and carrying it at arm's length, threw it into the iron safe, which he closed upon it.

Such are the true facts of the death of Dr Grimesby Roylott, of Stoke Moran. It is not necessary that I should prolong a narrative which has already run to too great a length, by telling how we broke the sad news to the terrified girl, how we conveyed her by the morning train to the care of her good aunt at Harrow, of how the slow process of official inquiry came to the conclusion that the Doctor met his fate while indiscreetly playing with a dangerous pet. The little which I had yet to learn of the case was told me by Sherlock Holmes as we travelled back next day.

'I had,' said he, 'come to an entirely erroneous conclusion, which shows, my dear Watson, how dangerous it always is to reason from insufficient data. The presence of the gipsies, and the use of the word "band", which was used by the poor girl, no doubt, to explain the appearance which she had caught a horrid glimpse of by the light of her match, were sufficient to put me upon an entirely wrong scent. I can only claim the merit that I instantly reconsidered my position when, however, it became clear to me that whatever danger threatened an occupant of the room could not come either from the window or the door. My attention was speedily drawn, as I have already remarked to you, to this ventilator, and to the bell-rope which hung down to the bed. The discovery that this was a dummy, and that the bed was clamped to the floor, instantly gave rise to the suspicion that the rope was there as a bridge for something passing through the hole, and coming to the bed. The idea of a snake instantly occurred to me, and when I coupled it with my knowledge that the Doctor was furnished with a supply of creatures from India, I felt that I was probably on the right track. The idea of using a form of poison which could not possibly be discovered by any chemical test was just such a one as would occur to a clever and ruthless man who had had an Eastern training. The rapidity with which such a poison would take effect would also, from his point of view, be an advantage. It would be a sharp-eyed coroner indeed who could distinguish the two little dark punctures which would show where the poison fangs had done their work. Then I thought of the whistle. Of course, he must recall the snake before the morning light revealed it to the victim. He had trained it, probably by the use of the milk which we saw, to return to him when summoned. He would put it through this ventilator at the hour that he thought best, with the certainty that it would crawl down the rope, and land on the bed. It might or might not bite the occupant, perhaps she might escape every night for a week, but sooner or later she must fall a victim.

'I had come to these conclusions before ever I had entered his room. An inspection of his chair showed me that he had been in the habit of standing on it, which, of course, would be necessary in order that he should reach the ventilator. The sight of the safe, the saucer of milk, and the loop of whipcord were really enough to finally dispel any doubts which may have remained. The metallic clang heard by Miss Stoner was obviously caused by her father hastily closing the door of his safe upon its terrible occupant. Having once made up my mind, you know the steps which I took in order to put the matter to the proof. I heard the creature hiss, as I have no doubt that you did also, and I instantly lit the light and attacked it.'

'With the result of driving it through the ventilator.'

'And also with the result of causing it to turn upon its master at the other side. Some of the blows of my cane came home, and roused its snakish temper, so that it flew upon the first person it saw. In this way I am no doubt indirectly responsible for Dr Grimesby Roylott's death, and I cannot say that it is likely to weigh very heavily upon my conscience.'

The Engineer's Thumb

OF all the problems which have been submitted to my friend Mr Sherlock Holmes for solution during the years of our intimacy, there were only two which I was the means of introducing to his notice, that of Mr Hatherley's thumb and that of Colonel Warburton's madness.* Of these the latter may have afforded a finer field for an acute and original observer, but the other was so strange in its inception and so dramatic in its details, that it may be the more worthy of being placed upon record, even if it gave my friend fewer openings for those deductive methods of reasoning by which he achieved such remarkable results. The story has, I believe, been told more than once in the newspapers, but, like all such narratives, its effect is much less striking when set forth *en bloc** in a single half-column of print than when the facts slowly evolve before your own eyes and the mystery clears gradually away as each new discovery furnishes a step which leads on to the complete truth. At the time the circumstances made a deep impression upon me, and the lapse of two years has hardly served to weaken the effect.

It was in the summer of '89, not long after my marriage, that the events occurred which I am now about to summarize. I had returned to civil practice, and had finally abandoned Holmes in his Baker Street rooms, although I continually visited him, and occasionally even persuaded him to forgo his Bohemian habits so far as to come and visit us. My practice had steadily increased, and as I happened to live at no very great distance from Paddington Station, I got a few patients from among the officials. One of these whom I had cured of a painful and lingering disease was never weary of advertising my virtues, and of endeavouring to send me on every sufferer over whom he might have any influence.

One morning, at a little before seven o'clock, I was awakened by the maid tapping at the door, to announce that two men had come from Paddington, and were waiting in the consulting-room. I dressed hurriedly, for I knew by experience that railway cases were seldom trivial, and hastened downstairs. As I descended, my old ally, the guard, came out of the room, and closed the door tightly behind him.

'I've got him here,' he whispered, jerking his thumb over his shoulder; 'he's all right.'

'What is it, then?' I asked, for his manner suggested that it was some strange creature which he had caged up in my room.

'It's a new patient,' he whispered. 'I thought I'd bring him round myself; then he couldn't slip away. There he is, all safe and sound. I must go now, Doctor, I have my dooties, just the same as you.' And off he went, this trusty tout, without even giving me time to thank him.

I entered my consulting-room, and found a gentleman seated by the table. He was quietly dressed in a suit of heather tweed,* with a soft cloth cap, which he had laid down upon my books. Round one of his hands he had a handkerchief wrapped, which was mottled all over with bloodstains. He was young, not more than five-and-twenty, I should say, with a strong masculine face; but he was exceedingly pale, and gave me the impression of a man who was suffering from some strong agitation, which it took all his strength of mind to control.

'I am sorry to knock you up so early, Doctor,' said he. 'But I have had a very serious accident during the night. I came in by train this morning, and on inquiring at Paddington as to where I might find a doctor, a worthy fellow very kindly escorted me here. I gave the maid a card, but I see that she has left it upon the side table.'

I took it up and glanced at it. 'Mr Victor Hatherley,* hydraulic engineer, 16a Victoria Street (3rd floor).'* That was the name, style, and abode of my morning visitor. 'I regret that I have kept you waiting,' said I, sitting down in my library chair. 'You are fresh from a night journey, I understand, which is in itself a monotonous occupation.'

'Oh, my night could not be called monotonous,' said he, and laughed. He laughed very heartily, with a high ringing note, leaning back in his chair, and shaking his sides. All my medical instincts rose up against that laugh.

'Stop it!' I cried. 'Pull yourself together!' And I poured some water from a carafe.

It was useless, however. He was off in one of those hysterical outbursts which come upon a strong nature when some great crisis is over and gone. Presently he came to himself once more, very weary and blushing hotly.

'I have been making a fool of myself,' he gasped.

'Not at all. Drink this!' I dashed some brandy into the water, and the colour began to come back to his bloodless cheeks.

'That's better!' said he. 'And now, Doctor, perhaps you would kindly attend to my thumb, or rather to the place where my thumb used to be.'

He unwound the handkerchief and held out his hand. It gave even my hardened nerves a shudder to look at it. There were four protruding fingers and a horrid red spongy surface where the thumb should have been. It had been hacked or torn right out from the roots.

'Good heavens!' I cried, 'this is a terrible injury. It must have bled considerably.'

'Yes, it did. I fainted when it was done; and I think that I must have been senseless for a long time. When I came to, I found that it was still bleeding, so I tied one end of my handkerchief very tightly round the wrist, and braced it up with a twig.'

'Excellent! You should have been a surgeon.'

'It is a question of hydraulics, you see, and came within my own province.'

'This has been done,' said I, examining the wound, 'by a very heavy and sharp instrument.'

'A thing like a cleaver,' said he.

'An accident, I presume?'

'By no means.'

'What, a murderous attack!'

'Very murderous indeed.'

'You horrify me.'

I sponged the wound, cleaned it, dressed it; and, finally, covered it over with cotton wadding and carbolized bandages.* He lay back without wincing, though he bit his lip from time to time.

'How is that?' I asked, when I had finished.

'Capital! Between your brandy and your bandage, I feel a new man. I was very weak, but I have had a good deal to go through.'

'Perhaps you had better not speak of the matter. It is evidently trying to your nerves.'

'Oh, no; not now. I shall have to tell my tale to the police; but, between ourselves, if it were not for the convincing evidence of this wound of mine, I should be surprised if they believed my statement, for it is a very extraordinary one, and I have not much in the way of proof with which to back it up. And, even if they believe me, the clues which I can give them are so vague that it is a question whether justice will be done.'

'Ha!' cried I, 'if it is anything in the nature of a problem which you desire to see solved, I should strongly recommend you to come to my friend Mr Sherlock Holmes before you go to the official police.'

'Oh, I have heard of that fellow,' answered my visitor, 'and I should be very glad if he would take the matter up, though of course I must use the official police as well. Would you give me an introduction to him?'

'I'll do better. I'll take you round to him myself.'

'I should be immensely obliged to you.'

'We'll call a cab and go together. We shall just be in time to have a little breakfast with him. Do you feel equal to it?'

'Yes. I shall not feel easy until I have told my story.'

'Then my servant will call a cab, and I shall be with you in an instant.' I rushed upstairs, explained the matter shortly to my wife, and in five minutes was inside a hansom, driving with my new acquaintance to Baker Street.

Sherlock Holmes was, as I expected, lounging about his sitting-room in his dressing-gown, reading the agony column of *The Times*,* and smoking his before-breakfast pipe, which was composed of all the plugs and dottles left from his smokes of the day before, all carefully dried and collected on the corner of the mantelpiece.* He received us in his quietly genial fashion, ordered fresh rashers and eggs, and joined us in a hearty meal. When it was concluded he settled our new acquaintance upon the sofa, placed a pillow beneath his head, and laid a glass of brandy and water within his reach.

'It is easy to see that your experience has been no common one, Mr Hatherley,' said he. 'Pray lie down there and make yourself absolutely at home. Tell us what you can, but stop when you are tired, and keep up your strength with a little stimulant.'

'Thank you,' said my patient, 'but I have felt another man since the doctor bandaged me, and I think that your breakfast has completed the cure. I shall take up as little of your valuable time as possible, so I shall start at once upon my peculiar experiences.'

Holmes sat in his big armchair, with the weary, heavy-lidded expression which veiled his keen and eager nature, while I sat opposite to him, and we listened in silence to the strange story which our visitor detailed to us.

'You must know,' said he, 'that I am an orphan and a bachelor, residing alone in lodgings in London. By profession I am a hydraulic engineer, and I have had considerable experience of my work during the seven years that I was apprenticed to Venner & Matheson, the well-known firm of Greenwich.* Two years ago, having served my time, and having also come into a fair sum of money through my poor father's death, I determined to start in business for myself, and took professional chambers in Victoria Street.

'I suppose that everyone finds his first independent start in business a dreary experience. To me it has been exceptionally so. During two years I have had three consultations and one small job, and that is absolutely all that my profession has brought me. My gross takings amount to twenty-seven pounds ten. Every day, from nine in the morning until four in the afternoon,* I waited in my little den, until at last my heart began to sink, and I came to believe that I should never have any practice at all.

'Yesterday, however, just as I was thinking of leaving the office, my clerk entered to say there was a gentleman waiting who wished to see me upon business. He brought up a card, too, with the name of "Colonel Lysander Stark"* engraved upon it. Close at his heels came the Colonel himself, a man rather over the middle size but of an exceeding thinness. I do not think that I have ever seen so thin a man. His whole face sharpened away into nose and chin, and the skin of his cheeks was drawn quite tense over his outstanding bones. Yet this emaciation seemed to be his natural habit, and due to no disease, for his eye was bright, his step brisk, and his bearing assured. He was plainly but neatly dressed, and his age, I should judge, would be nearer forty than thirty.

' "Mr Hatherley?" said he, with something of a German accent. "You have been recommended to me, Mr Hatherley, as being a man who is not only proficient in his profession, but is also discreet and capable of preserving a secret."

'I bowed, feeling as flattered as any young man would at such an address. "May I ask who it was who gave me so good a character?" I asked.

' "Well, perhaps it is better that I should not tell you just at this moment. I have it from the same source that you are both an orphan and a bachelor, and are residing alone in London."

' "That is quite correct," I answered, "but you will excuse me if I say that I cannot see how all this bears upon my professional qualifications. I understood that it was on a professional matter that you wished to speak to me?"

' "Undoubtedly so. But you will find that all I say is really to the point. I have a professional commission for you, but absolute secrecy is quite essential—*absolute* secrecy, you understand, and of course we may expect that more from a man who is alone than from one who lives in the bosom of his family."

' "If I promise to keep a secret," said I, "you may absolutely depend upon my doing so."

'He looked very hard at me as I spoke, and it seemed to me that I had never seen so suspicious and questioning an eye.

' "You do promise, then?" said he at last.

' "Yes, I promise."

' "Absolute and complete silence, before, during, and after? No reference to the matter at all, either in word or writing?"

' "I have already given you my word."

' "Very good." He suddenly sprang up, and darting like lightning across the room he flung open the door. The passage outside was empty.

' "That's all right," said he, coming back. "I know that clerks are sometimes curious as to their masters' affairs. Now we can talk in safety." He drew up his chair very close to mine, and began to stare at me again with the same questioning, and thoughtful look.

'A feeling of repulsion and of something akin to fear had begun to rise within me at the strange antics of this fleshless man. Even my dread of losing a client could not restrain me from showing my impatience.

' "I beg that you will state your business, sir," said I; "my time is of value." Heaven forgive me for that last sentence, but the words came to my lips.

' "How would fifty guineas for a night's work suit you?" he asked.

' "Most admirably."

' "I say a night's work, but an hour's would be nearer the mark. I simply want your opinion about a hydraulic stamping machine which has got out of gear. If you show us what is wrong we shall soon set it right ourselves. What do you think of such a commission as that?"

' "The work appears to be light, and the pay munificent."

' "Precisely so. We shall want you to come tonight by the last train."

' "Where to?"

' "To Eyford, in Berkshire.* It is a little place near the borders of Oxfordshire, and within seven miles of Reading. There is a train from Paddington which would bring you in there at about 11.15."

' "Very good."

' "I shall come down in a carriage to meet you."

' "There is a drive, then?"

' "Yes, our little place is quite out in the country. It is a good seven miles from Eyford station."

' "Then we can hardly get there before midnight. I suppose there would be no chance of a train back. I should be compelled to stop the night."

' "Yes, we could easily give you a shakedown."*

' "That is very awkward. Could I not come at some more convenient hour?"

' "We have judged it best that you should come late. It is to recompense you for any inconvenience that we are paying you, a young and unknown man, a fee which would buy an opinion from the very heads of your profession. Still, of course, if you would like to draw out of the business, there is plenty of time to do so."

'I thought of the fifty guineas, and of how very useful they would be to me. "Not at all," said I; "I shall be very happy to accommodate myself to your wishes. I should like, however, to understand a little more clearly what it is that you wish me to do."

' "Quite so. It is very natural that the pledge of secrecy which we have exacted from you should have aroused your curiosity. I have no wish to commit you to anything without your having it all laid before you. I suppose that we are absolutely safe from eavesdroppers?"

' "Entirely."

' "Then the matter stands thus. You are probably aware that fuller's earth* is a valuable product, and that it is only found in one or two places in England?"

' "I have heard so."

' "Some little time ago I bought a small place—a very small place—within ten miles of Reading. I was fortunate enough to discover that there was a deposit of fuller's earth in one of my fields. On examining it, however, I found that this deposit was a comparatively small one, and that it formed a link between two very much larger ones upon the right and the left—both of them, however, in the grounds of my neighbours. These good people were absolutely ignorant that their land contained that which was quite as valuable as a gold mine. Naturally, it was to my interest to buy their land before they discovered its true value; but, unfortunately, I had no capital by which I could do this. I took a few of my friends into the secret, however, and they suggested that we should quietly and secretly work our own little deposit, and that in this way we should earn the money which would enable us to buy the neighbouring fields. This we have now been doing for some time, and in order to help us in our operations we erected a hydraulic press. This press, as I have already explained, has got out of order, and we wish your advice upon the subject. We guard our secret very jealously, however, and if it once became known that we had hydraulic engineers coming to our little house, it would soon rouse inquiry, and then, if the facts came out, it would be good-bye to any chance of getting these fields and carrying out our plans. That is why I have made you promise me that you will not tell a human being that you are going to Eyford to-night. I hope that I make it all plain?"

' "I quite follow you," said I. "The only point which I could not quite understand, was what use you could make of a hydraulic press in excavating fuller's earth, which, as I understand, is dug out like gravel from a pit."

' "Ah!" said he carelessly, "we have our own process. We compress the earth into bricks, so as to remove them without revealing what they are. But that is a mere detail. I have taken you fully into my confidence now, Mr Hatherley, and I have shown you how I trust you." He rose as he spoke. "I shall expect you, then, at Eyford, at 11.15."

' "I shall certainly be there."

' "And not a word to a soul." He looked at me with a last long, questioning gaze, and then, pressing my hand in a cold, dank grasp, he hurried from the room.

'Well, when I came to think it all over in cool blood I was very much astonished, as you may both think, at this sudden commission which had been entrusted to me. On the one hand, of course, I was glad, for the fee was at least tenfold what I should have asked had I set a price upon my own services, and it was possible that this order might lead to other ones. On the other hand, the face and manner of my patron had made an unpleasant impression upon me, and I could not think that his explanation of the fuller's earth was sufficient to explain the necessity for my coming at midnight, and his extreme anxiety lest I should tell anyone of my errand. However, I threw all my fears to the winds, ate a hearty supper, drove to Paddington, and started off, having obeyed to the letter the injunction as to holding my tongue.

'At Reading I had to change not only my carriage but my station.* However, I was in time for the last train to Eyford, and I reached the little dim-lit station after eleven o'clock. I was the only passenger who got out there, and there was no one upon the platform save a single sleepy porter with a lantern. As I passed out through the wicket-gate, however, I found my acquaintance of the morning waiting in the shadow upon the other side. Without a word he grasped my arm and hurried me into a carriage, the door of which was standing open. He drew up the windows on either side, tapped on the woodwork, and away we went as hard as the horse could go.'

'One horse?' interjected Holmes.

'Yes, only one.'

'Did you observe the colour?'

'Yes, I saw it by the sidelights when I was stepping into the carriage. It was a chestnut.'

'Tired-looking or fresh?'

'Oh, fresh and glossy.'

'Thank you. I am sorry to have interrupted you. Pray continue your most interesting statement.'

'Away we went then, and we drove for at least an hour. Colonel Lysander Stark had said that it was only seven miles, but I should think, from the rate that we seemed to go, and the time we took, that it must have been nearer twelve. He sat at my side in silence all the time, and I was aware, more than once when I glanced in his direction, that he was looking at me with great intensity. The country roads seem to be not very good in that part of the world, for we lurched and jolted terribly. I tried to look out of the windows to see something of where we were, but they were made of frosted glass, and I could make out nothing save an occasional blur of a passing light. Now and then I hazarded some remark to break the monotony of the journey, but the Colonel answered only in monosyllables, and the conversation soon flagged. At last, however, the bumping of the road was exchanged for the crisp smoothness of a gravel drive and the carriage came to a stand. Colonel Lysander Stark sprang out, and, as I followed after him, pulled me swiftly into a porch which gaped in front of us. We stepped, as it were, right out of the carriage and into the hall, so that I failed to catch the most fleeting glance of the front of the house. The instant that I had crossed the threshold the door slammed heavily behind us, and I heard faintly the rattle of the wheels as the carriage drove away.

'It was pitch dark inside the house, and the Colonel fumbled about looking for matches, and muttering under his breath. Suddenly a door opened at the other end of the passage, and a long, golden bar of light shot out in our direction. It grew broader, and a woman appeared with a lamp in her hand, which she held above her head, pushing her face forward and peering at us. I could see that she was pretty, and from the gloss with which the light shone upon her dark dress I knew that it was a rich material. She spoke a few words in a foreign tongue in a tone as though asking a question, and when my companion answered in a gruff monosyllable she gave such a start that the lamp nearly fell from her hand. Colonel Stark went up to her, whispered something in her ear, and then, pushing her back into the room from whence she had come, he walked towards me again with the lamp in his hand.

' "Perhaps you will have the kindness to wait in this room for a few minutes," said he, throwing open another door. It was a quiet little plainly furnished room, with a round table in the centre, on which several German books were scattered. Colonel Stark laid down the lamp on the top of a harmonium beside the door. "I shall not keep you waiting an instant," said he, and vanished into the darkness.

'I glanced at the books upon the table, and in spite of my ignorance of German I could see that two of them were treatises on science, the others being volumes of poetry. Then I walked across to the window, hoping that I might catch some glimpse of the country-side, but an oak shutter, heavily barred, was folded across it. It was a wonderfully silent house. There was an old clock ticking loudly somewhere in the passage, but otherwise everything was deadly still. A vague feeling of uneasiness began to steal over me. Who were these German people, and what were they doing, living in this strange, out-of-the-way place? And where was the place? I was ten miles or so from Eyford, that was all I knew, but whether north, south, east, or west, I had no idea. For that matter, Reading, and possibly other large towns, were within that radius, so the place might not be so secluded after all. Yet it was quite certain from the absolute stillness that we were in the country. I paced up and down the room, humming a tune under my breath to keep up my spirits, and feeling that I was thoroughly earning my fifty-guinea fee.

'Suddenly, without any preliminary sound in the midst of the utter stillness, the door of my room swung slowly open. The woman was standing in the aperture, the darkness of the hall behind her, the yellow light from my lamp beating upon her eager and beautiful face. I could see at a glance that she was sick with fear, and the sight sent a chill to my own heart. She held up one shaking finger to warn me to be silent, and she shot a few whispered words of broken English at me, her eyes glancing back, like those of a frightened horse, into the gloom behind her.

' "I would go," said she, trying hard, as it seemed to me, to speak calmly; "I would go. I should not stay here. There is no good for you to do."

' "But, madam," said I, "I have not yet done what I came for. I cannot possibly leave until I have seen the machine."

' "It is not worth your while to wait," she went on. "You can pass through the door; no one hinders." And then, seeing that I smiled and shook my head, she suddenly threw aside her constraint, and made a step forward, with her hands wrung together. "For the love of Heaven!" she whispered, "get away from here before it is too late!"

'But I am somewhat headstrong by nature, and the more ready to engage in an affair when there is some obstacle in the way. I thought of my fifty-guinea fee, of my wearisome journey, and of the unpleasant night which seemed to be before me. Was it all to go for nothing? Why should I slink away without having carried out my commission, and without the payment which was my due? This woman might, for all I knew, be a monomaniac.* With a stout bearing, therefore, though her manner had shaken me more than I cared to confess, I still shook my head, and declared my intention of remaining where I was. She was about to renew her entreaties when a door slammed overhead, and the sound of several footsteps was heard upon the stairs. She listened for an instant, threw up her hands with a despairing gesture, and vanished as suddenly and noiselessly as she had come.

'The newcomers were Colonel Lysander Stark, and a short thick man with a chinchilla beard* growing out of the creases of his double chin, who was introduced to me as Mr Ferguson.

' "This is my secretary and manager," said the Colonel. "By the way, I was under the impression that I left this door shut just now. I fear that you have felt the draught."

' "On the contrary," said I, "I opened the door myself, because I felt the room to be a little close."

'He shot one of his suspicious glances at me. "Perhaps we had better proceed to business, then," said he. "Mr Ferguson and I will take you up to see the machine."

' "I had better put my hat on, I suppose."

' "Oh no, it is in the house."

' "What, do you dig fuller's earth in the house?"

' "No, no. This is only where we compress it. But never mind that! All we wish you to do is to examine the machine and to let us know what is wrong with it."

'We went upstairs together, the Colonel first with the lamp, the fat manager and I behind him. It was a labyrinth of an old house, with corridors, passages, narrow winding staircases, and little low doors, the thresholds of which were hollowed out by the generations who had crossed them. There were no carpets, and no signs of any furniture above the ground floor, while the plaster was peeling off the walls, and the damp was breaking through in green, unhealthy blotches. I tried to put on as unconcerned an air as possible, but I had not forgotten the warnings of the lady, even though I disregarded them, and I kept a keen eye upon my two companions. Ferguson appeared to be a morose and silent man, but I could see from the little that he said that he was at least a fellow-countryman.

'Colonel Lysander Stark stopped at last before a low door, which he unlocked. Within was a small square room, in which the three of us could hardly get at one time. Ferguson remained outside, and the Colonel ushered me in.

' "We are now," said he, "actually within the hydraulic press, and it would be a particularly unpleasant thing for us if anyone were to turn it on. The ceiling of this small chamber is really the end of the descending piston, and it comes down with the force of many tons upon this metal floor. There are small lateral columns of water outside which receive the force, and which transmit and multiply it in the manner which is familiar to you. The machine goes readily enough, but there is some stiffness in the working of it and it has lost a little of its force. Perhaps you will have the goodness to look it over, and to show us how we can set it right."

'I took the lamp from him, and I examined the machine very thoroughly. It was indeed a gigantic one, and capable of exercising enormous pressure. When I passed outside, however, and pressed down the levers which controlled it, I knew at once by the whishing sound that there was a slight leakage, which allowed a regurgitation of water through one of the side cylinders. An examination showed that one of the india-rubber bands which was round the head of a driving-rod had shrunk so as not quite to fill the socket along which it worked. This was clearly the cause of the loss of power, and I pointed it out to my companions, who followed my remarks very carefully, and asked several practical questions as to how they should proceed to set it right. When I had made it clear to them, I returned to the main chamber of the machine, and took a good look at it to satisfy my own curiosity. It was obvious at a glance that the story of the fuller's earth was the merest fabrication, for it would be absurd to suppose that so powerful an engine could be designed for so inadequate a purpose. The walls were of wood, but the floor consisted of a large iron trough, and when I came to examine it I could see a crust of metallic deposit all over it. I had stooped and was scraping at this to see exactly what it was, when I heard a muttered exclamation in German, and saw the cadaverous face of the Colonel looking down at me.

' "What are you doing there?" he asked.

'I felt angry at having been tricked by so elaborate a story as that which he had told me. "I was admiring your fuller's earth," said I; "I think that I should be better able to advise you as to your machine if I knew what the exact purpose was for which it was used."

'The instant that I uttered the words I regretted the rashness of my speech. His face set hard, and a baleful light sprang up in his grey eyes.

' "Very well," said he, "you shall know all about the machine." He took a step backward, slammed the little door, and turned the key in the lock. I rushed towards it and pulled at the handle, but it was quite secure, and did not give in the least to my kicks and shoves. "Hallo!" I yelled. "Hallo! Colonel! Let me out!"

'And then suddenly in the silence I heard a sound which sent my heart into my mouth. It was the clank of the levers, and the swish of the leaking cylinder. He had set the engine at work. The lamp still stood upon the floor where I had placed it when examining the trough. By its light I saw that the black ceiling was coming down upon me, slowly, jerkily, but, as none knew better than myself, with a force which must within a minute grind me to a shapeless pulp. I threw myself, screaming, against the door, and dragged with my nails at the lock. I implored the Colonel to let me out, but the remorseless clanking of the levers drowned my cries. The ceiling was only a foot or two above my head, and with my hand upraised I could feel its hard, rough surface. Then it flashed through my mind that the pain of my death would depend very much upon the position in which I met it. If I lay on my face the weight would come upon spine, and I shuddered to think of that dreadful snap. Easier the other way, perhaps, and yet had I the nerve to lie and look up at that deadly black shadow wavering down upon me? Already I was unable to stand erect, when my eye caught something which brought a gush of hope back to my heart.

'I have said that though floor and ceiling were of iron, the walls were of wood. As I gave a last hurried glance around, I saw a thin line of yellow light between two of the boards, which broadened and broadened as a small panel was pushed backwards. For an instant I could hardly believe that here was indeed a door which led away from death. The next I threw myself through, and lay half-fainting upon the other side. The panel had closed again behind me, but the crash of the lamp, and a few moments afterwards the clang of the two slabs of metal, told me how narrow had been my escape.

'I was recalled to myself by a frantic plucking at my wrist, and I found myself lying upon the stone floor of a narrow corridor, while a woman bent over me and tugged at me with her left hand, while she held a candle in her right. It was the same good friend whose warning I had so foolishly rejected.

' "Come! Come!" she cried, breathlessly. "They will be here in a moment. They will see that you are not there. Oh, do not waste the so precious time, but come!"

'This time, at least, I did not scorn her advice. I staggered to my feet, and ran with her along the corridor and down a winding stair. The latter led to another broad passage, and, just as we reached it, we heard the sound of running feet, and the shouting of two voices—one answering the other—from the floor on which we were, and from the one beneath. My guide stopped, and looked about her like one who is at her wits' end. Then she threw open a door which led into a bedroom, through the window of which the moon was shining brightly.

' "It is your only chance," said she. "It is high, but it may be that you can jump it."

'As she spoke a light sprang into view at the further end of the passage, and I saw the lean figure of Colonel Lysander Stark rushing forward with a lantern in one hand, and a weapon like a butcher's cleaver in the other. I rushed across the bedroom, flung open the window, and looked out. How quiet and sweet and wholesome the garden looked in the moonlight, and it could not be more than thirty feet down. I clambered out upon the sill, but hesitated to jump, until I should have heard what passed between my saviour and the ruffian who pursued me. If she were ill-used, then at any risks I was determined to go back to her assistance. The thought had hardly flashed through my mind before he was at the door, pushing his way past her; but she threw her arms round him, and tried to hold him back.

' "Fritz! Fritz!" she cried in English, "remember your promise after the last time. You said it should not be again. He will be silent! Oh, he will be silent!"

' "You are mad, Elise!" he shouted, struggling to break away from her. "You will be the ruin of us. He has seen too much. Let me pass, I say!" He dashed her to one side, and, rushing to the window, cut at me with his heavy weapon. I had let myself go, and was hanging with my fingers in the window slot and my hands across the sill, when his blow fell. I was conscious of a dull pain, my grip loosened, and I fell into the garden below.

'I was shaken, but not hurt by the fall; so I picked myself up and rushed off among the bushes as hard as I could run, for I understood that I was far from being out of danger yet. Suddenly, however, as I ran, a deadly dizziness and sickness came over me. I glanced down at my hand, which was throbbing painfully, and then, for the first time, saw that my thumb had been cut off, and that the blood was pouring from my wound. I endeavoured to tie my handkerchief round it, but there came a sudden buzzing in my ears, and next moment I fell in a dead faint among the rose-bushes.

'How long I remained unconscious I cannot tell. It must have been a very long time, for the moon had sunk and a bright morning was breaking when I came to myself. My clothes were all sodden with dew, and my coat-sleeve was drenched with blood from my wounded thumb. The smarting of it recalled in an instant all the particulars of my night's adventure, and I sprang to my feet with the feeling that I might hardly yet be safe from my pursuers. But, to my astonishment, when I came to look round me neither house nor garden were to be seen. I had been lying in an angle of the hedge close by the highroad, and just a little lower down was a long building, which proved, upon my approaching it, to be the very station at which I had arrived upon the previous night. Were it not for the ugly wound upon my hand, all that had passed during those dreadful hours might have been an evil dream.

'Half dazed, I went into the station, and asked about the morning train. There would be one to Reading in less than an hour. The same porter was on duty, I found, as had been there when I arrived. I inquired from him whether he had ever heard of Colonel Lysander Stark. The name was strange to him. Had he observed a carriage the night before waiting for me? No, he had not. Was there a police station anywhere near? There was one about three miles off.

'It was too far for me to go, weak and ill as I was. I determined to wait until I got back to town before telling my story to the police. It was a little past six when I arrived, so I went first to have my wound dressed, and then the doctor was kind enough to bring me along here. I put the case into your hands, and shall do exactly what you advise.'

We both sat in silence for some little time after listening to this extraordinary narrative. Then Sherlock Holmes pulled down from the shelf one of the ponderous commonplace books in which he placed his cuttings.

'Here is an advertisement which will interest you,' said he. 'It appeared in all the papers about a year ago. Listen to this—"Lost on the 9th inst., Mr Jeremiah Hayling,* aged 26, a hydraulic engineer. Left his lodgings at ten o'clock at night, and has not been heard of since. Was dressed in," etc. etc. Ha! That represents the last time that the Colonel needed to have his machine overhauled, I fancy.'

'Good heavens!' cried my patient. 'Then that explains what the girl said.'

'Undoubtedly. It is quite clear that the Colonel was a cool and desperate man, who was absolutely determined that nothing should stand in the way of his little game, like those out-and-out pirates who will leave no survivor from a captured ship. Well, every moment now is precious, so, if you feel equal to it, we shall go down to Scotland Yard at once as a preliminary to starting for Eyford.'

Some three hours or so afterwards we were all in the train together, bound from Reading to the little Berkshire village. There were Sherlock Holmes, the hydraulic engineer, Inspector Bradstreet of Scotland Yard, a plain-clothes man, and myself. Bradstreet had spread an ordnance map of the county* out upon the seat, and was busy with his compasses drawing a circle with Eyford for its centre.

'There you are,' said he. 'That circle is drawn at a radius of ten miles from the village. The place we want must be somewhere near that line. You said ten miles, I think, sir?'

'It was an hour's good drive.'

'And you think that they brought you back all that way when you were unconscious?'

'They must have done so. I have a confused memory, too, of having been lifted and conveyed somewhere.'

'What I cannot understand,' said I, 'is why they should have spared you when they found you lying fainting in the garden. Perhaps the villain was softened by the woman's entreaties.'

'I hardly think that likely. I never saw a more inexorable face in my life.'

'Oh, we shall soon clear up all that,' said Bradstreet. 'Well, I have drawn my circle, and I only wish I knew at what point upon it the folk that we are in search of are to be found.'

'I think I could lay my finger on it,' said Holmes quietly.

'Really, now!' cried the inspector, 'you have formed your opinion! Come now, we shall see who agrees with you. I say south, for the country is more deserted there.'

'And I say east,' said my patient.

'I am for west,' remarked the plain-clothes man. 'There are several quiet little villages up there.'

'And I am for north,' said I; 'because there are no hills there, and our friend says that he did not notice the carriage go up any.'

'Come,' said the inspector, laughing; 'it's a very pretty diversity of opinion. We have boxed the compass* among us. Who do you give your casting vote to?'

'You are all wrong.'

'But we can't *all* be.'

'Oh, yes, you can. This is my point,' he placed his finger on the centre of the circle. 'This is where we shall find them.'

'But the twelve-mile drive?' gasped Hatherley.

'Six out and six back. Nothing simpler. You say yourself that the horse was fresh and glossy when you got in. How could it be that, if it had gone twelve miles over heavy roads?'

'Indeed it is a likely ruse enough,' observed Bradstreet thoughtfully. 'Of course there can be no doubt as to the nature of this gang.'

'None at all,' said Holmes. 'They are coiners on a large scale, and have used the machine to form the amalgam which has taken the place of silver.'*

'We have known for some time that a clever gang was at work,' said the inspector. 'They have been turning out half-crowns by the thousand. We even traced them as far as

Reading, but could get no further; for they had covered their traces in a way that showed that they were very old hands. But now, thanks to this lucky chance, I think that we have got them right enough.'

But the inspector was mistaken, for those criminals were not destined to fall into the hands of justice. As we rolled into Eyford station we saw a gigantic column of smoke which streamed up from behind a small clump of trees in the neighbourhood, and hung like an immense ostrich feather over the landscape.

'A house on fire?' asked Bradstreet, as the train steamed off again on its way.

'Yes, sir,' said the station-master.

'When did it break out?'

'I hear that it was during the night, sir, but it has got worse, and the whole place is in a blaze.'

'Whose house is it?'

'Dr Becher's.'

'Tell me,' broke in the engineer, 'is Dr Becher a German,* very thin, with a long sharp nose?'

The station-master laughed heartily. 'No, sir, Dr Becher is an Englishman, and there isn't a man in the parish who has a better-lined waistcoat. But he has a gentleman staying with him, a patient as I understand, who is a foreigner, and he looks as if a little good Berkshire beef would do him no harm.'

The station-master had not finished his speech before we were all hastening in the direction of the fire. The road topped a low hill, and there was a great widespread white-washed building in front of us, spouting fire at every chink and window, while in the garden in front three fire-engines were vainly striving to keep the flames under.

'That's it!' cried Hatherley, in intense excitement. 'There is the gravel drive, and there are the rose-bushes where I lay. That second window is the one that I jumped from.'

'Well, at least,' said Holmes, 'you have had your revenge upon them. There can be no question that it was your oil lamp which, when it was crushed in the press, set fire to the wooden walls, though no doubt they were too excited in the chase after you to observe it at the time. Now keep your eyes open in this crowd for your friends of last night, though I very much fear that they are a good hundred miles off by now.'

And Holmes's fears came to be realized, for from that day to this no word has ever been heard either of the beautiful woman, the sinister German, or the morose Englishman. Early that morning a peasant had met a cart, containing several people and some very bulky boxes, driving rapidly in the direction of Reading, but there all traces of the fugitives disappeared, and even Holmes's ingenuity failed to discover the least clue to their whereabouts.

The firemen had been much perturbed at the strange arrangements which they found within, and still more so by discovering a newly severed human thumb upon a window-sill of the second floor. About sunset, however, their efforts were at last successful, and they subdued the flames, but not before the roof had fallen in, and the whole place reduced to such absolute ruin that, save some twisted cylinders and iron piping, not a trace remained of the machinery which had cost our unfortunate aquaintance so dearly. Large masses of nickel and of tin were discovered stored in an outhouse, but no coins were to be found, which may have explained the presence of those bulky boxes which have been already referred to.

How our hydraulic engineer had been conveyed from the garden to the spot where he recovered his senses might have remained for ever a mystery were it not for the soft mould which told us a very plain tale. He had evidently been carried down by two persons, one of whom had remarkably small feet, and the other unusually large ones. On the whole, it was most probable that the silent Englishman, being less bold or less murderous than his companion, had assisted the woman to bear the unconscious man out of the way of danger.

'Well,' said our engineer ruefully, as we took our seats to return to London, 'it has been a pretty business for me! I have lost my thumb, and I have lost a fifty-guinea fee, and what have I gained!'

'Experience,' said Holmes, laughing. 'Indirectly it may be of value, you know; you have only to put it into words to gain the reputation of being excellent company for the remainder of your existence.'

The Noble Bachelor

THE Lord St Simon* marriage, and its curious termination, have long since ceased to be a subject of interest in those exalted circles in which the unfortunate bridegroom moves. Fresh scandals have eclipsed it, and their more piquant details have drawn the gossips away from this four-year-old drama.* As I have reason to believe, however, that the full facts have never been revealed to the general public, and as my friend Sherlock Holmes had a considerable share in clearing the matter up, I feel that no memoir of him would be complete without some little sketch of this remarkable episode.

It was a few weeks before my own marriage, during the days when I was still sharing rooms with Holmes in Baker Street, that he came home from an afternoon stroll to find a letter on the table waiting for him. I had remained indoors all day, for the weather had taken a sudden turn to rain, with high autumnal winds, and the jezail bullet which I had brought back in one of my limbs as a relic of my Afghan campaign,* throbbed with dull persistency. With my body in one easy chair and my legs upon another, I had surrounded myself with a cloud of newspapers, until at last, saturated with the news of the day, I tossed them all aside and lay listless, watching the huge crest and monogram upon the envelope upon the table, and wondering lazily who my friend's noble correspondent could be.

'Here is a very fashionable epistle,' I remarked as he entered. 'Your morning's letters, if I remember right, were from a fishmonger and a tide-waiter.'*

'Yes, my correspondence has certainly the charm of variety,' he answered, smiling, 'and the humbler are usually the more interesting. This looks like one of those unwelcome social summonses which call upon a man either to be bored or to lie.'

He broke the seal, and glanced over the contents.

'Oh, come, it may prove to be something of interest after all.'

'Not social, then?'

'No, distinctly professional.'

'And from a noble client?'

'One of the highest in England.'

'My dear fellow, I congratulate you.'

'I assure you, Watson, without affectation, that the status of my client is a matter of less moment to me than the interest of his case. It is just possible, however, that that also may not be wanting in this new investigation. You have been reading the papers diligently of late, have you not?'

'It looks like it,' said I, ruefully, pointing to a huge bundle in the corner. 'I have had nothing else to do.'

'It is fortunate, for you will perhaps be able to post me up. I read nothing except the criminal news and the agony column. The latter is always instructive. But if you have followed recent events so closely you must have read about Lord St Simon and his wedding?'

'Oh, yes, with the deepest interest.'

'That is well. The letter which I hold in my hand is from Lord St Simon. I will read it to you, and in return you must turn over these papers and let me have whatever bears upon the matter. This is what he says:

MY DEAR MR SHERLOCK HOLMES,

Lord Backwater* tells me that I may place implicit reliance upon your judgment and discretion. I have determined, therefore, to call upon you, and to consult you in reference to the very painful event which has occurred in connection with my wedding. Mr Lestrade, of Scotland Yard, is acting already in the matter, but he assures me that he sees no objection to your co-operation, and that he even thinks that it might be of some assistance. I will call at four o'clock in the afternoon, and should you have any other engagement at that time, I hope you will postpone it, as this is a matter of paramount importance.

Yours faithfully,
ROBERT ST SIMON*

'It is dated from Grosvenor Mansions,* written with a quill pen, and the noble lord has had the misfortune to get a smear of ink upon the outer side of his right little finger,' remarked Holmes, as he folded up the epistle.

'He says four o'clock. It is three now. He will be here in an hour.'

'Then I have just time, with your assistance, to get clear upon the subject. Turn over those papers, and arrange the extracts in their order of time, while I take a glance as to who our client is.' He picked a red-covered volume* from a line of books of reference beside the mantelpiece. 'Here he is,' said he, sitting down and flattening it out upon his knee. ' "Robert Walsingham de Vere St Simon, second son of the Duke of Balmoral"*—Hum! "Arms: Azure, three caltrops in chief over a fess sable.* Born in 1846." He's forty-one years of age, which is mature for marriage. Was Under-Secretary for the Colonies in a late Administration. The Duke, his father, was at one time Secretary for Foreign Affairs.* They inherit Plantagenet blood by direct descent, and Tudor on the distaff side.* Ha! Well, there is nothing very instructive in all this. I think I must turn to you, Watson, for something more solid.'

'I have very little difficulty in finding what I want,' said I, 'for the facts are quite recent, and the matter struck me as remarkable. I feared to refer them to you, however, as I knew that you had an inquiry on hand, and that you disliked the intrusion of other matters.'

'Oh, you mean the little problem of the Grosvenor Square furniture van.* That is quite cleared up now—though, indeed, it was obvious from the first. Pray give me the results of your newspaper selections.'

'Here is the first notice which I can find. It is in the personal column of the *Morning Post*,* and dates, as you see, some weeks back. "A marriage has been arranged,"* it says, "and will, if rumour is correct, very shortly take place, between Lord Robert St Simon, second son of the Duke of Balmoral, and Miss Hatty Doran,* the only daughter of Aloysius Doran, Esq., of San Francisco, Cal., U.S.A." That is all.'

'Terse and to the point,' remarked Holmes, stretching his long thin legs towards the fire.

'There was a paragraph amplifying this in one of the society papers of the same week. Ah, here it is. "There will soon be a call for protection in the marriage market, for the present free-trade principle appears to tell heavily against our home product. One by one the management of the noble houses of Great Britain is passing into the hands of our fair cousins from across the Atlantic.* An important addition has been made during the last week to the list of prizes which have been borne away by these charming invaders. Lord St Simon, who has shown himself for over twenty years proof against the little god's arrows,* has now definitely announced his approaching marriage with Miss Hatty Doran, the fascinating daughter of a Californian millionaire. Miss Doran, whose graceful figure and striking face attracted much attention at the Westbury House festivities,* is an only child, and it is currently reported that her dowry will run to considerably over the six figures, with expectancies for the future. As it is an open secret that the Duke of Balmoral has been compelled to sell his pictures within the last few years, and as Lord St Simon has no property of his own, save the small estate of Birchmoor,* it is obvious that the Californian heiress is not the only gainer by an alliance which will enable her to make the easy and common transition from a republican lady* to a British title." '

'Anything else?' asked Holmes, yawning.

'Oh, yes; plenty. Then there is another note in the *Morning Post* to say that the marriage would be an absolutely quiet one,* that it would be at St George's, Hanover Square,* that only half a dozen intimate friends would be invited, and that the party would return to the furnished house at Lancaster Gate* which has been taken by Mr Aloysius Doran. Two days later—that is, on Wednesday last—there is a curt announcement that the wedding had taken place, and that the honeymoon would be passed at Lord Back-water's place, near Petersfield.* Those are all the notices which appeared before the disappearance of the bride.'

'Before the what?' asked Holmes, with a start.

'The vanishing of the lady.'

'When did she vanish, then?'

'At the wedding breakfast.'

'Indeed. This is more interesting than it promised to be; quite dramatic, in fact.'

'Yes; it struck me as being a little out of the common.'

'They often vanish before the ceremony, and occasionally during the honeymoon; but I cannot call to mind anything quite so prompt as this. Pray let me have the details.'

'I warn you that they are very incomplete.'

'Perhaps we may make them less so.'

'Such as they are, they are set forth in a single article of a morning newspaper of yesterday, which I will read to you. It is headed, "Singular Occurrence at a Fashionable Wedding":

' "The family of Lord Robert St Simon has been thrown into the greatest consternation by the strange and painful episodes which have taken place in connection with his wedding. The ceremony, as shortly announced in the papers of yesterday, occurred on the previous morning; but it is only now that it has been possible to confirm the strange rumours which have been so persistently floating about. In spite of the attempts of the friends to hush the matter up, so much public attention has now been drawn to it that no good purpose can be served by affecting to disregard what is a common subject for conversation.

' "The ceremony, which was performed at St George's, Hanover Square, was a very quiet one, no one being present save the father of the bride, Mr Aloysius Doran, the Duchess of Balmoral, Lord Backwater, Lord Eustace and Lady Clara St Simon (the younger brother and sister of the bridegroom), and Lady Alicia Whittington.* The whole party proceeded afterwards to the house of Mr Aloysius Doran, at Lancaster Gate, where breakfast had been prepared. It appears that some little trouble had been caused by a woman, whose name has not been ascertained, who endeavoured to force her way into the house after the bridal party, alleging that she had some claim upon Lord St Simon.

It was only after a painful and prolonged scene that she was ejected by the butler and the footman. The bride, who had fortunately entered the house before this unpleasant interruption, had sat down to breakfast with the rest, when she complained of a sudden indisposition, and retired to her room. Her prolonged absence having caused some comment, her father followed her; but learned from her maid that she had only come up to her chamber for an instant, caught up an ulster and bonnet, and hurried down to the passage. One of the footmen declared that he had seen a lady leave the house thus apparelled: but had refused to credit that it was his mistress, believing her to be with the company. On ascertaining that his daughter had disappeared, Mr Aloysius Doran, in conjunction with the bridegroom, instantly put themselves into communication with the police, and very energetic inquiries are being made, which will probably result in a speedy clearing up of this very singular business. Up to a late hour last night, however, nothing had transpired as to the whereabouts of the missing lady. There are rumours of foul play in the matter, and it is said that the police have caused the arrest of the woman who had caused the original disturbance, in the belief that, from jealousy or some other motive, she may have been concerned in the strange disappearance of the bride." '

'And is that all?'

'Only one little item in another of the morning papers, but it is a suggestive one.'

'And it is?'

'That Miss Flora Millar,* the lady who had caused the disturbance, has actually been arrested. It appears that she was formerly a *danseuse** at the Allegro,* and that she had known the bridegroom for some years. There are no further particulars, and the whole case is in your hands now—so far as it has been set forth in the public press.'

'And an exceedingly interesting case it appears to be. I would not have missed it for worlds. But there is a ring at the bell, Watson, and as the clock makes it a few minutes after four, I have no doubt that this will prove to be our noble client. Do not dream of going, Watson, for I very much prefer having a witness, if only as a check to my own memory.'

'Lord Robert St Simon,' announced our page-boy, throwing open the door. A gentleman entered, with a pleasant, cultured face, high-nosed and pale, with something perhaps of petulance about the mouth, and with the steady, well-opened eye of a man whose pleasant lot it had ever been to command and to be obeyed. His manner was brisk, and yet his general appearance gave an undue impression of age, for he had a slight forward stoop, and a little bend of the knees as he walked. His hair, too, as he swept off his very curly brimmed hat, was grizzled round the edges, and thin upon the top. As to his dress, it was careful to the verge of foppishness, with high collar, black frock-coat, white waistcoat, yellow gloves, patent-leather shoes, and light-coloured gaiters. He advanced slowly into the room, turning his head from left to right, and swinging in his right hand the cord which held his golden eye-glasses.

'Good day, Lord St Simon,' said Holmes, rising and bowing. 'Pray take the basket chair. This is my friend and colleague, Dr Watson. Draw up a little to the fire, and we shall talk this matter over.'

'A most painful matter to me, as you can most readily imagine, Mr Holmes. I have been cut to the quick. I understand you have already managed several delicate cases of this sort, sir, though I presume that they were hardly from the same class of society.'

'No, I am descending.'

'I beg pardon?'

'My last client of the sort was a king.'

'Oh, really! I had no idea. And which king?'

'The King of Scandinavia.*

'What! Had he lost his wife?'

'You can understand,' said Holmes suavely, 'that I extend to the affairs of my other clients the same secrecy which I promise to you in yours.'

'Of course! Very right! very right! I'm sure I beg pardon. As to my own case, I am ready to give you any information which may assist you in forming an opinion.'

'Thank you. I have already learned all that is in the public prints,* nothing more. I presume that I may take it as correct—this article, for example, as to the disappearance of the bride.'

Lord St Simon glanced over it. 'Yes, it is correct, as far as it goes.'

'But it needs a great deal of supplementing before anyone could offer an opinion. I think that I may arrive at my facts most directly by questioning you.'

'Pray do so.'

'When did you first meet Miss Hatty Doran?'

'In San Francisco, a year ago.'

'You were travelling in the States?'

'Yes.'

'Did you become engaged then?'

'No.'

'But you were on a friendly footing?'

'I was amused by her society, and she could see that I was amused.'

'Her father is very rich?'

'He is said to be the richest man on the Pacific Slope.*'

'And how did he make his money?'

'In mining. He had nothing a few years ago. Then he struck gold, invested it, and came up by leaps and bounds.'

'Now, what is your own impression as to the young lady's—your wife's character?'

The nobleman swung his glasses a little faster and stared down into the fire. 'You see, Mr Holmes,' said he, 'my wife was twenty before her father became a rich man. During that time she ran free in a mining camp, and wandered through woods or mountains, so that her education has come from nature rather than from the schoolmaster. She is what we call in England a tomboy,* with a strong nature, wild and free, unfettered by any sort of traditions. She is impetuous—volcanic, I was about to say. She is swift in making up her mind, and fearless in carrying out her resolutions. On the other hand, I would not have given her the name which I have the honour to bear' (he gave a little stately cough) 'had I not thought her to be at bottom a noble woman. I believe she is capable of heroic self-sacrifice, and that anything dishonourable would be repugnant to her.'

'Have you her photograph?'

'I brought this with me.' He opened a locket, and showed us the full face of a very lovely woman. It was not a photograph, but an ivory miniature, and the artist had brought out the full effect of the lustrous black hair, the large dark eyes, and the exquisite mouth. Holmes gazed long and earnestly at it. Then he closed the locket and handed it back to Lord St Simon.

'The young lady came to London, then, and you renewed your acquaintance?'

'Yes, her father brought her over for this last London season. I met her several times, became engaged to her, and have now married her.'

'She brought, I understand, a considerable dowry.'

'A fair dowry. Not more than is usual in my family.'

'And this, of course, remains to you, since the marriage is a *fait accompli*?'*

'I really have made no inquiries on the subject.'

'Very naturally not. Did you see Miss Doran on the day before the wedding?'

'Yes.'

'Was she in good spirits?'

'Never better. She kept talking of what we should do in our future lives.'

'Indeed. That is very interesting. And on the morning of the wedding?'

'She was as bright as possible—at least, until after the ceremony.'

'And did you observe any change in her then?'

'Well, to tell the truth, I saw then the first signs that I had ever seen that her temper was just a little sharp. The incident, however, was too trivial to relate, and can have no possible bearing upon the case.'

'Pray let us have it, for all that.'

'Oh, it is childish. She dropped her bouquet as we went towards the vestry. She was passing the front pew at the time, and it fell over into the pew. There was a moment's delay, but the gentleman in the pew handed it up to her again, and it did not appear to be the worse for the fall. Yet, when I spoke to her of the matter, she answered me abruptly; and in the carriage, on our way home, she seemed absurdly agitated over this trifling cause.'

'Indeed. You say that there was a gentleman in the pew. Some of the general public were present, then?'

'Oh, yes. It is impossible to exclude them when the church is open.'

'This gentleman was not one of your wife's friends?'

'No, no; I call him a gentleman by courtesy, but he was quite a common-looking person. I hardly noticed his appearance. But really I think that we are wandering rather far from the point.'

'Lady St Simon, then, returned from the wedding in a less cheerful frame of mind than she had gone to it. What did she do on re-entering her father's house?'

'I saw her in conversation with her maid.'

'And who is her maid?'

'Alice is her name. She is an American, and came from California with her.'

'A confidential servant?'

'A little too much so. It seemed to me that her mistress allowed her to take great liberties. Still, of course, in America they look upon these things in a different way.'

'How long did she speak to this Alice?'

'Oh, a few minutes. I had something else to think of.'

'You did not overhear what they said?'

'Lady St Simon said something about "jumping a claim".* She was accustomed to use slang of the kind. I have no idea what she meant.'

'American slang is very expressive sometimes. And what did your wife do when she had finished speaking to her maid?'

'She walked into the breakfast-room.'

'On your arm?'

'No, alone. She was very independent in little matters like that. Then, after we had sat down for ten minutes or so, she rose hurriedly, uttered some words of apology, and left the room. She never came back.'

'But this maid Alice, as I understand, deposes that she went to her room, covered her bride's dress with a long ulster, put on a bonnet, and went out.'

'Quite so. And she was afterwards seen walking into Hyde Park in company with Flora Millar, a woman who is now in custody, and who had already made a disturbance at Mr Doran's house that morning.'

'Ah, yes. I should like a few particulars as to this young lady, and your relations to her.'

Lord St Simon shrugged his shoulders, and raised his eyebrows. 'We have been on a friendly footing for some years—I may say on a *very* friendly footing. She used to be at the Allegro. I have not treated her ungenerously, and she has no just cause of complaint against me, but you know what women are, Mr Holmes. Flora was a dear little thing, but exceedingly hot-headed, and devotedly attached to me. She wrote me dreadful letters when she heard that I was to be married, and to tell the truth the reason why I had the marriage celebrated so quietly was that I feared lest there might be a scandal in the church. She came to Mr Doran's door just after we returned, and she endeavoured to push her way in, uttering very abusive expressions towards my wife, and even threatening her, but I had foreseen the possibility of something of the sort, and I had given instructions to the servants, who soon pushed her out again. She was quiet when she saw that there was no good in making a row.'

'Did your wife hear all this?'

'No, thank goodness, she did not.'

'And she was seen walking with this very woman afterwards?'

'Yes. That is what Mr Lestrade, of Scotland Yard, looks upon as so serious. It is thought that Flora decoyed my wife out, and laid some terrible trap for her.'

'Well, it is a possible supposition.'

'You think so, too?'

'I did not say a probable one. But you do not yourself look upon this as likely?'

'I do not think Flora would hurt a fly.'

'Still, jealousy is a strange transformer of characters. Pray what is your own theory as to what took place?'

'Well, really, I came to seek a theory, not to propound one. I have given you all the facts. Since you ask me, however, I may say that it has occurred to me as possible that the excitement of this affair, the consciousness that she had made so immense a social stride, had the effect of causing some little nervous disturbance in my wife.'

'In short, that she had become suddenly deranged?'

'Well, really, when I consider that she has turned her back—I will not say upon me, but upon so much that many have aspired to without success—I can hardly explain it in any other fashion.'

'Well, certainly that is also a conceivable hypothesis,' said Holmes, smiling. 'And now, Lord St Simon, I think that I have nearly all my data. May I ask whether you were seated at the breakfast-table so that you could see out of the window?'

'We could see the other side of the road, and the Park.'

'Quite so. Then I do not think that I need detain you any longer. I shall communicate with you.'

'Should you be fortunate enough to solve this problem,' said our client, rising.

'I have solved it.'

'Eh? What was that?'

'I say that I have solved it.'

'Where, then, is my wife?'

'That is a detail which I shall speedily supply.'

Lord St Simon shook his head. 'I am afraid that it will take wiser heads than yours or mine,' he remarked, and bowing in a stately, old-fashioned manner, he departed.

'It is very good of Lord St Simon to honour my head by putting it on a level with his own,' said Sherlock Holmes, laughing. 'I think that I shall have a whisky and soda and a cigar after all this cross-questioning. I had formed my conclusions as to the case before our client came into the room.'

'My dear Holmes!'

'I have notes of several similar cases, though none, as I remarked before, which were quite as prompt. My whole examination served to turn my conjecture into a certainty. Circumstantial evidence is occasionally very convincing, as when you find a trout in the milk, to quote Thoreau's example.'*

'But I have heard all that you have heard.'

'Without, however, the knowledge of pre-existing cases which serves me so well. There was a parallel instance in Aberdeen some years back, and something on very much the same lines at Munich the year after the Franco-Prussian War.* It is one of these cases—but hullo, here is Lestrade! Good afternoon, Lestrade! You will find an extra tumbler upon the sideboard, and there are cigars in the box.'

The official detective was attired in a pea-jacket and cravat, which gave him a decidedly nautical appearance, and he carried a black canvas bag in his hand. With a short greeting he seated himself, and lit the cigar which had been offered to him.

'What's up, then?' asked Holmes, with a twinkle in his eye. 'You look dissatisfied.'

'And I feel dissatisfied. It is this infernal St Simon marriage case. I can make neither head nor tail of the business.'

'Really! You surprise me.'

'Who ever heard of such a mixed affair? Every clue seems to slip through my fingers. I have been at work upon it all day.'

'And very wet it seems to have made you,' said Holmes, laying his hand upon the arm of the pea-jacket.

'Yes, I have been dragging the Serpentine.'*

'In Heaven's name, what for?'

'In search of the body of Lady St Simon.'

Sherlock Holmes leaned back in his chair and laughed heartily.

'Have you dragged the basin of the Trafalgar Square fountain?'* he asked.

'Why? What do you mean?'

'Because you have just as good a chance of finding this lady in the one as in the other.'

Lestrade shot an angry glance at my companion. 'I suppose you know all about it,' he snarled.

'Well, I have only just heard the facts, but my mind is made up.'

'Oh, indeed! Then you think that the Serpentine plays no part in the matter?'

'I think it very unlikely.'

'Then perhaps you will kindly explain how it is that we found this in it?' He opened his bag as he spoke, and tumbled on to the floor a wedding dress of watered silk, a pair of white satin shoes, and a bride's wreath and veil, all discoloured and soaked in water. 'There,' said he, putting a new wedding-ring upon the top of the pile. 'There is a little nut for you to crack, Master Holmes.'

'Oh, indeed,' said my friend, blowing blue rings into the air. 'You dragged them from the Serpentine?'

'No. They were found floating near the margin by a park-keeper. They were identified as her clothes, and it seemed to me that if the clothes were there the body would not be far off.'

'By the same brilliant reasoning, every man's body is to be found in the neighbourhood of his wardrobe. And pray what did you hope to arrive at through this?'

'At some evidence implicating Flora Millar in the disappearance.'

'I am afraid you will find it difficult.'

'Are you indeed, now?' cried Lestrade, with some bitterness. 'I am afraid, Holmes, that you are not very practical with your deductions and your inferences. You have made two blunders in as many minutes. This dress does implicate Miss Flora Millar.'

'And how?'

'In the dress is a pocket. In the pocket is a card-case. In the card-case is a note. And here is the very note.' He slapped it down upon the table in front of him. 'Listen to this. "You will see me when all is ready. Come at once, F.H.M." Now my theory all along has been that Lady St Simon was decoyed away by Flora Millar, and that she, with confederates no doubt, was responsible for her disappearance. Here, signed with her initials, is the very note which was no doubt quietly slipped into her hand at the door, and which lured her within their reach.'

'Very good, Lestrade,' said Holmes, laughing. 'You really are very fine indeed. Let me see it.' He took up the paper in a listless way, but his attention instantly became riveted, and he gave a little cry of satisfaction. 'This is indeed important,' said he.

'Ha, you find it so?'

'Extremely so. I congratulate you warmly.'

Lestrade rose in his triumph and bent his head to look. 'Why,' he shrieked, 'you're looking on the wrong side.'

'On the contrary, this is the right side.'

'The right side? You're mad! Here is the note written in pencil over here.'

'And over here is what appears to be a fragment of a hotel bill, which interests me deeply.'

'There's nothing in it. I looked at it before,' said Lestrade. ' "Oct. 4th, rooms 8s., breakfast 2s. 6d., cocktail 1s., lunch 2s. 6d., glass sherry 8d." I see nothing in that.'

'Very likely not. It is most important all the same. As to the note, it is important also, or at least the initials are, so I congratulate you again.'

'I've wasted time enough,' said Lestrade, rising, 'I believe in hard work, and not in sitting by the fire spinning fine theories. Good-day, Mr Holmes, and we shall see which gets to the bottom of the matter first.' He gathered up the garments, thrust them into the bag, and made for the door.

'Just one hint to you, Lestrade,' drawled Holmes, before his rival vanished; 'I will tell you the true solution of the matter. Lady St Simon is a myth. There is not, and there never has been, any such person.'

Lestrade looked sadly at my companion. Then he turned to me, tapped his forehead three times, shook his head solemnly, and hurried away.

He had hardly shut the door behind him, when Holmes rose and put on his overcoat. 'There is something in what the fellow says about outdoor work,' he remarked, 'so I think, Watson, that I must leave you to your papers for a little.'

It was after five o'clock when Sherlock Holmes left me, but I had no time to be lonely, for within an hour there arrived a confectioner's man with a very large flat box. This he unpacked with the help of a youth whom he had brought with him, and presently, to my very great astonishment, a quite epicurean little cold supper began to be laid out upon our humble lodging-house mahogany. There were a couple of brace of cold woodcock, a pheasant, a *pâté de foie gras* pie, with a group of ancient and cobwebby bottles. Having laid out all these luxuries, my two visitors vanished away, like the genii of the Arabian Nights,* with no explanation save that the things had been paid for, and were ordered to this address.

Just before nine o'clock Sherlock Holmes stepped briskly into the room. His features were gravely set, but there was a light in his eye which made me think that he had not been disappointed in his conclusions.

'They have laid the supper, then,' he said, rubbing his hands.

'You seem to expect company. They have laid for five.'

'Yes, I fancy we may have some company dropping in,' said he. 'I am surprised that Lord St Simon has not already arrived. Ha! I fancy that I hear his step now upon the stairs.'

It was indeed our visitor of the morning who came bustling in, dangling his glasses more vigorously than ever, and with a very perturbed expression upon his aristocratic features.

'My messenger reached you, then?' asked Holmes.

'Yes, and I confess that the contents startled me beyond measure. Have you good authority for what you say?'

'The best possible.'

Lord St Simon sank into a chair, and passed his hand over his forehead.

'What will the Duke say,' he murmured, 'when he hears that one of the family has been subjected to such a humiliation?'

'It is the purest accident. I cannot allow that there is any humiliation.'

'Ah, you look on these things from another standpoint.'

'I fail to see that anyone is to blame. I can hardly see how the lady could have acted otherwise, though her abrupt method of doing it was undoubtedly to be regretted. Having no mother, she had no one to advise her at such a crisis.'

'It was a slight, sir, a public slight,' said Lord St Simon, tapping his fingers upon the table.

'You must make allowance for this poor girl, placed in so unprecedented a position.'

'I will make no allowance. I am very angry indeed, and I have been shamefully used.'

'I think I heard a ring,' said Holmes. 'Yes, there are steps on the landing. If I cannot persuade you to take a lenient view of the matter, Lord St Simon, I have brought an advocate here who may be more successful.' he opened the door and ushered in a lady and gentleman. 'Lord St Simon,' said he, 'allow me to introduce you to Mr and Mrs Francis Hay Moulton.* The lady, I think, you have already met.'

At the sight of these newcomers our client had sprung from his seat, and stood very erect, with his eyes cast down and his hand thrust into the breast of his frock-coat, a picture of offended dignity. The lady had taken a quick step forward and had held out her hand to him, but he still refused to raise his eyes. It was as well for his resolution, perhaps, for her pleading face was one which it was hard to resist.

'You're angry, Robert,' said she. 'Well, I guess you have every cause to be.'

'Pray make no apology to me,' said Lord St Simon, bitterly.

'Oh, yes, I know that I treated you real bad, and that I should have spoken to you before I went; but I was kind of rattled, and from the time when I saw Frank here again, I just didn't know what I was doing or saying. I only wonder that I didn't fall down and do a faint right there before the altar.'

'Perhaps, Mrs Moulton, you would like my friend and me to leave the room while you explain this matter?'

'If I may give an opinion,' remarked the strange gentleman, 'we've had just a little too much secrecy over this business already. For my part, I should like all Europe and America to hear the rights of it.' He was a small, wiry, sunburned man, with a sharp face and alert manner.

'Then I'll tell our story right away,' said the lady. 'Frank here and I met in '81, in McQuire's camp,* near the Rockies, where Pa was working a claim. We were engaged to each other, Frank and I; but then one day father struck a rich pocket, and made a pile, while poor Frank here had a claim that petered out and came to nothing. The richer Pa grew, the poorer was Frank; so at last Pa wouldn't hear of our engagement lasting any longer, and he took me away to 'Frisco.* Frank wouldn't throw up his hand, though; so he followed me there, and he saw me without Pa knowing anything about it. It would only have made him mad to know, so we just fixed it all up for ourselves. Frank said that he would go and make his pile, too, and never come back to claim me until he had as much as Pa. So then I promised to wait for him to the end of time, and pledged myself not to marry anyone else while he lived. "Why shouldn't we be married right away, then," said he, "and then I will feel sure of you; and I won't claim to be your husband until I come back." Well, we talked it over, and he had fixed it all up so nicely, with a clergyman all ready in waiting, that we just did it right there; and then Frank went off to seek his fortune and I went back to Pa.

'The next that I heard of Frank was that he was in Montana, and then he went prospecting into Arizona, and then I heard of him from New Mexico.* After that came a long newspaper story about how a miners' camp had been attacked by Apache Indians,* and there was my Frank's name among the killed. I fainted dead away, and I was very sick for months after. Pa thought I had a decline, and took me to half the doctors in 'Frisco. Not a word of news came for a year or more, so that I never doubted that Frank was really dead. Then Lord St Simon came to 'Frisco, and we came to London, and a marriage was arranged, and Pa was very pleased, but I felt all the time that no man on this earth would ever take the place in my heart that had been given to my poor Frank.

'Still, if I had married Lord St Simon, of course I'd have done my duty by him. We can't command our love, but we can our actions. I went to the altar with him with the intention that I would make him just as good a wife as it was in me to be. But you may imagine what I felt when, just as I came to the altar rails, I glanced and saw Frank standing looking at me out of the first pew. I thought it was his ghost at first; but, when I looked again, there he was still, with a kind of question in his eyes as if to ask me whether I were glad or sorry to see him. I wonder I didn't drop. I know that everything was turning round, and the words of the clergy-man were just like the buzz of a bee in my ear. I didn't know what to do. Should I stop the service and make a scene in the church?* I glanced at him again, and he seemed to know what I was thinking, for he raised his finger to his lips to tell me to be still. Then I saw him scribble on a piece of paper, and I knew he was writing me a note. As I passed his pew on the way out I dropped my bouquet over to him, and he slipped the note into my hand when he returned me the flowers. It was only a line asking me to join him when he made the sign to me to do so. Of course I never doubted for a moment that my first duty was now to him, and I determined to do just whatever he might direct.

'When I got back I told my maid, who had known him in California, and had always been his friend. I ordered her to say nothing, but to get a few things packed and my ulster ready. I know I ought to have spoken to Lord St Simon, but it was dreadful hard before his mother and all those great people. I just made up my mind to run away, and explain afterwards. I hadn't been at the table ten minutes before I saw Frank out of the window at the other side of the road. He beckoned to me, and then began walking into the Park. I slipped out, put on my things, and followed him. Some woman came talking something or other about Lord St Simon to me—seemed to me from the little I heard as if he had a little secret of his own before marriage also—but I managed to get away from her, and soon overtook Frank. We got into a cab together, and away we drove to some lodgings he had taken in Gordon Square,* and that was my true wedding after all those years of waiting. Frank had been a prisoner among the Apaches, had escaped, came on to 'Frisco, found that I had given him up for dead and had gone to England, followed me there, and had come upon me at last on the very morning of my second wedding.'

'I saw it in a paper,' explained the American. 'It gave the name and the church, but not where the lady lived.'

'Then we had a talk as to what we should do, and Frank was all for openness, but I was so ashamed of it all that I felt as if I would like to vanish away and never see any of them again, just sending a line to Pa, perhaps, to show him that I was alive. It was awful to me to think of all those lords and ladies sitting round that breakfast-table, and waiting for me to come back. So Frank took my wedding clothes and things, and made a bundle of them so that I should not be traced, and dropped them away somewhere where no one should find them. It is likely that we should have gone on to Paris to-morrow, only that this good gentleman, Mr Holmes, came round to us this evening, though how he found us is more than I can think, and he showed us very clearly and kindly that I was wrong and that Frank was right, and that we should put ourselves in the wrong if we were so secret. Then he offered to give us a chance of talking to Lord St Simon alone, and so we came right away and I am very sorry if I have given you pain, and I hope that you do not think very meanly of me.'

Lord St Simon had by no means relaxed his rigid attitude, but had listened with a frowning brow and a compressed lip to this long narrative.

'Excuse me,' he said, 'but it is not my custom to discuss my most intimate personal affairs in this public manner.'

'Then you won't forgive me? You won't shake hands before I go?'

'Oh, certainly, if it would give you any pleasure.' He put out his hand and coldly grasped that which she extended to him.

'I had hoped,' suggested Holmes, 'that you would have joined us in a friendly supper.'

'I think that there you ask a little too much,' responded his lordship. 'I may be forced to acquiesce in these recent developments, but I can hardly be expected to make merry over them. I think that, with your permission, I will now wish you all a very good night.' He included us all in a sweeping bow, and stalked out of the room.

'Then I trust that you at least will honour me with your company,' said Sherlock Holmes. 'It is always a joy to me to meet an American, Mr Moulton, for I am one of those who believe that the folly of a monarch and the blundering of a Minister in far gone years will not prevent our children from being some day citizens of the same world-wide country under a flag which shall be a quartering of the Union Jack with the Stars and Stripes.'*

'The case has been an interesting one,' remarked Holmes, when our visitors had left, 'because it serves to show very clearly how simple the explanation may be of an affair which at first sight seems to be almost inexplicable. Nothing could be more natural than the sequence of events as narrated by this lady, and nothing stranger than the result when viewed, for instance, by Mr Lestrade of Scotland Yard.'

'You were not yourself at fault, then?'

'From the first, two facts were very obvious to me, the one that the lady had been quite willing to undergo the wedding ceremony, the other that she had repented of it within a few minutes of returning home. Obviously something had occurred during the morning, then, to cause her to change her mind. What could that something be? She could not have spoken to anyone when she was out, for she had been in the company of the bridegroom. Had she seen someone, then? If she had, it must be someone from America, because she had spent so short a time in this country that she could hardly have allowed anyone to acquire so deep an influence over her that the mere sight of him would induce her to change her plans so completely. You see we have already arrived, by a process of exclusion, at the idea that she might have seen an American. Then who could this American be, and why should he possess so much influence over her? It might be a lover; it might be a husband. Her young womanhood had, I knew, been spent in rough scenes, and under strange conditions. So far had I got before I ever heard Lord St Simon's narrative. When he told us of a man in a pew, of the change in the bride's manner, of so transparent a device of obtaining a note as the dropping of a bouquet, of her resort to her confidential maid, and of her very significant allusion to claim-jumping, which in miners' parlance means taking possession of that which another person has prior claim to, the whole situation became absolutely clear. She had gone off with a man, and the man was either a lover or was a previous husband, the chances being in favour of the latter.'

'And how in the world did you find them?'

'It might have been difficult, but friend Lestrade held information in his hands the value of which he did not himself know. The initials were of course of the highest importance, but more valuable still was it to know that within a week he had settled his bill at one of the most select London hotels.'

'How did you deduce the select?'

'By the select prices. Eight shillings for a bed and eight-pence for a glass of sherry, pointed to one of the most expensive hotels. There are not many in London which charge at that rate. In the second one which I visited in Northumberland Avenue,* I learned by an inspection of the book that Francis H. Moulton, an American gentleman, had left only the day before, and on looking over the entries against him, I came upon the very items which I had seen in the duplicate bill. His letters were to be forwarded to 226, Gordon Square, so thither I travelled, and being fortunate enough to find the loving couple at home, I ventured to give them some paternal advice, and to point out to them that it would be better in every way that they should make their position a little clearer, both to the general public and to Lord St Simon in particular. I invited them to meet him here, and, as you see, I made him keep the appointment.'

'But with no very good results,' I remarked. 'His conduct was certainly not very gracious.'

'Ah! Watson,' said Holmes, smiling, 'perhaps you would not be very gracious either, if, after all the trouble of wooing and wedding, you found yourself deprived in an instant of wife and of fortune. I think that we may judge Lord St Simon very mercifully, and thank our stars that we are never likely to find ourselves in the same position. Draw your chair up, and hand me my violin, for the only problem which we have still to solve is how to while away these bleak autumnal evenings.'

The Beryl Coronet

'HOLMES,' said I, as I stood one morning in our bow-window* looking down the street, 'here is a madman coming along. It seems rather sad that his relatives should allow him to come out alone.'

My friend rose lazily from his armchair, and stood with his hands in the pockets of his dressing-gown, looking over my shoulder. It was a bright, crisp February morning, and the snow of the day before still lay deep upon the ground, shimmering brightly in the wintry sun. Down the centre of Baker Street it had been ploughed into a brown crumbly band by the traffic, but at either side and on the heaped-up edges of the footpaths it still lay as white as when it fell. The grey pavement had been cleaned and scraped, but was still dangerously slippery, so that there were fewer passengers than usual. Indeed, from the direction of the Metropolitan station* no one was coming save the single gentleman whose eccentric conduct had drawn my attention.

He was a man of about fifty, tall, portly, and imposing, with a massive, strongly marked face and a commanding figure. He was dressed in a sombre yet rich style, in black frock-coat, shining hat, neat brown gaiters, and well-cut pearl-grey trousers. Yet his actions were in absurd contrast to the dignity of his dress and features, for he was running hard, with occasional little springs, such as a weary man gives who is little accustomed to set any tax upon his legs. As he ran he jerked his hands up and down, waggled his head, and writhed his face into the most extraordinary contortions.

'What on earth can be the matter with him?' I asked. 'He is looking up at the numbers of the houses.'

'I believe that he is coming here,' said Holmes, rubbing his hands.

'Here?'

'Yes; I rather think he is coming to consult me profession-
ally. I think that I recognize the symptoms. Ha! did I not tell
you?' As he spoke, the man, puffing and blowing, rushed at
our door, and pulled at our bell until the whole house
resounded with the clanging.

A few moments later he was in our room, still puffing,
still gesticulating, but with so fixed a look of grief and
despair in his eyes that our smiles were turned in an instant
to horror and pity. For a while he could not get his words
out, but swayed his body and plucked at his hair like one
who has been driven to the extreme limits of his reason.
Then, suddenly springing to his feet, he beat his head
against the wall with such force that we both rushed upon
him, and tore him away to the centre of the room. Sherlock
Holmes pushed him down into the easy-chair, and, sitting beside him, patted his hand, and chatted with him in
the easy, soothing tones which he knew so well how to
employ.

'You have come to me to tell me your story, have you
not?' said he. 'You are fatigued with your haste. Pray wait
until you have recovered yourself, and then I shall be most
happy to look into any little problem which you may submit
to me.'

The man sat for a minute or more with a heaving chest,
fighting against his emotion. Then he passed his handkerchief over his brow, set his lips tight, and turned his face
towards us.

'No doubt you think me mad?' said he.

'I see that you have had some great trouble,' responded
Holmes.

'God knows I have!—a trouble which is enough to unseat
my reason, so sudden and so terrible is it. Public disgrace I
might have faced, although I am a man whose character has
never yet borne a stain. Private affliction also is the lot of
every man; but the two coming together, and in so frightful
a form, have been enough to shake my very soul. Besides, it
is not I alone. The very nobles in the land may suffer, unless
some way be found out of this horrible affair.'

'Pray compose yourself, sir,' said Holmes, 'and let me have a clear account of who you are, and what it is that has befallen you.'

'My name,' answered our visitor, 'is probably familiar to your ears. I am Alexander Holder,* of the banking firm of Holder & Stevenson, of Threadneedle Street.'*

The name was indeed well known to us, as belonging to the senior partner in the second largest private banking concern in the City of London. What could have happened, then, to bring one of the foremost citizens of London to this most pitiable pass? We waited, all curiosity, until with another effort he braced himself to tell his story.

'I feel that time is of value,' said he, 'that is why I hastened here when the police inspector suggested that I should secure your co-operation. I came to Baker Street by the Underground, and hurried from there on foot, for the cabs go slowly through this snow.* That is why I was so out of breath, for I am a man who takes very little exercise. I feel better now, and I will put the facts before you as shortly and yet as clearly as I can.

'It is, of course, well known to you, that in a successful banking business as much depends upon our being able to find remunerative investments for our funds, as upon our increasing our connection and the number of our depositors. One of our most lucrative means of laying out money is in the shape of loans, where the security is unimpeachable. We have done a good deal in this direction during the last few years, and there are many noble families to whom we have advanced large sums upon the security of their pictures, libraries, or plate.

'Yesterday morning I was seated in my office at the Bank, when a card was brought in to me by one of the clerks. I started when I saw the name, for it was that of none other than—well, perhaps even to you I had better say no more than that it was a name which is a household word all over the earth—one of the highest, noblest, most exalted names in England.* I was overwhelmed by the honour, and attempted, when he entered, to say so, but he plunged at once into business with the air of a man who wishes to hurry quickly through a disagreeable task.

' "Mr Holder," said he, "I have been informed that you are in the habit of advancing money."

' "The firm do so when the security is good," I answered.

' "It is absolutely essential to me," said he, "that I should have fifty thousand pounds at once. I could of course borrow so trifling a sum ten times over from my friends, but I much prefer to make it a matter of business, and to carry out that business myself. In my position you can readily understand that it is unwise to place oneself under obligations."

' "For how long, may I ask, do you want this sum?" I asked.

' "Next Monday I have a large sum due to me, and I shall then most certainly repay what you advance, with whatever interest you think it right to charge. But it is very essential to me that the money should be paid at once."

' "I should be happy to advance it without further parley* from my own private purse," said I, "were it not that the strain would be rather more than it could bear. If, on the other hand, I am to do it in the name of the firm, then in justice to my partner I must insist that, even in your case, every business-like precaution should be taken."

' "I should much prefer to have it so," said he, raising up a square, black morocco case which he had laid beside his chair. "You have doubtless heard of the Beryl Coronet?"*

' "One of the most precious public possessions of the Empire,"* said I.

' "Precisely." He opened the case, and there, embedded in soft, flesh-coloured velvet, lay the magnificent piece of jewellery which he had named. "There are thirty-nine enormous beryls," said he, "and the price of the gold chasing is incalculable. The lowest estimate would put the worth of the coronet at double the sum which I have asked. I am prepared to leave it with you as my security."

'I took the precious case into my hands and looked in some perplexity from it to my illustrious client.

' "You doubt its value?" he asked.

' "Not at all. I only doubt—"

' "The propriety of my leaving it. You may set your mind at rest about that. I should not dream of doing so were it not absolutely certain that I should be able in four days to reclaim it. It is a pure matter of form. Is the security sufficient?"

' "Ample."

' "You understand, Mr Holder, that I am giving you a strong proof of the confidence which I have in you, founded upon all that I have heard of you. I rely upon you not only to be discreet and to refrain from all gossip upon the matter, but, above all, to preserve this coronet with every possible precaution, because I need not say that a great public scandal would be caused if any harm were to befall it. Any injury to it would be almost as serious as its complete loss, for there are no beryls in the world to match these, and it would be impossible to replace them. I leave it with you, however, with every confidence, and I shall call for it in person on Monday morning."

'Seeing that my client was anxious to leave, I said no more; but, calling for my cashier, I ordered him to pay over fifty thousand-pound notes. When I was alone once more, however, with the precious case lying upon the table in front of me, I could not but think with some misgivings of the immense responsibility which it entailed upon me. There could be no doubt that, as it was a national possession, a horrible scandal would ensue if any misfortune should occur to it. I already regretted having ever consented to take charge of it. However, it was too late to alter the matter now, so I locked it up in my private safe, and turned once more to my work.

'When evening came, I felt that it would be an imprudence to leave so precious a thing in the office behind me. Bankers' safes had been forced before now, and why should not mine be? If so, how terrible would be the position in which I should find myself! I determined, therefore, that for the next few days I would always carry the case backwards and forwards with me, so that it might never be really out of my reach. With this intention, I called a cab, and drove out to my house at Streatham,* carrying the jewel with me. I did not breathe freely until I had taken it upstairs, and locked it in the bureau of my dressing-room.

'And now a word as to my household, Mr Holmes, for I wish you to thoroughly understand the situation. My groom and my page sleep out of the house, and may be set aside altogether. I have three maid-servants who have been with me a number of years, and whose absolute reliability is quite above suspicion. Another, Lucy Parr,* the second waiting-maid, has only been in my service a few months. She came with an excellent character, however, and has always given me satisfaction. She is a very pretty girl, and has attracted admirers who have occasionally hung about the place. That is the only drawback which we have found to her, but we believe her to be a thoroughly good girl in every way.

'So much for the servants. My family itself is so small that it will not take me long to describe it. I am a widower, and have an only son, Arthur. He has been a disappointment to me, Mr Holmes—a grievous disappointment. I have no doubt that I am myself to blame. People tell me that I have spoiled him. Very likely I have. When my dear wife died I felt that he was all I had to love. I could not bear to see the smile fade even for a moment from his face. I have never denied him a wish. Perhaps it would have been better for both of us had I been sterner, but I meant it for the best.

'It was naturally my intention that he should succeed me in my business, but he was not of a business turn. He was wild, wayward, and, to speak the truth, I could not trust him in the handling of large sums of money. When he was young he became a member of an aristocratic club, and there, having charming manners, he was soon the intimate of a number of men with long purses and expensive habits. He learned to play heavily at cards and to squander money on the turf, until he had again and again to come to me and implore me to give him an advance upon his allowance, that he might settle his debts of honour. He tried more than once to break away from the dangerous company which he was keeping, but each time the influence of his friend Sir George Burnwell* was enough to draw him back again.

'And, indeed, I could not wonder that such a man as Sir George Burnwell should gain an influence over him, for he has frequently brought him to my house, and I have found myself that I could hardly resist the fascination of his manner. He is older than Arthur, a man of the world to his finger-tips, one who has been everywhere, seen everything, a brilliant talker, and a man of great personal beauty. Yet when I think of him in cold blood, far away from the glamour of his presence, I am convinced from his cynical speech, and the look which I have caught in his eyes, that he is one who should be deeply distrusted. So I think, and so, too, thinks my little Mary,* who has a woman's quick insight into character.

'And now there is only she to be described. She is my niece; but when my brother died five years ago and left her alone in the world I adopted her, and have looked upon her ever since as my daughter. She is a sunbeam in my house—sweet, loving, beautiful, a wonderful manager and housekeeper, yet as tender and quiet and gentle as a woman could be. She is my right hand. I do not know what I could do without her. In only one matter has she ever gone against my wishes. Twice my boy has asked her to marry him, for he loves her devotedly, but each time she has refused him. I think that if anyone could have drawn him into the right path it would have been she, and that his marriage might have changed his whole life; but now, alas! it is too late—for ever too late!

'Now, Mr Holmes, you know the people who live under my roof, and I shall continue with my miserable story.

'When we were taking coffee in the drawing-room that night, after dinner, I told Arthur and Mary my experience, and of the precious treasure which we had under our roof, suppressing only the name of my client. Lucy Parr, who had brought in the coffee, had, I am sure, left the room; but I cannot swear that the door was closed. Mary and Arthur were much interested, and wished to see the famous coronet, but I thought it better not to disturb it.

' "Where have you put it?" asked Arthur.

' "In my own bureau."

' "Well, I hope to goodness the house won't be burgled during the night," said he.

' "It is locked up," I answered.

' "Oh, any old key will fit that bureau. When I was a youngster I have opened it myself with the key of the box-room cupboard."

'He often had a wild way of talking, so that I thought little of what he said. He followed me to my room, however, that night with a very grave face.

' "Look here, dad," said he, with his eyes cast down. "Can you let me have two hundred pounds?"

' "No, I cannot!" I answered sharply. "I have been far too generous with you in money matters."

' "You have been very kind," said he; "but I must have this money, or else I can never show my face inside the club again."

' "And a very good thing, too!" I cried.

' "Yes, but you would not have me leave it a dishonoured man," said he. "I could not bear the disgrace. I must raise the money in some way, and if you will not let me have it, then I must try other means."

'I was very angry, for this was the third demand during the month. "You shall not have a farthing* from me," I cried, on which he bowed and left the room without another word.

'When he was gone I unlocked my bureau, made sure that my treasure was safe, and locked it again. Then I started to go round the house to see that all was secure—a duty which I usually leave to Mary, but which I thought it well to perform myself that night. As I came down the stairs I saw Mary herself at the side window of the hall, which she closed and fastened as I approached.

' "Tell me, dad," said she, looking, I thought, a little disturbed, "did you give Lucy, the maid, leave to go out to-night?"

' "Certainly not."

' "She came in just now by the back door. I have no doubt that she has only been to the side gate to see someone but I think that it is hardly safe, and should be stopped."

' "You must speak to her in the morning, or I will, if you prefer it. Are you sure that everything is fastened?"

' "Quite sure, dad."

' "Then, good-night." I kissed her, and went to my bedroom, where I was soon asleep.

'I am endeavouring to tell you everything, Mr Holmes, which may have any bearing upon the case, but I beg that you will question me upon any point which I do not make clear.'

'On the contrary, your statement is singularly lucid.'

'I come to a part of my story now in which I should wish to be particularly so. I am not a very heavy sleeper, and the anxiety in my mind tended, no doubt, to make me even less so than usual. About two in the morning, then, I was awakened by some sound in the house. It had ceased ere I was wide awake, but it had left an impression behind it as though a window had gently closed somewhere. I lay listening with all my ears. Suddenly, to my horror, there was a distinct sound of footsteps moving softly in the next room. I slipped out of bed, all palpitating with fear, and peeped round the corner of my dressing-room door.

' "Arthur!" I screamed, "you villain! you thief! How dare you touch that coronet?"

'The gas was half up, as I had left it, and my unhappy boy, dressed only in his shirt and trousers, was standing beside the light, holding the coronet in his hands. He appeared to be wrenching at it, or bending it with all his strength. At my cry he dropped it from his grasp, and turned as pale as death. I snatched it up and examined it. One of the gold corners, with three of the beryls in it, was missing.

' "You blackguard!" I shouted, beside myself with rage. "You have destroyed it! You have dishonoured me for ever! Where are the jewels you have stolen?"

' "Stolen!" he cried.

' "Yes, you thief!" I roared, shaking him by the shoulder.

' "There are none missing. There cannot be any missing," said he.

' "There are three missing. And you know where they are. Must I call you a liar as well as a thief? Did I not see you trying to tear off another piece?"

' "You have called me names enough," said he; "I will not stand it any longer. I shall not say another word about this business since you have chosen to insult me. I will leave your house in the morning, and make my own way in the world."

' "You shall leave it in the hands of the police!" I cried, half mad with grief and rage. "I shall have this matter probed to the bottom."

' "You shall learn nothing from me," said he, with a passion such as I should not have thought was in his nature. "If you choose to call the police, let them find what they can."

'By this time the whole house was astir, for I had raised my voice in my anger. Mary was the first to rush into my room, and at the sight of the coronet and of Arthur's face, she read the whole story, and, with a scream, fell down senseless on the ground. I sent the housemaid for the police, and put the investigation into their hands at once. When the inspector and a constable entered the house, Arthur, who had stood sullenly with his arms folded, asked me whether it was my intention to charge him with theft. I answered that it had ceased to be a private matter, but had become a public one, since the ruined coronet was national property. I was determined that the law should have its way in everything.

' "At least," said he, "you will not have me arrested at once. It would be to your advantage as well as mine if I might leave the house for five minutes."

' "That you may get away, or perhaps that you may conceal what you have stolen," said I. And then realizing the dreadful position in which I was placed, I implored him to remember that not only my honour, but that of one who was far greater than I was at stake; and that he threatened to raise a scandal which would convulse the nation. He might avert it all if he would but tell me what he had done with the three missing stones.

' "You may as well face the matter," said I; "you have been caught in the act, and no confession could make your guilt more heinous. If you make such reparation as is in your power, by telling us where the beryls are, all shall be forgiven and forgotten."

' "Keep your forgiveness for those who ask for it," he answered, turning away from me with a sneer. I saw that he was too hardened for any words of mine to influence him. There was but one way for it. I called in the inspector, and gave him into custody. A search was made at once, not only of his person, but of his room, and of every portion of the house where he could possibly have concealed the gems; but no trace of them could be found, nor would the wretched boy open his mouth for all our persuasions and our threats. This morning he was removed to a cell, and I, after going through all the police formalities, have hurried round to you, to implore you to use your skill in unravelling the matter. The police have openly confessed that they can at present make nothing of it. You may go to any expense which you think necessary. I have already offered a reward of a thousand pounds. My God, what shall I do! I have lost my honour, my gems, and my son in one night. Oh, what shall I do!'

He put a hand on either side of his head, and rocked himself to and fro, droning to himself like a child whose grief has got beyond words.

Sherlock Holmes sat silent for some minutes, with his brows knitted and his eyes fixed upon the fire.

'Do you receive much company?' he asked.

'None, save my partner with his family, and an occasional friend of Arthur's. Sir George Burnwell has been several times lately. No one else, I think.'

'Do you go out much in society?'

'Arthur does. Mary and I stay at home. We neither of us care for it.'

'That is unusual in a young girl.'

'She is of a quiet nature. Besides, she is not so very young. She is four-and-twenty.'

'This matter, from what you say, seems to have been a shock to her also.'

'Terrible! She is even more affected than I.'

'You have neither of you any doubt as to your son's guilt?'

'How can we have, when I saw him with my own eyes with the coronet in his hands?'

'I hardly consider that a conclusive proof. Was the remainder of the coronet at all injured?'

'Yes, it was twisted.'

'Do you not think, then, that he might have been trying to straighten it?'

'God bless you! You are doing what you can for him and for me. But it is too heavy a task. What was he doing there at all? If his purpose were innocent, why did he not say so?'

'Precisely. And if he were guilty, why did he not invent a lie? His silence appears to me to cut both ways. There are several singular points about the case. What did the police think of the noise which awoke you from your sleep?'

'They considered that it might be caused by Arthur's closing his bedroom door.'

'A likely story! As if a man bent on felony would slam the door so as to awake a household. What did they say, then, of the disappearance of these gems?'

'They are still sounding the planking and probing the furniture* in the hope of finding them.'

'Have they thought of looking outside the house?'

'Yes, they have shown extraordinary energy. The whole garden has already been minutely examined.'

'Now, my dear sir,' said Holmes, 'is it not obvious to you now that this matter really strikes very much deeper than either you or the police were at first inclined to think? It appeared to you to be a simple case; to me it seems exceedingly complex. Consider what is involved by your theory. You suppose that your son came down from his bed, went, at great risk, to your dressing-room, opened your bureau, took out your coronet, broke off by main force a small portion of it, went off to some other place, concealed three gems out of the thirty-nine, with such skill that nobody can find them, and then returned with the other thirty-six into the room in which he exposed himself to the greatest danger of being discovered. I ask you now, is such a theory tenable?'

'But what other is there?' cried the banker with a gesture of despair. 'If his motives were innocent, why does he not explain them?'

'It is our task to find out,' replied Holmes, 'so now, if you please, Mr Holder, we will set off for Streatham together, and devote an hour to glancing a little more closely into details.'

My friend insisted upon my accompanying them in their expedition, which I was eager enough to do, for my curiosity and sympathy were deeply stirred by the story to which we had listened. I confess that the guilt of the banker's son appeared to me to be as obvious as it did to his unhappy father, but still I had such faith in Holmes's judgment that I felt that there must be some grounds for hope as long as he was dissatisfied with the accepted explanation. He hardly spoke a word the whole way out to the southern suburb, but sat with his chin upon his breast, and his hat drawn over his eyes, sunk in the deepest thought. Our client appeared to have taken fresh heart at the little glimpse of hope which had been presented to him, and he even broke into a desultory chat with me over his business affairs. A short railway journey, and a shorter walk, brought us to Fairbank,* the modest residence of the great financier.

Fairbank was a good-sized square house of white stone, standing back a little from the road. A double carriage sweep,* with a snow-clad lawn, stretched down in front to the two large iron gates which closed the entrance. On the right side was a small wooden thicket which led into a narrow path between two neat hedges stretching from the road to the kitchen door, and forming the tradesmen's entrance. On the left ran a lane which led to the stables, and was not itself within the grounds at all, being a public,

though little used, thoroughfare. Holmes left us standing at
the door, and walked slowly all round the house, across the
front, down the tradesmen's path, and so round by the
garden behind into the stable lane. So long was he that Mr
Holder and I went into the dining-room, and waited by the
fire until he should return. We were sitting there in silence
when the door opened, and a young lady came in. She was
rather above the middle height, slim, with dark hair and
eyes, which seemed the darker against the absolute pallor of
her skin. I do not think that I have ever seen such deadly
paleness in a woman's face. Her lips, too, were bloodless,
but her eyes were flushed with crying. As she swept silently
into the room she impressed me with a greater sense of her
grief than the banker had done in the morning, and it was
the more striking in her as she was evidently a woman of
strong character, with immense capacity for self-restraint.
Disregarding my presence, she went straight to her uncle,
and passed her hand over his head with a sweet womanly
caress.

'You have given orders that Arthur should be liberated,
have you not, dad?' she asked.

'No, no, my girl, the matter must be probed to the
bottom.'

'But I am so sure that he is innocent. You know what
women's instincts are. I know that he has done no harm,
and that you will be sorry for having acted so harshly.'

'Why is he silent, then, if he is innocent?'

'Who knows? Perhaps because he was so angry that you
should suspect him.'

'How could I help suspecting him, when I actually saw
him with the coronet in his hand?'

'Oh, but he had only picked it up to look at it. Oh, do,
do take my word for it that he is innocent. Let the matter
drop, and say no more. It is so dreadful to think of our dear
Arthur in prison!'

'I shall never let it drop until the gems are found—never,
Mary! Your affection for Arthur blinds you as to the awful
consequences to me. Far from hushing the thing up, I have

brought a gentleman down from London to inquire more deeply into it.'

'This gentleman?' she asked, facing round to me.

'No, his friend. He wished us to leave him alone. He is round in the stable lane now.'

'The stable lane?' She raised her dark eyebrows. 'What can he hope to find there! Ah, this, I suppose, is he. I trust, sir, that you will succeed in proving, what I feel sure is the truth, that my cousin Arthur is innocent of this crime.'

'I fully share your opinion, and, I trust with you, that we may prove it,' returned Holmes, going back to the mat to knock the snow from his shoes. 'I believe I have the honour of addressing Miss Mary Holder. Might I ask you a question or two?'

'Pray do, sir, if it may help, to clear this horrible affair up.'

'You heard nothing yourself last night?'

'Nothing, until my uncle here began to speak loudly. I heard that, and I came down.'

'You shut up the windows and doors the night before. Did you fasten all the windows?'

'Yes.'

'Were they all fastened this morning?'

'Yes.'

'You have a maid who has a sweetheart? I think that you remarked to your uncle last night that she had been out to see him?'

'Yes, and she was the girl who waited in the drawing-room, and who may have heard uncle's remarks about the coronet.'

'I see. You infer that she may have gone out to tell her sweetheart, and that the two may have planned the robbery.'

'But what is the good of all these vague theories,' cried the banker, impatiently, 'when I have told you that I saw Arthur with the coronet in his hands?'

'Wait a little, Mr Holder. We must come back to that. About this girl, Miss Holder. You saw her return by the kitchen door, I presume?'

'Yes; when I went to see if the door was fastened for the night I met her slipping in. I saw the man, too, in the gloom.'

'Do you know him?'

'Oh, yes; he is the greengrocer who brings our vegetables round. His name is Francis Prosper.'*

'He stood,' said Holmes, 'to the left of the door—that is to say, further up the path than is necessary to reach the door?'

'Yes, he did.'

'And he is a man with a wooden leg?'

Something like fear sprang up in the young lady's expressive black eyes. 'Why, you are like a magician,' said she. 'How do you know that?' She smiled, but there was no answering smile in Holmes's thin, eager face.

'I should be very glad now to go upstairs,' said he. 'I shall probably wish to go over the outside of the house again. Perhaps I had better take a look at the lower windows before I go up.'

He walked swiftly round from one to the other, pausing only at the large one which looked from the hall on to the stable lane. This he opened, and made a very careful examination of the sill with his powerful magnifying lens. 'Now we shall go upstairs,' said he, at last.

The banker's dressing-room was a plainly furnished little chamber with a grey carpet, a large bureau, and a long mirror. Holmes went to the bureau first, and looked hard at the lock.

'Which key was used to open it?' he asked.

'That which my son himself indicated—that of the cupboard of the lumber-room.'

'Have you it here?'

'That is it on the dressing-table.'

Sherlock Holmes took it up and opened the bureau.

'It is a noiseless lock,' said he. 'It is no wonder that it did not wake you. This case, I presume, contains the coronet. We must have a look at it.' He opened the case, and, taking out the diadem, he laid it upon the table. It was a magnificent specimen of the jeweller's art, and the thirty-six stones were the finest that I have ever seen. At one side of the coronet was a crooked cracked edge, where a corner holding three gems had been torn away.

'Now, Mr Holder,' said Holmes; 'here is the corner which corresponds to that which has been so unfortunately lost. Might I beg that you will break it off.'

The banker recoiled in horror. 'I should not dream of trying,' said he.

'Then I will.' Holmes suddenly bent his strength upon it, but without result. 'I feel it give a little,' said he; 'but, though I am exceptionally strong in the fingers, it would take me all my time to break it. An ordinary man could not do it. Now, what do you think would happen if I did break it, Mr Holder? There would be a noise like a pistol shot. Do you tell me that all this happened within a few yards of your bed, and that you heard nothing of it?'

'I do not know what to think. It is all dark to me.'

'But perhaps it may grow lighter as we go. What do you think, Miss Holder?'

'I confess that I still share my uncle's perplexity.'

'Your son had no shoes or slippers on when you saw him?'

'He had nothing on save only his trousers and shirt.'

'Thank you. We have certainly been favoured with extraordinary luck during this inquiry, and it will be entirely our own fault if we do not succeed in clearing the matter up. With your permission, Mr Holder, I shall now continue my investigations outside.'

He went alone, at his own request, for he explained that any unnecessary footmarks might make his task more difficult. For an hour or more he was at work, returning at last with his feet heavy with snow and his features as inscrutable as ever.

'I think that I have seen now all that there is to see, Mr Holder,' said he; 'I can serve you best by returning to my rooms.'

'But the gems, Mr Holmes. Where are they?'

'I cannot tell.'

The banker wrung his hands. 'I shall never see them again!' he cried. 'And my son? You give me hopes?'

'My opinion is in no way altered.'

'Then for God's sake what was this dark business which was acted in my house last night?'

'If you can call upon me at my Baker Street rooms tomorrow morning between nine and ten I shall be happy to do what I can to make it clearer. I understand that you give me *carte blanche* to act for you, provided only that I get back the gems, and that you place no limit on the sum I may draw.'

'I would give my fortune to have them back.'

'Very good. I shall look into the matter between this and then. Good-bye; it is just possible that I may have to come over here again before evening.'

It was obvious to me that my companion's mind was now made up about the case, although what his conclusions were was more than I could even dimly imagine. Several times during our homeward journey I endeavoured to sound him upon that point, but he always glided away to some other topic, until at last I gave it over in despair. It was not yet three when we found ourselves in our room once more. He hurried to his chamber, and was down again in a few minutes dressed as a common loafer.* With his collar turned up, his shiny seedy coat, his red cravat, and his worn boots, he was a perfect sample of the class.

'I think that this should do,' said he, glancing into the glass above the fireplace. 'I only wish that you could come with me, Watson, but I fear that it won't do. I may be on the trail in this matter, or I may be following a will-o'-the-wisp,* but I shall soon know which it is. I hope that I may be back in a few hours.' He cut a slice of beef from the joint upon the sideboard, sandwiched it between two rounds of bread, and, thrusting this rude meal into his pocket, he started off upon his expedition.

I had just finished my tea when he returned, evidently in excellent spirits, swinging an old elastic-sided boot in his hand. He chucked it down into a corner and helped himself to a cup of tea.

'I only looked in as I passed,' said he. 'I am going right on.'

'Where to?'

'Oh, to the other side of the West End. It may be some time before I get back. Don't wait up for me in case I should be late.'

'How are you getting on?'

'Oh, so so. Nothing to complain of. I have been out to Streatham since I saw you last, but I did not call at the house. It is a very sweet little problem, and I would not have missed it for a good deal. However, I must not sit gossiping here, but must get these disreputable clothes off and return to my highly respectable self.'

I could see by his manner that he had stronger reasons for satisfaction than his words alone would imply. His eyes twinkled, and there was even a touch of colour upon his sallow cheeks. He hastened upstairs, and a few minutes later I heard the slam of the hall door, which told me that he was off once more upon his congenial hunt.

I waited until midnight, but there was no sign of his return, so I retired to my room. It was no uncommon thing for him to be away for days and nights on end when he was hot upon a scent, so that his lateness caused me no surprise. I do not know at what hour he came in, but when I came down to breakfast in the morning, there he was with a cup of coffee in one hand and the paper in the other, as fresh and trim as possible.

'You will excuse my beginning without you, Watson,' said he; 'but you remember that our client has rather an early appointment this morning.'

'Why, it is after nine now,' I answered. 'I should not be surprised if that were he. I thought I heard a ring.'

It was, indeed, our friend the financier. I was shocked by the change which had come over him, for his face, which was naturally of a broad and massive mould, was now pinched and fallen in, while his hair seemed to be at least a shade whiter. He entered with a weariness and lethargy which was even more painful than his violence of the morning before, and he dropped heavily into the armchair which I pushed forward for him.

'I do not know what I have done to be so severely tried,'
said he. 'Only two days ago I was a happy and prosperous
man, without a care in the world. Now I am left to a lonely
and dishonoured age. One sorrow comes close upon the
heels of another. My niece Mary has deserted me.'

'Deserted you?'

'Yes. Her bed this morning had not been slept in, her
room was empty, and a note lay for me upon the hall table.
I had said to her last night, in sorrow and not in anger, that
if she had married my boy all might have been well with
him. Perhaps it was thoughtless of me to say so. It is to that
remark that she refers in this note:

My Dearest Uncle—I feel that I have brought this trouble upon
you, and that if I had acted differently this terrible misfortune
might never have occurred. I cannot, with this thought in my
mind, ever again be happy under your roof, and I feel that I must
leave you for ever. Do not worry about my future, for that is
provided for; and, above all, do not search for me, for it will be
fruitless labour, and an ill service to me. In life or in death, I am
ever your loving,

MARY

'What could she mean by that note, Mr Holmes? Do you
think it points to suicide?'

'No, no, nothing of the kind. It is perhaps the best possible
solution. I trust, Mr Holder, that you are nearing the end of
your troubles.'

'Ha! You say so! You have heard something, Mr Holmes:
you have learned something! Where are the gems?'

'You would not think a thousand pounds apiece an
excessive sum for them?'

'I would pay ten.'

'That would be unnecessary. Three thousand will cover
the matter. And there is a little reward, I fancy. Have you
your cheque-book? Here is a pen. Better make it out for four
thousand pounds.'

With a dazed face the banker made out the required
cheque. Holmes walked over to his desk, took out a little

triangular piece of gold with three gems in it, and threw it down upon the table.

With a shriek of joy our client clutched it up.

'You have it?' he gasped. 'I am saved! I am saved!'

The reaction of joy was as passionate as his grief had been, and he hugged his recovered gems to his bosom.

'There is one other thing you owe, Mr Holder,' said Sherlock Holmes, rather sternly.

'Owe!' He caught up a pen. 'Name the sum, and I will pay it.'

'No, the debt is not to me. You owe a very humble apology to that noble lad, your son, who has carried himself in this matter as I should be proud to see my own son do, should I ever chance to have one.'

'Then it was not Arthur who took them?'

'I told you yesterday, and I repeat to-day, that it was not.'

'You are sure of it! Then let us hurry to him at once, to let him know that the truth is known.'

'He knows it already. When I had cleared it all up I had an interview with him, and, finding that he would not tell me the story, I told it to him, on which he had to confess that I was right, and to add the very few details which were not yet quite clear to me. Your news of this morning, however, may open his lips.'

'For Heaven's sake, tell me, then, what is this extraordinary mystery!'

'I will do so, and I will show you the steps by which I reached it. And let me say to you, first, what it is hardest for me to say and for you to hear. There has been an understanding between Sir George Burnwell and your niece, Mary. They have now fled together.'

'My Mary? Impossible!'

'It is, unfortunately, more than possible; it is certain. Neither you nor your son knew the true character of this man when you admitted him into your family circle. He is one of the most dangerous men in England—a ruined gambler, an absolutely desperate villain; a man without heart or conscience. Your niece knew nothing of such men.

When he breathed his vows to her, as he had done to a hundred before her, she flattered herself that she alone had touched his heart. The devil knows best what he said, but at last she became his tool, and was in the habit of seeing him nearly every evening.'

'I cannot, and I will not, believe it!' cried the banker with an ashen face.

'I will tell you, then, what occured in your house that night. Your niece, when you had, as she thought, gone to your room, slipped down and talked to her lover through the window which leads into the stable lane. His footmarks had pressed right through the snow, so long had he stood there. She told him of the coronet. His wicked lust for gold kindled at the news, and he bent her to his will. I have no doubt that she loved you, but there are women in whom the love of a lover extinguishes all other loves, and I think that she must have been one. She had hardly listened to his instructions when she saw you coming downstairs, on which she closed the window rapidly, and told you about one of the servants' escapade with her wooden-legged lover, which was all perfectly true.

'Your boy, Arthur, went to bed after his interview with you, but he slept badly on account of his uneasiness about his club debts. In the middle of the night he heard a soft tread pass his door, so he rose, and looking out, was surprised to see his cousin walking very stealthily along the passage, until she disappeared into your dressing-room. Petrified with astonishment the lad slipped on some clothes, and waited there in the dark to see what would come of this strange affair. Presently she emerged from the room again, and in the light of the passage lamp your son saw that she carried the precious coronet in her hands. She passed down the stairs, and he, thrilling with horror, ran along and slipped behind the curtain near your door, whence he could see what passed in the hall beneath. He saw her stealthily open the window, hand out the coronet to someone in the gloom, and then closing it once more hurry back to her room, passing quite close to where he stood hid behind the curtain.

'As long as she was on the scene he could not take any action without a horrible exposure of the woman whom he loved. But the instant she was gone he realized how crushing a misfortune this would be for you, and how all-important it was to set it right. He rushed down, just as he was, in his bare feet, opened the window, sprang out into the snow, and ran down the lane, where he could see a dark figure in the moonlight. Sir George Burnwell tried to get away, but Arthur caught him, and there was a struggle between them, your lad tugging at one side of the coronet, and his opponent at the other. In the scuffle, your son struck Sir George, and cut him over the eye. Then something suddenly snapped, and your son, finding that he had the coronet in his hands, rushed back, closed the window, ascended to your room, and had just observed that the coronet had been twisted in the struggle, and was endeavouring to straighten it, when you appeared upon the scene.'

'Is it possible?' gasped the banker.

'You then roused his anger by calling him names at a moment when he felt that he had deserved your warmest thanks. He could not explain the true state of affairs without betraying the one who certainly deserved little enough consideration at his hands. He took the more chivalrous view, however, and preserved her secret.'

'And that was why she shrieked and fainted when she saw the coronet,' cried Mr Holder. 'Oh, my God! what a blind fool I have been. And his asking to be allowed to go out for five minutes! The dear fellow wanted to see if the missing piece were at the scene of the struggle. How cruelly I have misjudged him!'

'When I arrived at the house,' continued Holmes, 'I at once went very carefully round it to observe if there were any traces in the snow which might help me. I knew that none had fallen since the evening before, and also that there had been a strong frost to preserve impressions. I passed along the tradesmen's path, but found it all trampled down and indistinguishable. Just beyond it, however, at the far side of the kitchen door, a woman had stood and talked with

a man, whose round impression on one side showed that he
had a wooden leg. I could even tell that they had been
disturbed, for the woman had run back swiftly to the door,
as was shown by the deep toe and light heel-marks, while
Wooden-leg had waited a little, and then had gone away. I
thought at the time that this might be the maid and her
sweet-heart, of whom you had already spoken to me, and
inquiry showed it was so. I passed round the garden without
seeing anything more than random tracks, which I took to
be the police; but when I got into the stable lane a very long
and complex story was written in the snow in front of me.

'There was a double line of tracks of a booted man, and
a second double line which I saw with delight belonged to
a man with naked feet. I was at once convinced from what
you had told me that the latter was your son. The first had
walked both ways, but the other had run swiftly, and, as his
tread was marked in places over the depression of the boot,
it was obvious that he had passed after the other. I followed
them up, and found that they led to the hall window, where
Boots had worn all the snow away while waiting. Then I
walked to the other end, which was a hundred yards or
more down the lane. I saw where Boots had faced round,
where the snow was cut up, as though there had been a
struggle, and, finally, where a few drops of blood had fallen,
to show me that I was not mistaken. Boots had then run
down the lane, and another little smudge of blood showed
that it was he who had been hurt. When he came to the
high-road at the other end, I found that the pavement had
been cleared, so there was an end to that clue.

'On entering the house, however, I examined, as you
remember, the sill and framework of the hall window with
my lens, and I could at once see that someone had passed
out. I could distinguish the outline of an instep where the
wet foot had been placed in coming in. I was then beginning
to be able to form an opinion as to what had occurred. A
man had waited outside the window, someone had brought
him the gems; the deed had been overseen by your son, he
had pursued the thief, had struggled with him, they had

each tugged at the coronet, their united strength causing injuries which neither alone could have effected. He had returned with the prize, but had left a fragment in the grasp of his opponent. So far I was clear. The question now was, who was the man, and who was it brought him the coronet?

'It is an old maxim of mine that when you have excluded the impossible, whatever remains, however improbable, must be the truth.* Now, I knew that it was not you who had brought it down, so there only remained your niece and the maids. But if it were the maids, why should your son allow himself to be accused in their place? There could be no possible reason. As he loved his cousin, however, there was an excellent explanation why he should retain her secret—the more so as the secret was a disgraceful one. When I remembered that you had seen her at that window, and how she had fainted on seeing the coronet again, my conjecture became a certainty.

'And who could it be who was her confederate? A lover evidently, for who else could outweigh the love and gratit-ude which she must feel to you? I knew that you went out little, and that your circle of friends was a very limited one. But among them was Sir George Burnwell. I had heard of him before as being a man of evil reputation among women. It must have been he who wore those boots, and retained the missing gems. Even though he knew that Arthur had discovered him, he might still flatter himself that he was safe, for the lad could not say a word without compromising his own family.

'Well, your own good sense will suggest what measures I took next. I went in the shape of a loafer to Sir George's house, managed to pick up an acquaintance with his valet, learned that his master had cut his head the night before, and finally, at the expense of six shillings, made all sure by buying a pair of his cast-off shoes. With those I journeyed down to Streatham, and saw that they exactly fitted the tracks.'

'I saw an ill-dressed vagabond in the lane yesterday evening,' said Mr Holder.

'Precisely. It was I. I found that I had my man, so I came home and changed my clothes. It was a delicate part which I had to play then, for I saw that a prosecution must be avoided to avert scandal, and I knew that so astute a villain would see that our hands were tied in the matter. I went and saw him. At first, of course, he denied everything. But when I gave him every particular that had occured, he tried to bluster, and took down a life-preserver* from the wall. I knew my man, however, and I clapped a pistol to his head before he could strike. Then he became a little more reasonable. I told him that we would give him a price for the stones he held—a thousand pounds apiece. That brought out the first signs of grief he had shown. "Why, dash it all!" said he, "I've let them go at six hundred for the three!" I soon managed to get the address of the receiver* who had them, on promising him that there would be no prosecution. Off I set to him, and after much chaffering* I got our stones at a thousand apiece. Then I looked in upon your son, told him that all was right, and eventually got to my bed about two o'clock after what I may call a really hard day's work.'

'A day which has saved England from a great public scandal,' said the banker, rising. 'Sir, I canot find words to thank you. But you shall not find me ungrateful for what you have done. Your skill has indeed exceeded all that I have ever heard of it. And now I must fly to my dear boy to apologize to him for the wrong which I have done him. As to what you tell me of poor Mary, it goes to my heart. Not even your skill can inform me where she is now.'

'I think that we may safely say,' returned Holmes, 'that she is wherever Sir George Burnwell is. It is equally certain, too, that whatever her sins are, they will soon receive a more than sufficient punishment.'

The Copper Beeches

'TO the man who loves art for its own sake,'* remarked Sherlock Holmes, tossing aside the advertisement sheet of the *Daily Telegraph*,* 'it is frequently in its least important and lowliest manifestations that the keenest pleasure is to be derived. It is pleasant to me to observe, Watson, that you have so far grasped this truth that in these little records of our cases which you have been good enough to draw up, and, I am bound to say, occasionally to embellish, you have given prominence not so much to the many *causes célèbres** and sensational trials in which I have figured, but rather to those incidents which may have been trivial in themselves, but which have given room for those faculties of deduction and of logical synthesis which I have made my special province.'

'And yet,' said I, smiling, 'I cannot quite hold myself absolved from the charge of sensationalism which has been urged against my records.'

'You have erred, perhaps,' he observed, taking up a glowing cinder with the tongs, and lighting with it the long cherrywood pipe which was wont to replace his clay* when he was in a disputatious rather than a meditative mood— 'you have erred, perhaps, in attempting to put colour and life into each of your statements, instead of confining yourself to the task of placing upon record that severe reasoning from cause to effect which is really the only notable feature about the thing.'

'It seems to me that I have done you full justice in the matter,' I remarked, with some coldness, for I was repelled by the egotism which I had more than once observed to be a strong factor in my friend's singular character.

'No, it is not selfishness or conceit,' said he, answering, as was his wont, my thoughts rather than my words. 'If I claim full justice for my art, it is because it is an impersonal thing—a thing beyond myself. Crime is common. Logic is rare.* Therefore it is upon the logic rather than upon the crime that you should dwell. You have degraded what should have been a course of lectures into a series of tales.'

It was a cold morning of the early spring, and we sat after breakfast on either side of a cheery fire in the old room in Baker Street. A thick fog rolled down between the lines of dun-coloured houses, and the opposing windows loomed like dark, shapeless blurs, through the heavy yellow wreaths. Our gas was lit, and shone on the white cloth, and glimmer of china and metal, for the table had not been cleared yet. Sherlock Holmes had been silent all the morning, dipping continuously into the advertisement columns of a succession of papers, until at last, having apparently given up his search, he had emerged in no very sweet temper to lecture me upon my literary shortcomings.

'At the same time,' he remarked, after a pause, during which he had sat puffing at his long pipe and gazing down into the fire, 'you can hardly be open to a charge of sensationalism, for out of these cases which you have been so kind as to interest yourself in, a fair proportion do not treat of crime, in its legal sense,* at all. The small matter in which I endeavoured to help the King of Bohemia, the singular experience of Miss Mary Sutherland, the problem connected with the man with the twisted lip, and the incident of the noble bachelor, were all matters which are outside the pale of the law. But in avoiding the sensational, I fear that you may have bordered on the trivial.'

'The end may have been so,' I answered, 'but the methods I hold to have been novel and of interest.'

'Pshaw, my dear fellow, what do the public, the great unobservant public, who could hardly tell a weaver by his tooth or a compositor by his left thumb,* care about the finer shades of analysis and deduction! But, indeed, if you are trivial, I cannot blame you, for the days of the great cases are past. Man, or at least criminal man, has lost all enterprise and originality. As to my own little practice, it seems to be degenerating into an agency for recovering lost lead pencils and giving advice to young ladies from boarding-schools.* I think that I have touched bottom at last, however. This note I had this morning marks my zero point, I fancy. Read it!' He tossed a crumpled letter across to me.

It was dated from Montague Place* upon the preceding evening, and ran thus:

DEAR MR HOLMES—I am very anxious to consult you as to whether I should or should not accept a situation which has been offered to me as governess. I shall call at half past ten tomorrow, if I do not inconvenience you.

Yours faithfully,
VIOLET HUNTER.

'Do you know the young lady?' I asked.
'Not I.'
'It is half-past ten now.'
'Yes, and I have no doubt that is her ring.'
'It may turn out to be of more interest than you think. You remember that the affair of the blue carbuncle, which appeared to be a mere whim at first, developed into a serious investigation. It may be so in this case also.'
'Well, let us hope so! But our doubts will very soon be solved, for here, unless I am much mistaken, is the person in question.'

As he spoke the door opened, and a young lady entered the room. She was plainly but neatly dressed, with a bright, quick face, freckled like a plover's egg,* and with the brisk manner of a woman who has had her own way to make in the world.

'You will excuse my troubling you, I am sure,' said she, as my companion rose to greet her; 'but I have had a very strange experience, and as I have no parents or relations of any sort from whom I could ask advice, I thought that perhaps you would be kind enough to tell me what I should do.'

'Pray take a seat, Miss Hunter. I shall be happy to do anything that I can to serve you.'

I could see that Holmes was favourably impressed by the manner and speech of his new client. He looked her over in his searching fashion, and then composed himself with his lids drooping and his finger-tips together to listen to her story.

'I have been a governess for five years,' said she, 'in the family of Colonel Spence Munro,* but two months ago the Colonel received an appointment at Halifax, in Nova Scotia,* and took his children over to America with him, so that I found myself without a situation. I advertised and I answered advertisements, but without success. At last the little money which I had saved began to run short, and I was at my wits' end as to what I should do.

'There is a well-known agency for governesses in the West End called Westaway's, and there I used to call about once a week in order to see whether anything had turned up which might suit me. Westaway was the name of the founder of the business, but it is really managed by Miss Stoper.* She sits in her own little office, and the ladies who are seeking employment wait in an ante-room, and are then shown in one by one, when she consults her ledgers, and sees whether she has anything which would suit them.

'Well, when I called last week I was shown into the little office as usual, but I found that Miss Stoper was not alone. A prodigiously stout man with a very smiling face, and a great heavy chin which rolled down in fold upon fold over his throat, sat at her elbow with a pair of glasses on his nose, looking very earnestly at the ladies who entered. As I came in he gave quite a jump in his chair, and turned quickly to Miss Stoper:

' "That will do," said he; "I could not ask for anything better. Capital! capital!" He seemed quite enthusiastic, and rubbed his hands together in the most genial fashion. He was such a comfortable-looking man that it was quite a pleasure to look at him.

' "You are looking for a situation, miss?" he asked.

' "Yes, sir."

' "As governess?"

' "Yes, sir."

' "And what salary do you ask?"

' "I had four pounds a month in my last place with Colonel Spence Munro."

' "Oh, tut, tut! sweating—rank sweating!"* he cried, throwing his fat hands out into the air like a man who is in a boiling passion. "How could anyone offer so pitiful a sum to a lady with such attractions and accomplishments?"

' "My accomplishments, sir, may be less than you imagine," said I. "A little French, a little German, music and drawing—"

' "Tut, tut!" he cried. "This is all quite beside the question. The point is, have you or have you not the bearing and deportment of a lady? There it is in a nutshell. If you have not, you are not fitted for the rearing of a child who may some day play a considerable part in the history of the country. But if you have, why, then how could any gentleman ask you to condescend to accept anything under the three figures? Your salary with me, madam, would commence at a hundred pounds a year."

'You may imagine, Mr Holmes, that to me, destitute as I was, such an offer seemed almost too good to be true. The gentleman, however, seeing perhaps the look of incredulity upon my face, opened a pocket-book and took out a note.

' "It is also my custom," said he, smiling in the most pleasant fashion until his eyes were just two shining slits, amid the white creases of his face, "to advance to my young ladies half their salary beforehand, so that they may meet any little expenses of their journey and their wardrobe."

'It seemed to me that I had never met so fascinating and so thoughtful a man. As I was already in debt to my tradesmen, the advance was a great convenience, and yet there was something unnatural about the whole transaction which made me wish to know a little more before I quite committed myself.

' "May I ask where you live, sir?" said I.

' "Hampshire. Charming rural place. The Copper Beeches, five miles on the far side of Winchester.* It is the most lovely country, my dear young lady, and the dearest old country house."

' "And my duties, sir? I should be glad to know what they would be."

' "One child—one dear little romper* just six years old. Oh, if you could see him killing cockroaches with a slipper!* Smack! smack! smack! Three gone before you could wink!" He leaned back in his chair and laughed his eyes into his head again.

'I was a little startled at the nature of the child's amusement, but the father's laughter made me think that perhaps he was joking.

' "My sole duties, then," I asked, "are to take charge of a single child?"

' "No, no, not the sole, not the sole, my dear young lady," he cried. "Your duty would be, as I am sure your good sense would suggest, to obey any little commands which my wife might give, provided always that they were such commands as a lady might with propriety obey. You see no difficulty, heh?"

' "I should be happy to make myself useful."

' "Quite so. In dress now, for example! We are faddy* people, you know—faddy, but kind-hearted. If you were asked to wear any dress which we might give you, you would not object to our little whim. Heh?"

' "No," said I, considerably astonished at his words.

' "Or to sit here, or sit there, that would not be offensive to you?"

' "Oh, no."

' "Or to cut your hair quite short before you come to us?"

'I could hardly believe my ears. As you may observe, Mr Holmes, my hair is somewhat luxuriant, and of a rather peculiar tint of chestnut. It has been considered artistic.* I could not dream of sacrificing it in this off-hand fashion.

' "I am afraid that that is quite impossible," said I. He had been watching me eagerly out of his small eyes and I could see a shadow pass over his face as I spoke.

' "I am afraid that it is quite essential," said he. "It is a little fancy of my wife's, and ladies' fancies, you know, madam, ladies' fancies must be consulted. And so you won't cut your hair?"

' "No, sir, I really could not," I answered firmly.

275

' "Ah, very well; then that quite settles the matter. It is a pity, because in other respects you would really have done very nicely. In that case, Miss Stoper, I had best inspect a few more of your young ladies."

'The manageress had sat all this while busy with her papers without a word to either of us, but she glanced at me now with so much annoyance upon her face that I could not help suspecting that she had lost a handsome commission through my refusal.

' "Do you desire your name to be kept upon the books?" she asked.

' "If you please, Miss Stoper."

' "Well, really, it seems rather useless, since you refuse the most excellent offers in this fashion," said she sharply. "You can hardly expect us to exert ourselves to find another such opening for you. Good-day to you, Miss Hunter." She struck a gong upon the table, and I was shown out by the page.

'Well, Mr Holmes, when I got back to my lodgings and found little enough in the cupboard, and two or three bills upon the table, I began to ask myself whether I had not done a very foolish thing. After all, if these people had strange fads, and expected obedience on the most extraordinary matters, they were at least ready to pay for their eccentricity. Very few governesses in England are getting a hundred a year. Besides, what use was my hair to me? Many people are improved by wearing it short, and perhaps I should be among the number. Next day I was inclined to think that I had made a mistake, and by the day after I was sure of it. I had almost overcome my pride, so far as to go back to the agency and inquire whether the place was still open, when I received this letter from the gentleman himself. I have it here, and I will read it to you:

The Copper Beeches, near Winchester

DEAR MISS HUNTER,

Miss Stoper has very kindly given me your address, and I write from here to ask you whether you have reconsidered your decision. My wife is very anxious that you should come, for she has been much attracted by my description of you. We are willing to give

thirty pounds a quarter, or £120 a year, so as to recompense you
for any little inconvenience which our fads may cause you. They
are not very exacting after all. My wife is fond of a particular
shade of electric blue,* and would like you to wear such a dress
indoors in the morning. You need not, however, go to the expense
of purchasing new, as we have one belonging to my dear daughter
Alice (now in Philadelphia) which would, I should think, fit you
very well. Then, as to sitting here or there, or amusing yourself in
any manner indicated, that need cause you no inconvenience. As
regards your hair, it is no doubt a pity, especially as I could not
help remarking its beauty during our short interview, but I am
afraid that I must remain firm upon this point, and I only hope
that the increased salary may recompense you for the loss. Your
duties, as far as the child is concerned, are very light. Now do try
to come, and I shall meet you with the dogcart at Winchester. Let
me know your train.

> Yours faithfully,
> JEPHRO RUCASTLE.*

'That is the letter which I have just received, Mr Holmes,
and my mind is made up that I will accept it. I thought,
however, that before taking the final step, I should like to
submit the whole matter to your consideration.'

'Well, Miss Hunter, if your mind is made up, that settles
the question,' said Holmes, smiling.

'But you would not advise me to refuse?'

'I confess that it is not the situation which I should like to
see a sister of mine* apply for.'

'What is the meaning of it all, Mr Holmes?'

'Ah, I have no data. I cannot tell. Perhaps you have
yourself formed some opinion?'

'Well, there seems to me to be only one possible solution.
Mr Rucastle seemed to be a very kind, good-natured man.
Is it not possible that his wife is a lunatic, that he desires to
keep the matter quiet for fear she should be taken to an
asylum, and that he humours her fancies in every way in
order to prevent an outbreak.'

'That is a possible solution—in fact, as matters stand, it is
the most probable one. But in any case it does not seem to
be a nice household for a young lady.'

'But the money, Mr Holmes, the money!'

'Well, yes, of course, the pay is good—too good. That is what makes me uneasy. Why should they give you £120 a year, when they could have their pick for £40? There must be some strong reason behind.'

'I thought that if I told you the circumstances you would understand afterwards if I wanted your help. I should feel so much stronger if I felt that you were at the back of me.'

'Oh, you may carry that feeling away with you. I assure you that your little problem promises to be the most interesting which has come my way for some months. There is something distinctly novel about some of the features. If you should find yourself in doubt or in danger—'

'Danger! What danger do you foresee?'

Holmes shook his head gravely. 'It would cease to be a danger if we could define it,' said he. 'But at any time, day or night, a telegram would bring me down to your help.'

'That is enough.' She rose briskly from her chair with the anxiety all swept from her face. 'I shall go down to Hampshire quite easy in my mind now. I shall write to Mr Rucastle at once, sacrifice my poor hair tonight, and start for Winchester to-morrow.' With a few grateful words to Holmes she bade us both good-night, and bustled off upon her way.

'At least,' said I, as we heard her quick, firm step descending the stairs, 'she seems to be a young lady who is very well able to take care of herself.'

'And she would need to be,' said Holmes, gravely; 'I am much mistaken if we do not hear from her before many days are past.'

It was not very long before my friend's prediction was fulfilled. A fortnight went by, during which I frequently found my thoughts turning in her direction, and wondering what strange side-alley of human experience this lonely woman had strayed into. The unusual salary, the curious conditions, the light duties, all pointed to something abnormal, though whether a fad or a plot, or whether the man were a philanthropist or a villain, it was quite beyond my powers to determine. As to Holmes, I observed that he sat frequently for half an hour on end, with knitted brows and an abstracted air, but he swept the matter away with a wave of his hand when I mentioned it. 'Data! data! data!' he cried impatiently. 'I can't make bricks without clay.'* And yet he would always wind up by muttering that no sister of his should ever have accepted such a situation.

The telegram which we eventually received came late one night, just as I was thinking of turning in, and Holmes was settling down to one of those all-night researches which he frequently indulged in, when I would leave him stooping over a retort and a test-tube at night, and find him in the same position when I came down to breakfast in the morning. He opened the yellow envelope,* and then, glancing at the message, threw it across to me.

'Just look up the trains in Bradshaw,'* said he, and turned back to his chemical studies.

The summons was a brief and urgent one.

Please be at the Black Swan Hotel* at Winchester at midday tomorrow (it said). Do come! I am at my wits' end.
        HUNTER.

'Will you come with me?' asked Holmes, glancing up.

'I should wish to.'

'Just look it up, then.'

'There is a train at half-past nine,' said I, glancing over my Bradshaw. 'It is due at Winchester at 11.30.'

'That will do very nicely. Then perhaps I had better postpone my analysis of the acetones,* as we may need to be at our best in the morning.'

By eleven o'clock the next day we were well upon our way to the old English capital.* Holmes had been buried in the morning papers all the way down, but after we had passed the Hampshire border he threw them down, and began to admire the scenery. It was an ideal spring day, a light blue sky, flecked with little fleecy white clouds drifting across from west to east. The sun was shining very brightly, and yet there was an exhilarating nip in the air, which set an edge to a man's energy. All over the countryside, away to the rolling hills around Aldershot,* the little red and grey roofs of the farm-steadings peeped out from amidst the light green of the new foliage.

'Are they not fresh and beautiful?'. I cried, with all the enthusiasm of a man fresh from the fogs of Baker Street.

But Holmes shook his head gravely.

'Do you know, Watson,' said he, 'that it is one of the curses of a mind with a turn like mine that I must look at everything with reference to my own special subject. You look at these scattered houses, and you are impressed by their beauty. I look at them, and the only thought which comes to me is a feeling of their isolation, and of the impunity with which crime may be committed there.'

'Good heavens!' I cried. 'Who would associate crime with these dear old homesteads?'

'They always fill me with a certain horror. It is my belief, Watson, founded upon my experience, that the lowest and vilest alleys in London do not present a more dreadful record of sin than does the smiling and beautiful countryside.'

'You horrify me!'

'But the reason is very obvious. The pressure of public opinion can do in the town what the law cannot accomplish. There is no lane so vile that the scream of a tortured child, or the thud of a drunkard's blow, does not beget sympathy and indignation among the neighbours, and then the whole machinery of justice is ever so close that a word of complaint can set it going, and there is but a step between the crime and the dock. But look at these lonely houses, each in its own fields, filled for the most part with poor ignorant folk who know little of the law. Think of the deeds of hellish cruelty, the hidden wickedness which may go on, year in, year out, in such places, and none the wiser. Had this lady who appeals to us for help gone to live in Winchester, I should never have had a fear for her. It is the five miles of country which makes the danger. Still, it is clear that she is not personally threatened.'

'No. If she can come to Winchester to meet us she can get away.'

'Quite so. She has her freedom.'

'What *can* be the matter, then? Can you suggest no explanation?'

'I have devised seven separate explanations, each of which would cover the facts as far as we know them. But which of these is correct can only be determined by the fresh information which we shall no doubt find waiting for us. Well, there is the tower of the Cathedral, and we shall soon learn all that Miss Hunter has to tell.'

The 'Black Swan' is an inn of repute in the High Street, at no distance from the station, and there we found the young lady waiting for us. She had engaged a sitting-room, and our lunch awaited us upon the table.

'I am so delighted that you have come,' she said earnestly, 'it is so kind of you both; but indeed I do not know what I should do. Your advice will be altogether invaluable to me.'

'Pray tell us what has happened to you.'

'I will do so, and I must be quick, for I have promised Mr Rucastle to be back before three. I got his leave to come into town this morning, though he little knew for what purpose.'

'Let us have everything in its due order.' Holmes thrust his long thin legs out towards the fire, and composed himself to listen.

'In the first place, I may say that I have met, on the whole, with no actual ill-treatment from Mr and Mrs Rucastle. It is only fair to them to say that. But I cannot understand them, and I am not easy in my mind about them.'

'What can you not understand?'

'Their reasons for their conduct. But you shall have it all just as it occurred. When I came down Mr Rucastle met me here, and drove me in his dog-cart to Copper Beeches. It is, as he said, beautifully situated, but it is not beautiful in itself, for it is a large square block of a house, whitewashed, but all stained and streaked with damp and bad weather. There are grounds round it, woods on three sides, and on the fourth a field which slopes down to the Southampton high-road, which curves past about a hundred yards from the front door. This ground in front belongs to the house, but the woods all round are part of Lord Southerton's preserves.* A clump of copper beeches immediately in front of the hall door has given its name to the place.

'I was driven over by my employer, who was as amiable as ever, and was introduced by him that evening to his wife and the child. There was no truth, Mr Holmes, in the conjecture which seemed to us to be probable in your rooms at Baker Street. Mrs Rucastle is not mad. I found her to be a silent, pale-faced woman, much younger than her husband, not more than thirty, I should think, while he can hardly be less than forty-five. From their conversation I have gathered that they have been married about seven years, that he was a widower, and that his only child by the first wife was the daughter who has gone to Philadelphia. Mr Rucastle told me in private that the reason why she had left them was that she had an unreasoning aversion to her stepmother. As the daughter would not have been less than twenty, I can quite imagine that her position must have been uncomfortable with her father's young wife.

'Mrs Rucastle seemed to me to be colourless in mind as well as in feature. She impressed me neither favourably nor the reverse. She was a nonentity. It was easy to see that she was passionately devoted both to her husband and to her little son. Her light grey eyes wandered continually from one to the other, noting every little want and forestalling it if possible. He was kind to her also in his bluff boisterous fashion, and on the whole they seemed to be a happy couple. And yet she had some secret sorrow, this woman. She would often be lost in deep thought, with the saddest look upon her face. More than once I have surprised her in tears. I have thought sometimes that it was the disposition of her child which weighed upon her mind, for I have never met so utterly spoilt and so ill-natured a little creature. He is small for his age, with a head which is quite disproportionately large. His whole life appears to be spent in an alternation between savage fits of passion and gloomy intervals of sulking. Giving pain to any creature weaker than himself seems to be his one idea of amusement, and he shows quite remarkable talent in planning the capture of mice, little birds, and insects. But I would rather not talk about the creature, Mr Holmes, and, indeed, he has little to do with my story.'

'I am glad of all details,' remarked my friend, 'whether they seem to you to be relevant or not.'

'I shall try not to miss anything of importance. The one unpleasant thing about the house, which struck me at once, was the appearance and conduct of the servants. There are only two, a man and his wife. Toller,* for that's his name, is a rough, uncouth man, with grizzled hair and whiskers, and a perpetual smell of drink. Twice since I have been with them he has been quite drunk, and yet Mr Rucastle seemed to take no notice of it. His wife is a very tall and strong woman with a sour face, as silent as Mrs Rucastle, and much less amiable. They are a most unpleasant couple, but fortunately I spend most of my time in the nursery and my own room, which are next to each other in one corner of the building.

'For two days after my arrival at the Copper Beeches my life was very quiet; on the third, Mrs Rucastle came down just after breakfast and whispered something to her husband.

' "Oh yes," said he, turning to me, "we are very much obliged to you, Miss Hunter, for falling in with our whims so far as to cut your hair. I assure you that it has not detracted in the tiniest iota from your appearance. We shall now see how the electric blue dress will become you. You will find it laid out upon the bed in your room, and if you would be so good as to put it on we should both be extremely obliged."

'The dress which I found waiting for me was of a peculiar shade of blue. It was of excellent material, a sort of beige,* but it bore unmistakable signs of having been worn before. It could not have been a better fit if I had been measured for it. Both Mr and Mrs Rucastle expressed a delight at the look of it which seemed quite exaggerated in its vehemence. They were waiting for me in the drawing-room, which is a very large room, stretching along the entire front of the house, with three long windows reaching down to the floor. A chair had been placed close to the central window, with its back turned towards it. In this I was asked to sit, and then Mr Rucastle, walking up and down on the other side of the room, began to tell me a series of the funniest stories that I have ever listened to. You cannot imagine how comical he was, and I laughed until I was quite weary. Mrs Rucastle, however, who has evidently no sense of humour, never so much as smiled, but sat with her hands in her lap, and a sad, anxious look upon her face. After an hour or so Mr Rucastle suddenly remarked that it was time to commence the duties of the day, and that I might change my dress, and go to little Edward in the nursery.

'Two days later this same performance was gone through under exactly similar circumstances. Again I changed my dress, again I sat in the window, and again I laughed very heartily at the funny stories of which my employer had an immense *répertoire,* and which he told inimitably. Then he handed me a yellow-backed novel, and, moving my chair a little sideways, that my own shadow might not fall upon the page, he begged me to read aloud to him. I read for about ten minutes, beginning in the heart of a chapter, and then suddenly, in the middle of a sentence, he ordered me to cease and change my dress.

'You can easily imagine, Mr Holmes, how curious I became as to what the meaning of this extraordinary performance could possibly be. They were always very careful, I observed, to turn my face away from the window, so that I became consumed with the desire to see what was going on behind my back. At first it seemed to be impossible, but I soon devised a means. My hand mirror had been broken, so a happy thought seized me, and I concealed a little of the glass in my handkerchief. On the next occasion, in the midst of my laughter, I put my handkerchief up to my eyes, and was able with a little management to see all that there was behind me. I confess that I was disappointed. There was nothing.

'At least, that was my first impression. At the second glance, however, I perceived that there was a man standing in the Southampton Road, a small bearded man in a grey suit, who seemed to be looking in my direction. The road is an important highway, and there are usually people there. This man, however, was leaning against the railings which bordered our field, and was looking earnestly. I lowered my handkerchief, and glanced at Mrs Rucastle to find her eyes fixed upon me with a most searching gaze. She said nothing, but I am convinced that she had divined that I had a mirror in my hand, and had seen what was behind me. She rose at once.

' "Jephro," said she, "there is an impertinent fellow upon the road there who stares up at Miss Hunter."

' "No friend of yours, Miss Hunter?" he asked.

' "No; I know no one in these parts."

' "Dear me! How very impertinent! Kindly turn round, and motion him to go away."

' "Surely it would be better to take no notice?"

' "No, no, we should have him loitering here always. Kindly turn round, and wave him away like that."

'I did as I was told, and at the same instant Mrs Rucastle drew down the blind. That was a week ago, and from that time I have not sat again in the window, nor have I worn the blue dress, nor seen the man in the road.'

'Pray continue,' said Holmes. 'Your narrative promises to be a most interesting one.'

'You will find it rather disconnected, I fear, and there may prove to be little relation between the different incidents of which I speak. On the very first day I was at Copper Beeches, Mr Rucastle took me to a small outhouse which stands near the kitchen door, as we approached it I heard the sharp rattling of a chain, and the sound as of a large animal moving about.

' "Look in here!" said Mr Rucastle, showing a slit between two planks. "Is he not a beauty?"

'I looked through, and was conscious of two glowing eyes, and of a vague figure huddled up in the darkness.

' "Don't be frightened," said my employer, laughing at the start which I had given. "It's only Carlo,* my mastiff. I call him mine, but really old Toller, my groom, is the only man who can do anything with him. We feed him once a day, and not too much then, so that he is always as keen as mustard.* Toller lets him loose every night, and God help the trespasser whom he lays his fangs upon. For goodness' sake don't you ever on any pretext set your foot over the threshold at night, for it is as much as your life is worth."

'The warning was no idle one, for two nights later I happened to look out of my bedroom window about two o'clock in the morning. It was a beautiful moonlight night, and the lawn in front of the house was silvered over and almost as bright as day. I was standing, wrapt* in the peaceful beauty of the scene, when I was aware that something was moving under the shadow of the copper beeches. As it emerged into the moonshine I saw what it was. It was a giant dog, as large as a calf, tawny-tinted, with hanging jowl, black muzzle, and huge projecting bones. It walked slowly across the lawn and vanished into the shadow upon the other side. That dreadful silent sentinel sent a chill to my heart, which I do not think that any burglar could have done.

'And now I have a very strange experience to tell you. I had, as you know, cut off my hair in London, and I had placed it in a great coil at the bottom of my trunk. One evening, after the child was in bed, I began to amuse myself by examining the furniture of my room and by rearranging my own little things. There was an old chest of drawers in the room, the two upper ones empty and open, the lower one locked. I had filled the two first with my linen and, as I had still much to pack away, I was naturally annoyed at not having the use of the third drawer. It struck me that it might have been fastened by a mere oversight, so I took out my bunch of keys and tried to open it. The very first key fitted to perfection, and I drew the drawer open. There was only one thing in it, but I am sure that you would never guess what it was. It was my coil of hair.

'I took it up and examined it. It was of the same peculiar tint, and the same thickness. But then the impossibility of the thing obtruded itself upon me. How *could* my hair have been locked in the drawer? With trembling hands I undid my trunk, turned out the contents, and drew from the bottom my own hair. I laid the two tresses together, and I assure you they were identical. Was it not extraordinary? Puzzle as I would, I could make nothing at all of what it meant. I returned the strange hair to the drawer, and I said nothing of the matter to the Rucastles, as I felt that I had put myself in the wrong by opening a drawer which they had locked.

'I am naturally observant as you may have remarked, Mr Holmes, and I soon had a pretty good plan of the whole house in my head. There was one wing, however, which appeared not to be inhabited at all. A door which faced that which led into the quarters of the Tollers opened into this suite, but it was invariably locked. One day, however, as I ascended the stair, I met Mr Rucastle coming out through this door, his keys in his hand, and a look on his face which made him a very different person to the round jovial man to whom I was accustomed. His cheeks were red, his brow was all crinkled with anger, and the veins stood out at his temples with passion. He locked the door, and hurried past me without a word or a look.

'This aroused my curiosity; so when I went out for a walk in the grounds with my charge, I strolled round to the side from which I could see the windows of this part of the house. There were four of them in a row, three of which were simply dirty, while the fourth was shuttered up. They were evidently all deserted. As I strolled up and down, glancing at them occasionally, Mr Rucastle came out to me, looking as merry and jovial as ever.

' "Ah!" said he, "you must not think me rude if I passed you without a word, my dear young lady. I was preoccupied with business matters."

'I assured him that I was not offended. "By the way," said I, "you seem to have quite a suite of spare rooms up there, and one of them has the shutters up."

' "Photography is one of my hobbies,"* said he. "I have made my dark room up there. But, dear me! what an observant young lady we have come upon. Who would have believed it? Who would have ever believed it?" He spoke in a jesting tone, but there was no jest in his eyes as he looked at me. I read suspicion there, and annoyance, but no jest.

'Well, Mr Holmes, from the moment that I understood that there was something about that suite of rooms which I was not to know, I was all on fire to go over them. It was not mere curiosity, though I have my share of that. It was more a feeling of duty—a feeling that some good might come from my penetrating to this place. They talk of woman's instinct; perhaps it was woman's instinct which gave me that feeling. At any rate, it was there; and I was keenly on the look-out for any chance to pass the forbidden door.

'It was only yesterday that the chance came. I may tell you that, besides Mr Rucastle, both Toller and his wife find something to do in these deserted rooms, and I once saw him carrying a large black linen bag with him through the door. Recently he has been drinking hard, and yesterday evening he was drunk; and, when I came upstairs, there was a key in the door. I have no doubt at all that he had left it there. Mr and Mrs Rucastle were both downstairs, and the child was with them, so that I had an admirable opportunity. I turned the key gently in the lock, opened the door, and slipped through.

'There was a little passage in front of me, unpapered and uncarpeted, which turned at a right angle at the farther end. Round this corner were three doors in a line, the first and third of which were open. They each led into an empty room, dusty and cheerless, with two windows in the one, and one in the other, so thick with dirt that the evening light glimmered dimly through them. The centre door was closed, and across the outside of it had been fastened one of the broad bars of an iron bed, padlocked at one end to a ring in the wall, and fastened at the other with stout cord. The door itself was locked as well, and the key was not there. This barricaded door corresponded clearly with the shuttered window outside, and yet I could see by the glimmer from beneath it that the room was not in darkness. Evidently there was a skylight which let in light from above. As I stood in the passage gazing at this sinister door, and wondering what secret it might veil, I suddenly heard the sound of steps within the room, and saw a shadow pass backwards and forwards against the little slit of dim light which shone out from under the door. A mad, unreasoning terror rose up in me at the sight, Mr Holmes. My overstrung nerves failed me suddenly, and I turned and ran—ran as though some dreadful hand were behind me, clutching at the skirt of my dress. I rushed down the passage, through the door, and straight into the arms of Mr Rucastle, who was waiting outside.

' "So," said he, smiling, "it was you, then. I thought it must be when I saw the door open."

' "Oh, I am so frightened!" I panted.

' "My dear young lady! my dear young lady!"—you cannot think how caressing and soothing his manner was—"and what has frightened you, my dear young lady?"

'But his voice was just a little too coaxing. He overdid it. I was keenly on my guard against him.

' "I was foolish enough to go into the empty wing," I answered. "But it is so lonely and eerie in this dim light that I was frightened and ran out again. Oh, it is so dreadfully still in there!"

' "Only that?" said he, looking at me keenly.

' "Why, what do you think?" I asked.

' "Why do you think that I lock this door?"

' "I am sure that I do not know."

' "It is to keep people out who have no business there. Do you see?" He was still smiling in the most amiable manner.

' "I am sure if I had known—"

' "Well, then, you know now. And if you ever put your foot over that threshold again—"here in an instant the smile hardened into a grin of rage, and he glared down at me with the face of a demon, "I'll throw you to the mastiff."

'I was so terrified that I do not know what I did. I suppose that I must have rushed past him into my room. I remember nothing until I found myself lying on my bed trembling all over. Then I thought of you, Mr Holmes. I could not live there longer without some advice. I was frightened of the house, of the man, of the woman, of the servants, even of the child. They were all horrible to me. If I could only bring you down all would be well. Of course I might have fled from the house, but my curiosity was almost as strong as my fears. My mind was soon made up. I would send you a wire. I put on my hat and cloak, went down to the office, which is about half a mile from the house, and then returned, feeling very much easier. A horrible doubt came into my mind as I approached the door lest the dog might be loose, but I remembered that Toller had drunk himself into a state of insensibility that evening, and I knew that he was the only one in the household who had any influence with the savage creature, or who would venture to set him free. I slipped in in safety, and lay awake half the night in my joy at the thought of seeing you. I had no difficulty in getting leave to come into Winchester this morning, but I must be back before three o'clock, for Mr and Mrs Rucastle are going on a visit, and will be away all the evening, so that I must look after the child. Now I have told you all my adventures, Mr Holmes, and I should be very glad if you could tell me what it all means, and, above all, what I should do.'

Holmes and I had listened spellbound to this extraordinary story. My friend rose now, and paced up and down the room, his hands in his pockets, and an expression of the most profound gravity upon his face.

'Is Toller still drunk?' he asked.

'Yes. I heard his wife tell Mrs Rucastle that she could do nothing with him.'

'That is well. And the Rucastles go out to-night?'

'Yes.'

'Is there a cellar with a good strong lock?'

'Yes, the wine cellar.'

'You seem to me to have acted all through this matter like a brave and sensible girl, Miss Hunter. Do you think that you could perform one more feat? I should not ask it of you if I did not think you a quite exceptional woman.'

'I will try. What is it?'

'We shall be at the Copper Beeches by seven o'clock, my friend and I. The Rucastles will be gone by that time, and Toller will, we hope, be incapable. There only remains Mrs Toller, who might give the alarm. If you could send her into the cellar, on some errand, and then turn the key upon her, you would facilitate matters immensely.'

'I will do it.'

'Excellent! We shall then look thoroughly into the affair. Of course there is only one feasible explanation. You have been brought there to personate someone, and the real person is imprisoned in this chamber. That is obvious. As to who this prisoner is, I have no doubt that it is the daughter, Miss Alice Rucastle, if I remember right, who was said to have gone to America. You were chosen, doubtless, as resembling her in height, figure, and the colour of your hair. Hers had been cut off, very possibly in some illness through which she has passed, and so, of course, yours had to be sacrificed also. By a curious chance you came upon her tresses. The man in the road was, undoubtedly, some friend of hers—possibly her *fiancé*—and no doubt as you wore the girl's dress, and were so like her, he was convinced from your laughter, whenever he saw you, and afterwards from your gesture, that Miss Rucastle was perfectly happy, and that she no longer desired his attentions. The dog is let loose at night to prevent him from endeavouring to communicate with her. So much is fairly clear. The most serious point in the case is the disposition of the child.'

'What on earth has that to do with it?' I ejaculated.

'My dear Watson, you as a medical man are continually gaining light as to the tendencies of a child by the study of the parents. Don't you see that the converse is equally valid. I have frequently gained my first real insight into the character of parents by studying their children. This child's disposition is abnormally cruel, merely for cruelty's sake, and whether he derives this from his smiling father, as I should suspect, or from his mother, it bodes evil for the poor girl who is in their power.'

'I am sure that you are right, Mr Holmes,' cried our client. 'A thousand things come back to me which make me certain that you have hit it. Oh, let us lose not an instant in bringing help to this poor creature.'

'We must be circumspect, for we are dealing with a very cunning man. We can do nothing until seven o'clock. At that hour we shall be with you, and it will not be long before we solve the mystery.'

We were as good as our word, for it was just seven when we reached the Copper Beeches, having put up our trap at a wayside public-house. The group of trees, with their dark leaves shining like burnished metal in the light of the setting sun, were sufficient to mark the house even had Miss Hunter not been standing smiling on the doorstep.

'Have you managed it?' asked Holmes.

A loud thudding noise came from somewhere downstairs. 'That is Mrs Toller in the cellar,' said she. 'Her husband lies snoring on the kitchen rug. Here are his keys, which are the duplicates of Mr Rucastle's.'

'You have done well indeed!' cried Holmes, with enthusiasm. 'Now lead the way, and we shall soon see the end of this black business.'

We passed up the stair, unlocked the door, followed on down a passage, and found ourselves in front of the barricade which Miss Hunter had described. Holmes cut the cord and removed the transverse bar. Then he tried the various keys in the lock, but without success. No sound came from within, and at the silence Holmes's face clouded over.

'I trust that we are not too late,' said he. 'I think, Miss Hunter, that we had better go in without you. Now, Watson, put your shoulder to it, and we shall see whether we cannot make our way in.'

It was an old rickety door and gave at once before our united strength. Together we rushed into the room. It was empty. There was no furniture save a little pallet bed,* a small table, and a basketful of linen. The skylight above was open, and the prisoner gone.

'There has been some villainy here,' said Holmes; 'this beauty has guessed Miss Hunter's intentions, and has carried his victim off.'

'But how?'

'Through the skylight. We shall soon see how he managed it.' He swung himself up on to the roof. 'Ah, yes,' he cried, 'here's the end of a long light ladder against the eaves. That is how he did it.'

'But it is impossible,' said Miss Hunter, 'the ladder was not there when the Rucastles went away.'

'He has come back and done it. I tell you that he is a clever and dangerous man. I should not be very much surprised if this were he whose step I hear now upon the stair. I think, Watson, that it would be as well for you to have your pistol ready.'

The words were hardly out of his mouth before a man appeared at the door of the room, a very fat and burly man, with a heavy stick in his hand. Miss Hunter screamed and shrunk against the wall at the sight of him, but Sherlock Holmes sprang forward and confronted him.

'You villain!' said he, 'where's your daughter?'

The fat man cast his eyes round, and then up at the open skylight.

'It is for me to ask you that,' he shrieked, 'you thieves! Spies and thieves! I have caught you, have I? You are in my power. I'll serve you!' He turned and clattered down the stairs as hard as he could go.

'He's gone for the dog!' cried Miss Hunter.

'I have my revolver,' said I.

'Better close the front door,' cried Holmes, and we all rushed down the stairs together. We had hardly reached the hall when we heard the baying of a hound, and then a scream of agony, with a horrible worrying sound which it was dreadful to listen to. An elderly man with a red face and shaking limbs came staggering out at a side door.

'My God!' he cried. 'Someone has loosed the dog. It's not been fed for two days. Quick, quick, or it'll be too late!'

Holmes and I rushed out, and round the angle of the house, with Toller hurrying behind us. There was the huge famished brute, its black muzzle buried in Rucastle's throat, while he writhed and screamed upon the ground. Running up, I blew its brains out, and it fell over with its keen white teeth still meeting in the great creases of his neck. With much labour we separated them, and carried him, living but horribly mangled, into the house. We laid him upon the drawing-room sofa, and having despatched the sobered Toller to bear the news to his wife, I did what I could to relieve his pain. We were all assembled round him when the door opened, and a tall, gaunt women entered the room.

'Mrs Toller!' cried Miss Hunter.

'Yes, miss. Mr Rucastle let me out when he came back before he went up to you. Ah, miss, it is a pity you didn't let me know what you were planning, for I would have told you that your pains were wasted.'

'Ha!' said Holmes, looking keenly at her. 'It is clear that Mrs Toller knows more about this matter than anyone else.'

'Yes, sir, I do, and I am ready enough to tell what I know.'

'Then pray sit down, and let us hear it, for there are several points on which I must confess that I am still in the dark.'

'I will soon make it clear to you,' said she; 'and I'd have done so before now if I could ha' got out from the cellar. If there's police-court business over this, you'll remember that I was the one that stood your friend, and that I was Miss Alice's friend too.

'She was never happy at home, Miss Alice wasn't, from the time that her father married again. She was slighted like, and had no say in anything; but it never really became bad for her until after she met Mr Fowler* at a friend's house. As well as I could learn, Miss Alice had rights of her own by will, but she was so quiet and patient, she was, that she never said a word about them, but just left everything in Mr Rucastle's hands. He knew he was safe with her; but when there was a chance of a husband coming forward, who would ask for all that the law could give him, then her father thought it time to put a stop on it. He wanted her to sign a paper so that whether she married or not, he could use her money. When she wouldn't do it, he kept on worrying her until she got brain fever,* and for six weeks was at death's door. Then she got better at last, all worn to a shadow, and with her beautiful hair cut off; but that didn't make no change in her young man, and he stuck to her as true as man could be.'

'Ah,' said Holmes, 'I think that what you have been good enough to tell us makes the matter fairly clear, and that I can deduce all that remains. Mr Rucastle, then, I presume, took to this system of imprisonment?'

'Yes, sir.'

'And brought Miss Hunter down from London in order to get rid of the disagreeable persistence of Mr Fowler.'

'That was it, sir.'

'But Mr Fowler, being a persevering man, as a good seaman should be, blockaded the house, and having met you, succeeded by certain arguments, metallic or otherwise,* in convincing you that your interests were the same as his.'

'Mr Fowler was a very kind-spoken, free-handed gentleman,' said Mrs Toller serenely.

'And in this way he managed that your good man should have no want of drink, and that a ladder should be ready at the moment when your master had gone out.'

'You have it, sir, just as it happened.'

'I am sure we owe you an apology, Mrs Toller,' said Holmes, 'for you have certainly cleared up everything which puzzled us. And here comes the country surgeon and Mrs Rucastle, so I think, Watson, that we had best escort Miss Hunter back to Winchester, as it seems to me that our *locus standi** now is rather a questionable one.'

And thus was solved the mystery of the sinister house with the copper beeches in front of the door. Mr Rucastle survived, but was always a broken man, kept alive solely through the care of his devoted wife. They still live with their old servants, who probably know so much of Rucastle's past life that he finds it difficult to part from them. Mr Fowler and Miss Rucastle were married, by special licence,* in Southampton the day after their flight, and he is now the holder of a Government appointment in the Island of Mauritius.* As to Miss Violet Hunter,* my friend Holmes, rather to my disappointment, manifested no further interest in her when once she had ceased to be the centre of one of his problems, and she is now the head of a private school at Walsall,* where I believe that she has met with considerable success.

EXPLANATORY NOTES

The Adventures of Sherlock Holmes was published by George Newnes Ltd on 14 Oct. 1892 in an edition of 10,000 copies. The first American edition was published by Harper & Brothers, New York, on the following day (4,500 copies). A colonial edition (the second English edition) was issued by Longmans, Green, & Co. in their Colonial Library in Apr. 1894.

A SCANDAL IN BOHEMIA

First published in the *Strand Magazine*, 2 (July 1891), 61–75, with 10 illustrations by Sidney Paget; *Strand Magazine*, New York (Aug. 1891); S.S. McClure Newspaper Syndicate, USA, various dates between 11 July and 18 Oct. 1891, with woodcut illustrations. Alternative titles: 'A Scandal of Bohemia' (*Chicago Inter-Ocean*); 'A Bohemian Scandal' (*New Orleans Daily Picayune*); 'Woman's Wit' (*Baltimore Weekly Sun*); 'The King's Sweetheart' (*Boston Sunday Globe*).

Written at 2 Upper Wimpole Street and 23 Montague Place; dispatched 3 Apr. 1891.

Text: collated with MS and printed versions; pp. 13–19 are in another hand ('Large sitting-room on the right hand side . . . when he became a specialist in crime'). All the printed texts divide the story into three sections, numbered II and III in the *Strand*, and I–III in Newnes (1892) and Murray (1928); but this is the only story with such subdivisions and they have been omitted from the present edition.

There are two documents in the library at Austin, Texas referring to the 'second hand' in the MS. One by John Dickson Carr claiming it was the hand of the author, and one by Adrian Conan Doyle stating it was that of the author's sister, Lottie. Carr says:

Sir Arthur Conan Doyle, as a schoolboy at Stonyhurst, cultivated two styles of handwriting—his own famous script, and another, more angular style which he adopted to rest his hand. This appears in his school and college letters, where his mother sharply criticizes the second handwriting, and he explains how he came to adopt it. Indeed, the second handwriting may be seen in the letters as late as his days at Norwood, and in his Norwood notebook. Having examined dozens of examples, I can testify that the second handwriting which appears in 'A Scandal in Bohemia', and which appears to be an interpolation by someone else, is actually by Conan Doyle himself—John Dickson Carr.

Adrian Conan Doyle in a letter dated 30 Apr. 1962 (acknowledging the photostats of the 'Conan Doyle documentation' at Texas) wrote:

In the holograph manuscript of 'A Scandal in Bohemia', you may have noticed some five or six pages not in my father's handwriting, occur in the middle of the manuscript, and I thought that you might like to know that this is the handwriting of his sister Lottie, to whom, when my father's hand became tired, he would dictate. This happened on very rare occasions and among the family collection of manuscripts there are only two which carry one or two pages in dictation in his sister's handwriting.

The MS was acquired by David Randall for the Scribner Bookstore, New York, in 1946 and sold to Carroll A. Wilson, thence to Frederic A. Dannay. Present location (since 1959), the Ellery Queen Collection, Humanities Research Center, Austin, Texas.

[Title]: originally 'A Scandal of Bohemia'. *Scènes de la vie de Bohème* (1848) by Henri Murger (1822–61), which is referred to in *A Study in Scarlet*, may have inspired the title and mood; it was adapted for the stage in 1851 and for opera in 1896. The title may also have been suggested by 'A Pompeii in Bohemia' (which appeared alongside the first part of *The White Company* in the *Cornhill Magazine* for Jan. 1891), or by a current book, *Sketches from Bohemia*, by S. J. Adair Fitzgerald (1891). 'Bohemia' is used of the country and of the lifestyle adopted by artists (named after 'Bohemiens', who were gypsies). 'Bohemianism' is defined by Henri Murger as 'the manners and customs of those belonging to a class which has hitherto been unfairly condemned, and whose greatest vice is an irregularity for which they have this excuse—that the life they must lead forces irregularity upon them'. There is also 'The Queen of Bohemia' found on inn signs—named after Elizabeth (1596–1662), the daughter of James I, and wife of Friedrich V (1596–1632) elector of the Palatinate whose election to the throne of Bohemia touched off the Thirty Years War. The diversion outside the house recalls 'The Purloined Letter' (1844) by Edgar Allan Poe, in which a musket is fired in the street by a 'pretended lunatic' in the pay of Dupin—and that story provided the format for the series. Further inspiration came from the works of Robert Louis Stevenson, in particular the *New Arabian Nights* (1882), in which Prince Florizel of Bohemia is the protagonist.

5 *Irene Adler:* the first name perhaps suggested by Samuel Johnson's unsuccessful tragedy, *Irene* (written 1737, performed 1749); the surname is that of a river in Bohemia. Irene Adler could have been suggested by Lola Montez, alias Maria Dolores Gilbert (1818–61), the mistress of Ludwig I of Bavaria (1786–1868), or Elizabeth Anne Howard (1822–64), mistress of Napoleon III (1808–73), though her character differs greatly from theirs. Her operatic past could have been suggested by the careers of great singers of the day, such as the Canadian Marie Louise Lajeunesse (1852–1930), whose stage name was (Dame) Emma Albani; (Dame) Nellie Melba *née* Mitchell of Melbourne (1861–1931); and Adelina Patti (1843–1919), born in Madrid but of Italian parentage who began singing in New York at the age of seven. The King of Bohemia has echoes of Ludwig I, who sacrificed his rule for Lola Montez, and Napoleon III, but the Austrian Archduke Rudolf (1858–89) whose love life had caused a scandal in Bohemia and throughout the Habsburg dominions, and Wilhelm II of Germany (1859–1941), who had recently dismissed Bismarck, are stronger candidates, as is Queen Victoria's son, the future Edward VII (1841–1910), who had a three-year liaison with Emily Charlotte ('Lillie') Langtry (1852–1929).

the most perfect reasoning and observing machine that the world has seen: ACD had in mind the calculating machine constructed by Charles Babbage (1791–1871), for he wrote to Joseph Bell (16 June 1892) that Holmes was 'as inhuman as Babbage's Calculating Machine, and just about as likely to fall in love' (Stisted Papers). The remark was perhaps in reply to the suggestion of a romantic plot featuring Holmes.

to introduce a distracting factor: MS 'to admit a distracting factor'.

the late Irene Adler: the cause of her death is not given.

I had seen little of Holmes . . . away from each other: this was altered in the *Strand* (from which the book editions were taken) to read: 'I had seen little of Holmes lately. My marriage had drifted us away from each other'. The marriage was to Mary Morstan (*The Sign of the Four*).

6 *He was still . . . the official police*: these lines were added at the proof stage and are not in the MS.

his summons to Odessa in the case of the Trepoff murder: perhaps an allusion to General Fedor Fedorovich Trepov (1812–89), who was shot by a Nihilist on 24 Jan. 1878. ACD had previously referred to Odessa in *A Study in Scarlet*, where Holmes cites the imaginary case of Dolsky who was murdered by the forcible administration of poison, but the use of the name might have been prompted by Wilde's 'Lord Arthur Savile's Crime' where Herr Winckelkopf, the explosives expert, 'instanced the case of a barometer that he had once sent to the military Governor at Odessa, which, though timed to explode in ten days, had not done so for something like three months'. Wilde's story had appeared in the *Court and Society Review* (11, 18, 25 May 1887) and was published in book form in July 1891.

the singular tragedy of the Atkinson brothers: perhaps from H. J. Atkinson, the MP for Boston in Lincolnshire, who in February 1891 asked the government to bring in a bill to compel leader writers to sign their articles, and perhaps also an allusion to the Ryan Brothers, one of whom was ACD's closest friend, James Paul Emile Ryan (1859–1920), who at short notice left Edinburgh to take charge of the family estates in Ceylon.

Trincomalee: a town and fortress with a large natural harbour on the north-east side of Ceylon (Sri Lanka), acquired by the British in 1795 for use as a naval base.

the reigning family of Holland: the House of Orange, presided over by William III, King of the Netherlands and Grand Duke of Luxembourg (ruled 1849–90), and thereafter by his daughter, Wilhelmina (born 1880) under the regency of the Queen-mother.

returned to civil practice: i.e. returned to medical practice on leaving the Army medical corps, from which he had been invalided.

a spirit case: a lockable stand containing decanters (a tantalus).

a gasogene: also known as a Seltzogene or by its French name 'Gazogene'; an early form of soda syphon, consisting of two strong glass globes connected one above the other by a wide glass tube and covered in wire mesh. The lower globe was filled with water and the upper one with sodium bicarbonate and tartaric acid, which when mixed produced carbon dioxide which aerated the water.

7 *You would certainly have been burned*: i.e. burned at the stake as a warlock (a common practice until the end of the 17th century). ACD had attended a lecture by David Nicholson on 'Witches and Witchcraft' at the Portsmouth Literary and Scientific Society on 1 Apr. 1890, and in proposing a vote of thanks said: 'Modern Science, far from having destroyed the original idea underlying this topic, has gone a long way to confirm it (*Hampshire Telegraph*, 5 Apr. 1890).

Mary Jane: a generic name for a maid (equivalent to 'Tommy Atkins' for a soldier); the 'slavey' was a term used for maid-servants primarily with drudgery duties. Possible originals would be Mary Smith or Lillie Brereton, the servants at 23 Montague Place where ACD had his lodgings. 'Mary Jane' also occurs in ACD's works as slang for a transvestite ('The Man With the Watches', *Round the Fire Stories*).

iodoform: a compound of iodine chemically analogous to chloroform; a pale yellow solid with antiseptic properties. In the first edition the word is incorrectly given as 'idioform'.

nitrate of silver: a compound produced by dissolving silver in nitric acid; used externally as a caustic to destroy unhealthy tissue and stimulate healing.

stethoscope: used to measure the heartbeat; originally monaural (held against one ear); a short tube of wood or rubber about six inches long, belled at one end and flanged at the other. 'Doctors were in the habit of carrying them in their hats, and as these caused a slight bulge it was always an elementary matter to pick out doctors from other wearers of silk hats' (W. J. Cairns, *Daily Telegraph*, 24 May 1951). The modern binaural stethoscope was in use by 1891. Dr John Ward Cousins, the Honorary Secretary of the Portsmouth Literary and Scientific Society when ACD joined it, described himself in the *Medical Directory* (1881) as the inventor of the 'Convertible Stethoscope (single and double)'.

9 *half-a-crown*: a pre-decimal coin, worth two shillings and sixpence [12½ new pence].

Continental Gazetteer: a geographical dictionary of the continent of Europe, arranged alphabetically, but ACD may have been thinking of Walter Graham Blackie's *Imperial Gazetteer* (2 vols., 1855), or the *Gazetteer of the World* (7 vols., 1850–7).

Eglow, Eglonitz: two invented places; perhaps suggested by Eglon in Western Virginia, or Elgon in British East Africa.

Egria . . . a German-speaking country—in Bohemia: the Latin form of Eger, a frontier town of Bohemia, and centre of a German-speaking district; now known as Cheb.

Carlsbad: (Karlsbad/Karlovy Vary) a celebrated watering place, 116 miles west of Prague.

the scene of the death of Wallenstein: (MS: 'Wollenstein') Albrecht Eusebius Wensel von Wallenstein (1583–1634), the Duke of Friedland, led the Imperial Troops during the Thirty Years' War and was assassinated at the burgomaster's house at Eger on 25 Feb. 1634. His life and death is the subject of the *Wallenstein* trilogy by Friedrich Schiller (1759–1805). The misspelling in the MS was a confusion with Wollstein, a town to which ACD had referred in his article on Dr Robert Koch in the *Review of Reviews* (Dec. 1890).

its numerous glass factories and paper mills: Bohemia was famous for its paper and crystal-glass, but Eger was a centre for the textile industry.

brougham: a four-wheeled closed carriage, seating two or more persons, drawn by a single horse or pair; named after a carriage designed by the essayist, Lord Chancellor, and Founder of the *Edinburgh Review*, Henry Brougham (1778–1868).

10 *Boswell*: James Boswell (1740–95), the biographer of Samuel Johnson, 'a keen young Scot with a mind which was reverent and impressionable . . . If Boswell had not lived I wonder how much we should hear now of his huge friend?' (*Through the Magic Door*).

a Hercules: (Greek: Heracles) the son of Zeus and Alcmene; a man of powerful physique, resembling the Farnese Hercules in the National Museum of Naples.

astrakhan: fine wool, similar to fur; named after the Russian city and province on the Caspian Sea. 'Astrachan, the passing rage in fashionable shops at present, is originally taken from the back of the Persian lamb, which abounds in Armenia and other parts of Asia Minor . . . Before giving birth to its offspring the mother ewe is slaughtered and its young disembowelled, the delicate hides of these embryos constituting the best pattern from which the garment is made' ('How Astrachan Fur is Obtained', *Tit-Bits*, 28 Feb. 1891).

a black vizard mask: 'vizard' or 'visor' (from the movable part of a helmet), a mask which conceals the eyes.

a man of strong character: MS originally 'a man with pronounced features'. The Habsburgs had marked family characteristics, such as a prominent lip.

11 *Count von Kramm*: from the German name, 'von Cramm'; or perhaps from 'Krumau' in Bohemia. 'Crammer' was also Victorian schoolboy slang for a liar.

the great House of Ormstein, hereditary kings of Bohemia: the Kings of Bohemia were elected until 1647, and thereafter became hereditary, within the House of Habsburg.

12 *Wilhelm Gottsreich Sigismond von Ormstein, Grand Duke of Cassel-Felstein*: a fictitious name and place. Wilhelm was the name of the German Kaiser; Gottsreich means 'God's Kingdom'; Sigismond, perhaps from an earlier King of Bohemia (Sigismund, 1419–38). Ormstein ('worm-stone') possibly from Dr Bernhard Ornstein (1809–96). Cassel-Felstein (which in Murray (1928) becomes 'Cassel-Falstein') from Schleswig-Holstein. Cassel (Kassel) is a town in Germany, and there is a Carlstein in Bohemia, but the name may have been suggested by Carl A. Falstedt, the Swedish Consul who was a fellow lodger with ACD at 23 Montague Place. Feldkirch, where ACD was at school in 1875–6, would be another possible antecedent.

incognito: (Latin) unknown, in disguise, or here 'under an assumed name'.

Prague: the capital of Bohemia, and now of the Czech Republic.

Warsaw: a city of Russia and former capital of the Kingdom of Poland, now capital of the Republic of Poland.

a Hebrew Rabbi: the Revd Dr Nathan Marcus Adler (1803–90), the Chief Rabbi of the United Congregations of the British Empire, or his son, the Revd Dr Hermann Adler (1839–1911), who succeeded him as the Chief Rabbi.

12 *a staff-commander . . . deep-sea fishes*: a Staff Commander in the Royal Navy is equivalent to a Lieutenant-Colonel in the Army, but this is an allusion to Cort Siverstein Adeler (1622–75), a Danish naval commander, whose name appears in contemporary biographical dictionaries above that of the Chief Rabbi. 'Deep-sea Fish' was the title of an article by Grant Allen which appeared in the *Cornhill Magazine* (Nov. 1890).

La Scala: Teatro alla Scala, the great opera house in Milan (built by Piermarini, 1776–8, and named after Regina della Scala, the wife of the Duke Barnabo Visconti who founded a church on the site in the 14th century).

Imperial Opera of Warsaw: Warsaw was part of the Russian Empire, so the opera performed at the National Theatre or at the Grand Theatre in Warsaw would have been 'Imperial'.

14 *Clotilde Lothman von Saxe-Meningen . . . King of Scandinavia*: the first name is taken from Princess Clotilde, the daughter of the King of Italy whose husband, Prince Napoleon died on 17 March 1891. 'Saxe-Meningen' is from Saxe-Meiningen, a duchy of south-central Germany. Adelaide of Saxe-Meiningen (1792–1849) was the wife of King William IV, and Charlotte, Duchess of Saxe-Meiningen (1860–1919) was the sister of the German Kaiser and grand-daughter of Queen Victoria. The King of Scandinavia was Oscar II (1829–1907), King of Sweden and of Norway, which was then annexed to it.

the face of the most beautiful of women, and the mind of the most resolute of men: MS originally 'the mind and spirit of the most resolute of men'. Perhaps suggested by the famous speech of Elizabeth I at Tilbury (1588): 'I know I have the body of a weak and feeble woman, but I have the heart and stomach of a king.'

the Langham: the Langham Hotel in Portland Place; designed by Giles and Murray (1863–5), damaged 1940, used as an annex of the BBC, and now restored to its original use. ACD dined here with J. M. Stoddart (and Oscar Wilde) on 30 Aug. 1889, when he was commissioned to write the story which became *The Sign of the Four*.

carte blanche: literally, ' a blank paper'; a paper with only the signature written upon it, on which the recipient may write his own terms; so, absolute freedom of action, an open hand, or unlimited resources.

15 *provinces*: the districts or provinces of Bohemia should correctly be called 'divisions' or 'circles'.

Briony Lodge, Serpentine Avenue, St John's Wood: from Bryony, a climbing plant with heart-shaped leaves (*Bryonia dioica*). St John's Wood was an area of London favoured by artists and authors, and was the home of several noted courtesans, including Elizabeth Anne Howard. 'Serpentine Avenue' is an invented street name, from the Serpentine in Hyde Park.

Was the photograph a cabinet?: a cabinet photograph, 5½ inches by 4 inches, on a mount 6½ inches by 4¼ inches, embossed at the foot and on the verso with the photographer's name. The successor to the *carte-de-visite* size. It was first used for portraits in 1866 and was in universal use by 1868. The term 'cabinet' is from small old master paintings which were kept in cabinets.

the two crimes which I have elsewhere recorded: in *A Study in Scarlet* (1887) and *The Sign of the Four* (1890); the reading in Newnes (1892); the *Strand* has 'the two crimes which I have already recorded'.

16 *a bijou villa*: literally, 'a jewel', small and elegant. As in *More New Arabian Nights: The Dynamiter* (1885) by Robert Louis Stevenson and his wife: 'Here, on the one hand, framed in the walls and the green tops of trees, were several of those discreet, *bijou* residences on which propriety is apt to look askance'.

Chubb lock: a lock made by Chubb and Sons (founded in 1818), the inventors of the 'unpickable lock'.

a glass of half-and-half: a mixture of two liquors, such as porter and ale, old and mild, or mild and bitter.

shag tobacco: 'Shag tobacco has obtained its distinctive name from its being so finely cut that the filaments appear like so much "shag"—the old name for short and matted wool or hair. It is manufactured of the strongest and very worst kind of leaf, and is chiefly consumed by the poorer classes' (Joseph Fune, *A Paper: of Tobacco*, 1839).

17 *Mr Godfrey Norton*: perhaps suggested by the Hon. George Norton (1800–75), the husband of Caroline Elizabeth Sarah Norton (1808–77), granddaughter of the Irish playwright Richard Brinsley Sheridan (1751–1816) and a famous defender

of the rights of married women. In 1853 Caroline Norton resisted attempts by her alienated husband to claim the profits of her considerable literary earnings, and the case led to the Matrimonial Causes Act of 1857 and the establishment of the first Divorce Court. ACD became a strong advocate of divorce law reform.

17 *the Inner Temple*: one of the four Inns of Court. The Inner and Middle Temples lie between Fleet Street and the Victoria Embankment and contain the chambers and living quarters of barristers and law students.

18 *Gross and Hankey's in Regent Street*: an invented name, perhaps from Hancock and Company, the New Bond Street jewellers.

the church of St Monica in the Edgware Road: perhaps suggested by the Roman Catholic chapel of St Monica in Hoxton Square, though the location implies St Agnes in Cricklewood, or St Anthony's at the far end of the Edgware Road.

Half a guinea: originally a gold coin worth ten shillings and sixpence [52½ new pence], afterwards used of that amount of money.

landau: a two-seated, four-wheeled, covered vehicle with a divided top; named after the German town in which it was first manufactured.

half a sovereign: a gold coin, worth ten shillings [50 new pence].

It was twenty-five minutes to twelve: at the time of ACD's wedding in 1885 the law required marriages to be solemnized before noon, but in May 1886 the hours had been extended to 3.00 p.m. The change in the law, however, did not apply to marriages within the Roman Catholic Church.

19 *I found myself mumbling responses*: the marriage law requires two witnesses; they take part in the prayers, but do not speak during the ceremony. In a Roman Catholic marriage, however, the Latin rite then in use involved Latin prayers from a priest with Latin responses from an acolyte, in addition to the promises and statements from the bride and groom in English. (ACD had been an altar-boy at Stonyhurst and may have been an acolyte at a wedding if an old boy decided on a wedding in Stonyhurst chapel.)

the bride gave me a sovereign . . . in memory of the occasion: ACD had been given a spade guinea early in his career which he wore on his watch chain. Perhaps also a memory of the tips given to the altar-boy after a wedding.

in the Park: either Hyde Park or Regent's Park.

20 *Mrs Turner*: this should perhaps have been 'Mrs Hudson'. The slip was repeated in the MS of 'The Empty House' in the *Return* but was corrected.

an ordinary plumber's smoke rocket: used by plumbers to test pipes for leakage (perhaps suggested by the German article 'Testing Gas Pipes for Leakage' which ACD translated for the *Gas and Water Review* of 19 Nov. 1886).

21 *Mr John Hare*: a character actor (1844–1921), knighted in 1907. He was included among the 'Portraits of Celebrities at Different Times of their Lives' in the *Strand* for Feb. 1891 and referred to as 'the finest actor of old men at present on the stage—if not, indeed, the finest ever seen . . . Mr Hare as an old man is old all over. Yet no two of his old men are like each other.' The character of the 'amiable and simple minded Noncomformist clergyman' may have been suggested by his portrayal of Benjamin Goldfinch in *The Pair of Spectacles* (at the Garrick Theatre, London, from 22 Feb. 1890) which he claimed as his favourite role: 'I take about a month to study up a character. I always wear the clothes I am going to play in for some time previously, so as to get them to my figure' ('Actors' Dressing Rooms', *Strand*, Feb. 1891).

a scissors-grinder with his wheel: a knife grinder. 'The periodical visit of the scissors grinder, with his impressive machinery, is an event in the more gloomy streets of the Metropolis. It could not well be otherwise seeing the fuss his wheel makes, not to speak of the sparks he sends flying when a knife bearing signs of long and arduous service is submitted to his tender mercies' (*Living London*, ed. G. R. Sims, 1902–3).

nurse-girl: a nurse maid.

24 *ulster*: a long, loose overcoat of frieze or rough cloth. The 'Ulster' overcoat was introduced by J. G. McGee & Co., of Belfast, in 1867, and the term 'Ulster' was in common use from 1879.

25 *the Darlington Substitution Scandal*: perhaps inspired by Dupin's substitution of a facsimile for the purloined letter in Edgar Allan Poe's story of 'The Purloined Letter' (1844). Darlington,

in south Durham, was the terminus of the first passenger railway (1825).

25 *the Arnsworth Castle business*: an invented name, perhaps from Alnwick and Warkworth Castles (mentioned in an article on the former—alongside the serialization of *The White Company*—in the *Cornhill Magazine* for Feb. 1891); or from Farnworth and Unsworth in Lancashire; or from *Windsor Castle* (1843) by William Harrison Ainsworth (1805–82).

27 *a sardonic eye*: a sardonic expression (from 'risus sardonicus'—a sardonic smile).

Charing Cross: the terminus of the South-Eastern Railway (1864), near Trafalgar Square.

28 *she was not on my level*: cf. 'I have tried thee, and joy to find that thou deservest to be loved by Mahomet—with a mind great as his own' (Mahomet to Irene, early draft of Johnson's *Irene*, quoted by Boswell, *Life of Johnson* (1791)).

A CASE OF IDENTITY

First published in the *Strand Magazine*, 2 (Sept. 1891), 248–59, with seven illustrations by Sidney Paget; *Strand Magazine*, New York (Oct. 1891); S.S. McClure Newspaper Syndicate, USA, various dates between 5 Sept. and 4 Oct. 1891, with woodcut illustrations.

Written at 2 Upper Wimpole Street and 23 Montague Place; finished 10 April 1891. MS: whereabouts unknown.

[Title]: a variant of the common phrase 'a case of mistaken identity'. The inspiration may have come in part from the description given by Edgar Allan Poe of the way Dupin traced the purloined letter by adopting 'a pair of green spectacles' as a disguise: 'I complained of my weak eyes, and lamented the necessity of spectacles, under cover of which I cautiously and thoroughly surveyed the apartment' ('The Purloined Letter', 1844).

30 *life is infinitely stranger . . . invent*: an echo of Byron: ''Tis strange—but true; for truth is always strange; / Stranger than fiction' (*Don Juan*, XIV. ci). This passage may be compared with Wilde's 'The Decay of Lying', originally published in the *Nineteenth Century* (Jan. 1889), where life is presented as an imitation of art.

outré: extraordinary, bizarre, shocking, outside the bounds of propriety; a word borrowed from Edgar Allan Poe: 'In the manner of thrusting the corpse up the chimney, you will admit there was something *excessively outré*—something altogether irreconcilable with our common notions of human action, even when we suppose the actors the most depraved of men' ('The Murders in the Rue Morgue', 1841).

most stale and unprofitable: *Hamlet*, I. ii: 'How weary, stale, flat, and unprofitable / Seem to me all the uses of this world'.

31 *the Dundas separation case*: perhaps suggested by the Dundas Seduction Case of May 1831, when Major Philip Dundas, a nephew of the second Viscount Melville, was found guilty of the seduction of a 17-year-old girl.

his snuff-box of old gold, with a great amethyst in the centre of the lid: amethysts are manganese-coloured quartz, purple or violet in colour. The 'little souvenir from the King of Bohemia' may have been based on the 'Presents of Royal Visitors' described in *Tit-Bits* on 24 Jan. 1891: 'When Emperor Napoleon came to England in 1855, the six lords who were in waiting each received a splendid gold snuff box with the Emperor's portrait set in diamonds; the equerries and grooms in waiting got similar boxes with the Emperor's cipher.' The article also describes the gifts given by the King of the Netherlands when he attended the wedding of Queen Victoria's fourth son, Leopold, Duke of Albany (1853–84), to the daughter of the Prince of Waldeck-Pyrmont in 1882.

32 *tilted in a coquettish Duchess-of-Devonshire fashion*: a reference to the portrait of Georgiana Spencer (1757–1806), the wife of William Cavendish, 5th Duke of Devonshire, painted in 1783 by Thomas Gainsborough (1727–88). The painting was stolen by Adam Worth from Agnew and Company of Bond Street in 1876 and was known as the 'Stolen Duchess' until its return in March 1901: 'The fact of his celebrated Duchess of Devonshire having been stolen has probably had much to do with making the public regard it as the finest thing that Gainsborough ever did' ('Pictures with Histories', *Strand*, Apr. 1891). The 'Gainsborough hat' was mentioned by G. A. Storey in one of the 'Letters from Artists on Ladies' Dress' in the *Strand* for Feb. 1891.

panoply: originally, 'a complete suit of armour'; a display of finery.

32 *an affaire du coeur*: 'affair of the heart', a love affair.

the boy in buttons: a page boy (from the line of small buttons on the tunic running from collar to waist). William Gillette in the play *Sherlock Holmes* (1899) gave him the name 'Billy', which ACD afterwards adopted.

Miss Mary Sutherland: perhaps from Jane Sutherland, who was a fellow lodger at 23 Montague Place, or from Mary, Duchess of Sutherland (1848–1912), the second wife of George Granville William Leveson-Gower, third Duke of Sutherland (1828–92).

33 *Mrs Etherege*: perhaps named after Sir George Etherege (1634–88), whose plays include *The Comical Revenge: or, Love in a Tub* (1664) and *She Would if She Could* (1667).

Hosmer Angel: the first name is of American origin. Harriet Goodhue Hosmer (1830–1908) was an American sculptor; Frederic Lucian Hosmer (1840–79), an American hymn writer; and an E. S. Hosmer acted as general assistant on an expedition to St Elias in Alaska. The latter was referred to in an article on 'Two Expeditions to Mount St Elias' in the *Century Magazine* (Apr. 1891): 'On account of uncertain health, Mr Hosmer left us at our first camp.' The name might otherwise be a variant of 'Rosmer', from Henrik Ibsen's play *Rosmersholm* (1887), which was first performed in London on 23 Feb. 1891. 'Making an Angel' was the title of a story in the *Strand* for Feb. 1891, and the 'Story of the Destroying Angel' is the title of the Mormon episode in the Stevensons' *More New Arabian Nights* (to which ACD was indebted in *A Study in Scarlet*). There is also a suggestion of 'angel visits': 'Like angel visits, few and far between' (Thomas Campbell, 'The Pleasures of Hope').

Mr Windibank: perhaps from Sir Francis Windebank (1582–1646), the secretary of state to Charles I. Liberton Bank, where ACD had lived in Edinburgh as a small boy, was a very windy bank.

34 *the Tottenham Court Road*: a street running north from Oxford Street, which ACD passed when going from his lodgings at Montague Place to his consulting-room in Upper Wimpole Street.

uncle Ned: ACD's wife, Louisa, had an 'Uncle Ned' (Edwin Butt, her mother's brother, who died when she was 6); and it was the name of the 'Squirradical' in *The Wrong Box* (1889) by Robert Louis Stevenson and Lloyd Osbourne. ACD may also have had in mind his own Uncle Tom, his mother's brother, who died in Queensland in 1885.

New Zealand Stock: securities issued by the government.

35 *the gasfitters' ball*: perhaps inspired by 'A Few Queer Trade Societies' (*Tit-Bits*, 1 Nov. 1890), which lists unusual clubs and institutes, such as those of the rag-pickers, paper-bag makers, undertakers, pipemakers, and lamplighters; or it could have been suggested by an announcement in the *Gas and Water Review* (to which ACD contributed in 1886).

purple plush: a type of cloth made of silk or cotton, similar in appearance to velvet.

36 *Leadenhall Street*: a road running from the Cornhill to Aldgate in the City of London. A Post Office or 'Postal Telegraph Office, Receiving House, Money Order Office, and Savings Bank' was to be found in the Rochester Buildings at 138 Leadenhall Street.

quinsy: (medical Latin, *quinancia*) 'dog-throttling', an inflammation of the throat, caused by suppuration of the tonsils.

37 *the Testament*: the Bible, or the New Testament, upon which oaths were sworn by Christians.

Bordeaux: a town and port in the south-west of France; the centre of the largest wine growing region of the country.

St Saviour's near King's Cross: St Saviour's is in Southwark (and there were twelve other churches of that name in London); but the location suggests St Pancras Old Church, in the Pancras Road, or the neo-classical New Church, in the Euston Road. King's Cross (1852) was the terminus of the Great Northern Railway—named after a monument to George IV which formerly stood there.

St Pancras Hotel: the Midland Grand Hotel (1872) at St Pancras Station, a large neo-Gothic building by George Gilbert Scott, renamed St Pancras Chambers when the hotel closed in 1935.

39 *Chronicle*: the *Daily Chronicle* (originally the *Clerkenwell News*, 1855) which took the name on 25 Nov. 1872 and was merged into the *News Chronicle* in 1930.

Lyon Place, Camberwell: an invented address, perhaps from Lyon Street, Camden, in the Borough of St Pancras. Camberwell is a district of south London, which may have been familiar to ACD as his friend, David George Thomson (1856–1923), was for a time Assistant Physician at the Camberwell House Asylum.

39 *Westhouse and Marbank, the great claret importers*: an imaginary firm, suggested by companies such as Mears and Stainbank (the Whitechapel Bell Foundry), or Westfield and Moss (the brewers of the Mile End Road). Westhouse is the name of a hamlet next to Masongill where ACD's mother lived. 'Claret' is the English name for the red wines from the Bordeaux region (from an old French word for 'clear').

Fenchurch Street: in the City of London, near Leadenhall Street.

Andover in '77: an imaginary case, perhaps suggested by the Penge Case of 1877, when Louis A. E. Staunton was found guilty of neglect towards his wife. Andover is a small town in Hampshire which gave its name to Andover in Massachusetts, the site of the Andover Theological Seminary (publishers of the *Andover Review*, 1884–93), and of the Phillips Academy at which Oliver Wendell Holmes (1809–94) was a student.

The Hague: (Den Haag, 's Gravenhage) the capital and seat of government of the Netherlands (which ACD visited in August 1891).

40 *I can never bring you to realise . . . a bootlace*: the remark echoes the instruction given by Joseph Bell: 'I always impressed over and over again upon all my scholars—Conan Doyle among them—the vast importance of little distinctions, the endless significance of the trifles' (*Pall Mall Budget*, 4 Jan. 1894). It also recalls an article in the *Strand*: 'The river police could tell of many a remarkable clue to identification—a piece of lace, or the button of a man's trousers' ('A Night with the Thames Police', Feb. 1891). The winner of a Sherlock Holmes Examination Paper in *Tit-Bits* provided fifteen examples of the way bootlaces could offer 'a tolerably reliable index both to the character of the wearer and the extent of his worldly possessions', such as 'Laces of a different colour to the boots indicate that the wearer possibly is wanting in taste; is eccentric; likes at all cost to attract attention' (*Tit-Bits*, 16 Dec. 1893).

jet: hard black lignite which takes a high polish; a popular and inexpensive form of beadwork and jewellery.

41 *gold Albert chain*: a watch-chain with stout links, popularized by and named after Prince Albert of Saxe-Coburg-Gotha (1819–61), the consort of Queen Victoria.

grey Harris tweed trousers: a variety of tweed, from Harris, in the Outer Hebrides. 'My tailor tells me that Harris tweed cannot wear out. This is a mere theory, and will not stand a thorough scientific test' ('An Alpine Pass on "Ski" ', *Strand*, Dec. 1894).

Balzac: Honoré de Balzac (1799–1850), French novelist, author of the series of novels, *La Comedie Humaine*. A translation of his short stories, *Don Juan, or the Elixir of Life*, was published at the end of 1890, and 'A Passion in the Desert' was included in the *Strand* for Feb. 1891. 'There are some authors from whom I shrink because they are so voluminous that I feel that, do what I may, I can never hope to be well read in their works. Therefore, and very weakly, I avoid them altogether. There is Balzac, for example, with his hundred odd volumes. I am told that some of them are masterpieces and the rest pot-boilers, but that no one is agreed which is which. Such an author makes an undue claim upon the little span of mortal years. Because he asks too much one is inclined to give him nothing' (*Through the Magic Door*).

43 *the denouement of the little mystery*: the final revelation or conclusion; as in 'The Mystery of Marie Rogêt' (1843) where Poe talks of 'tracing to its *denouement* the mystery which surrounded her'.

bisulphate of baryta: barium hydrogen sulphate; a chemical curiosity first prepared by J. J. Berzelius in 1843. It is decomposed by water and has no practical use.

44 *a typewriter . . . a man's handwriting*: this is an obvious exaggeration, but was more true of typewriters a century ago, as the keys got out of alignment and were sometimes wrongly set. ACD purchased his first typewriter during the summer of 1890. 'My getting a machine is rather in the nature of an experiment,' he told George Augustus Sala (13 Aug. 1890, Huntington Library, MSS).

47 *a hunting-crop*: a short straight whipstock with a handle and a short leather loop in place of the lash, used in the hunting field.

48 *Voilà tout*: 'that is all'; that is the whole of it.

the old Persian saying . . . Hafiz as in Horace: the 'saying' is not specifically ascribed to Hafiz and Persian scholars agree that it is almost certainly not by him. It may possibly come from another Persian poet, such as Muslih Addin (*c*.1184?–?1294), known as Sa'di, or could be an old Persian saying of unknown origin. The comparison of Shams-ud-Din Mahommed, known as Hafiz of Shiraz, and Quintus Horatius Flaccus (63–8 BC), author of the *Odes*, *Epodes*, *Satires*, and the *Ars Poetica*, is only intended to imply that the wisdom of medieval Persia is as great as that of ancient Rome, a Holmes counterpoint to Watson's Horatian end of *A Study in Scarlet*.

THE RED-HEADED LEAGUE

First published in the *Strand Magazine*, 2 (Aug. 1891), 190–204, with ten illustrations by Sidney Paget; *Strand Magazine*, New York (Sept. 1891); S.S. McClure Newspaper Syndicate, USA, various dates between 8 Aug. and 6 Dec. 1891, with woodcut illustrations.

Written at 2 Upper Wimpole Street and 23 Montague Place; dispatched 20 Apr. 1891. MS: whereabouts unknown.

Part of the inspiration for the story almost certainly comes from *The Autocrat of the Breakfast-Table* (1858) by Oliver Wendell Holmes which mentions a man who had memorized the first volume of an encyclopaedia:

> The talk ran upon mountains. He was wonderfully well acquainted with the leading facts about the Andes, the Apennines, and the Appalachians; he had nothing in particular to say about Ararat, Ben Nevis, and various other mountains that were mentioned. By and by some Revolutionary anecdote came up, and he showed singular familiarity with the lives of the Adamses, and gave many details relating to Major André. A point of Natural History being suggested, he gave an excellent account of the air-bladder of fishes. He was very full upon the subject of agriculture, but retired from the conversation when horticulture was introduced in the discussion. So he seemed well acquainted with the geology of anthracite, but did not pretend to know anything of other kinds of coal. There was something so odd about the extent and limitations of his knowledge, that I suspected all at once what might be the meaning of it, and waited till I got an opportunity.—Have you seen the *New American Cyclopaedia*? said I.—I have, he replied; I received an early copy.—How far does it go?—He turned red, and answered,—To Araguay.—Oh, said I to myself, not quite so far as Ararat;—that is the reason he knew nothing about it.

Further inspiration could have come from articles in *Tit-Bits*, such as: 'A Journey with a Million of Money' (28 Feb. 1891), a description of the transfer of gold bullion from the Bank of England to the Bank of France; 'In Business as a Pawnbroker' (7 Mar. 1891) and 'More Experiences in Pawning' (14 Mar. 1891). Or those concerned with red hair: 'I have met with thousands of articles and paragraphs about red hair—"funny" articles, laudatory articles, historical articles, apologetic articles, and so forth. But never yet, I think, have I seen what a red-haired man thinks on the subject,' wrote one contributor to *Tit-Bits* ('Confessions of a Red-Headed Man', 16 May 1891), followed by 'Confessions of a Red-Haired Woman' and 'More about Red-Haired People' (30 May 1891); and in *Answers*, 'Are Red-Haired People Bad-Tempered?' (4 July 1891). The unusual hair colour also recalls the description of John Williams, the Marrs murderer, in Thomas De Quincey's 'Murder as One of the Fine Arts': 'A lady, who saw him under examination (I think at Thames Police Office), assured me that his hair was of the most extraordinary and vivid colour, viz. bright yellow, something between an orange and a lemon colour.'

The bank theft probably has several sources, and there is perhaps a recollection of the sewer man who in 1836 found his way into the bullion room of the Bank of England. He sent an anonymous note to the Directors offering to meet them there at any hour they chose; they did so at a 'dark and midnight hour' and gave him a large reward for his honesty.

49   *the very simple problem presented by Miss Mary Sutherland*: i.e. 'A Case of Identity', which appeared in the *Strand* the following month due to a confusion over the order of the stories.

50   *Mr Jabez Wilson*: Jabez ('sorrowful', from 1 Chronicles, 4: 9: 'And Jabez was more honourable than his brethren: and his mother called his name Jabez, saying, Because I bare him with sorrow'). Perhaps from Jabez Spencer Balfour, JP, Mayor of Croydon, MP, and founder of the Liberator Building Society, whose companies collapsed the following year leaving debts of eight million pounds. It was also the name of a confectioner living at 123 Trafalgar Road, Greenwich (Redmond, 40).

  grey shepherd's check trousers: shepherd's plaid, grey cloth trousers with a small black and white check pattern; as worn by John Hare in his role as Benjamin Goldfinch: 'the actor finds plenty of "character" even in a coat—and the shepherd's-plaid trousers' ('Actors' Dressing Rooms', *Strand*, Feb. 1891).

51 *a Freemason*: a member of the fraternity of 'Free and Accepted Masons' who meet in private to conduct semi-religious rituals based on the tools and practices of the stonemason's trade. Masonically expressed, Freemasonry is 'a peculiar system of morality, veiled in allegory, and illustrated by symbols' which is intended to improve the man and to offer him support in times of hardship. The United Grand Lodge was established in London in 1717 and there were nearly two thousand local lodges in England by the end of the nineteenth century. ACD was a member of the Phoenix Lodge, No. 257, Portsmouth.

Your right hand is quite a size larger than your left: said to be the mark of a ship's carpenter. This may be compared to 'Peculiarities of Workmen' (*Tit-Bits*, 10 Jan. 1891): 'A carpenter's shoulder is almost invariably higher than his left, in consequence of having to use his right arm all the time in planing and hammering. With every shaving his body rises with a jerk, and it finally becomes natural to him to hold himself in that way.' Dr Joseph Bell told Harry How: 'Nearly every handicraft writes its sign manual on the hands. The scars of the miner differ from those of the quarryman. The carpenter's callosities are not those of the mason. The shoemaker and the tailor are quite different' ('A Day with Dr Conan Doyle', *Strand*, Aug. 1892).

rather against the strict rules of your order: Freemasons were obliged to keep secret the several words and various signs revealed to them, and the motto of the order was 'Audi Vide Tace' (Hear, See, Keep Silent). It was commonly supposed that Masons would reveal themselves to other members by secret hand grips, signs, and code words.

an arc and compass breastpin: correctly a 'square and compass' breastpin; the emblems of the craft. The compasses are to remind the wearer 'to keep in due bounds with mankind, particularly our brethren in Freemasonry'; the square (set square) is the implement with which the mason gauges right angles. 'The Square and Compass combined were at one time a fairly common object of personal adornment in the form of watch-chain ornaments or on signet rings. This has long been discouraged in England and the display of "Masonic" jewellery is now regarded as improper' (F. L. Pick and G. Norman Knight, *The Freemason's Pocket Reference Book*, 1955).

The fish . . . done in China: 'In London there is a man who follows the business of tattooing. The majority of his patients are men who have designs of a naval character pricked into their skin, but there are also a great many women who employ his art, if it may be termed such. With women the decoration is usually a bee, a butterfly, a spray of flowers, or a monogram. These ornaments are worn inside the wrist, so that they may be hidden by the glove, if necessary' (*Tit-Bits*, 14 Feb. 1891). Tattooing was practised in China, but the most extravagant were made in Japan. The 'tattoo marks on hand or arm will tell their own tale as to voyages' (Joseph Bell to Harry How, 16 June 1892, Stisted Papers—a remark perhaps suggested by his having read this story).

52 *a Chinese coin hanging from your watch-chain*: earlier referred to as a 'square pierced bit of metal'; either a square coin, pierced, or more probably the 'Tsien', a round coin pierced with a square.

Omne ignotum pro magnifico: 'the unknown is always thought to be magnificent', 'distance lends enchantment to the view'; Tacitus, *Agricola*, 30.4: 'Atque omne ignotum pro magnifico est; sed nunc terminus Britanniae patet' ('Now the farthest bounds of Britain lie open to our enemies; and what men know nothing about they always assume to be a valuable prize', tr. Mattingly/Handford, Penguin, 1970).

TO THE RED-HEADED LEAGUE . . . Fleet Street: the Stoll Film Company placed a similar advertisement in the agony columns of *The Times* on 20 Jan. 1920 when filming the story: 'The Red-Headed League. On account of circumstances not unconnected with the bequest of the late Hezekiah Hopkins of Lebanon, Penn., USA, lucrative employment for One Day Only is now available for twenty CURLY, RED-HEADED MEN who are sound in mind and body. Those who have served in HM Forces and have some knowledge of acting preferred.' Forty curly, red-haired, ex-servicemen applied to the Cricklewood Studio and the producer decided to engage them all (*Stoll's Editorial News*, 2 June 1921).

Ezekiah Hopkins: from Hezekiah, the King of Judah (in Isaiah). The name recalls 'Elias B. Hopkins—The Parson of Jackman's

Gulch', an early story by ACD reprinted in *The Captain of the Pole-Star.*

52 *Lebanon, Penn., U.S.A.*: a county and its county town in Pennsylvania.

7, Pope's Court, Fleet Street: possibly Mitre Court, which connects Fleet Street with the Temple, or Pope's Head Alley, off the Cornhill (originally a footpath running through the yard of the Pope's Head Tavern). Or perhaps suggested by the oranges in the Pope's court: 'The Pope has no fewer than 10,000 of the most delicious oranges growing in the gardens of the Vatican. His Holiness distributes these to his friends throughout Europe, prepares the list to whom they are to be sent, and practically superintends the despatching of them' (*Tit-Bits*, 27 June 1891).

at scratch: the line at the starting-point of a race, a mark which is scratched or chalked on the ring; thus 'from the beginning'.

the Morning Chronicle: a newspaper (1769–1862) which was for a time edited by William Ewart Gladstone and included Charles Dickens among its contributors. 'He who loves his London, more especially he who loves his Strand, will not forget that No. 332, now the office of the *Weekly Times*, was the scene of Dickens' early work in journalism for the *Morning Chronicle*' ('The Story of the Strand', *Strand*, Jan. 1891).

April 27, 1890. Just two months ago: two months before the dissolution of the League on 9 October could not have been 27 April 1890, as that was a Sunday six months before, so it seems August was intended; perhaps 'Ag' (August) was misread as 'Ap' (April).

Coburg Square, near the City: also called 'Saxe-Coburg Square'. There are Coburg Streets in London (near the Old Kent Road and in Teddington); a Coburg Dock in Liverpool (from which ACD sailed in the *Mayumba* in 1881), and a Saxe-Coburg Place and Saxe-Coburg Street in Edinburgh. Queen Victoria was the daughter of Victoire of Saxe-Coburg Saalfield; Albert, her husband and cousin, was the son of the Duke of Saxe-Coburg Gotha; and Princess Charlotte, the daughter of George IV, was married to Prince Leopold of Saxe-Coburg (after whom the Royal Coburg Theatre or 'Old Vic' was named).

53 *Vincent Spaulding*: perhaps suggested by St Vincent de Paul (ACD's father was secretary of the St Vincent de Paul Society in Edinburgh); or from the Spalding Club in Aberdeen, or the town of Spalding in Lincolnshire.

I am a widower, and never had any family: Duncan Ross is therefore wrong when he says later, 'It is exceedingly unfortunate that you should be a bachelor'.

54 *a nice little crib*: (popular slang) a 'job' or 'situation'.

55 *a coster's orange barrow*: a costermonger's fruit barrow.

56 *cobbler's wax*: a resin used by shoemakers to make thread supple, but here suggesting shoe polish or leather dye.

Mr Duncan Ross: 'Duncan' and 'Ross' are characters in Shakespeare's *Macbeth*.

58 the *Encylopedia Britannica*: first published in Edinburgh (1768–71), but this presumably refers to the Ninth Edition (1875–1889).

the first volume of it in that press: a book press (in which books could be kept flat by means of a screw), or a cupboard or shelf.

will you be ready to-morrow: 'to-morrow' would have been a Sunday.

the letter A: the first entry in the *Encyclopaedia Britannica*.

59 *planked down*: (American and old English) to pay down money. It is derived from 'boards', a cant word for shillings, and was used for racecourse betting where 'to plank down' meant 'to lay money on a horse'.

Abbots, and Archery, and Armour, and Architecture, and Attica: *Encyclopaedia Britannica*, 9th Edition: vol. i, 22–4, 'Abbot' (by the Revd Canon Venables, MA, Precentor of Lincoln); vol. ii, 371–8, 'Archery', (by James Sharpe Salisbury); 553–8, 'Arms and Armour' (by Joseph Anderson, Secretary of the Society of Antiquaries, Scotland); 382–475, 'Architecture' (by T. Hayter Lewis and George Edmund Street); vol. iii, 57–60, 'Attica', (by the Revd Henry F. Tozer). It would have been impossible to copy out the contents of these volumes in the time stated.

60 *the gentleman at No. 4*: though the address was previously given as 'No. 7'.

William Morris: the name of the artist, writer and printer (1834–96); who founded the Kelmscott Press in 1891, and is mentioned by ACD in an article 'On the Geographical Distribution of British Intellect' (*Nineteenth Century*, Aug. 1888).

60 *17 King Edward Street, near St Paul's*: the street runs north from Newgate Street; No. 17 was the premises of a carpet and lace manufacturer.

a manufactory of artificial knee-caps: there were seventeen 'Artificial Leg and Arm Makers' in London, one of which was near King Edward Street at 44 Little Britain; but ACD may have been thinking of J. & E. Ferris, of 48 Great Russell Street, who were 'the only makers of legs with sub-astragalus ankle movement'; or of the false arm and silver tracheotomy tube which were deposited at a pawnbroker ('In Business as a Pawnbroker', *Tit-Bits*, 7 Mar. 1891).

61 *it cost them two-and-thirty pounds*: Wilson was not paid on the Saturday when he came to see Sherlock Holmes and says that Spaulding 'came down to the office just this day eight weeks', so one week's pay is unaccounted for.

62 *Today is Saturday*: yet the League was dissolved on 9 Oct. 1890—'this morning' according to Jabez Wilson—which was a Thursday.

his hawk-like nose: this and the subsequent reference to the 'black clay pipe thrusting out like the bill of some strange bird' were ignored by Sidney Paget in the illustrations. ACD approved of Paget's drawings, but originally envisaged Holmes as 'a more beaky-nosed, hawk-faced man, approaching more to the Red-Indian type' ('Conan Doyle Tells the True Story of Sherlock Holmes', *Tit-Bits*, 15 Dec. 1900).

Sarasate: Pablo Martin Meliton Sarasate y Navascues, Spanish violinist (1844–1908); Sarasate trained at the Paris Conservatoire and made his London debut in 1861. 'The concerts of Sarasate, the eminent violinist, are evidently regarded by music lovers as the most enjoyable of all entertainments which depend upon the skill and fascination of a single artist for success. His manipulation of the violin is altogether marvellous, and yet he gets through his programmes with such apparent ease that even a second-rate player might almost fancy he could do as well. He is a Spaniard, and, besides being in the plenitude of his artistic power, he is in the prime of his manhood, having been born in 1844' ('Personal Tit-Bits', *Tit-Bits*, 14 Feb. 1891).

St James's Hall: a concert hall (built in 1857 and demolished in 1905) between Air Street and Swallow Street near Piccadilly Circus, with the main entrance in the Regent Street Quadrant and a side entrance in Piccadilly. Sarasate gave twenty-eight concerts in Great Britain during the autumn of 1890, but he did not perform at the St James's Hall during October.

I observe ... German music ... I want to introspect: perhaps the Lieder by Mendelssohn, which Holmes played in *A Study in Scarlet*. 'I always feel that there is music which would move me greatly,' ACD said later, 'but I never quite seem to get it. Yet I have an average ear and a good memory for music' ('Music and the Writer', *John O' London's Weekly*, 20 July 1920).

63 *Aldersgate*: Aldersgate Street Station on the Circle Line of the Metropolitan ('Underground') Railway (also a terminus for the London, Chatham, and Dover Railway); opened in 1865 and re-named the 'Barbican' in 1968.

Three gilt balls: the pawnbrokers's sign (said to come from the coat of arms of the Medici family; and to have been introduced to London by the Lombard bankers).

The knees of his trousers: ACD was thinking ahead to this story when he wrote 'A Case of Identity', in which Holmes comments on the importance of small details: 'In a man it is perhaps better first to take the knee of the trouser.'

64 *one of the main arteries ... north and west*: perhaps Aldersgate Street or the Farringdon Road.

Mortimer's, the tobacconist: perhaps Francis Albine Mortimer, a tobacconist at 86 Church Street, Edgware Road, or suggested by Mortimer Street which ACD passed on the way to his consulting-room.

the Coburg branch of the City and Suburban Bank: (later called 'the City branch of one of the principal London banks') an invented name, perhaps from the 'City and Suburban' Handicap Race run at Epsom on 8 Apr. 1891 and won in 1889 by 'Goldseeker' and in 1890 by 'Rêve d'Or'; or based on real banks, such as the London and Provincial, the Capital and Counties (at which ACD had his account), the City Bank, the London and County, or the London and General, which was founded by Jabez Spencer Balfour in 1882 to process dubious cheques from his own companies.

64 *a composer of no ordinary merit*: 'This is the only reference to Holmes as a composer, and it is difficult to believe that he really was one in the accepted sense' (Guy Warrack, *Sherlock Holmes and Music*, 1947).

the dual nature alternately asserted itself: a concept borrowed from Edgar Allan Poe whose narrator notes that Dupin assumed a 'frigid and abstract' manner when analysing people: 'Observing him in these moods, I often dwelt meditatively upon the old philosophy of the Bi-Part Soul, and amused myself with the fancy of a double Dupin—the creative and the resolvent' ('The Murders in the Rue Morgue', 1841).

65 *black-letter*: Gothic or German type used in the early days of printing, from the heavy black appearance when compared to Roman type, and thus the editions which used it. The library of Raffles Haw had 'some hundred black-letters, with five very fine specimens of Schoffer and Fust' (*The Doings of Raffles Haw*, 1892, written Jan. 1891).

66 *across the Park, and so through Oxford Street to Baker Street*: i.e. across Kensington Gardens and Hyde Park to Marble Arch, then along Oxford Street and north to Baker Street.

Two hansoms: a two-wheeled carriage (or 'cabriolet'), drawn by one horse, with the driver mounted behind; named after J. A. Hansom (1803–82) who patented the design.

whom I recognized as Peter Jones, the official police agent: the context shows that he is the same as Athelney Jones (whose name recalls that of the prominent Welsh Radical politician, L. A. Atherley-Jones, MP) found in *The Sign of the Four*. Peter Jones is the name of a department store on the west side of Sloane Square which opened in 1877.

pea-jacket: from the Dutch *pie* or *pij*; a 'coat of coarse woollen stuff' (*OED*).

Mr Merryweather: perhaps from the line-filling advertisement of the period: 'Merryweather's Water Supply to Mansions and Fire Protection of Mansions', or from Frederick Somner Merryweather (1847–1900), the editor of the *Surrey Comet*.

that business of the Sholto murder and the Agra treasure: i.e. *The Sign of the Four*.

67 *I miss my rubber*: 'The rubber is the best of three games. If the first two games be won by the same players, the third game

322

is not played' (from the rules of the game, as quoted by Major-General Drayson, *The Art of Practical Whist*, 1879). *A Quiet Rubber* (adapted by C. F. Coghlan) was given by the Garrick Theatre Company at a command performance at Windsor Castle on 17 Mar. 1891.

John Clay, the murderer, thief, smasher, and forger: the name may have been suggested by John Clayton, the oldest and richest solicitor on the Rolls, who died in July 1890; James Clay (1804–73), the author of *The Laws of Short Whist, and a Treatise on the Game* (1864); Richard Clay and Sons, of London and Bungay, the largest book printers in the country; Alice Clay, the author of *The Agony Column* (1881); or Henry Clay (1777–1852), the American orator and statesman. 'Smasher' is thieves' slang for a person who passes counterfeit money or forged notes; as in an earlier reference to Raffles Haw: ' "I know one or two things about him. What is it they call him at *The Three Pigeons*? A 'smasher'—that's the word—a coiner of false money" ' (*The Doings of Raffles Haw*, 1892, written Jan. 1891).

His grandfather was a Royal Duke: the grandfather would have been one of the four sons of George III (1738–1820) who were not enthroned.

He'll crack a crib in Scotland . . . an orphanage in Cornwall the next: to 'crack a crib' (thieves' slang) is to commit a burglary, to break into a house.

labyrinth of gas-lit streets . . . Farringdon Street: Farringdon Street runs from Ludgate Circus at the end of Fleet Street to the Holborn Viaduct, where it becomes the Farringdon Road. It was the one part of London which was not gas lit, as electric light was installed between Fleet Street and Aldgate in 1889.

69 *thirty thousand napoleons*: gold coins worth 20 francs, first struck by Napoleon I between 1803 and 1815, restored to favour under the Second Empire, and last minted in 1921. Thirty thousand napoleons would have weighed over 425 pounds. Poe had said that 'four Napoleons' were among the objects discovered on the floor after the murder in the Rue Morgue, and the 'Napoleon' or 'Nap' is also a term used in whist.

that dark lantern: a bull's eye lantern; the fluted chimney formed part of an inner screen which could be turned to obscure the light.

69 *a partie carrée*: *partie* (a game, match); *carrée* or *quarrée* (square, quadrate)—a square or quadrate party, a party of four.

71 *Jump, Archie, jump, and I'll swing for it!*: 'Archie' was presumably the real name of 'Duncan Ross'; 'jump' means 'make a run for it'. John Clay would presumably 'swing' (be hanged), not for the attempted robbery, but for the murders he had committed, though this is not clear from the context, nor was it taken as such by T. S. Eliot who asked: 'Was bank robbery subject to capital punishment at that epoch? or else why should John Clay, when caught, have exclaimed "I'll swing for it" ' (*Criterion*, Apr. 1929). Dakin (p. 52) suggests that the most recent murder committed by Clay may have been that of Jabez Wilson, and that this would be the crime for which he would swing.

Jones clutched at his skirts: 'coat-tails'; leading T. S. Eliot to ask: 'And what sort of garments did burglars wear, when Athelney Jones [*sic*] tore off Clay's accomplice's coat-tails?' (*op. cit.*).

derbies: (darbies), slang for handcuffs (as in Charles Reade's *It's Never Too Late to Mend*, 'he won't know me till I put the darbies on him'). The phrase 'father Derbies bands' (found as early as 1576) is thought to come from a rigid form of usurer's bond (Father Derby's bond).

73 *it would give them two days for their escape*: the theft was attempted on Sunday morning, so they only had one day for their escape.

74 *It saved me from ennui*: Holmes is here 'seeking like all distinguished aesthetes of his century—like Des Esseintes and Dorian Gray, like Poe, Baudelaire, Swinburne and Pater—to escape from the commonplace, to free himself from what Baudelaire denominates *les noirs ennuis*' (Paul Barolsky, *Walter Pater's Renaissance*, 1987). 'The only horrible thing in the world is *ennui*, Dorian,' says Lord Henry Wotton. 'That is the one sin for which there is no forgiveness' (*The Picture of Dorian Gray*).

'L'homme c'est rien—l'œuvre c'est tout,' as Gustave Flaubert wrote to George Sand: properly, 'L'homme n'est rien, l'oeuvre tout!' ('The man is nothing, the work is everything') from a letter of Dec. 1875 (*Lettres de Gustave Flaubert à George Sand*, Paris: Charpentier, 1884, 272–6). 'His constant refrain in his letters is the impersonality, as he calls it, of the artist, whose work should consist exclusively of his subject and his style, without

an emotion, an idiosyncrasy that is not utterly transmuted' (Henry James, 'Gustave Flaubert', *Macmillan's Magazine*, Mar. 1893). The correspondence between Gustave Flaubert (1821–80), the author of *Madame Bovary*, and George Sand (Amantine Lucille Aurore Dupin Dudevant, 1804–76), the author of *Consuelo*, began in 1866 and continued up to her death.

THE BOSCOMBE VALLEY MYSTERY:

First published in the *Strand Magazine*, 2 (Oct. 1891), 401–16, with ten illustrations by Sidney Paget; *Strand Magazine*, New York (Nov. 1891); S.S. McClure Newspaper Syndicate, USA, various dates between 17 Oct. and 1 Nov. 1891, with woodcut illustrations. Alternative title: 'The Mystery of Boscombe Valley' (*St Louis Post-Dispatch*).

Written at 2 Upper Wimpole Street and 23 Montague Place; dispatched 27 April 1891. MS: whereabouts unknown.

This is the only Sherlock Holmes story with 'mystery' in the title, which is surprising given the frequency of its use, as in 'The Mystery of Marie Rogêt' (1842) by Edgar Allan Poe, *The Mystery of Edwin Drood* (1870) by Charles Dickens, *The Mystery of a Hansom Cab* (1886) by Fergus W. Hume, or *The Mystery of Cloomber* (1889) by ACD himself.

The exploits of bushrangers was a popular subject for fiction, and ACD may have been influenced by writers such as Ralph Boldrewood (Thomas Alexander Browne, 1826–1915), a pioneer squatter in Victoria in 1870 and afterwards Police Magistrate and Warden of the Goldfields in New South Wales, whose best known work is *Robbery Under Arms* (1888). ACD may also have discussed the subject with Carl A. Falstedt, the Swedish Consul from Sydney, New South Wales, who was a fellow lodger at 23 Montague Place, or have heard reports from his uncle, Thomas Foley, who died in Queensland in 1885.

The story is derived from Australian bank robberies and hold-ups of the early 1860s, such as the attack on a gold coach near Hartley Vale in the Blue Mountains on 24 Feb. 1863, the Eugowra Rocks Robbery of 15 June 1862 (when a coach carrying £14,500 in gold from the Lachlan diggings was waylaid between Forbes and Sydney), and the Mudgee Mail Robbery of 13 July 1863.

75 *wired*: telegraphed (an American term, used in England from the end of the 1850s).

75 *Boscombe Valley*: from Boscombe Chine, in Hampshire, a narrow ravine near the seaside resort of Boscombe Spa, a 'villa-suburb' of Bournemouth. 'The mineral spring, which is mildly chalybeate, is situated in a neat thatched cottage near the foot of Boscombe Chine. Boscombe Manor, the seat of Sir Percy Shelley, adjoins the grounds of the hotel. It is a hand-some edifice, well situated on an eminence, and surrounded with pine trees. Another residence here which may be noted is the Tower, the seat of Sir H. Drummond Wolff, the proprietor of a large part of Boscombe' (*Black's Guide to Hampshire*, 1881). The name may have been suggested by the reference to Boscombe in the dedication to Sir Percy and Lady Shelley in *The Master of Ballantrae* (1889), which Robert Louis Stevenson says was written 'by the loud shores of a subtropical island [Waikiki] near upon ten thousand miles from Boscombe Chine and Manor: scenes which rise before me as I write, along with the faces and voices of my friends'.

Paddington: the terminus of the Great Western Railway; designed by Isambard Kingdom Brunel (1806–59), and built 1850–4.

Anstruther would do your work for you: ACD had this arrangement with Dr Claude Clarke Claremont in Southsea: 'At present I have strained both muscles of my back at cricket and can hardly rise from a chair, yet in spite of it I am doing Claremont's work as well as my own, he being away' (ACD to Reginald Ratcliff Hoare, 24 July 1890: Berg Collection, New York Public Library). Anstruther is the name of the port in Fife from which ACD sailed to the Isle of May in 1881 ('After Cormorants with a Camera', *British Journal of Photography*, 14/21 Oct. 1881); Henry Torrens Anstruther was the Member of Parliament for the St Andrews Burghs; and 'The Notorious Miss Anstruther' was the title of a story by E. W. Hornung in the *Strand* for May 1891.

seeing what I gained: Dr Watson became engaged to his future wife, Mary Morstan, at the end of *The Sign of the Four*.

his long grey travelling-cloak and close-fitting cloth cap: Sidney Paget interpreted this as a long cape and deerstalker hat, thereby providing Sherlock Holmes with the headgear by which he is best known. The illustration in the *Strand*, 'We had the carriage to ourselves', was the first by Paget to show Holmes dressed in this way.

76 *Ross, in Herefordshire*: a market town on the River Wye, twelve miles south-east of Hereford and eighteen miles north-west of Gloucester. ACD travelled by the same route when visiting his wife's relations in Gloucestershire.

John Turner: perhaps suggested by 'Thomas Turner', the alias used by the bushranger Harry Manns, when arrested in July 1863 for his part in the Eugowra robbery.

Hatherley: a Gloucestershire place-name. Down Hatherley is three and half miles north-east of Cheltenham; Up Hatherley is two miles south-west of Cheltenham. ACD's early 'Our Derby Sweepstakes' is set around Hatherley House, Hatherley (*Uncollected Stories*).

Charles McCarthy: perhaps from Sir Charles M'Carthy (1764–1824), who served in the West Indies with the Irish Brigade 1794–96, governed Sierra Leone 1812–24, and was killed fighting the Ashantis, or from Justin McCarthy (1830–1912), the Parliamentary leader of the anti-Parnellite majority, whose novels and histories ACD praised at the Portsmouth Literary and Scientific Society on 31 Jan. 1888.

the Colonies: Australia consisted of six independent colonies before Federation (as the Commonwealth of Australia) in 1900.

77 *June 3—that is, on Monday last*: possibly implying that the year was 1889, when 3 June fell on a Monday.

William Crowder: perhaps from Thomas Crowder (1758–1824), an emancipated convict who was superintendent of convicts at Hobart Town (and thus a 'poacher turned gamekeeper').

Patience Moran: perhaps from Henry Moran, the constable wounded during the ambush of the gold escort coach near the Eugowra station in 1862; or from 'Dan Moran', in Ralph Boldrewood's *Robbery Under Arms* (1888). 'Patience' recalls the dairy maid in the comic opera (1881) by William Schwenck Gilbert (1836–1911) and Arthur Seymour Sullivan (1842–1900).

78 *Assizes*: general assizes ('sittings') when judges 'go their circuit'; periodical sittings of courts across England and Wales to try criminal cases in the presence of a jury. The assizes for Herefordshire were held in Hereford, where there was a

Court of Quarter Sessions, divided into eleven petty sessional divisions.

78 *Lestrade*: Inspector Lestrade, of Scotland Yard, who is introduced in *A Study in Scarlet*. Barristers are 'retained', but it would have been impossible to 'retain' an inspector from Scotland Yard as a fee would be involved which would be illegal.

79 *métier*: calling, trade, profession.

80 *the local Herefordshire paper*: there was one local daily paper, the *Hereford Mercury and Independent* (established 1832). The 'weekly county paper' referred to later could have been the *Hereford Journal* (established 1713), the *Hereford Times* (established 1832), or the *Hereford Weekly Marvel* (established 1869).

81 *John Cobb*: perhaps from Cobb and Co., the Australian mail and passenger coach company, founded by Freeman Cobb (1830–78) at the height of the Ballarat gold rush; or from Cobb's Hole, the fishing village in *The Moonstone* (1868); or from 'cob', a short legged, stout variety of horse.

a cry of 'Cooee!': (Cooey), an aboriginal signal borrowed by Australian settlers. Perhaps suggested by an incident in E. W. Hornung's novel, *A Bride from the Bush* (1890), when the bride causes a commotion in Hyde Park by giving voice to this call: ' "Coo-ee." / 'That was the startling cry as nearly as it can be written. But no letters can convey the sustained shrillness of the long, penetrating note represented by the first syllable, nor the weird die-away wail of the second. It is the well-known Bush call, the "jodel" of the black-fellow; but it has seldom been heard from a white throat as Gladys Bligh let it out that afternoon in Hyde Park in the presence of Royalty.' Or from *'Cooee.' Tales of Australian Life*, edited by Mrs Patchett Martin (May 1891).

82 *a plaid*: a long piece of twilled woollen cloth, with a chequered or tartan pattern. The item of clothing may have been the cape of an Inverness coat which can blow off, unobserved by the wearer, as it is attached only by a button on each shoulder.

83 *Petrarch*: Francesco Petrarca (1304–74), the Italian poet. *Selections from the Canzoniere of Francesco Petrarch* (translated by Cyfaill) and May Alden Ward's *Petrarch, A Sketch of His Life and Works* were published at the beginning of 1891.

We lunch at Swindon: 'this was in the days when the Swindon Hotel Company still exercised its right of holding up all trains for ten minutes whilst the passengers refreshed themselves in its dining rooms' (J. Alan Rannie, 'The Railway Journeys of Mr Sherlock Holmes', *Railway Magazine*, May 1935). The Refreshment Rooms at Swindon were in decline by 1891 and in 1895 the Great Western Railway paid £100,000 for the unexpired forty-five years of the lease allowing their trains to travel non-stop to Bristol.

84 *Stroud Valley*: named after the market town of Stroud, nine miles south of Gloucester, on the Thames and Severn Canal.

the broad gleaming Severn: a river rising in mid-Wales to empty in the Bristol Channel. It is broad in places, but not where this railway line crosses it.

dustcoat: a coat worn to keep off the dust.

the 'Hereford Arms': an invented hotel (the arms would be those of the City of Hereford, the Bishop of Hereford, or Viscount Hereford).

It is entirely a question of barometric pressure: atmospheric pressure measured by a barometer or 'glass'. At the earth's surface the pressure or weight of a column of air is about 14½ lb. per square inch. Holmes's concern with the weather may be compared to that shown by Gaboriau's Lecoq whose mood changed as he became aware that misfortune threatened his investigation: 'A very great misfortune. Do you not perceive that the weather has undesirably changed. It is evident that the wind is now coming from the south. The fog has disappeared, but the sky is cloudy and threatening. It will rain in less than an hour.' Father Absinthe could not see the connection. 'His companion took pity on his anxiety. "What!" he exclaimed, as he still hastened forward, "you do not understand that our investigation, my success, and your reward, are dependent upon those black clouds which the wind is driving towards us . . . Twenty minutes of merely gentle rain, and our time and labour will be lost. If it rains, the snow will melt, and then farewell to our proofs' (Émile Gaboriau, *Monsieur Lecoq*, 1869).

Twenty-nine: atmospheric pressure is expressed by the perpendicular height measured by a column of mercury in a closed glass tube of just over thirty inches. When the pressure increases the level rises (high pressure) and when it decreases the level falls (low pressure). 'Twenty-nine' or 'twenty-nine inches' means that the pressure will sustain a column of mercury of that height. The register plates of cistern barometers and the dials of wheel barometers are marked from a low of 28 ('Stormy') to a high of 31 ('Very Dry'), and between them come 28.5 ('Much Rain'), 29 ('Rain'), 29.5 ('Change'), 30 ('Fair'), and 30.5 ('Set Fair'). 'Twenty-nine' therefore implies rain, but the weather should properly be judged by observing the movement of the mercury—a gradual rise would indicate settled weather and a rapid fall would suggest stormy weather.

84 *as plain as a pikestaff*: the phrase is a reference to the plain surface of the staff on which a pedlar supported his pack (originally 'as plain as a packstaff').

violet eyes: the pigment of the iris comes in many shades, but 'violet' eyes are uncommon outside the pages of fiction, as in the Stevensons' 'Story of the Destroying Angel' (*More New Arabian Nights*): 'Never was there a smile of more touching sweetness; never were eyes more deeply violet, more honestly eloquent of the soul! I speak with knowledge, for these were the same eyes that smiled upon me in the cradle.' The ultimate origin for both passages is perhaps Sir Walter Scott, *The Lord of the Isles*, I. iv:

> The dew that on the violet lies
> Mocks the dark lustre of thine eyes.

86 *Victoria*: a British colonial territory (now a state) in south-eastern Australia, with Melbourne as its capital. It was settled in 1804 and formed a dependency of New South Wales until 1851.

a train to Hereford: Ross and Hereford were connected by a direct line of the Great Western Railway. The prison for Hereford and Radnorshire was in Commercial Road, near the railway station.

a yellow-backed novel: a cheap (sixpenny or shilling) edition of a book with illustrated covers of glazed and predominantly yellow paper over boards. The first 'yellowbacks' were published in 1847 by Simms and McIntyre, and other publishers quickly followed suit, namely Routledge, Chapman & Hall, Frederick Warne, Maxwell, Chatto & Windus, and Ward, Lock, & Co. ACD's work twice appeared in this format: the reissue of the anthology *Strange Secrets*, issued by Chatto &

Windus in 1890, and *A Study in Scarlet* issued by Lever Brothers in 1894. The yellowback was superseded by the sixpenny paperback novel at the end of the century.

87 *the posterior . . . had been shattered*: the two parietal bones form part of the sides and top of the skull, and the 'occipital bone' makes up the back.

88 *thereby hangs a rather painful tale*: *As You Like It*, II. ii. 28 ('And thereby hangs a tale'); *The Taming of the Shrew*, IV. i. 60 ('And thereby hangs a tale').

89 *the Bermuda Dockyard*: the Royal Dockyard on Ireland Isle in the Bermudas where the British North American squadron refitted. It had an iron dry dock which was built at Woolwich and towed across the Atlantic in July 1869. The islands in the mid-Atlantic were settled by the English in 1609.

let us talk about George Meredith: the English novelist and poet (1828–1909), author of *The Egotist* (1879), of whom Oscar Wilde said: 'His style is chaos illumined by flashes of lightning. As a writer he has mastered everything except language: as a novelist he can do everything, except tell a story: as an artist he is everything except articulate' ('The Decay of Lying', 1889). ACD talked about 'The Genius of George Meredith' to the Portsmouth Literary and Scientific Society on 20 Nov. 1888. 'Meredith was made to be imitated. His mission is not so much to tell stories himself, as to initiate a completely new method in the art of fiction, to infuse fresh spirit into a branch of literature which was in much need of regeneration' ('Mr Stevenson's Methods in Fiction', *National Review*, Jan. 1890). Meredith was sent copies of *Micah Clarke* and *The White Company*, and he twice invited ACD to Box Hill (cf. Pierre Nordon, 'George Meredith vu par Sir Arthur Conan Doyle', *Etudes Anglaises*, Juillet–Septembre 1959, XIIe Année, No. 3). Meredith referred to Sherlock Holmes when complimenting ACD (14 Jan. 1907) on his *Daily Telegraph* articles concerning the case of George Edalji: 'I shall not mention the name which must have become wearisome to your ears, but the creator of the marvellous Amateur Detective has shown what he can do in the life of breath.'

90 *the merest moonshine*: appearance without substance; something that is unsubstantial (as in *Love's Labour's Lost*, V. xi. 208: 'Thou now request'st but moonshine in the water').

91 *Sherlock Holmes was transformed*: the description echoes that of Lecoq when tracing footprints in the snow: 'A bloodhound in pursuit of his prey would have been less alert, less discerning, and less agile. He came and went, now turning, now pausing, now retreating, now hurrying on again without any apparent reason; he scrutinized, he questioned every surrounding object; the ground, the logs of wood, the blocks of stone, in a word, nothing escaped his glance. For a moment he would remain standing, then fall upon his knees, and at times lie flat upon his stomach with his face so near the ground that his breath must have melted the snow' (*Monsieur Lecoq*, 1869).

whip-cord: tightly twisted cord, for making whip-lashes.

92 *He drew out a lens*: a magnifying glass (which in the popular mind he never afterwards put away).

93 *a tall man, left-handed, limps with the right leg*: a further echo of Lecoq, who after tracing the footprints, says: 'He was a tall man of middle age; he wore a soft hat and a shaggy brown overcoat; he was, moreover, probably married, or had been so, as he had a wedding-ring on the little finger of his right hand' (*Monsieur Lecoq*).

95 *BALLARAT*: the second city of Victoria, seventy-four miles by rail from Melbourne, where gold was discovered on 25 Aug. 1851. In *The Wrong Box* (1889) Stevenson and Osbourne make a passing reference to the possibility of an uncle 'returning from Ballarat with a large fortune'; and in *The Sign of the Four* Dr Watson claims to have been there, for he says of the disorder at Pondicherry Lodge: 'It looks as though all the moles in England had been let loose in it. I have seen something of the sort on the side of a hill near Ballarat, where the prospectors had been at work.'

96 *a little monograph . . . tobacco*: the title is given in *The Sign of the Four* as 'Upon the Distinction between the Ashes of the Various Tobaccos', and Holmes says: 'In it I enumerate a hundred and forty forms of cigar, cigarette, and pipe tobacco, with colour plates illustrating the difference in ash.' ACD told his American publisher that he had been asked for a copy: 'It's a triumph ever to get a rise out of you shrewd people on the other side, but a Philadelphia tobacconist actually wrote to me under cover to you, to ask me where he could get a copy of the monograph in which Sherlock Holmes describes

the difference in the ashes of 140 different kinds of tobacco. Rather funny, isn't it?' (19 Mar. 1890, to Joseph Marshall Stoddart (Redmond A. Burke Collection)).

98 *in the early 'sixties at the diggings*: which confirms that ACD was thinking of the ambush of the Eugowra gold escort in June 1862 or the Mudgee Mail Robbery of July 1863.

troopers: the mounted infantry, established in 1825, who dealt with escaped convicts. They were armed with sabres, carbines and horse-pistols, and wore the uniform of the Light Dragoons until 1862 when the uniform was changed to a blue tunic with grey breeches and a waterproof cape.

I put my pistol to the head of the wagon-driver: in the Mudgee Mail Robbery of July 1863, two of the bushrangers put their pistols to the head of the driver.

100 *I never hear ... Sherlock Holmes*: a paraphrase of the words uttered by John Bradford (1510?–55), the Protestant martyr. 'There is a tradition that on seeing some criminals going to execution he exclaimed: "But for the grace of God there goes John Bradford" ' (*DNB*, 1886), here wrongly attributed to the English divine, Richard Baxter (1615–91).

THE FIVE ORANGE PIPS

First published in the *Strand Magazine*, 2 (Nov. 1891), 481–8, with 6 illustrations by Sidney Paget; *Strand Magazine*, New York (Dec. 1891); S.S. McClure Newspaper Syndicate, USA, various dates between 7 and 21 Nov. 1891, with woodcut illustrations. Alternative titles: 'Adventures of Five Orange Pips' (syndication title); 'The Story of Five Orange Pips' (*St Louis Post-Dispatch*).

Written at 23 Montague Place, London, and dispatched on 18 May 1891. MS: whereabouts unknown.

The Ku Klux Klan was created in Pulaski, Tennessee soon after the final overthrow of the Southern forces in 1865. The institution was put on a serious footing by the Tennessee Democratic leadership in Apr. 1867 and was headed by the Confederacy's leading guerrilla tactician, General Nathan Bedford Forrest (1821–77). The Klan quickly became conspicuous for intimidation of the ex-slaves, and imitation groups were organized in Kentucky and other ex-Confederate states, not always with the Ku Klux Klan name but with the same white uniforms, head-dresses, masks, hierarchies, and, above all, Negrophobia. The Florida organization, operating in a thinly populated state (eight of whose thirty-nine counties had blacks outnumbering whites), accounted for between 153 and 235 racial murders between 1867 and 1871, although it was in decline from 1869 (after failing to capture power in the election of 1868). Forrest and his associates at first denied under oath that they were involved; later it was accepted that they had been, as had even more respectable ex-Confederate leaders (among them the great Confederate General Robert E. Lee (1807–70) who gave the Klan his blessing); but the murders were ascribed to thugs who had supposedly taken over the organization after persons of social consequence had left it. In fact there seems no truth in this: the ex-Confederate leadership maintained close links with the Klan in its various forms, and were frequently associated with its most active murder chiefs. Hence a body of papers which could have proved that the supposed alien rough element who had taken over the Klans were in fact the original élite would have been very damaging to Southern Democratic leaders politically, and might have resulted in very prominent people being brought to trial.

So the background of the story is historically sound, especially Holmes's demythologizing—that 'some of the first [i.e. foremost] men in the South' could be implicated, a deduction he evidently makes from the encyclopaedia's whitewashing of 'the better classes'. What is wrong is the date. By 1891, or indeed from the return of the Democratic party to presidential power in 1885, such revelations would have had little effect, and ex-Confederate white power in the ex-Confederate states would have quashed any attempt to bring prosecutions. In 1881–2, on the other hand, something might have been made of serious proofs of participation in the Klan murders of 1867–8 by members of the social élite. ACD's three-day conversation with the dying black abolitionist leader and US Minister to Liberia, Henry Highland Garnet (1815–82), on the *Mayumba* in Jan. 1882 is the one source we know him to have possessed on these matters, though several books had appeared on this subject, such as *K.K.K. Sketches* (1877) by James Melville Beard. Garnet would clearly have hoped that evidence might yet appear to bring home the guilt of ex-slaveholder and ex-Confederate politicians. This would also explain why the story says relatively little that is reminiscent of the white version of the Klan, with its emphasis on the hierarchies of Wizard, Dragons, Kleagles, and on the Greek-derived name; on the other hand, it is quite consistent with a black version of it that stressed violence, terror, and a ruthless disregard for legal authorities. No white source mentions melon seeds or orange pips amongst the Klan's terror tactics; but ACD may have been told of their being used against blacks in a specific Southern locality known to Garnet but never publicly documented.

The immediate impetus seems to have been a reminder of white Southern mob violence when, in the words of the *Annual Register* for 1891, 'On March 14, eleven Italian subjects, inhabiting New Orleans, had been lynched in prison by the mob, on the ground that they belonged to the secret society of the Mafia. The execution had been planned and carried out in a particularly horrible manner.' The US federal authorities refused to intervene, arguing that it was a state matter, and as a consequence, the Italian government withdrew its Minister to Washington. The continued trial of 169 members of the Mala Vita in Italy while ACD was writing 'The Five Orange Pips' would also have brought the subject of secret societies to his attention.

ACD placed the story sixth on his list of the twelve best. 'There are a number of stories which really are a little hard to separate. On the whole I think I should find a place for "The Five Orange Pips", for though it is short it has a certain dramatic quality of its own' ['How I Made My List', *Strand*, June 1927].

102 *the adventure of the Paradol chamber*: possibly a reference to Lucien Anatole Prevost-Paradol (1829–70), the French writer and envoy to the USA, who shot himself in the chamber of his Washington hotel on 11 July 1870; or the 'Lethal Chamber' of Dr Richardson in which dogs were put to death by anaesthesia: ' "If I had," says Dr Richardson, "to elect whether I would die by drowning or anaesthesia, I should choose anaesthesia, without a moment's hesitation. I give the dog the benefit of my own choice, which is, I think, fair to him" ' ('The Lethal Chamber', *Tit-Bits*, 21 Mar. 1891).

the Amateur Mendicant Society . . . furniture warehouse: perhaps suggested by an article in *Chambers's Journal* on 20 Sept. 1890, 'Paris: Syndicate of Professional Mendicants', or an article in *Cassell's Saturday Journal*, 1 Oct. 1890, 'A School for Beggars', which describes the contents of the museum of the 'Mendicity Society' in London.

the facts . . . Sophy Anderson: the ship (of which there is no record in *Lloyd's Register*) may have been named after Sophie Anderson

(1823–98), a painter, and was perhaps suggested by the *Mary Celeste* (which had inspired ACD's 'J. Habakuk Jephson's Statement' (1884)), or the events connected with the barque *Martha M. Stubbs*, of Windsor, NS, the subject of William Clark Russell's story, 'Captain Jones of the Rose', which appeared in the *Strand* in May 1891.

102 *the singular adventures of the Grice Patersons in the island of Uffa*: from Captain W. G. Grice-Hutchinson, a Conservative (Unionist), who achieved an unexpected by-election victory on 20 Mar. 1891 at Aston Manor, Birmingham (where ACD had served as a doctor). Uffa is an imaginary island which was used as the setting for 'Our Midnight Visitor' (*Temple Bar*, Feb. 1891): 'On the western side of the island of Arran, seldom visited, and almost unknown to tourists, is the little island named Uffa.' It is based on the island of Pladda, off the coast of Arran, and takes its name from the islands of Ulva and Staffa, near the west coast of Mull. In *Memories and Adventures* (1924) ACD refers to the case as 'The Curious Experience of the Patterson Family in the Island of Uffa'.

the Camberwell poisoning case: Camberwell is in south London (cf. note to p. 39, 'Lyon Place, Camberwell'), but this could be an allusion to the 'Camberley Poisoning Case' of 1888, or to the Liverpool poisoning case of 1889 when Mrs Florence Elizabeth Maybrick was charged with the murder of her husband.

103 *the equinoctial gales*: gales that occur during the vernal or spring equinox in March, and the autumnal equinox in September. ACD had experienced gales at sea in 1882, and the equinoctial gales of 1891 were unusually severe.

the wind cried and sobbed like a child in the chimney: the simile may have been suggested by one found in Clark Russell's novel *A Sea Queen* (1883), where the tempest 'shrieked like tortured children at the hall-door and the window-casements, and roared like the discharge of heavy ordnance in the chimneys'.

one of Clark Russell's fine sea stories: perhaps *A Sea Queen*, or 'Captain Jones of the Rose' (*Strand*, May 1891), or *My Danish Sweetheart* (serialized in the *Illustrated London News*, 3 Jan.– 27 June 1891). Clark Russell (1844–1911) was the author of many novels of the sea and wrote the *Daily Telegraph* 'Seafarer' column which ACD saved in his commonplace book. 'Clark

Russell deserves a whole shelf for himself,' he said, when listing the twelve greatest sea stories, 'but anyhow you could not miss out *The Wreck of the Grosvenor*' (*Through the Magic Door*, 1907).

My wife was on a visit to her aunt's: Newnes, 1892; in the *Strand* this appeared as 'on a visit to her mother's', contradicting Mary Morstan's statement in *The Sign of the Four* that 'My mother was dead'.

104 *Horsham*: a town in Sussex, then served by the London, Brighton, and South Coast Railway.

that clay and chalk mixture . . . is quite distinctive: Horsham stands on the Tunbridge Wells Sands and is surrounded by the Weald clay, but there is no chalk. ACD was thinking of Joseph Bell who had correctly surmised from the clay on a pair of boots that a patient had walked over Bruntsfield Links (actually very near the Infirmary) from the south: 'Conan Doyle could not see how I knew that, absurdly simple as it was,' Bell explained: 'On a showery day, such as that had been, the reddish clay at bare parts of the links adheres to the boot, and a tiny part is bound to remain. There is no such clay anywhere else round the town for miles' ('The Original of Sherlock Holmes', *Pall Mall Budget*, 4 Jan. 1894).

I heard from Major Prendergast . . . the Tankerville Club Scandal: perhaps from General Sir Harry North Dalrymple Prendergast, VC (1834–1913), a hero of the Indian Mutiny. Tankerville derives from the Earls of Tankerville. Forde Grey (d. 1701), Earl of Tankerville, who commanded Monmouth's horse at Sedgemoor was made Earl of Tankerville in 1695. Wilde's 'The Canterville Ghost' had appeared but not yet in book form (it was collected soon after in *Lord Arthur Savile's Crime*), but if ACD knew it, the similarity of names is suggestive ('He remembered the terrible night when the wicked Lord Canterville was found choking in his dressing-room, with the knave of diamonds half-way down his throat, and confessed, just before he died, that he had cheated Charles James Fox out of £50,000 at Crockford's by means of that very card, and swore that the ghost had made him swallow it'). The scandal suggests the Baccarat Case where Sir William Gordon-Cumming was accused of cheating at Tranby Croft, near Doncaster, in Sept. 1890; or it could refer to a card scandal which forced the closure of the Walsingham Club in 1887. It could also be compared with ACD's short story 'A Regimental Scandal' (1891) in which a Major Errington cheats in order to lose at cards (*Uncollected Stories*).

105 *John Openshaw*: a Lancashire JP of this name is listed in *Kelly's Handbook* for 1891, but ACD perhaps took it from Thomas Horrocks Openshaw (1856–1929), a London surgeon, or from the manufacturing district of Openshaw, near Manchester.

a small factory at Coventry . . . the invention of bicycling: there is no firm date for the invention of the bicycle, though pedals were introduced *c*.1840. The reference may be an allusion to James Starley (1830–81), who helped to found the Coventry Sewing Machine Company in 1857. The Coventry Machinists' Company, as it then became, began manufacturing rubber tyred bicycles on the French model in 1868. 'The Coventry Machinists' Co. were firmly established as makers of reputation; Smith and Starley started making at St. Agnes Works, also in Coventry, and the elder Starley quickly gained the title of "Father of the Bicycle". No man introduced more improvements. This was in 1872. Starley was one of the first to add the much-needed step and he invented the Ariel wheel.' ('Who is the "Father of the Bicycle"', *Tit-Bits*, 24 Oct. 1891). James Starley's nephew, J. K. Starley, patented the tangent wheel in 1874, and his 'Rover' cycle of 1885 was the first with wheels of an equal size. As 'Ku Klux' is derived from the same Greek root as 'cycle' there may be a somewhat sinister joke involved as to the choice of interests in the Openshaw clan.

the patentee of the Openshaw unbreakable tyre: this would have been a tyre made of narrow strips of solid rubber, which were in use until the invention of the pneumatic tyre by J. R. Dunlop in 1888.

My uncle Elias: 'Elias' is the Roman Catholic (Douai) biblical form of 'Elijah'. See also note to p. 52 ('Ezekiah Hopkins').

the war: the American Civil War (1861–5).

Jackson's army: the army of Thomas Jonathan ('Stonewall') Jackson, the Confederate general (1824–63), who died of wounds received at Chancellorsville.

Hood: John Bell Hood (1831–79), a Confederate general, who commanded the troops during the Atlanta Campaign and had his forces annihilated at Nashville.

When Lee laid down his arms: Robert Edward Lee (1807–70), promoted General-in-chief of the Confederate armies after the defeat at Gettysburg. He surrendered on 9 Apr. 1865 at Appomattox Court House, Virginia, but other armies remained in the field, the last military force holding out under General Edmund Kirby-Smith (1824–93) until 2 June 1865.

his aversion to the negroes: Negrophobia, as a motivation for self-exile after Klan warfare, is obviously a realistic analysis, though it would seldom be put forward publicly. [ODE]

extending the franchise to them: the Republican policy was realized in the Fifteenth Amendment to the US Constitution, ratified in 1870, but it was tacitly dropped in 1877.

106 *Pondicherry*: a city on the south-east coast of India, eighty-six miles south-west of Madras, capital of the French settlement (1672) of the same name. It is used as the name of a house in *The Sign of the Four*.

107 *Fordham*: perhaps from Fordham near Newmarket, or from Fordham, in Westchester County, New York, the site of St John's College and home of Edgar Allan Poe between 1844 and 1849. 'We have spent one Sunday afternoon hunting out the little cottage at Fordham near New York where Edgar Allan Poe spent the last years of his life. There is a doll's kitchen, a small sitting-room, with tea-things still upon the table, and the tiny bedroom where Virginia Poe passed away. His face looks at you from every wall, austere, coldly intellectual, cruel in its precise accuracy. He had every quality save humour, and of that there was not a trace . . . There was a suggestion of the rarefied literary atmosphere in which he lived in the desk and the bookshelves, with a little written criticism in his exquisite script in which he accuses Coleridge of plagiarism from Schiller—with very complete proofs' (*Our American Adventure*, 1922).

109 *the reconstruction of the Southern States*: in the initial instance the victorious North offered mild terms of reunion which were answered by Southern choice of ex-Confederate Congressional representation, thus putting the war gains, and perhaps even the Union, at further risk. Congress therefore refused to seat the Southern states until they accepted the Fourteenth Amendment which, amongst other provisions, safeguarded the Union war debt, denied the Confederate war debt, and

protected the blacks. All the ex-Confederate states except Tennessee refused, as a result of which Alabama, Arkansas, Florida, Georgia, Louisiana, Mississippi, North Carolina, South Carolina, Virginia, and Texas were occupied by Union troops, given new constitutions and governments, and administered by military authorities and civilians including collaborative white and black Southerners.

109 *the carpet-bag politicians*: an opprobrious term invented by white Southerners who asserted that the occupying Union troops brought with them northern civilians with no more personal property than would fill a carpet-bag. In fact, some carpet-baggers were schoolteachers, philanthropists, and others who sought to give the blacks security and skills. But they also included some corrupt figures, and those who mixed philanthropic and political or economic motives.

my cock-and-bull story: an unlikely or incredible story, said to have originated in the old fables. 'Lord! said my mother, what is all this story about? / A Cock and a Bull, said Yorick—And one of the best of its kind, I ever heard' (Laurence Sterne, *Tristram Shandy*, 1759).

Dundee: a Scottish sea port on the River Tay, 42 miles north of Edinburgh.

110 *Major Freebody*: possibly an association of ideas with the Freedman's Bureau, the organization entrusted by Congress with preservation of the interests of the ex-slaves. Or perhaps suggested by Clement Freebody, who married the daughter of William Debenham in 1818, and gave his name as a partner to Debenham and Freebody, the drapery store in Cavendish Square.

one of the forts upon Portsdown Hill: one of five red-brick forts, Fort Nelson, Fort Widley, Fort Wallington, Fort Purbrook, or Fort Southwick (near which ACD watched the large Volunteer Review on 14 Apr. 1884) which defend the hill above Portsmouth. 'There is not a finer natural theatre in the world than Portsdown Hill and the country around it, nor any place where such a large number of spectators can follow operations upon a large scale and grasp the drift of them' ('Easter Monday with a Camera', *British Journal of Photography*, 23 May 1884).

Fareham: a town below Portsdown Hill, at the north-west extremity of Portsmouth Harbour.

111   *The postmark is London—eastern division*: the Post Office divided the city into eight postal districts (West Central, East Central, East, South East, South West, West, North West, and North).

   This is no time for despair: the advice given by Horace (*Odes*, I. vii): 'Nil desperandum'.

112   *the following enigmatical notices . . . Same old platform*: implies that the principles are what they always were: subordination or death to blacks, expulsion of Northerners and white collaborators. 'Cleared', as Holmes, says, means 'left the country'. Three days were customary: 'At Houston several teachers of colored schools were attacked; one of them told me that they ordered him to leave in three days or they would take his life. His wife was about to be confined, but he had to leave' (US Congress, *Report of the Joint Select Committee to Inquire into the Condition of Affairs in the Late Insurrectionary States* (1872): evidence of 'Cornelius McBride, a young Scotchman', schoolteacher of blacks during the week and of whites on Sunday at Sparta, Miss., where he received 175 lashes from the Klan and escaped before being hanged).

113   *Waterloo*: the terminus of the London and South-Western Railway, opened in 1848, with buildings dating from 1853–1885 (reconstructed 1900–22).

114   *even greater perils than did the Sholtos*: i.e. Bartholomew and Thaddeus Sholto, the twin sons of Major John Sholto, in *The Sign of the Four*.

   As Cuvier could correctly describe . . . a single bone: Georges Leopold Chretien Frederic Dagobert, Baron Cuvier (1769–1832), the French naturalist and anatomist. Gaboriau says of Père Tabaret: 'He will pretend, unassisted, to reconstruct all the scenes of a murder, as a professor reconstructs a prehistoric beast from a single bone' (*L'Affaire Lerouge*); and Oliver Wendell Holmes, discussing the Latin axiom 'Ex pede Herculem' ('you can judge the size of Hercules from his foot') says: 'Tell me about Cuvier's getting up a megatherium from a tooth, or Agassiz's drawing a portrait of an undiscovered fish from a single scale! As the "O" revealed Giotto—as the one word "moi" betrayed the Strattford-atte-Bowe-taught Anglais, so all a man's antecedents and possibilities are summed up in a single utterance which gives at once the gauge of his education and his mental organisation' (*The Autocrat of the Breakfast-Table*, 1858).

115 *It was a singular document*: 'Sherlock Holmes — His Limits'. 'I enumerated in my own mind all the various points upon which he had shown me that he was exceptionally well-informed. I even took a pencil and jotted them down. I could not help smiling at the document when I had completed it' (*A Study in Scarlet*).

the American Encyclopedia: Alvin J. Johnson's *New Universal Cyclopaedia* (1875–7), reprinted as *Johnson's Universal Cyclopaedia* (1893–5), contains an entry on the Ku Klux Klan which most closely resembles the one quoted by ACD. There was also the *American Cyclopaedia* (New York, 1873–6), the *International Encyclopaedia* (New York, 1884), and the *Encyclopaedia Americana* (Philadelphia, 1886).

117 *Ku Klux Klan . . . cocking a rifle*: *Johnson's Universal Cyclopedia* says it was named 'in imitation of the click heard in cocking the rifle'. D. L. Wilson, in 'The Ku Klux Klan. Its Origin, Growth, and Disbandment' (*Century Magazine*, July 1884), describes how the name was chosen by a committee: 'They mentioned several names which they had been considering. In this number was the name "kukloi", from the Greek word "κυκλος" (kuklos), meaning a band or circle. At mention of this, someone cried out: "Call it Ku Klux!" / "Klan" at once suggested itself, and was added to complete the alliteration.'

Its outrages . . . melon seeds or orange pips in others: there is no known source for this statement, though the *Encyclopaedia Britannica*, in its entry for the Ku Klux Klan, says 'Mysterious signs and warnings were sent to disorderly negro politicians'. Sprigs of oak were worn in England on 29 May, the birthday of Charles II; and oak sprays were worn on the hats of Protestant agrarian rioters in Ulster in the 1760s. In Louisiana the KKK called itself 'the Knights of the White Camellia', and it is supposed to have issued warnings with flower-shoots, sprigs, or petals. One other possible association of ideas is linked to the Tankerville card-games; the pips on playing-cards were named from the seeds of fruit, and 'to pip' means to take a trick in cards. It was also used of a black ball, and being 'pipped' is equivalent to being 'black-balled'.

In the year 1869, the movement rather suddenly collapsed: the Ku Klux Klan was disbanded by the 'Grand Wizard of the Invisible Order' after the proclamation of Martial Law in

Tennessee on 20 Feb. 1869—though others continued to use the name until suppressed by an act of Congress in 1871.

119 *Waterloo Bridge*: built (1811–17) by John Rennie, originally the 'Strand Bridge', but renamed after the Battle of Waterloo, and sometimes known as the 'English Bridge of Sighs' because of the large number of suicide attempts made from it. It was demolished in 1936 to make way for the present bridge (of 1942).

H Division: a division of the Metropolitan Police assigned to Whitechapel (rather than to Westminster); and perhaps familiar to ACD from press reports of the Whitechapel Murders, the most recent of which had been that of Frances Coles on 13 Feb. 1891.

The Embankment: the Victoria Embankment, running along the side of the Thames between Westminster and Blackfriars; one of the three great Embankments built between 1868 and 1874 which reclaimed the foreshore of the river.

120 *Captain James Calhoun*: probably suggested by John Caldwell Calhoun (1782–1850) of South Carolina, who was the great defender of slavery and advocate of states' rights.

Barque Lone Star, Savannah, Georgia: *Lloyd's Register* lists two ships of this name: an iron screw steamer, and a brigantine (built 1864). It is also said to be found in the 'Georgia register' with the owner given as 'Johannsen Brothers of Savannah' (Richard W. Clarke, *Baker Street Journal*, Apr. 1946). But more probably based on ships named after the stars used for navigation, as in *The Mystery of the Ocean Star* (1888) by William Clark Russell, or *The Captain of the Pole-Star* (1890) by ACD.

121 *Lloyd's registers and the files of old papers*: *Lloyd's Register of Shipping* (begun in 1764) classifies vessels (from A1 to C4); and the *Shipping and Mercantile Gazette and Lloyd's List* (started in 1838) gives the arrival and departure times of ships in Port of London.

the Albert Dock: the Royal Albert Dock (1880) on the Plaistow Marshes to the north of the Thames, which covered three-quarters of a mile and formed an eastern extension of the Victoria Dock.

Gravesend: a town in Kent, the boundary port of London, twenty-four miles from the city centre, where custom-house officers and pilots were embarked and disembarked.

121 *the Goodwins*: the Goodwin sands, an extensive and dangerous shoal or sandbank, off the eastern coast of Kent, opposite Sandwich and Deal (named after Earl Godwine).

122 *the best laid of human plans*: after Robert Burns (1759–96), 'The best laid schemes o' mice and men / Gang aft a-gley' ('To a Mouse').

  a shattered sternpost . . . the letters 'L.S.' carved upon it: the sternpost is the upright timber on which the rudder is hung. The name of the ship would be given in full on a board fixed across the stern.

THE MAN WITH THE TWISTED LIP

First published in the *Strand Magazine*, 2 (Dec. 1891), 623–37, with 10 illustrations by Sidney Paget; *Strand Magazine*, New York (Jan. 1892); S. S. McClure Newspaper Syndicate, USA, various dates between 5 and 20 Dec. 1891, with woodcut illustrations. Alternative title: 'The Strange Tale of a Beggar' (*Philadelphia Inquirer*).

Written at 12 Tennison Road, South Norwood, and completed by the second week of Aug. 1891. MS: whereabouts unknown.

The title may be compared with 'The Man with the Thumb' in *Casell's Saturday Journal* (from 27 Sept. 1890), which was also perhaps an influence on 'The Engineer's Thumb'.

The sources can be clearly identified:

(a) 'A Day as a Professional Beggar' (*Tit-Bits* 17 Jan. 1891). The author, a hard-working journalist, was seized with the idea for 'original copy', he would become a beggar for a day. He sought out old clothes. 'I also engaged a small room in a back street, where I should be able to change after the ordeal. My face, of course, would require making up a little, and after practising once or twice I succeeded to my satisfaction.' He took the precaution of providing himself with a few matches to escape being 'run-in' for begging and stationed himself in the street. He received a severe fright when he saw his closest friend with a lady whom he knew advancing towards him, but thereafter his fortunes improved and by the end of the day he had earned three shillings and sixpence. There is also a second article, 'A Day as an Amateur Crossing Sweeper' (*Tit-Bits*, 18 Apr. 1891) in which the author earned one shilling and three-halfpence for twelve hours work in the West End.

(b) An earlier fictional treatment is found in 'Miss Shum's Husband' in *The Memoirs of Mr C. J. Yellowplush* (1861) by W. M.

Thackeray. Mystery surrounds the birth and profession of Yellow-plush's master, Mr Frederic Altamont, who spends eight hours each day in the city but refuses to reveal the nature of his business. His mother-in-law decides to investigate after he admits seeing her husband twice in one day near the Bank. The discovery of a Queen Anne sixpence dated 1703 in the money given by Altamont to his wife provides the answer: 'Mr Haltamont SWEP THE CROSSING FROM THE BANK TO CORNHILL!' The earnings of Mr Altamont were between thirty and fifty shillings a day; both he and 'Hugh Boone' favoured a pitch near the Bank of England and made a living from their profession. The similarity was noted by Andrew Lang ('The Novels of Sir Arthur Conan Doyle', *Quarterly Review*, July 1904): 'Readers who remember the case of Mr Altamont are not puzzled by the disappearance of Mr Neville St Clair.'

(c) A second major source of inspiration was *The Moonstone* (1868) by Wilkie Collins. A sailor is observed entering the 'Wheel of Fortune' in Shore Lane, near Lower Thames Street. When no reply is forthcoming, the door is broken down and the man dressed as a sailor is discovered dead upon the bed. 'Look at the man's face,' says Sergeant Cuff. 'It is a face disguised—and here's proof of it!' He seizes the black hair and pulls it off. The beard follows. A further comparison can be made with Gaboriau's *Monsieur Lecoq* (1869), where the Count is disguised as a tramp and detained as a suspect, but manages to communicate with his wife by code words.

The opium den described by Charles Dickens in *The Mystery of Edwin Drood* (1870) is the literary prototype for many of those that followed; but the inspiration in this instance came from articles such as 'Ratcliff Highway and the Opium Dens of To-Day', by J. Hall Richardson (*Cassell's Saturday Journal*, 17 Jan. 1891); 'A Night in an Opium Den', by the Author of 'A Dead Man's Diary' [Coulson Kernahan] (*Strand*, July 1891); or 'In a London Opium Den' (*Tit-Bits*, 31 Oct. 1891). The first includes a description of the 'Mahogany Bar' and other dockside haunts of 'wiry Lascars'; the second describes Johnstone's opium den (which was thought to have inspired Dickens), and the third describes a visit to a den near the East India Docks within the sound of the big bell of St Paul's: 'we turn down a dreary side street, at the corners of which are loafing some rather ugly customers of the Lascar type' and reach what appears to be a shop. Within lies the kitchen with a tin pan on a fire of coke and coal in which the opium is prepared; a staircase leads up to a pair of rooms where the customers wander 'through scenes which none but a De Quincey can portray'.

ACD studied the effects of drugs as part of his medical course, and his earliest known letter to the press describes the effect of the drug gelseminum upon himself: 'The system may learn to tolerate gelseminum as it may opium' (*British Medical Journal*, 20 Sept. 1879).

Several sources are suggested for the 'twisted lip': '*L'Homme Qui Rit*' by Victor Hugo (*By Order of the King*, 1870), where the man of the title was disfigured as a child so that his lips were set in a perpetual smile; or Zola's novel *Thérèse Raquin* (1867), where the paintings by Laurent all show the face of the murdered man: 'Each had a slight contraction to the left of the mouth which distorted the lips and made them grimace. This twist, which Laurent remembered seeing in the contorted face of the drowning man, showed that they all belonged to the same horrible family' (Penguin, 1962, tr. by Leonard Tancock). A twisted lip is also found in the description of a man in 'Across Rannoch Moor' (by Charles Batherwick, *Blackwood's Magazine*, Sept. 1891): 'His features were contorted by a curious cicatrix on the cheek, which drew up one corner of his mouth into a permanent grin. The lower eyelid, too, was drawn down and averted' (quoted by Redmond, 55).

123 *Isa*: an American name, or variant of the Jewish name, Iser; perhaps intended here as a contraction for Isaiah or (Douai version) Isaias, as the brother's name is also that of a major Old Testament prophet. In England it is more commonly a shortened form of Isabella—as in 'Isa' Bowman, the child friend of Lewis Carroll.

Elias Whitney: perhaps from Eli Whitney (1765–1825), the American gunsmith who invented gun cotton and made the first muskets with interchangeable parts; or from names found in an article in the *Century Magazine* for Apr. 1891, 'Two Expeditions to Mount St Elias'. The expedition of 1886 planned to use native canoes 'to reach the nearest point off the St Elias range; but we were not compelled to make use of the canoes at all, thanks to the kindness of Mr Whitney, the Secretary of the Navy, who authorised the use of the man-of-war *Pinta* in the Alaskan waters.' The reference is to Charles Collins Whitney (1841–1904), the American financier.

the Theological College of St George's: an invented college, named after St George's Street and the dockland district of St

George's-in-the-East, and perhaps based on the Theological College of St Joseph.

De Quincey's description of his dreams and sensations: *Confessions of an English Opium-Eater* (1822, 1856) by Thomas De Quincey (1785–1859), first published in the *London Magazine* (Sept. and Oct. 1821). The drug is central to the plot of *The Moonstone* (1868), in which a marked copy of 'the far-famed *Confessions of an English Opium Eater*' is offered to Franklin Blake by Mr Candy. ACD refers to De Quincey in an earlier story where an oriental wanderer who had strayed into a Yorkshire village 'reminded me of the description of the opium-eating Malay whom De Quincey saw in the farmhouse in Scotland' ('Uncle Jeremy's Household', *Boy's Own Paper*, Jan.–Feb. 1887).

laudanum: tincture of opium in alcohol, as taken by De Quincey and his contemporaries. Twenty-five drops of laudanum was equivalent to one grain of opium.

124 *James*: Watson's first name was John, as in *A Study in Scarlet*, which is described as 'a reprint from the Reminiscences of John H. Watson, M. D., Late of the Army Medical Department'. James Watson was a Southsea friend of ACD who organized the farewell banquet given in his honour by the Portsmouth Literary and Scientific Society in December 1890. ACD made the same slip when writing to the editor of the *Strand* on 4 Mar. 1908: 'I don't suppose so far as I see that I should write a new "Sherlock Holmes" series but I see no reason why I should not do an occasional scattered story under some such heading as "Reminiscences of Mr Sherlock Holmes (Extracted from the diaries of his friend, Dr James Watson)" ' (Metropolitan Toronto Library MSS). Several ingenious explanations are given to explain why Watson's wife used another name, such as Dorothy Sayers's theory that the middle initial stood for 'Hamish'—the Scottish form of 'James' ('Dr Watson's Christian Name', *Unpopular Opinions*, 1946).

the 'Bar of Gold': perhaps suggested by 'The Wheel of Fortune' in *The Moonstone*, or the Mahogany Bar described in *Cassell's Saturday Journal* (17 Jan. 1891).

Upper Swandam Lane: a fictitious name, perhaps for Trig Lane, near St Paul's Wharf, or suggested by Swan Lane to the west of London Bridge, near Upper Thames Street. 'Dam' is a

Dutch ending which ACD would have encountered during his visit to Holland in August 1891.

125 *slop shop*: a shop selling ready-made clothes (slops) and bedding for sailors. 'Here and there is a slop shop,' says an article in the *Strand* describing the old Ratcliff Highway, 'where many dangling oilskins and sou'westers wave in the breeze, and where, as often as not, an old figure-head or the effigy of a naval officer in the uniform of fifty years ago stands as a sign' ('Jamrach's', May 1891).

gin shop: a wine shop or liquor store. Gin shops were an 18th-century phenomenon—at one time there were 7,044 houses selling gin and a man could get drunk for a penny—but they were suppressed after the Gin Act of 1735.

lack-lustre eye: the contraction of the pupils is one of the first signs of opium use, as ACD noted in his copy of *The Essentials of Materia Medica and Therapeutics* by Alfred Baring Garrod (1819–1907). Jacques refers to a 'lack-lustre' eye in Shakespeare's *As You Like It* (I I. vii):

> And then he drew a dial from his poke,
> And, looking on it with lack-lustre eye,
> Says very wisely, 'It is ten o'clock:
> Thus we may see', quoth he, 'how the world wags:
> 'Tis but an hour ago since it was nine,
> And after one hour more 'twill be eleven;
> And so, from hour to hour, we ripe and ripe,
> And then, from hour to hour, we rot and rot;
> And thereby hangs a tale.'

a small brazier of burning charcoal: also encountered by Dorian Gray when he visits an opium den: 'Some Malays were crouching by a little charcoal stove playing with bone counters and showing their white teeth as they chattered' (Oscar Wilde, *The Picture of Dorian Gray*).

126 *Friday, June 19th*: 19 June 1889 was a Wednesday.

skirt: the lower part of a frock coat.

128 *Lascar*: (Urdu, *Lashkar*) an East Indian sailor. Most opium dens in London were run by Chinese, but the one in New Court, St George's-in-the-East, which Charles Dickens used as a model in *The Mystery of Edwin Drood* (1870), was kept by 'Lascar Sal'.

Paul's Wharf: a complex of buildings below St Paul's Cathedral, between Blackfriars Bridge and Southwark Bridge, leading to St Paul's Pier. 'St Paul's landing' and the neighbouring area were also used as settings for *Beyond the City* (1893, though written July 1891).

The Cedars: a common house name, as in The Cedars, Putney, the home of the author John Strange Winter (i.e. Henrietta Eliza Vaughan Stannard (1856–1911), Mrs Arthur Stannard), and also the name of a house on Belmont Hill, Lee, which suggests that ACD might have known the neighbourhood in which he set part of the story; or perhaps suggested by 'The Elms', the surgery of Dr Reginald Ratcliff Hoare at Gravelly Hill, in Aston, Birmingham, where ACD had worked as an assistant doctor in 1882.

129 *a broad balustraded bridge*: i.e. London Bridge, built 1821–31 by Sir John Rennie, the first Thames crossing until Tower Bridge was opened in 1894. The bridge was dismantled in 1967 and reconstructed at Lake Havasu City in Arizona.

wrack: (rack) a mass of clouds driven before the wind in the upper air.

You have a grand gift of silence, Watson: a phrase taken from Robert Louis Stevenson, to which ACD refers in his article on 'Mr Stevenson's Methods in Fiction': 'Mr Stevenson, like one of his own characters, has an excellent gift of silence' (*National Review*, Jan. 1890).

130 *Cannon Street*: The terminus of the South-Eastern Railway, completed in 1866.

the Capital and Counties Bank: a large clearing bank, with its head offices at 39 Threadneedle Street, which merged with Lloyds Bank in 1918. ACD had his account at the Oxford Street Branch (as did Sherlock Holmes in 'The Priory School' (*Return*)).

Aberdeen Shipping Company: i.e. the Aberdeen Steam Navigation Company which had a wharf in Limehouse, south of the London Docks, and offices at 102 Victoria Street.

Fresno Street: an invented name, perhaps suggested by 'Fresh Wharf' near the Old Swan Pier. Fresno (Spanish, 'ash-tree'), is the name of a river, city, and county, south-east of San Francisco.

131 *her husband looking down at her*: perhaps suggested by the 'Incident at the Window' in Robert Louis Stevenson's *Dr Jekyll and Mr Hyde* (1886) when Mr Utterson and his companion see the doctor at the window and witness a horrible transformation: 'They saw it but for a glimpse, for the window was instantly thrust down; but that glimpse had been sufficient, and they turned and left the court without a word.'

132 *Hugh Boone*: perhaps from Daniel Boone (1734–1820), the American frontiersman whose adventures form part of American folklore; or from 'Boone Street' in Lee, Kent; or from the word, 'boon', which means a request, or the asking of a favour.

a professional beggar: the words used in the title of the article which inspired the story, 'A Day as a Professional Beggar' (*Tit-Bits*, 17 Jan. 1891).

133 *wax vestas*: wax matches (from Vesta, the Roman goddess of the hearth).

Threadneedle Street: the site of the Bank of England.

Mrs St Clair had fainted at the sight of the blood: though she says, 'I am not hysterical, nor given to fainting'.

Inspector Barton: perhaps from *Mary Barton* (1848), the novel by Mrs Gaskell.

three English counties: the parts of London north of the river were formerly in Middlesex and those to south were in Surrey, but London had been constituted as an 'administrative county' by the Local Government Act of 1888. Lee is on the borders of Kent (a mile or so beyond Lewisham, of which it became a part in 1906).

136 *mousseline-de-soie*: 'muslin of silk', a thin silk fabric with a texture like that of muslin. 'Among the new creations is a lilac-hued dress of mousseline-de-soie, festooned *en baldequin*— that is to say, like the valance of a curtain—and edged with white lace' ('Paris Fashions', *Daily Telegraph*, 27 Apr. 1891).

137 *an old campaigner*: perhaps from Oliver Wendell Holmes, who said that men in public life were bound to speak decent English 'unless, indeed, they are rough old campaigners, like General Jackson or General Taylor' (*The Autocrat of the Breakfast Table*, 1858). General Andrew Jackson (1767–1845) won the Battle of New Orleans (1815), conquered Florida, and was President of the USA 1829–37; General Zachary Taylor

(1784–1850) conquered Northern Mexico 1846–7 and was President of the USA 1849–50.

galvanized: stimulated by means of galvanic current, a form of electricity developed by chemical action (from Luigi Galvani, who first described the phenomena in 1792).

138 *Gravesend*: a river port and market town in Kent, twenty-four miles east of London on the south bank of the Thames; the boundary port for the London docks at which customs-house officers and pilots embarked or were put ashore.

One of his hands: this supports John Dickson Carr's contention (quoted in the introductory note to 'A Scandal in Bohemia') that ACD cultivated two styles of handwriting, 'his own famous script, and another, more angular style which he adopted to rest his hand'.

a fly-leaf of a book: a blank page, between the end-papers and the body of a book.

139 *There is so keen a sympathy . . . if evil came upon him*: a theory which interested ACD (and which recurs in 'The Speckled Band', where two twins are supposed to be aware of each other's feelings) based on the experiments of Jean Martin Charcot (1825–93), to which ACD referred after hearing a paper on 'Witches and Witchcraft' at the Portsmouth Literary and Scientific Society on 1 Apr. 1890. He said that 'in Paris recently mesmerism and clairvoyance had been investigated by scientists, showing that in exceptional cases there was apparently a power in the human mind of knowing what was in another's mind and of exercising power over another' (*Portsmouth Times*, 5 Apr. 1890). Mesmerism afterwards provided the plot for *The Parasite* (1894).

140 *a large blue dressing-gown*: the discrepancy over the colour of the dressing-gown, which is described as purple in 'The Blue Carbuncle' and mouse-coloured in 'The Empty House' (*Return*), was discussed by Ronald Knox in the first great work of Sherlockian exegesis, 'Studies in the Literature of Sherlock Holmes' (1912), but one can assume that this one was borrowed from Neville St Clair.

141 *Eastern divan*: a Turkish and Persian word; a bench covered with cushions, or a sofa-bed of cushions, such as the 'divan of Persian saddle-bags' on which Lord Henry Wotton is first

encountered in Oscar Wilde's *The Picture of Dorian Gray*; also used of a smoking-room with comfortable sofas, as in the 'Bohemian Cigar Divan' in the Stevensons' *More New Arabian Nights*.

141 *Charing Cross*: a district on the east side of Trafalgar Square (named after the ancient village of Charing and the cross which Edward I erected in memory of Queen Eleanor).

Gladstone bag: a small leather travelling bag or portmanteau named after William Ewart Gladstone (1809–98).

142 *wheeled sharply . . . Bow Street*: Wellington Street leads directly into Bow Street. Holmes and Watson wheeled right into the inner courtyard of the Bow Street Police Station or into Broad Court, which runs alongside. People on remand would not be held there: 'Considering the important part which that famous police-court has played in fiction for the past century at least, the error was a natural one. As a fact, however, accused persons on remand are sent to one or other of the prisons until the day of their re-examination' (*Tit-Bits*, 19 Feb. 1898).

Bradstreet: Anne Bradstreet (*c*.1612–72) with her husband Simon (1603–97) and father Thomas Dudley (1576–1653) landed with the founding Puritans of the colony of Massachusetts Bay (1630), of which both men later became Governors. Her book *The Tenth Muse* (1650) is the earliest known poetry written by an American white settler; Oliver Wendell Holmes was a descendant of hers. Or the name may derive from Colonel John Bradstreet (1711–74), the British soldier involved in wars against the French and Indians in the American colonies.

frogged jacket: a jacket fastened or ornamented with frogs (spindle-shaped buttons covered with silk or other material which pass through loops on the other side of the garment).

beggarman, Boone: the phrase recalls the rhyme used when counting cherry stones: 'Tinker, Tailor, Soldier, Sailor, Rich man, Poor man, Beggarman, Thief'.

145 *Chesterfield*: a town in Derbyshire, twelve miles south of Sheffield.

the green-room: a common-room near the stage (originally painted or upholstered green) in which actors await their cues.

backed a bill: guaranteed a bill of exchange; stood surety.

146 *dollars*: (slang) crowns (five shilling pieces); but here a general term for small change.

THE BLUE CARBUNCLE

First published in the *Strand Magazine*, 3 (Jan. 1892), 73–85, with 8 illustrations by Sidney Paget; *Strand Magazine*, New York (Feb. 1892); S. S. McClure Newspaper Syndicate, USA, various dates between 9 Jan. and 14 Feb. 1892, with woodcut illustrations. Alternative title: 'The Christmas Goose that Swallowed the Diamond' (*Philadelphia Inquirer*).

Written at 12 Tennison Road, South Norwood, and completed during the last week of Oct. 1891. MS: whereabouts unknown.

The title may have been suggested by Nathaniel Hawthorne's story, 'The Great Carbuncle' (*Twice-Told Tales*, 1851), but the inspiration probably came from one of the following:

(a) 'Strange Recoveries of Lost Jewels' (*Cassell's Saturday Journal*, 25 Apr. 1891), in which the owner of a valuable ring was grouse shooting in Scotland and was on the point of firing when he noticed the stone had disappeared. Having examined the ground without success, he decided to turn out the charge. The diamond 'had slipped into the muzzle when he was loading it and without his observing it; and, but for that lucky thought, five hundred pounds' worth of pure carbon might have been blown into the inside of a bird, and have astonished the cook when she came to prepare it'.

(b) 'Clever Diamond Smuggling' (*Tit-Bits*, 5 Sept. 1891), which tells how a smuggler concealed three diamonds in pieces of meat and then fed them to his dog in order to evade the Customs in New York.

(c) 'Diamond-digging in South Africa' (Henry Knollys, *Blackwood's Magazine*, Sept. 1891): 'A diamond is wrapped in a piece of meat and given to a dog, which is conveyed out of the district and slaughtered, when the stone is removed from the intestines.'

(d) 'A Valley of Gold' (*Tit-Bits*, 17 Oct. 1891), which may be quoted in full: ' "Muddy Creek Valley" is the deceptive name of a place in North Carolina, whence have already come £200,000 of gold, besides rubies, sapphires, beryl, moonstones, jasper, garnets, silver, copper, platinum, lead, iron, mica, and so on—one of Nature's richest laboratories in fact. "They never kill a turkey or a chicken in the valley now," says a correspondent of the New York *Sun*, "without looking in its crop for a possible ruby or diamond." '

T. S. Blakeney noted a further parallel 'when reading *Studies in Social History*, edited by Dr J. H. Plumb. On page 193 one learns that Sir Robert Walpole's steward, John Wrott, used to secrete the rents he collected and sent to his master, inside geese, in order to hoodwink highwaymen, who in those days (early Eighteenth Century) infested the roads from Norfolk to London' (*Sherlock Holmes Journal*, Winter 1959). There is also the legend of St Winwaloe whose sister's eye was plucked out by a goose. He was taught by an angel how to identify the responsible goose and having caught it, cut it open, found the eye in its gizzard shining like a ruby, washed it clean, and put it carefully in his sister's head (where it saw as well as its companion). He forgave the goose, who was sent away alive and cackling for joy.

The Blue Carbuncle may be based on the Hope Diamond, which originated in India. It was sold to Louis XIV and disappeared during the French Revolution. It was then cut down, and reappeared in London—when it was bought by Henry Thomas Hope, the banker. It afterwards passed through several hands before being donated to the Smithsonian Institution in Washington. The deep-blue stone is traditionally associated with a dozen violent deaths and with disasters to two royal houses.

ACD's story also has echoes of fables, fairy tales, and nursery rhymes, such as the goose that laid a golden egg; Little Jack Horner (who 'pulled out a plum and said "What a good boy am I" '); and 'Persevere and Prosper', a story in *The Doyle Fairy Book* (by A. R. Montalba, illustrated by ACD's uncle, Richard Doyle), which concerns 'a carbuncle of inestimable value' lost in the Tigris and restored by the fish.

149 *four million human beings . . . a few square miles*: the Census results had shown that the population of London (on 5 Apr. 1891) was 4,231,431.

150 *commissionaire*: a member of the Corps of Commissionaires, founded by Captain Edward Walter in 1879 to give employment to crippled soldiers from the Crimean campaigns, with the headquarters at Sandringham Mansions in the Strand. By 1891 the Corps consisted of 1,834 men, of whom 1,250 were based in London. They wore uniform and were employed as porters, door-keepers, messengers, drill-instructors, caretakers, attendants in hospitals, and gatekeepers at Exhibitions ('How Old Soldiers are Employed', *Tit-Bits*, 7 Feb. 1891).

billycock: a hard (or soft) round-crowned felt hat or 'bowler'; named after William Coke, for whom it was first designed in 1850.

151 *the initials 'H. B.'*: they were also the initials used by ACD's grandfather, John Doyle (1789–1868), the political cartoonist (two Js making the H, and two Ds the B).

there are some thousands of Bakers . . . in this city of ours: there were 103 Bakers, and seven Henry Bakers listed as householders in the London *Post Office Directory* for 1891, but there were many others who lived in lodgings.

154 *its crop*: or craw, the pouch-like enlargement of the oseophagus or gullet found in poultry where the food is prepared for digestion. According to some experts a crop is not found in either geese or woodcock.

155 *the Countess of Morcar's blue carbuncle:* from Earl Morcar, who joined Hereward 'the Wake' in his stand against William the Conqueror on the Isle of Ely in 1071. Earl Morcar is a character in Charles Kingsley's *Hereward the Wake* (1866). Morcar is also introduced into Lewis Carroll's *Alice's Adventures in Wonderland* (1865):

> 'Ahem!' said the Mouse with an important air. 'Are you all ready? This is the driest thing I know. Silence all round, if you please! "William the Conqueror, whose cause was favoured by the pope, was soon submitted to by the English, who wanted leaders, and had been of late much accustomed to usurpation and conquest. Edwin and Morcar, the earls of Mercia and Northumbria—" '
>
> 'Ugh!' said the Lory, with a shiver.
>
> 'I beg your pardon!' said the Mouse, frowning, but very politely, 'Did you speak?'
>
> 'Not I!' said the Lory, hastily.
>
> 'I thought you did', said the Mouse. 'I proceed. "Edwin and Morcar, the earls of Mercia and Northumbria declared for him . . . " '

A 'carbuncle' (Latin, *carbunculus*, a little coal) is the jeweller's name for a garnet when it is cut *en cabochon* (in a boss form, hollowed out beneath to allow the colour of the stone to be seen).

absolutely unique: a blue carbuncle would be unique, as garnets come in various shades of red, white, yellow, green, brown, purple, and black, but never in blue.

155 *a thousand pounds . . . the market price*: this would be an improbable price for a stone of 12 carats (even if it were unique). The Russian or Orloff Diamond of 194 carats in the Russian Imperial Sceptre was valued in 1891 at £90,000, and the Hope Diamond (which had cost £18,000) was valued at £30,000. The moonstone, in the Wilkie Collins novel of the same name (1868) was said to be worth £20,000.

the Hotel Cosmopolitan: an invented hotel, possibly based on the Metropole near Charing Cross or the Continental in Regent Street. The *Cosmopolitan* was the title of an American magazine (first published in 1886).

John Horner: perhaps from 'Little Jack Horner' in the nursery rhyme, as in *Punch* for 10 Oct. 1891, where the 'International Nursery-Tale Congress' was said to have as its chairman 'Mr John Horner, P.R.I.N.T.C., lineal descendant of the celebrated "Jack" of that ilk'.

referred to the Assizes: Assize Courts are held in the English counties, but a criminal case in London would not be 'referred' to them as the capital is the seat of justice with the Courts of Justice and the Central Criminal Court.

James Ryder: perhaps from Lieutenant Ryder who outlined his plans for an expedition to the east coast of Greenland at the Danish Royal Geographical Society on 31 Mar. 1891.

upper-attendant: the head attendant, or the attendant on duty in the front or upper part of the hotel (rather than 'below stairs'); now known as the 'Duty Manager'.

solder the second bar of the grate: F. O. Louden said in a letter to the *Observer* on 29 July 1934 that he wrote to ACD on this matter; 'I pointed out to him that all grates at that time were cast, and there was no way in which cast iron could be soldered. He very kindly wrote back and said: "You are, of course, quite right." '

156 *the small morocco casket*: a casket covered in morocco-leather (leather made from goatskins, tanned with sumac).

Inspector Bradstreet, B Division: the Metropolitan Police District consisted of twenty-two divisions. 'B' Division covered Knightsbridge, Chelsea, and Fulham, so the Inspector was outside his area, as he was in 'The Man with the Twisted Lip', where he was described as being on duty at Bow Street (in E Division), and as he is again in 'The Engineer's Thumb', where he travels beyond its boundaries.

157 *run down to the advertising agency*: the MS is said to have read 'run down to Willing's Advertising Agency', and rumour has it that early copies of the *Strand* also contained the name. An advertisement for a copy with the name was inserted in the *Publisher's Circular* on 13 Apr. 1935, but there is no record of any such copy ever having been found. James Willing, of 125 the Strand and 162 Piccadilly, was a leading general and newspaper advertising agency who inserted advertisements in the London, provincial, and foreign newspapers.

the Globe . . . Standard, Echo: (the *Strand* has *St James's*; altered to *St James's Gazette* in Newnes, 1892) an almost complete list of the principal London evening papers. The *Globe* (1803–1921); the *Star* (1888–1960); the *Pall Mall Gazette* (1865–1923); the *St James's Gazette* (1880–1905); the *Evening News* (1881–1980); the *Evening Standard* (from 1827); and the *Echo* (1868–1905).

> The latest aspect of the latest boom,
> > The starting price of winners and of wheat,
> The thousand lives lost in a late simoom,
> > A conflagration, or a bursting leat,
> > How gallant gentlemen can stoop to cheat,
> The spicy current gossip of the Bar—
> > Can all be found in this or that news-sheet,
> *Globe, Evening News, Pall Mall, St James's, Star!*

> > > ('A Ballade of Evening Papers', *Punch*, 11 July 1891)

'At four o'clock the evening papers came in,' says Oscar Wilde in 'Lord Arthur Savile's Crime' (1887), 'and Lord Arthur disappeared into the library with the *Pall Mall*, the *St James's*, the *Globe*, and the *Echo*, to the immense indignation of Colonel Goodchild, who . . . for some reason or other had a strong prejudice against the *Evening News*.'

and any others that occur to you: the press guides of the period list three other evening papers: the *Shipping and Mercantile Gazette and Lloyd's List* (1836–1916), the *Public Ledger* (1870–1932), and the *Argus* (founded 1889); the London *Post Office Guide* adds: the *Evening Report*, the *National Press Journal*, *Dornbuschi Floating Cargoes List*, the *Evening Corn Trade List*, the *Eastern Evening News*, and the *Daily Bourse*—but none of these would have been suitable for the advertisement.

157   *the Amoy River in Southern China*: no garnet has ever been found in China and there is no Amoy River. Amoy is a city and seaport on an island of the same name, facing Taiwan (Formosa). It was seized by the British in 1841 and returned after the fulfilment of the terms of the Treaty of Nanking.

a vitriol-throwing: the hurling of concentrated sulphuric acid ('oil of vitriol') or any of its salts at the face as an act of revenge (as later described in 'The Illustrious Client' (*Case-Book*)).

this forty-grain weight: gems are usually weighed in carats and an English carat is 3.163 troy grains, so the weight of the Blue Carbuncle was 12.62 English carats.

crystallized charcoal: diamonds are pure crystallized carbon, but garnets contain no carbon; they are silicates of alumina, magnesia, lime, and iron. The remark may be compared to that made by Godfrey Ablewhite when Gabriel Betteredge is lost in wonder at the sight of the Moonstone: 'Carbon, Betteredge! mere carbon, after all, my good friend!' (Wilkie Collins, *The Moonstone*, 1868).

a purveyor to the gallows and the prison: a 'purveyor' is one who supplies goods or services, and the term was used by high-class emporia such as were 'Purveyors to Their Majesties' or 'to the Royal Household'.

158   *woodcock*: a general term for birds related to snipe.

Scotch bonnet: a round, flat, blue, woollen cap, with a tuft on the top, traditionally made in Ayrshire; Henry Baker's descent from gentility recalls the Scots term 'bonnet laird', denoting a small landowner wearing a bonnet, not the hat of the gentry.

your circulation: the 'circulation of the blood' (which would freeze in Arctic conditions).

159   *disjecta membra*: 'scattered limbs' (or as Stevenson translated it in *The Wrong Box*, 'disjected members'); fragments, scattered remains. A phrase in common usage, first found in Horace, *Satires* (1.4): *Invenias disjecti membra poetae*—'You would still find the limbs of the dismembered poet' (meaning that you can appreciate the greatness of a good poet from a short quotation or a bad translation).

160   *the 'Alpha' Inn near the Museum*: near the British Museum: perhaps the Museum Tavern, at 49 Great Russell Street, on the corner of Museum Street opposite the main gates to the Museum, or the Plough Tavern at 27 Museum Street; and

possibly named after the 'Alpha' Air Horse Collar and Saddlery Company of Charing Cross Road, or the Alpha Cigar Company of Bethnal Green Road. The leading star in the constellation of the Plough is Alpha.

Windigate: perhaps from 'Windygates' station on the North British Railway, near Thornton Junction, in Fife; or a variant of 'Windibank' used in 'A Case of Identity'.

through Wigmore Street: 'across' Wigmore Street, which runs parallel to Oxford Street. The route from Baker Street through the 'Doctors' quarter' (near Harley Street) was familiar to ACD as it was the one he took from his consulting-room in Upper Wimpole Street to his lodgings in Montague Place.

161 *Breckinridge*: perhaps from John Cabell Breckenridge (1821–75), the American Vice-President who stood against Lincoln in the 1860 presidential election.

across Holborn, down Endell Street: more probably across New Oxford Street (a continuation of Holborn), then down Endell Street and into Bow Street.

Covent Garden Market: London's fruit and flower market (until 1973) at which geese could not be purchased. Some birds were available at Smithfield Central Market (the meat market), but most poultry was sold at the Leadenhall Market. It stayed open throughout the Christmas week when some 50,000 geese and turkeys changed hands ('How London is Provided for Christmas', *Tit-Bits*, 26 Dec. 1890).

163 *Mrs Oakshott*: from Oakshott Station, four miles north-west of Leatherhead, in Surrey.

117, Brixton Road: a real address in South London, on the corner of Blackwell Street.

the 'Pink 'Un': the familiar name for the *Sporting Times* (1865–1931), from the pink paper on which it was printed. 'It was more than a mere journal for the sportsman and man about town; it had established itself as a social centre of a highly specialised nature, and its readers constituted a species of home and overseas club, whose bond of fellowship was good humour and good sportsmanship' (J. B. Booth, *Sporting Times. The 'Pink 'Un' World*, 1938).

164 *King of Proosia*: used here of a person remote and powerful, as Robert Louis Stevenson and his wife used the 'Queen of

Portugal' ('Suppose the lady were my friend's wife, suppose she were my fairy godmother, suppose she were the Queen of Portugal; and how should that affect yourself or Mr Jones?'— *More New Arabian Nights*). It could refer to Frederic the Great (1712–86) who made Prussia into a military power, or Frederic William III who was an ally of Great Britain at the Battle of Waterloo; but was perhaps suggested by the 'The King of Prussia' inns (of which there were eight in London). 'Proosia' is the anglicized German pronunciation, as found, for example, in Gilbert and Sullivan's *HMS Pinafore* (1878): 'For he might have been a Roosian, / A French, or Turk, or Proosian, / Or perhaps Itali-an'.

164 *It is my business to know what other people don't know*: an echo, perhaps, of the claim made by the blackmailer Montague Nevitt in Grant Allen's novel *What's Bred in the Bone*: 'It's my business to hear and find out everything' (*Tit-Bits*, 14 Feb. 1891).

165 *a four-wheeler*: the London 'growler', a closed carriage with the driver seated at the front.

John Robinson: a common false name; recalling the popular phrase, 'Before you can say "Jack Robinson" '.

the basket chair: a basket-work or wicker chair.

168 *Maudsley*: perhaps from Henry Maudsley (1835–1918), a specialist in forensic medicine and mental disease at University College, London.

Pentonville: the model prison in the Caledonian Road, built 1840–2.

Kilburn: an area north of Maida Vale in London.

white, with a barred tail: there are no white barred-tail geese, except among the Pink-footed Geese of Greenland and Iceland, where the proportion is one in ten thousand.

170 *I suppose that I am commuting a felony*: a punishment can be commuted by being lessened, but the prerogative belongs to the Crown. Holmes was not commuting a felony, but compounding it by taking a reward while refraining from prosecuting the person who had committed the felony, and thus was guilty of misprision of felony, 'the definition of which, according to Sir James Fitzjames Stephen, K.C.S.I., D.C.L., in his *Digest of the Criminal Law*, being: "Everyone who knows that any other person has committed felony and conceals or

procures the concealment thereof is guilty of misprision of felony" ' (J. D. Howard, 'Sherlock Holmes's Crime', *John O' London's Weekly*, 26 Aug. 1933).

I am saving a soul: 'Saving a soul' recalls the absolution offered by a Roman Catholic priest after confession.

THE SPECKLED BAND

First published in the *Strand Magazine*, 3 (Feb. 1892), 142–57, with 9 illustrations by Sidney Paget; *Strand Magazine*, New York (Mar. 1892); S. S. McClure Newspaper Syndicate, USA, various dates between 13 Feb. and 20 Nov. 1892, with woodcut illustrations. Alternative title: 'The Spotted Band' (*New York World*, 20 Aug. 1905).

Written at 12 Tennison Road, South Norwood, completed by the last week of Oct. 1891.

MS: pp. 15–16 copied by an amanuensis and corrected by ACD; formerly in the collection of the Comte de Suzannet; sold at Sotheby's, London, on 26 Mar. 1934 for £82 (Lot 49); sold by Scribner's Bookstore in 1935 to a Chicago dealer. Present location unknown. In the manuscript Helen Stoner and her sister appeared as Helen and Julia Roylott.

The story may be compared with 'The Murders in the Rue Morgue' (1841), by Edgar Allan Poe, where murder is committed by a gorilla, but the source appears to have been: 'Called on by a Boa Constrictor. A West African Adventure' in *Cassell's Saturday Journal* (14 Feb. 1891): A captain tells how he was dispatched to a remote camp in West Africa where the only house was a tumble-down shanty that had belonged to a Portuguese trader: 'The queerest thing about it, however, was a sort of wooden ventilator above the door of the inner room, which I had made into my bedroom.' On the first evening he is awoken by a creaking sound and on opening his eyes he looks towards the door and sees 'a dark queer-looking thing hanging down through the ventilator above it, which in another moment I saw to be the head of the largest boa constrictor I had ever seen.' He is paralysed with fear as the serpent begins to wriggle into the room, but then the unexpected happens and the flap which covered it comes down, driving a spike through its body. The 'hiss that the old brute set up . . . went through my head like a steam whistle'. Unable to cry out for help, and with the snake made furious by his attempts to kill it, the captain spots 'an old bell that hung from a projecting beam above one of the windows'. The cord had rotted away, but by means of a forked stick he is able to ring it and raise the alarm.

ACD referred to the story as a 'thriller' in a letter to his mother in Oct. 1891 and considered it the best of the series. When asked by Mortimer Menpes which was his favourite, he replied: 'Perhaps the one about the serpent, but I can't for the life of me remember the name of it' ('Conan Doyle at the Front', M[ainly] A[bout] P[eople], 14 July 1900). It was placed first on his list of the twelve best stories: 'There are certainly some few an echo of which has come to me from all parts of the world, and I think this is the final proof of merit of some sort. There is the grim snake story, "The Speckled Band". And that I am sure will be on every list' ('How I Made My List', Strand, June 1927).

A dramatized version of the story by ACD was first given at the Adelphi Theatre in London on 4 June 1910, with H. A. Saintsbury as Sherlock Holmes and Lyn Harding as Dr Grimesby Rylott (sic). The play (originally called 'The Stonor Case') differs from the story in several particulars. The first act is set in Stoke Place at Stoke Moran where an inquest is held into the death of Miss Violet Stonor. In the absence of Professor van Donop, Dr Watson, who had known the girls' mother in India, acts as the main witness. The characters include: Rodgers, a butler; Ali, an Indian servant; and Mrs Staunton, the housekeeper. Enid Stonor says she was awakened on the fateful night by a sound like low music and her sister had screamed out the words 'band' and 'speckled'. Various points are raised, one by Scott Wilson, the fiancé of the deceased, and the verdict is given as death by natural causes.

Two years are then supposed to have elapsed. Miss Enid Stonor makes known her forthcoming engagement and Rylott and Mrs Staunton plot together. The butler is dimissed. The act ends with the Indian servant placing a saucer of milk next to a basket, and then playing on an eastern flute. The next scene is at Baker Street, where Billy tells Watson of the cases in progress. Holmes enters disguised as a gasfitter. A succession of clients pass through, including Mr Milverton, and finally Miss Enid Stonor is announced. Holmes recalls Dr Rylott: 'Fifty-five years of age, killed his khitmutgar in India; once in a madhouse; married money—wife died; distinguished surgeon'. Miss Stonor seeks help and Holmes agrees to go down to Stoke Place. Rylott appears and threatens him, and the scene ends with Watson being asked to take the last train to Stoke Place.

The third act opens in the hall of the 'Stoke Moran Manor House' where Rylott is found to have engaged a new servant, Peters and his daughter, Amelia. Miss Enid Stonor is to be kept in the house. An argument ensues. Peters comes to her aid and is dismissed. The final scene takes place in Enid Stonor's bedroom. Holmes enters through the window, and reveals that he was Peters, and Amelia was Billy. Watson also infenestrates. Holmes examines the room. Then the flap opens and the snake descends. He lashes out and it returns into the neighbouring room. There is a scream and Dr Rylott appears at the door with 'the snake round his head and neck'. The snake is killed and Rylott collapses. 'The brute is dead,' says Watson. 'So is the other,' replies Holmes.

171 *Stoke Moran*: an invented place, perhaps suggested by Stoke D'Abernon House, seven miles west of Epsom, on the River Mole, or from Stoke Poges, the village whose churchyard was made famous by the 'Elegy' and the grave of the poet Thomas Gray (1716–71); or from Stoke Road and Stoke Lake in the Gosport district of Portsmouth.

Dr Grimesby Roylott: the first name perhaps suggested by Grimesthorpe in Sheffield (where ACD worked as a locum in the late 1870s) or by Grimsby, the largest British fishing port whose ancient name was Grimesbi. The surname is taken from a Leicestershire bowler, Arnold Rylott on ACD's own admission: 'I am afraid even my villains have a taint of cricket, and when I think of Dr Grimesby Rylott I feel I owe an apology to that excellent bowler' (speech at the Stoll Convention Dinner, 27 Sept. 1921).

173 *a dog-cart*: a two-wheeled open vehicle, with two transverse seats back to back, so called from the rear foot rest which could be raised to serve as a box for sporting dogs.

Leatherhead: a small town on the River Mole, four miles south-west of Epsom and eighteen miles south-west of London, on the London and South Western, and the London, Brighton, and South Coast Railways.

Mrs Farintosh: perhaps from Lord Farintosh, in *The Newcomes* (1854–5) and other works by W. M. Thackeray (1811–63).

174 *My name is Helen Stoner . . . one of the oldest Saxon families in England*: ACD was perhaps thinking of Stonor Park, near Henley-on-Thames, the home of the Stonor family since the

363

twelfth century, and of the Hon. Julia Stonor, the sister of Lord Camoys, who was married to the Marquis d'Hautpoul on 18 July 1891 (*Morning Post*, 20 July 1891). 'Stonor' is the spelling used in the play of 1910 where Helen Stoner becomes Enid Stonor (and her sister Julia is renamed Violet Stonor).

175 *Bengal Artillery*: the Bengal Artillery of the East India Company, comprising Horse, Foot, and Native Artillery, was merged with the Royal Artillery after the Indian Mutiny of 1857.

a railway accident near Crewe: a town in Cheshire and a major railway junction of the London and North Western Railway. There was a collision at Crewe on 30 Sept. 1882 when many people were injured, but ACD may have been thinking of the accident at Norwood Junction on 1 May 1891 when the Portland Bridge collapsed, wrecking an express train. In *The Stark Munro Letters* (1895) the hero was 'involved in the fatal railroad accident at Sittingfleet, where the express ran into a freight train which was standing in the depot'.

176 *wandering away with them sometimes for weeks on end*: perhaps in emulation of George Borrow (1803–81), the student of gypsy life and author of *Lavengro* (1851) and *The Romany Rye* (1857). ACD was an admirer of Borrow, as revealed in 'Borrowed Scenes' (*Danger! and Other Stories*), and his occasional use of unjust suspicion of gypsies as an incidental theme reflects it.

Indian animals: cheetahs are indigenous to India, but baboons would only be found in Africa or Arabia. In the play of 1910 Dr Rylott has a boar hound and a dog, Shiva.

correspondent: an agent, in another country, who transacts business on one's behalf.

Miss Honoria Westphail: perhaps from Westphalia in Germany, and from Honorius who ruled over the Western Roman Empire (395–423).

Harrow: Harrow on the Hill, an urban district, ten miles north-west of London (the site of the famous public school).

a half-pay Major of Marines: a soldier on a warship, placed on 'half pay' when not on active service. The 'Royal Marine Forces' consisted of artillery and light infantry, and in 1882 officers were given equal rank to those in the army and navy.

178 *revolved slowly upon its hinges*: or 'turned'. The old usage was rendered obsolete after the invention of a true 'revolving door'.

179 *what the county coroner asked me at the inquiry*: coroners for every county were first appointed in 1275. They are chosen for life and their duty is to inquire into the cause of unnatural death upon view of the body at an inquest. In the play of 1910, the coroner is called Mr Longbrace.

180 *His name is Armitage*: a common surname; also the name of a railway station, five miles north-west of Lichfield, on the main line to Crewe, which ACD passed when visiting his mother. In the play, Armitage is the name of the village grocer, while the fiancé is called Lieutenant Curtis.

Crane Water, near Reading: i.e. Virginia Water, the large artificial lake south of Windsor Great Park on the Surrey and Berkshire border; suggested by the Crane river which flows into the Thames at Isleworth.

the Crown Inn: perhaps based on the Plough Inn, near Stoke D'Abernon.

182 *high gaiters*: coverings of cloth or leather for the lower leg (as opposed to 'half gaiters', or 'spats', which cover the ankle); a form of dress favoured by farmers and country landowners.

bile-shot eyes: (from 'bloodshot') used in a figurative sense: 'angry', 'peevish'.

183 *jack-in-office*: an overbearing or self-important official. 'Jacks-in-Office' was the title of a letter to the *Daily Telegraph* on 8 Apr. 1891.

he picked up the steel poker . . . straightened it out again: considerable strength is required to bend a steel poker and even more is needed to bend it back. It is impossible to return it to its original condition and for this reason the incident, which was included in the script of the 1910 play, had to be omitted in performance as no suitable prop could be found.

184 *Doctors' Commons*: an anachronism, as the building near St Paul's Churchyard had been demolished in 1867, and the Wills had been transferred to Somerset House. The name was derived from the common table or dining-hall used by Doctors of Civil Law and was then used for the building. Charles Dickens said it was 'familiar by name to everybody, as the

place where they grant marriage-licenses to love-sick couples, and divorces to unfaithful ones; register the Wills of people who have any property to leave, and punish hasty gentlemen who call ladies by unpleasant names' ('Doctors' Commons', *Sketches by Boz*, 1836). ACD probably took the name from *The Moonstone* (1868) where Lady Verinder's Will is examined at Doctors' Commons; Wilkie Collins adds in parenthesis: 'I shall perhaps do well if I explain in this place, for the benefit of the few people who don't know it already, that the law allows all Wills to be examined at Doctors' Commons by anybody who applies, on the payment of a shilling fee.'

184 *the fall in agricultural prices*: there was an agricultural depression between 1877 and 1879 as a result of bad seasons and foreign imports, and this forced landlords to reduce or remit rents.

An Eley's No. 2: the Webley No. 2 is what was intended. ACD confused the revolver with the cartridges for reasons which Major Hugh Pollard explained in the notes to the catalogue of the Sherlock Holmes Exhibition of 1951: 'The Eley cartridges of the time were sold in boxes labelled to say which weapons they fitted; and "Eley No. 2" is probably a confusion arising out of a box marked in large letters "Eley" and, in smaller letters, "For the Webley Pistol No. 2". Moreover, some Webley pistols were marketed with "Eley .320" on the barrel to prevent confusion with the Smith and Wesson .32.'

a trap: a small two-wheeled spring carriage, a gig, or spring cart.

187 *Wilton carpet*: a type of Brussels carpet with loops cut open into thick pile, named after the town in Wiltshire where it is made.

188 *a camp bed*: a folding or collapsible wooden bed, used in the field, but of greater bulk than its modern equivalent.

190 *the hasp*: the fastening, or catch.

192 *Palmer and Pritchard*: two notorious poisoners. Dr William Palmer (1824–56), of Rugeley, was tried at the Old Bailey in May 1856 for the murder of John Parsons Cook and was hanged outside Stafford Gaol on 14 June 1856; Dr Edward William Pritchard (1825–65), of Glasgow, was tried in Edinburgh in July 1865 for the murder of his wife and mother-in-law and was hanged in Glasgow. Palmer qualified as a doctor at St Bartholomew's Hospital, London. Both he and Pritchard were Members of the Royal College of Surgeons.

193 *unrepaired breaches gaped in the old park wall*: ACD, like Watson, had perhaps forgotten the strange pets which roamed free in the grounds.

194 *a dark lantern*: or 'bull's-eye lantern', with a metal shutter that could be turned to cover the light.

195 *a swamp adder*: an invented name (as in 'swamp deer', 'swamp quail', or 'swamp rabbits'). The cobra (*Naja Naja*) is the snake which it most closely resembles (rather than the boa constrictor, which is not venomous). The cobra has black and white 'spectacle marks' and is one of the most deadly of the Indian *Thanatophidia* with a neurotoxic or fast-working venom which will often 'prove fatal in a few minutes' (*Encyclopaedia Britannica*). It is also a good climber and is used by Indian snake charmers. The puff adder from Africa, Russell's viper (described by the *Encylopaedia Britannica* as 'one of the most poisonous snakes in India'), and the Saw-scaled viper also bear a resemblance to the 'swamp adder', but they have 'haemotoxic' or slow-working venom. Snakes do not drink milk from choice (though they may do so when no water is available). They are deaf (though they respond to vibration); and they could not be kept in a safe without posing a risk to the handler.

196 *Violence does . . . digs for another*: an allusion to Ecclesiastes 1: 2: 'He that diggeth a pit shall fall into it; and whoso breaketh an hedge, a serpent shall bite him.'

THE ENGINEER'S THUMB

First published in the *Strand Magazine*, 3 (Mar. 1892), 276–88, with 8 illustrations by Sidney Paget; *Strand Magazine*, New York (Apr. 1892); S. S. McClure Newspaper Syndicate, USA, various dates between 3 and 30 Apr. 1892. Alternative title: 'A Strange Adventure' (*Baltimore Weekly Sun*).

Written at 12 Tennison Road, South Norwood, and completed by 11 Nov. 1891. MS: whereabouts unknown.

The title may have been suggested by 'The Man with a Thumb', by W.C. Hudson (serialized in *Cassell's Saturday Journal* on and after 27 Sept. 1890), or by the case which inspired it ('a jewel thief, who was well connected and went to extraordinary pains to effect the robbery, was ultimately apprehended because of his singular crooked thumb', *ibid.*, 8 Nov. 1890).

The story has points in common with *The Doings of Raffles Haw* (written in Jan. 1891) where clay is converted into gold, and further inspiration could have come from 'In the Engine Room' (*Tit-Bits*, 12 Sept. 1891) in which a young American physician witnesses an attempt on the life of an assistant engineer. The shaft of the ship in which they are travelling has become unsound and the assistant engineer is ordered into the heart of the engine. When he is directly below the crank, the second engineer sets the engine in motion, and he is only saved by the prompt action of the young doctor. The second engineer then goes below after the boilers have been put out, and a list by cargo or tide 'moved the machinery a half turn and crushed him'.

ACD may also have had in mind a case tried at the Central Criminal Court in Apr. 1891, when Charles Croft, alias Draker, alias Gibbs, together with his lover Sarah Collins and a woman named Worms, was indicted for 'possessing moulds and patterns for coining, and possessing counterfeit coin, well-knowing the same to be counterfeit' ('A Coiner Sentenced', *Daily Telegraph*, 8 Apr. 1891), and its sequel when Frederick Williams and Sarah Bishop were charged with counterfeiting at Lambeth Police Court on 16 Oct. 1891 ('Capture of a Coiner at Peckham', *Daily Telegraph*, 17 Oct. 1891).

There are echoes of the 'Waterloo Bridge Mystery' of Oct. 1857, when a bag containing severed limbs was found on a ledge; of 'A Terribly Strange Bed', by Wilkie Collins (*Household Words*, Feb. 1852; *After Dark*, 1856) in which the top of a four-poster bed descends to crush the drugged occupant; and of 'A Pair of Ears' (*Cornhill Magazine*, Aug. 1891), a source for 'The Cardboard Box' (*Memoirs*), in which ears are severed by the Mafia. The severed thumb also recalls 'The Story of Little Suck-a-Thumb' in *Struwwel-peter* (1845) by Dr Heinrich Hoffman:

> The door flew open, in he ran,
> The great, long, red-legg'd scissor-man.
> Oh! children, see! the tailor's come
> And caught out little Suck-a-Thumb.
> Snip! Snap! Snip! The scissors go;
> And Conrad cries out—Oh! Oh! Oh!
> Snip! Snap! Snip! They go so fast,
> That both his thumbs are off at last.

For Victor Hatherley, ACD may have drawn on what he learned of the profession and its skills from William Kinnimond Burton

(1856–99), the son of John Hill Burton and a close friend from Edinburgh (to whom he dedicated the *The Firm of Girdlestone* in 1890). Burton was apprenticed for five years (1873–8) to Brown Brothers & Co., hydraulic and mechanical engineers at the Rosebank Ironworks, after which he became their chief draughtsman.

Robert Louis Stevenson described to ACD the effect which the story had on a native of Samoa:

> I am reposing after a somewhat severe experience upon which I think it my duty to report to you. Immediately after dinner this evening it occurred to me to re-narrate to my native overseer Simele your story of 'The Engineer's Thumb'. And, sir, I have done it. It was necessary, I need hardly say, to go somewhat farther afield than you have done. To explain (for instance) what a railway is, what a steam hammer, what a coach and horse, what coining, what a criminal, and what the police. I pass over other and no less necessary explanations. But I did actually succeed; and if you could have seen the drawn, anxious features and the bright, feverish eyes of Simele, you would have (for the moment at least) tasted glory. You might perhaps think that, were you to come to Samoa, you might be introduced as the Author of 'The Engineer's Thumb'. Disabuse yourself. They do not know what it is to make up a story. 'The Engineer's Thumb' (God forgive me) was narrated as a piece of actual factual history. (*The Letters of Robert Louis Stevenson*, 1899; Vailima, 23 Aug. 1892).

198   *Colonel Warburton's madness*: perhaps named after William Warburton (1698–1779), the editor of Shakespeare and Pope; or Colonel William Pleace Warburton, who received his MD with ACD in 1885 and served as Superintendent of the Edinburgh Royal Infirmary.

     en bloc: 'in a block', the whole lot together.

199   *heather tweed*: a fabric of mixed hues supposed to resemble heather.

     Mr Victor Hatherley: the surname is used for a farm in 'The Boscombe Valley Mystery', but could here perhaps come from Lord Hatherley (William Page Wood, 1801–81), Lord Chancellor 1868–72 in Gladstone's first Administration and recently remembered in the news when his niece Katharine O'Shea (1845–1921) married Charles Stewart Parnell (1846–91) some months before his death on 6 Oct. 1891 following the famous divorce action *O'Shea* v. *O'Shea and Parnell* (1890), which split the Home Rule-Liberal alliance and the Parnell movement.

199 *16a Victoria Street (3rd floor)*: 16 Victoria Street is a real address. In 1891 seven of the nineteen offices within the building belonged to civil engineers, such as Mather and Platt, 'mechanical, hydraulic and electrical engineers'.

201 *carbolized bandages*: dressings impregnated with carbolic acid which served as an antiseptic.

202 *the agony column of The Times*: the personal column; so called from the advertisements for missing relatives or friends which gave evidence of distress. It is the subject of *The Agony Column* by Alice Clay (1881), and of an article in *Tit-Bits* (10 Oct. 1891), 'Twenty Years "Agony" Advertising'.

his before-breakfast pipe . . . corner of the mantelpiece: 'plugs' are pieces of tobacco pressed into a cake or stick; 'dottles' are the parts that remain after a pipe has been smoked. The same habit is ascribed to Dr Horton in *The Stark Munro Letters* (1895): 'He is the most abandoned smoker I have met with, collecting the dottles of his pipes in the evening, and smoking them the next morning before breakfast in the stable yard.'

Venner & Matheson . . . Greenwich: an invented name. Venner & Co. were electrical engineers in Old Queen Street, Westminster; Matheson and Grant were civil engineers in Walbrook; but ACD probably took the names from *Elsie Venner* (1861), the novel by Oliver Wendell Holmes, and from Robert Matheson, the Surveyor for Scotland at the Scottish Office of Works in Edinburgh where his father was employed as an assistant clerk.

from nine in the morning until four in the afternoon: ACD had similar experiences: 'Every morning I walked from the lodgings at Montague Place, reached my consulting room at ten and sat there until three or four, with never a ring to disturb my serenity' (*Memories and Adventures*).

203 *Colonel Lysander Stark*: the first name perhaps from Dr Lysander Maybury, who was elected to the Portsmouth Literary and Scientific Society on 20 Nov. 1888, or from Dr Lysander Munro, a police surgeon in Southsea; the second from

Arthur Cowell Stark, a medical graduate of Edinburgh University.

204 *Eyford, in Berkshire*: i.e. Twyford, a village four and a half miles north-east of Reading; named after the village of Eyford, near Stow-in-the-Wold, in Gloucestershire.

205 *a shakedown*: a makeshift, or improvised bed.

fuller's earth: hydrous silicate of alumina. A clay found at Nutfield near Redhill in Surrey and at Bala in North Wales. It was used by fullers to clean and thicken cloth by absorbing the grease and oil, and by others to filter mineral and vegetable oils for soap-making. The clay is mined or dug from the surface, and either dried naturally or ground into a slurry and dried in pans.

207 *At Reading . . . my station*: one belonged to the Great Western Railway on the direct line from Paddington; the other to the side of it belonged to the South-Eastern Railway.

210 *a monomaniac*: a person having an obsession with, or being irrational about, one subject.

a chinchilla beard: a grey beard, resembling the soft tufted fur of the South American rodent, but perhaps suggested by the 'chin-beard' favoured by Americans.

216 *Mr Jeremiah Hayling*: perhaps from Jeremiah Hawkins, ACD's father-in-law, and Hayling Island, near Portsmouth.

ordnance map of the county: an Ordnance Survey map on a scale of one inch to a mile; part of the official survey of Great Britain and Ireland started in 1791 under the direction of the Master-General of Ordnance.

217 *boxed the compass*: 'covered all points': a nautical expression (to name the thirty-two points of a compass in the correct order). A wind is said to 'box the compass' when it blows from every quarter in rapid succession.

the amalgam which has taken the place of silver: correctly, 'the alloy'. An amalgam is a mixture of solid metal with mercury and the 'large masses of nickel and tin' found in the out-house would not be suitable components.

218 *is Dr Becher a German*: perhaps named after Dr Johann Joachim Becher (1635–82), who held the chair of medicine at Mainz and superintended the chemical laboratory in Munich.

THE NOBLE BACHELOR

First published in the *Strand Magazine*, 3 (Apr. 1892), 386–99, with 8 illustrations by Sidney Paget; *Strand Magazine*, New York (May 1892); S. S. McClure Newspaper Syndicate, USA, various dates between 12 Mar. and 29 May 1892, with woodcut illustrations. Alternative titles: 'The Story of the Missing Bride' (*Philadelphia Inquirer*); 'The Adventures of a Nobleman' (*St Louis Post-Dispatch*); 'Adventures of a Noble Bachelor' (*Atlanta Constitution*). Incorrectly numbered 'IX' in the early printings.

Written at 12 Tennison Road, South Norwood, and completed by 11 Nov. 1891. MS: whereabouts unknown.

A possible source is *The Trumpet Call*, by G. R. Sims and Robert Buchanan, which was first produced at the Adelphi Theatre in London, on 1 Aug. 1891: Cuthbertson, a young gentleman marries a second time in the belief that his first wife is dead. He is then confronted by her and deserts the second, who, under the impression that she is not legally married, agrees to marry the villain. The wedding is about to take place in the Chapel Royal, Savoy, when Cuthbertson's first wife reveals that her marriage to him was bigamous. He rushes into the hands of his second wife, to whom he is legally married, and all is happiness. The theme was also used in earlier plays by G. R. Sims, such as *The Lights o' London* (1881), which was revived at the Olympic Theatre on 9 Feb. 1891, and *In the Ranks* (1883) and *Harbour Lights* (1885), which were written in collaboration with H. Pettitt.

The theme of the returning first spouse is very old and is found, for example, in Tennyson's 'Enoch Arden' (1864).

Marriages between American heiresses and impoverished members of the English aristocracy were a phenomenon of the age. Oscar Wilde ends 'The Canterville Ghost' by saying that the heroine 'received the coronet, which is the reward of all good little American girls ...', and in *The Picture of Dorian Gray* he has a conversation between Lord Henry Wotton and his uncle about the marriage of Lord Henry's elder brother, the Duke of Dartmoor:

'Who are her people?' grumbled the old gentleman. 'Has she got any?'

Lord Henry shook his head. 'American girls are as clever in concealing their parents as English women are at concealing their past', he said, rising to go.

'They are pork-packers, I suppose?'

'I hope so, Uncle George, for Dartmoor's sake. I am told that pork-packing is the most lucrative profession in America, after politics.'

'Is she pretty?'

'She behaves as if she was beautiful. Most American women do. It is the secret of their charm.'

'Why can't these American women stay in their own country? They are always telling us that it is the Paradise for women.'

'It is. That is the reason why, like Eve, they are so excessively anxious to get out of it . . .'

ACD came to have a low opinion of 'The Noble Bachelor'. When John Gore, in his column in the *Sphere* for 6 Nov. 1926, drew an unfavourable comparison between the later stories and the earlier ones, and singled out 'The Noble Bachelor' for praise, he replied that if he were to name the six best Holmes stories, two of the most recent, 'The Illustrious Client' and 'The Lion's Mane' would be among them, while 'The Noble Bachelor' would be 'about bottom of the list' (*Sphere*, 27 Nov. 1926).

221 *Lord St Simon*: perhaps from the Duc de Saint-Simon (1675–1755), whose *Memoirs* (1788) served as a source for *The Refugees* (1893). The eldest son of a Duke is by courtesy styled Marquis, while the younger son is styled Lord with the addition of his Christian name. Therefore, as the second son of the Duke of Balmoral, the noble bachelor should have been called Lord Robert St Simon. The solecism was noted by Andrew Lang, who also drew attention to Lord Robert St Simon's error in referring to Mrs Moulton as 'Lady St Simon' ('The Novels of Sir Arthur Conan Doyle', *Quarterly Review*, July 1904).

this four-year-old drama: ACD may have had in mind the marriage of Lilian Price Hammersley, the widow of a New York merchant, and George Charles Spencer Churchill, 8th Duke of Marlborough, which took place on 29 June 1888 and was widely seen as a trade of money for title.

the jezail bullet . . . my Afghan campaign: the jezail is an East Indian or Persian name for the heavy Afghan musket (based on the Lee Enfield Rifle). In *A Study in Scarlet* Watson says that he served at the Battle of Maiwand (in June 1880): 'There I was struck on the shoulder by a Jezail bullet, which shattered the bone and grazed the subclavian artery'. But in *The Sign of the Four* he sat nursing a 'wounded leg': 'I had a Jezail bullet

through it some time before, and though it did not prevent
me from walking, it ached wearily at every change of the
weather.'

221 *a tide-waiter*: a customs' officer who boarded overseas vessels
arriving in the Thames. The men were housed in a hulk
moored in Gravesend Reach (known as the 'tide-waiters'
depot') and were transferred to the incoming vessels, singly or
in pairs, by the quarantine examiner's boat. The practice was
discontinued in 1892.

222 *Lord Backwater*: an invented name, perhaps from the hamlet, north-west of Forfar, or from the Blackwater river in
Southern Ireland, near the Lismore property of ACD's maternal
relations.

ROBERT ST SIMON: this appeared as 'St Simon' in the *Strand*,
and was altered to 'Robert St Simon' in the first edition.

223 *Grosvenor Mansions*: there was a building with this name in
Victoria Street, but ACD had in mind grander addresses,
such as Grosvenor Square or Grosvenor Street (named after
the Grosvenor family, whose Hugh Lupus (1825–99) had
recently become Duke of Westminster).

a red-covered volume: the inclusion of the Arms suggests that it
was Debrett's *Illustrated Peerage* (started in 1863), or the *Red Book:
or Court and Fashionable Register* (published annually from 1849).

Robert Walsingham de Vere St Simon . . . Duke of Balmoral: 'Robert'
was the first name of Robert Arthur Talbot Gascoyne-Cecil,
third Marquess of Salisbury (1830–1903), whose second Administration was nearing its end (1886–92); 'Walsingham'
perhaps from Sir Francis Walsingham (?1539–90), the Elizabe-
than statesman; and 'De Vere' from Tennyson's 'Lady Clara
Vere de Vere' (1833), at least four passages of which have
relevance to the story:

> A simple maiden in her flower
> Is worth a hundred coats-of-arms . . .

> Her manners had not that repose
> Which stamps the caste of Vere de Vere . . .

> From yon blue heavens above us bent,
> The gardener Adam and his wife
> Smile at the claims of long descent . . .

> Kind hearts are more than coronets,
> And simple faith than Norman blood.

Balmoral is the name of a royal residence in west Aberdeen-shire, purchased by the Prince Consort in 1852.

Arms . . . a fess sable: ie., a blue ground, three calthrops (iron balls with four spikes) in blue on a fesse (black cross band). An heraldic solecism as colour should never be charged on colour. The heraldry here and in *The White Company* (1891) was imperfect. 'Everywhere *The White Company* encounters heraldry, and everywhere it is woefully wrong and topsy-turvy heraldry' (*Ancestor*, Oct. 1902).

Secretary for Foreign Affairs: the Secretary of State with respons-ibility for Foreign Affairs; the Foreign Secretary (a post held in 1891 by the Prime Minister, the Marquis of Salisbury).

They inherit Plantagenet . . . the distaff side: the only ducal family who could claim such descent were the Dukes of Beaufort. ACD was distantly related to the Percy family of Northum-berland: 'By this alliance we all connect up (and I have every generation by name, as marked out by my dear mother) with that illustrious line up to three marriages with the Plantaga-nets. One has, therefore, some strange strains in one's blood which are noble in origin and, one can but hope, are noble in tendency' (*Memories and Adventures*).

the Grosvenor Square furniture van: an association of ideas with Grosvenor Mansions or perhaps with the Grosvenor Hotel in Portsmouth at which a farewell banquet was held in ACD's honour on 12 Dec. 1890. The 'furniture van' may have been suggested by one of the two furniture vans which ACD had used to move his furniture from Bush Villa in Dec. 1890 and to South Norwood in June 1891, or by an anecdote from a German magazine reprinted in *Tit-Bits*. A man had forgotten to order a removal van, so he offered the contents of his house to a money-lender in return for a loan of three thousand marks at a rate of a third of one per cent per day. The money-lender then removed the furniture. The following day he was asked to return it to a different address and the full sum was returned, with ten marks to cover the interest ('The Furniture Van', *Tit-Bits*, 29 Nov. 1890).

223 *the Morning Post*: the main society newspaper (founded in 1772 and merged with the *Daily Telegraph* in 1937). 'One evening, in

the lantern-lit garden of a great London house, the young lord would listen to the American heiress's chatter and let himself get carried away. And the little American, who seemed such a child, saw that the thing was sealed as quickly as it was agreed with the obligatory announcement in the very next edition of the *Morning Post*' (MacColl and Wallace, *To Marry an English Lord*, 1989).

223 *A marriage has been arranged*: this was the form adopted by the *Morning Post*; for example: 'A marriage has been arranged to take place next month between the Earl of Westmorland and Lady Sybil St Clair-Erskine, second daughter of the late Earl of Rosslyn and Blanche, Countess of Rosslyn' (*Morning Post*, 7 Oct. 1891).

Hatty Doran: Hattie is the shortened form of Harriet, but it was probably suggested by Hetty Merton, the girl whom Dorian Gray left uncorrupted in *The Picture of Dorian Gray*.

224 *the management . . . across the Atlantic*: a constant refrain in the newspapers since the wedding of Jennie Jerome and Lord Randolph Churchill in Apr. 1874. There had been thirty such marriages by 1891, including that of Mary Burrows and Somerset Frederick Gough-Calthorpe, later Eighth Baron Calthorpe, in July 1891.

the little god's arrows: i.e. Cupid's darts.

Westbury House festivities: perhaps named after Westbury in Wiltshire (or from the first, second, or third Baron Westbury, whose title derived from it). The 'festivities' were inspired by glittering functions such as the Grosvenor House Ball given by the Duke of Westminster on 17 July 1890.

Birchmoor: an invented name, based on places such as Birchfield in Staffordshire, or Birchwood in Derbyshire.

a republican lady: 'republican' is capitalized in all other editions; it refers, of course, not to the Republican party but to the non-monarchical status of the USA.

another note . . . an absolutely quiet one: perhaps suggested by the note published in the *Morning Post*, 12 Oct. 1891: 'The marriage arranged between Mr Crawshay Bailey and Miss Edith Bacon, to take place the first week in November, will be a quiet one, owing to serious illness in the family.'

St George's, Hanover Square: St George's Church (1724), built by John James; the church of choice for society weddings. It was here that Jeannie Chamberlain, the original Self-Made Girl, married Captain Herbert Naylor Leyland in 1889. Benjamin Disraeli was married there, as was George Eliot ('A Few Interesting Records from the Marriage Registers of St George's, Hanover Square', *Tit-Bits*, 29 Nov. 1890).

Lancaster Gate: a fashionable area to the north of Hyde Park, abutting the Bayswater Road. It was developed in the 1860s and took its name from the Lancaster Gate of 1857 which is on the north side of Kensington Gardens.

Petersfield: a market town, nineteen miles north-east of Portsmouth, on the main railway line to London.

225 *Lady Alicia Whittington*: perhaps from Whittington in Derbyshire, or from 'Dick Whittington' (Sir Richard Whittington, *fl.*1400), the Lord Mayor of London.

226 *Millar*: Scots form of the name 'Miller'.

a danseuse: dancer; or here, 'a chorus girl'.

the Allegro: an invented theatre or music-hall; an Italian musical term meaning 'lively' or 'gay'; perhaps based on the Gaiety Theatre, which was the haunt of 'stage door Johnnies'.

227 *The King of Scandinavia*: Oscar II (1829–1907), who came to the throne in 1872.

228 *the public prints*: the newspapers, the press.

the Pacific Slope: the area in the United States of America between the Rocky Mountains and the Pacific Ocean.

a tomboy: a romping girl, a hoyden.

229 *a fait accompli*: 'a thing accomplished'; an unalterable, irreversible fact.

230 *jumping a claim*: (American slang) later explained as 'taking possession of that which another person has prior claim to'. Originally used of attempts to oust squatters or settlers on the virgin territories in the western states of America who had a first claim by law and custom, and later used of claims in the goldfields.

233 *Circumstantial evidence . . . a trout in the milk . . . example*: i.e. evidence that the milkman has been watering down the milk.

The phrase is from the *Journal* of Henry David Thoreau (1817–62), the American naturalist and author of *Walden* (1854): 'Some circumstantial evidence is very strong, as when you find a trout in the milk' (11 Nov. 1854). It was quoted by Ralph Waldo Emerson (1803–82) in an extended version of the address given at Thoreau's funeral which was first published in the *Atlantic Monthly* for Aug. 1862 (collected in *Miscellanies* (1862) and *Lectures and Biographical Sketches* (1883)). ACD re-read 'The Noble Bachelor' in Jan. 1927 when drawing up a list of the twelve best Sherlock Holmes stories, and repeated the aphorism in 'The Riddle of Houdini' (*Strand*, Aug. 1927; *The Edge of the Unknown*, 1930), where he claimed that Houdini was the 'greatest physical medium of modern times'; 'I do not see how it can ever be finally and definitely proved, but circumstantial evidence may be very strong, as Thoreau said when he found a trout in the milk jug.'

233 *the year after the Franco-Prussian War*: 1872 (the war ended on 28 Jan. 1871 and a Peace Treaty was signed in May 1871).

the Serpentine: a large ornamental lake in Hyde Park, dating from 1730, a short distance from Lancaster Gate, so named from its shape.

234 *the basin of the Trafalgar Square fountain*: one of two shallow granite fountains (dating from 1845).

236 *Having laid out . . . Arabian Nights*: the incident was suggested by the 'Narrative of the Spirited Old Lady' in the Stevensons' *More New Arabian Nights*, which describes a large van arriving outside the shuttered house which has been let to Colonel Geraldine. The door was immediately opened by one of the men. 'His companions—I counted seven of them in all—proceeded, with disciplined activity, to take from the van and carry into the house a variety of hampers, bottle-baskets, and boxes, such as are designed for plate and napery. The windows of the dining room were thrown open as though to air it, and I saw some of those within laying the table for a meal.' The men then disappear 'as though the whole affair had been a vision'.

237 *Mr and Mrs Francis Hay Moulton*: perhaps from the American poet, Louise Chandler Moulton (1835–1908), and from ACD's brother, John Francis Innes Hay Doyle (1873–1919); or from Francis Moulton who acted as a go-between for the Revd Henry Ward Beecher (1813–87) during the scandal over his

378

alleged relationship with Mrs Theodore Tilton in the early 1870s.

238 *McQuire's camp*: 'McQuire' was an incorrect spelling, favoured by ACD, of the Irish name Maguire or McGuire (or as the Stevensons rendered it in *More New Arabian Nights*, M'Guire).

'Frisco: the colloquial American shortening of San Francisco.

Montana . . . Arizona . . . New Mexico: Montana, extreme north-west point of Louisiana purchase (1803), was organized as a Territory in 1864, and admitted as a state in 1889. Arizona and New Mexico were acquired in 1848 by war against Mexico, and established as New Mexico Territory in 1850 becoming Arizona Territory and New Mexico Territory in 1863; but they were not admitted to the Union as states until 1912.

239 *Apache Indians*: a powerful and warlike tribe, which ranged over Arizona and New Mexico, and whose final surrender came in 1886.

Should I stop the service and make a scene in the church: legal opinion suggests that she should have done so, as she otherwise laid herself open to a charge of bigamy (under the Offences against the Person Act, 1861) by marrying another man while aware that her husband was alive. The priest asks the congregation and the bride and groom if they know of any just cause or impediment why they may not be lawfully joined together.

240 *Gordon Square*: in Bloomsbury, behind University College, a short distance from Montague Place where ACD had lodgings. The square was started by Thomas Cubitt in the 1820s and completed in the 1860s. It had 59 houses.

241 *It is always a joy to me to meet an American . . . Stars and Stripes*: i.e. the folly of George III and the blundering of Lord North, his Prime Minister, whose failure to remove tea duty caused the 'Boston Tea Party' and led to the War of Independence which resulted in the loss of North American colonies in 1783. The 'Anglo-American Reunion' was an idea fostered by William Thomas Stead (1849–1912), who found encouragement in the Supreme Court decision of Feb. 1891 that the seizure of a Canadian sealing vessel in Alaskan waters was a judicial, rather than a diplomatic, matter. Stead felt that this offered a 'glimpse into the future—the ultimate federation of the whole

English-speaking world' (*Review of Reviews*, Mar. 1891). ACD became an equally enthusiastic advocate, as in the dedication to *The White Company* (written on 29 Sept. 1891): 'To the Hope of the Future / The Reunion of the English-Speaking Races / This Little Chronicle of Our Common / Ancestry is Inscribed'. And in a letter to *The Times* in 1896 he called for the establishment of an Anglo-American Society to promote an Anglo-American Alliance: 'Such an organization would, I am sure, be easily founded, and would do useful work towards that greatest of all ends, the consolidation of the English-speaking races' ('England and America', *The Times*, 7 Jan. 1896; *Letters to the Press*, 1986).

243 *In the second one which I visited in Northumberland Avenue*: there were three large hotels in Northumberland Avenue: the Grand, facing Trafalgar Square; the Victoria or Northumberland Avenue Hotel; and the Metropole—of which the latter was deemed the most select.

THE BERYL CORONET

First published in the *Strand Magazine*, 3 (May 1892), 511–25, with 9 illustrations by Sidney Paget; *Strand Magazine*, New York (June 1892); S. S. McClure Newspaper Syndicate, USA, various dates between 16 and 24 Apr. 1892, with woodcut illustrations. Alternative titles: 'The Mystery of the Beryl Coronet' (*Cincinnati Commercial Gazette*), 'The Story of the Beryl Coronet' (*San Francisco Examiner*).

Written at 12 Tennison Road, South Norwood, and completed by 11 Nov. 1891. MS: whereabouts unknown.

The plot reworks various themes from Gaboriau (specifically the footprints in the snow, which are found in *Monsieur Lecoq*), and ACD resorts to the device of having a witness to a crime remain silent when wrongly accused of it, as was used by Fergus W. Hume in the popular bestseller *The Mystery of a Hansom Cab* (1886). The idea of the coronet was perhaps suggested by the reference in 'The Speckled Band' to the case of Mrs Farintosh which 'concerned an opal tiara'.

244 *our bow-window*: there are no bow-windows in Baker Street. There were bow-windows in the first-floor flats of 2 Argyle Park Terrace and 15 Lonsdale Terrace where the Doyles lived in Edinburgh in 1875–7 and 1881–2 respectively, both of

which afforded views of the fashionable park, the Meadows, but ACD was probably recalling his early days in Southsea when waiting for patients: 'I sat in the window of my consulting-room screened by the rather dingy curtain which I had put up, and watched the passing crowd' (*Memories and Adventures*).

the Metropolitan station: Baker Street was the main station on the Metropolitan Underground Railway (opened in 1863), and the terminus of the St John's Wood Railway.

246 *Alexander Holder*: perhaps suggested by the private London banks of Alexander, Fletcher, and Co., and Alexanders and Company; or from the generic term 'holder' which 'includes any person in possession of a bill who holds it either as payee, indorsee or bearer' ('Bill of Exchange', *Encyclopaedia Britannica*).

Holder & Stevenson, of Threadneedle Street: the second name perhaps in honour of Robert Louis Stevenson. Threadneedle Street is the site of the Bank of England and of the head offices of ACD's own bank, the Capital and Counties.

to Baker Street by the Underground . . . slowly through this snow: this may imply that 221B Baker Street lay at some distance from the station, but the intended meaning probably was that Holder came by underground from Scotland Yard, or from the mainline station, rather than taking a cab the whole way.

a household word . . . most exalted names in England: implying perhaps that of Albert Edward, Prince of Wales, afterwards Edward VII, or Albert Victor, Duke of Clarence and Avondale (1864–92), who was next in line.

247 *parley*: discussion of terms.

coronet: a 'cap or inferior crown' worn on state occasions by the five orders of peers. The one described here is that of a duke, consisting of a circlet of gold surmounted by eight strawberry or parsley leaves of equal height, set with gems. Beryls are aquamarine or yellow in colour and of the same chemical composition as an emerald.

one of the most precious public possessions of the Empire: this implies that the coronet belonged among the Crown Jewels, but ACD may have been thinking of the two beryl coronets ('single beryls, coronet mounted') in the Townshend Collection in

the South Kensington Museum; or of the coronet belonging to the Duke of Devonshire which was set with antique
gems.

249   *Streatham*: a 'southern suburb' of London, seven miles south-
west of Ludgate Hill, which ACD passed on the way to South
Norwood.

    Lucy Parr: Mary A. Parr was the ladies' maid at 2, Upper
Wimpole Street when ACD worked there.

250   *Sir George Burnwell*: perhaps from George Barnwell, the London
apprentice who 'thrice robbed his master, and murdered his
uncle in Ludlow' (*Percy's Reliques*, 1765) and who is the main
character in *The London Merchant* (1731) by George Lillo (1693–
1739); or from 'Burnwell' in West Virginia.

    Mary: ACD used his own name for the son and gave that of
his mother to the niece.

251   *a farthing*: ('fourthing') a quarter of an old penny; the smallest
coin (which remained in circulation until 31 Dec. 1960).

255   *sounding the planking and probing the furniture*: as in 'The Purloined
Letter' by Edgar Allan Poe, where floor-boards were 'exam-
ined with the microscope' and cushions 'probed with the fine
long needles'.

256   *Fairbank*: perhaps from Fairbrook or Fairburn. ACD had lived
as a boy in two houses which included 'bank' in their names,
Tower Bank and Liberton Bank.

    A double carriage sweep: a curved driveway, leading to and from
the house.

259   *Francis Prosper*: perhaps from the French writer, Prosper Merimée
(1803–70), whose story of 'How the Redoubt was Taken'
appeared in the second issue of the *Strand* (Feb. 1891).

261   *a common loafer*: (American slang, used in England from the
1850s) an idler; one who hangs about 'dependent on an inborn
instinct to keep him within gentle hail of fluid refreshment'.
'The East-End loafer differs in professional style from the
loafer of the West; the Fleet Street loafer, the park loafer, the
theatre loafer, the sporting loafer, the market loafer—all
have their departments, their particular manners, their views

of the world and of their own vocation, craft, or, as perhaps one should rather say, mystery' (*Living London*, ed. G. R. Sims, 1902–3).

a will-o'-the-wisp: Ignis Fatuus ('foolish fire'), the flame-like phosphorescence caused by spontaneous combustion of marsh gases which appears to flit across the ground, and deludes those who attempt to follow it.

268 *It is an old maxim of mine ... must be the truth*: the source was given by ACD in 'The Fate of the Evangeline', where a newspaper advises readers to 'bear in mind those simple rules as to the analysis of evidence laid down by Auguste Dupin. "Exclude the impossible," he remarks in one of Poe's immortal stories, "and what is left, however improbable, must be the truth" ' (*Boy's Own Paper*, Christmas Number, 1885).

269 *a life-preserver*: a short stick or bludgeon loaded with lead, and designed for self-defence.

the receiver: one who handles stolen goods without questioning their origin; or, in thieves' slang, a 'fence'.

chaffering: bargaining, haggling as to price.

THE COPPER BEECHES

First published in the *Strand Magazine*, 3 (June 1892), 613–28, with 9 illustrations by Sidney Paget; *Strand Magazine*, New York (July 1892); S. S. McClure Newspaper Syndicate, USA, various dates between 11 June and 9 Oct. 1892, with woodcut illustrations. Alternative titles: 'Adventures of the Copper Beeches' (*St Louis Post-Dispatch*); 'The Copper Breeches' (*sic*) (*Minneapolis Journal*).

Written at 12 Tennison Road, South Norwood, and completed by the end of Dec. 1891. MS: whereabouts unknown.

The plot was suggested by ACD's mother: 'It should concern a girl with beautiful golden hair, who, kidnapped and her hair shorn, should be made to impersonate some other girl for a villainous purpose' (Dickson Carr, 86–7). ACD was dubious at first: 'I don't see my way through the golden-hair episode', he told her; but in the end made use of it. 'During the holidays,' he wrote on 6 Jan. 1892, 'I finished my last Sherlock Holmes tale "The Adventure of the Copper Beeches" in which I used your lock of hair, so now a long farewell to Sherlock. He still lives, however, thanks to your entreaties' (Conan Doyle Foundation MSS).

The cutting of hair recalls Samson and Delilah, and *The Rape of the Lock* (1712) by Alexander Pope, but a more useful comparison would be with the story of Rapunzel by the Brothers Grimm. Rapunzel is held captive in a tower by a wicked witch who climbs up her hair. When the witch discovers that she has been seeing a prince, she cuts off the hair, ties it to the window latch, and lies in wait for the Prince. The fat, smiling villain recalls Count Fosco in *The Woman in White* (1860) by Wilkie Collins; the imprisoned daughter recalls the imprisoned wife in *Jane Eyre* (1847) by Charlotte Brontë, and there is a throwback to the Gothic novel in the closed and shuttered wing. Also evident are themes which recur throughout ACD's work: drunkenness (which he had seen first hand in his father) and the role of the governess (based on the experiences of his sisters). The dog who turns on his master is not unlike the 'speckled band' which turned against its handler.

Hair was often referred to in *Tit-Bits*, as in an inquiry concerning the longest tresses in the world: 'The lady possessing the longest hair in the world resides in Gainsville, Texas. It trails on the ground over 14 feet, and it is of beautiful red-gold colour' (*Tit-Bits*, 17 Oct. 1891). There was also an article on 'Strange Personal Resemblances' which described the confusion caused, for example, by a person who resembled Bismark (*Tit-Bits*, 14 Feb. 1891).

270   *the man who loves art for its own sake*: perhaps an allusion to the aesthetic ideal of 'L'art pour l'art', or 'art for art's sake', where art is independent of the man.

      Daily Telegraph: the newspaper (founded in 1855) to which ACD subscribed and which published letters from him in 1883 and 1890.

      causes célèbres: 'celebrated cases', sensational law suits.

      clay: a clay pipe, either with a short or long stem. The latter sometimes known as a 'churchwarden's' pipe.

271   *Crime is common. Logic is rare*: an aphorism suggested by 'Ars longa. Vita brevis' (Art is long. Life is short).

      a fair proportion . . . legal sense: ACD was defending himself against the charge of sensationalism, to which he later returned: 'There is one fact in connection with Holmes which will probably interest those who have followed his career from the beginning, and to which, so far as I am aware, attention has never been drawn. In dealing with criminal subjects one's natural endeavour is to keep crime in the background. In nearly half of the Sherlock Holmes stories, however, in a strictly legal sense no crime was actually committed at all. One heard a good deal about crime and the criminal, but the reader was completely bluffed. Of course, I could not bluff him always, so sometimes I had to give him a crime, and occasionally I had to make it a downright bad one' ('Conan Doyle Tells the True Story of Sherlock Holmes', *Tit-Bits*, 15 Dec. 1900).

tell a weaver . . . his left thumb: 'Tailors and seamstresses who are in the habit of cutting their thread with their teeth may show a characteristic tooth defect which consists of sharp V-shaped notches in the middle of the incisal edge of the incisors. The notching is most prominent on the upper incisors' (Burket, *Oral Medicine*, 1946). 'A compositor's left thumb is often characterised by the formation of a callous on the tip, often with abrasion of the skin lower down, across the "ball" of the digit' (Prof. Remsen Ten Eyck Schenck, 'The Effect of Trades Upon the Body', *Baker Street Journal*, Jan. 1953).

272 *an agency . . . young ladies from boarding schools*: perhaps a reference to ACD's own postbag, which contained 'letters from all over the country about Sherlock Holmes. Sometimes from school boys, sometimes from commercial travellers who are great readers, sometimes from lawyers pointing out mistakes in my law' (Raymond Blathwayt, 'A Talk with Dr Conan Doyle', *Bookman*, May 1892). He gave further details of these 'lunatic letters' when warning Joseph Bell of what to expect when he was identified as the model for Sherlock Holmes. He would hear from a 'mystic youth' who gave the precise time at which his letters were written. 'You will hear also from the youth in the South of Portugal, from the American lady with the curved spine, from the Liverpool merchant who burns to know who Jack the Ripper is, from many folks who believe that their neighbours are starving maiden aunts to death in hermetically sealed attics, and in short you will bless me and my yarns when you look at your post-box' (7 July 1892; Stisted Papers).

Montague Place: at the rear of the British Museum; perhaps number 23, where ACD lodged Mar.–June 1891.

272 *freckled like a plover's egg*: the spotted egg of the plover (a long-legged wading bird) is also mentioned by Wilkie Collins, who says that the moonstone, in the novel of that name, is 'as large, or nearly, as a plover's egg'.

273 *Colonel Spence Munro*: the first name is perhaps from James Spence (1812–82), ACD's Professor of Surgery at Edinburgh. 'Spencer' and 'Monroe' are names associated with Henry Highland Garnet. He was born into a slave family on the Maryland plantation of a Colonel Spencer, and when he was on the *Mayumba* as ACD's patient he was Minister to Monrovia, the capital of Liberia, named after US President James Monroe (1757–1831).

Halifax, in Nova Scotia: the major port of eastern Canada, the terminus of the Canadian Pacific Railway, and capital of the province. A British possession from 1758.

Miss Stoper: perhaps from 'stoper', a miner who excavates in layers; or a variant of 'Sloper', as in the humorous paper, *Ally Sloper's Half Holiday* (1884–1916).

274 *sweating—rank sweating*: gross exploitation, long hours for small pay; as in 'sweat shops' and 'sweated labour'.

The Copper Beeches, five miles on the far side of Winchester: placing it perhaps in the village of Otterbourne which is five miles south of Winchester on the Southampton High Road.

275 *romper*: one who plays in a boisterous manner.

killing cockroaches with a slipper: perhaps an echo of 'Cruel Frederick' in Dr Heinrich Hoffman's *Struwwelpeter* (1845):

> He caught the flies, poor little things,
> And then tore off their tiny wings,
> He killed the birds, and broke the
>   chairs,
> And threw the kitten down the stairs.

faddy: one who is given to fads, who has a peculiar notion about the correct way of doing something.

It has been considered artistic: bright golden auburn hair was favoured by the Venetian painter, Titian (Tiziano Vecelli, 1477–1570), and the 'Titian tint' was considered artistic by Pre-Raphaelite painters, such as Dante Gabriel Rossetti (1828–82).

277 *electric blue*: a trade name for a steely blue colour used for textile fabrics.

Jephro Rucastle: the spelling of the first name recalls Jephthah (Judges 11: 30–40), but it is more probably a variant of Jethro, the father-in-law of Moses (Exodus 3: 1, 4: 18), a name made famous by Jethro Tull (1674–1741), the great agricultural reformer.

a sister of mine: a sentiment from the heart, as ACD had three sisters who served as governesses.

279 *I can't make bricks without clay*: or perhaps 'without straw'; an allusion to the Israelites in Egypt who were faced with the impossibility of making bricks without the straw needed to bind them together. 'There is no straw given unto thy servants, and they say to us, Make brick: and, behold, thy servants are beaten; but the fault is in thine own people' (Exodus 5: 16).

the yellow envelope: telegrams were delivered in yellow, pink, or green envelopes.

Bradshaw: '*Bradshaw*—or, to give it its correct title, *Bradshaw's General Railway and Steam Navigation Guide* is essentially a British institution, like *The Times*, football, *Punch*, and cricket' ('The Story of *Bradshaw*', *Strand*, Feb. 1904). The timetable—first published by John Bradshaw (1801–51) in Dec. 1841—appeared monthly from June 1842 until June 1961.

the Black Swan Hotel: an 'inn of repute' in the High Street in Winchester. It was founded at the beginning of the 18th century and demolished in 1934.

my analysis of the acetones: correctly, 'ketones', a class of chemical compounds of which acetone (*dimethyl ketone*, $CO(CH_2)_2$) is the lowest; a colourless limpid liquid related to acetic acid. Perhaps suggested by 'A Test for Acetone in Expired Air' in the Supplement to the *British Medical Journal* (16 May 1891).

the old English capital: Winchester was the capital of the West Saxon kingdom under Cerlic (from *c.* AD 520), and of England under Egbert (from AD 827). It was the home of Alfred the Great (849–99) and a meeting place of Parliament until the reign of Henry VIII. The city is on the railway line between Southampton and London.

280 *Aldershot*: a town in Hampshire and the site of a permanent military camp (built 1854–5).

282 *Lord Southerton's preserves*: land set aside for the protection of game; perhaps from the village of Southerton on the edge of Dartmoor.

283 *Toller*: a 'toller' is a decoy and a small breed of dog; but the name may have been suggested by the 'tolley' used to beat boys at Stonyhurst—'a piece of india-rubber of the size and shape of a thick boot sole' (*Memories and Adventures*).

   beige: or beige cloth, a fine woollen fabric.

286 *Carlo*: a name ACD later gave to his own dog and to the spaniel in 'The Sussex Vampire' (*Case-Book*).

> To Carlo
>
> (Died July 1921)
>
> No truer, kinder soul
>   Was ever sped than thine.
> You lived without a growl,
>   You died without a whine.
>
> (*Collected Poems*, 1922)

   as keen as mustard: 'keen' means 'sharp' or 'pungent to the taste', and 'eager' or 'fervid'—hence the expression.

   wrapt: an erroneous form of 'rapt', enraptured.

288 *Photography is one of my hobbies*: ACD contributed articles to the *British Journal of Photography* in the 1880s and mentioned photography in 'The Red-Headed League'; but the reference was topical, for he told his mother on 14 Oct. 1891: 'I sold my eye instruments for £6.10.0 with which I shall buy photographic apparatus, so we have been able to start a hobby without any outlay.'

293 *pallet bed*: a small, mean bed; originally loose straw or a straw-filled mattress.

294 *Mr Fowler*: a common surname (from a 'fowler', one who hunts wild birds).

295 *brain fever ... at death's door*: 'brain fever' is a device of the novelist: an unspecified disease which renders a person delirious or dead to the world for any length of time necessary for the plot, and which has no harmful side-effects. In common usage it is applied to cerebral meningitis (an inflammation of the membranes around the brain) or to encephalitis lethargica (sleeping sickness). Cerebral meningitis claimed the life of

John Hawkins, the brother of ACD's future wife, and influenza claimed the life of his eldest sister, Annette in 1890.

certain arguments, metallic or otherwise: bribery (perhaps on oblique allusion to the arguments being used by the proprietor of the *Strand* to encourage ACD to continue the Sherlock Holmes stories).

locus standi: 'a place for standing', the right to appear before a court; 'our right to be here'.

296 *special licence*: the 'special licence' is granted with the approval of the Archbishop of Canterbury and enables a marriage to be solemnized in any place and at any time, without requiring a period of residence in the parish (as would be the case with an 'ordinary licence').

Mauritius: a volcanic island in the Indian Ocean, about 500 miles east of Madagascar; a British Colony from 1810. The Government appointments were to the Executive Council, the Council of Government, the Supreme Court, the Royal College, and the government-aided primary schools.

Miss Violet Hunter: printed as 'Miss Violent Hunter' in the first edition (Newnes, 1892) and the two subsequent impressions (called the 'Second' and 'Third Edition').

Walsall: a market town, eight miles north-west of Birmingham, near Aston where ACD had worked as a doctor.

TROLLOPE IN **OXFORD WORLD'S CLASSICS**

ANTHONY TROLLOPE

An Autobiography
The American Senator
Barchester Towers
Can You Forgive Her?
The Claverings
Cousin Henry
Doctor Thorne
The Duke's Children
The Eustace Diamonds
Framley Parsonage
He Knew He Was Right
Lady Anna
The Last Chronicle of Barset
Orley Farm
Phineas Finn
Phineas Redux
The Prime Minister
Rachel Ray
The Small House at Allington
The Warden
The Way We Live Now

The Oxford World's Classics Website

www.worldsclassics.co.uk

- Information about new titles
- Explore the full range of Oxford World's Classics
- Links to other literary sites and the main OUP webpage
- Imaginative competitions, with bookish prizes
- Peruse the Oxford World's Classics Magazine
- Articles by editors
- Extracts from Introductions
- A forum for discussion and feedback on the series
- Special information for teachers and lecturers

www.worldsclassics.co.uk

American Literature

British and Irish Literature

Children's Literature

Classics and Ancient Literature

Colonial Literature

Eastern Literature

European Literature

History

Medieval Literature

Oxford English Drama

Poetry

Philosophy

Politics

Religion

The Oxford Shakespeare

A complete list of Oxford Paperbacks, including Oxford World's Classics, Oxford Shakespeare, Oxford Drama, and Oxford Paperback Reference, is available in the UK from the Academic Division Publicity Department, Oxford University Press, Great Clarendon Street, Oxford OX2 6DP.

In the USA, complete lists are available from the Paperbacks Marketing Manager, Oxford University Press, 198 Madison Avenue, New York, NY 10016.

Oxford Paperbacks are available from all good bookshops. In case of difficulty, customers in the UK can order direct from Oxford University Press Bookshop, Freepost, 116 High Street, Oxford OX1 4BR, enclosing full payment. Please add 10 per cent of published price for postage and packing.